PRINCESSES OF THE AMAZONS

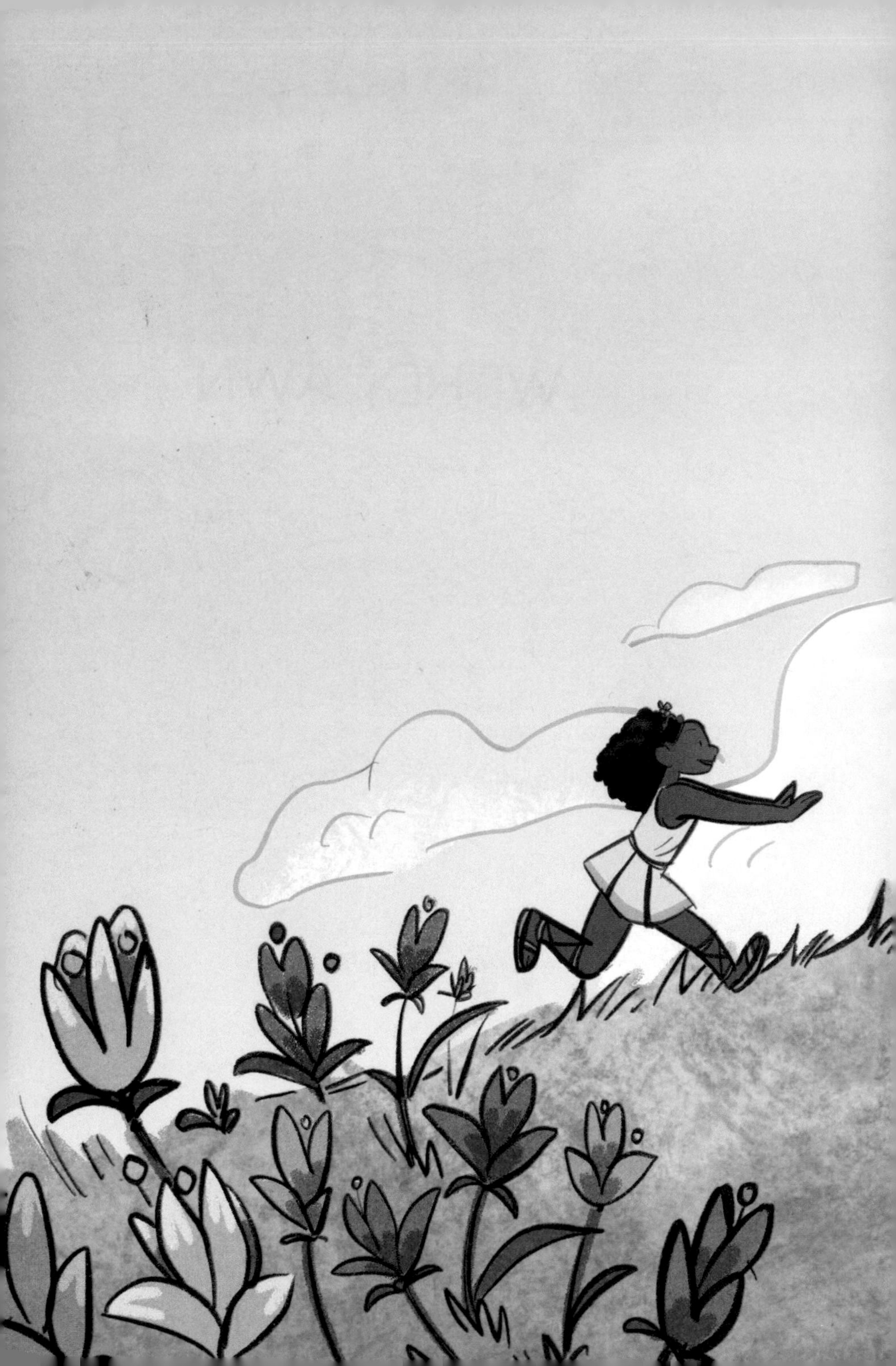

DIANA AND NUBIA:
PRINCESSES OF THE AMAZONS

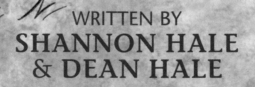

WRITTEN BY
SHANNON HALE
& DEAN HALE

DRAWN BY
VICTORIA YING

COLORED BY **LYNETTE WONG**

LETTERED BY **BECCA CAREY**

WONDER WOMAN CREATED BY WILLIAM MOULTON MARSTON

KRISTY QUINN Senior Editor
COURTNEY JORDAN Associate Editor
STEVE COOK Design Director – Books
AMIE BROCKWAY-METCALF Publication Design
DANIELLE RAMONDELLI Publication Production

MARIE JAVINS Editor-in-Chief, DC Comics

ANNE DePIES Senior VP – General Manager
JIM LEE Publisher & Chief Creative Officer
DON FALLETTI VP – Manufacturing Operations & Workflow Management
LAWRENCE GANEM VP – Talent Services
ALISON GILL Senior VP – Manufacturing & Operations
JEFFREY KAUFMAN VP – Editorial Strategy & Programming
NICK J. NAPOLITANO VP – Manufacturing Administration & Design
NANCY SPEARS VP – Revenue

DC Comics, 100 S. California Street,
Burbank, CA 91505

Printed by Worzalla, Stevens Point, WI,
USA. 9/30/22.

First Printing.

ISBN: 978-1-77950-769-3

MIX
Paper from
responsible sources
FSC
www.fsc.org
FSC® C002589

Library of Congress Cataloging-in-Publication Data

Names: Hale, Shannon, writer. | Hale, Dean, 1972- writer. | Ying, Victoria,
  illustrator. | Wong, Lynette, colorist. | Carey, Becca, letterer.
Title: Diana and Nubia, princesses of the Amazons / written by Shannon Hale
  & Dean Hale ; drawn by Victoria Ying ; colored by Lynette Wong ;
  lettered by Becca Carey.
Description: Burbank, CA : DC Comics, [2022] | Audience: Ages 8-12 |
  Audience: Grades 4-6 | Summary: Princess Nubia loves her mothers, their
  home on Themyscira, and all her Amazon aunties, but when Princess Diana
  is assigned to her bedroom she must learn to live and excel with her new
  sister.
Identifiers: LCCN 2022030457 | ISBN 9781779507693 (trade paperback)
Subjects: CYAC: Graphic novels. | Princesses--Fiction. | Amazons--Fiction.
  | LCGFT: Graphic novels.
Classification: LCC PZ7.7.H35 Df 2022 | DDC 741.5/973--dc23/eng/20220708
LC record available at https://lccn.loc.gov/2022030457

For Dinah and Wren:
twins, warriors, sisters, and friends.

—Shannon and Dean

For siblings who fight each other,
and who fight together.

—Victoria

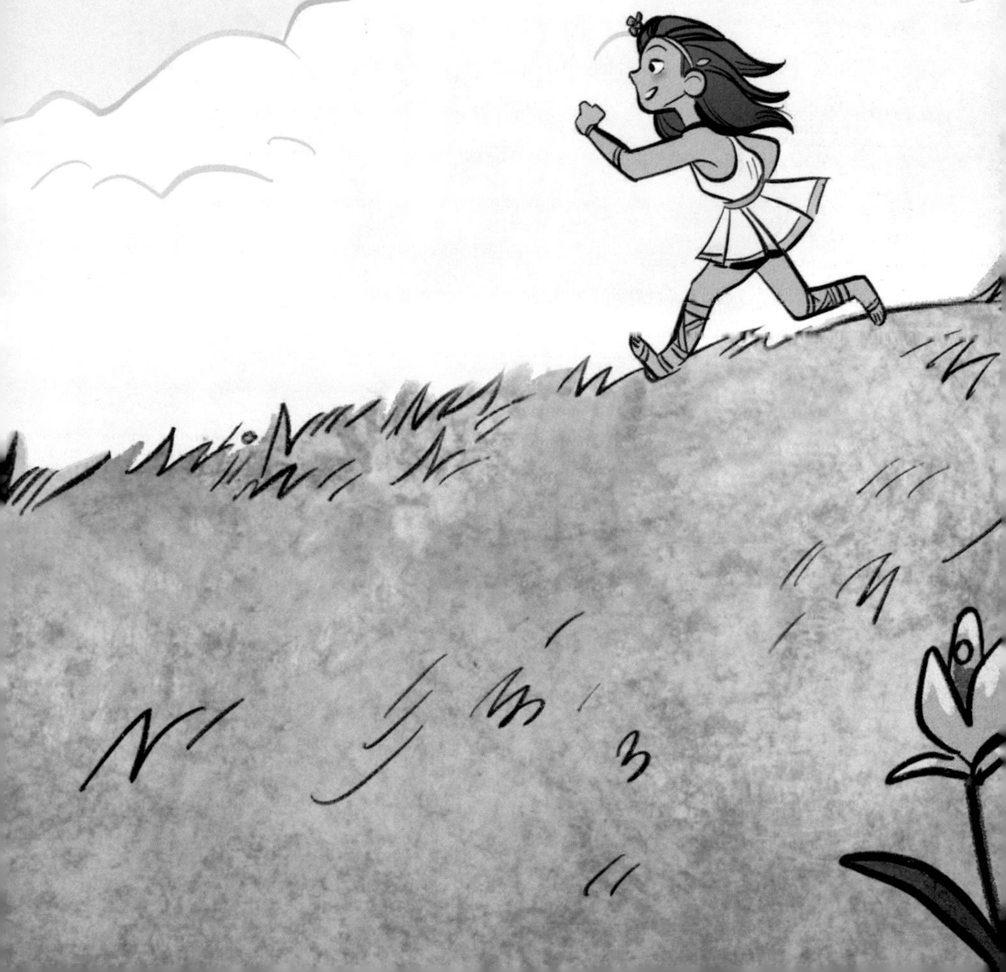

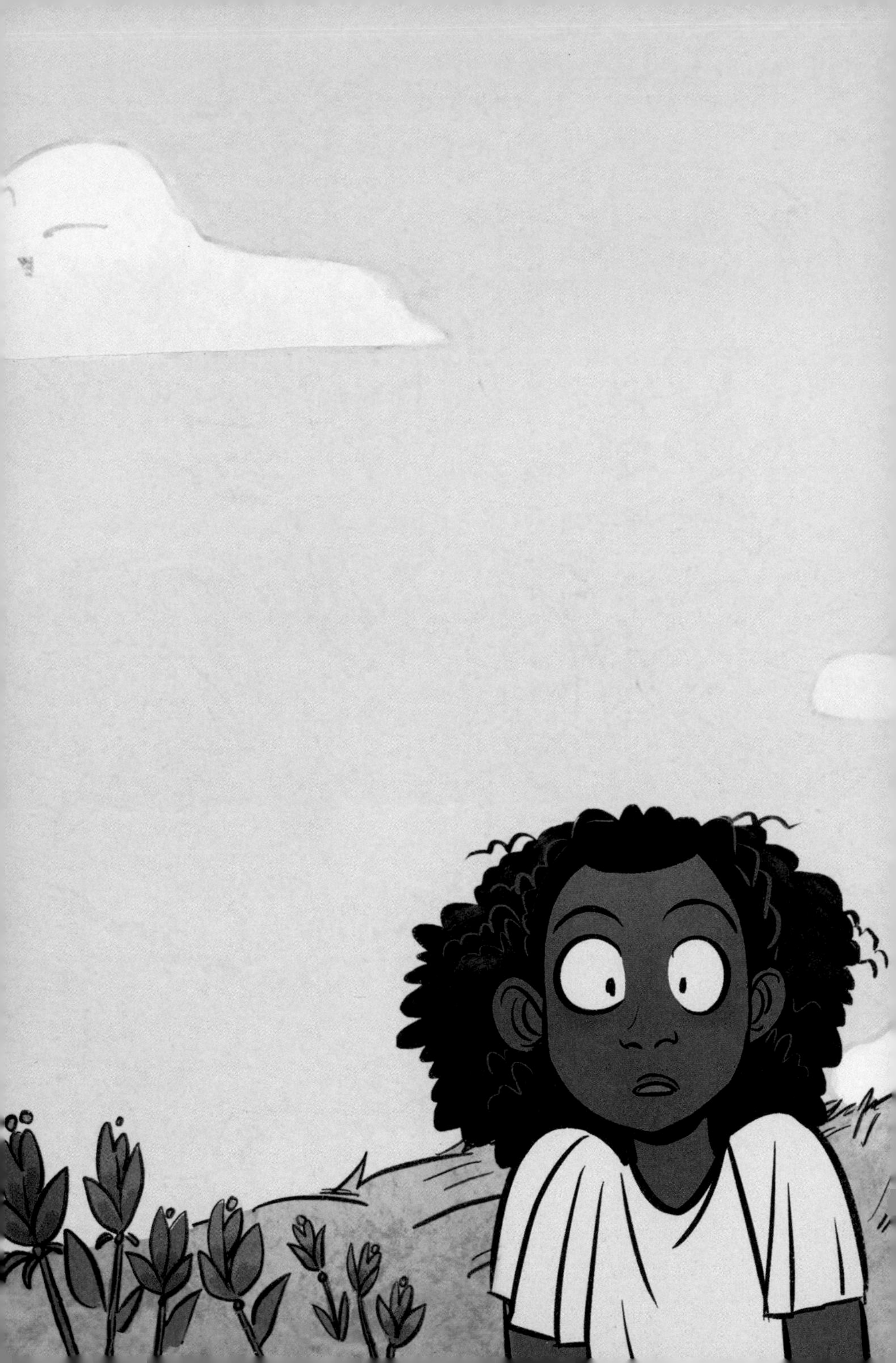

TABLE OF CONTENTS

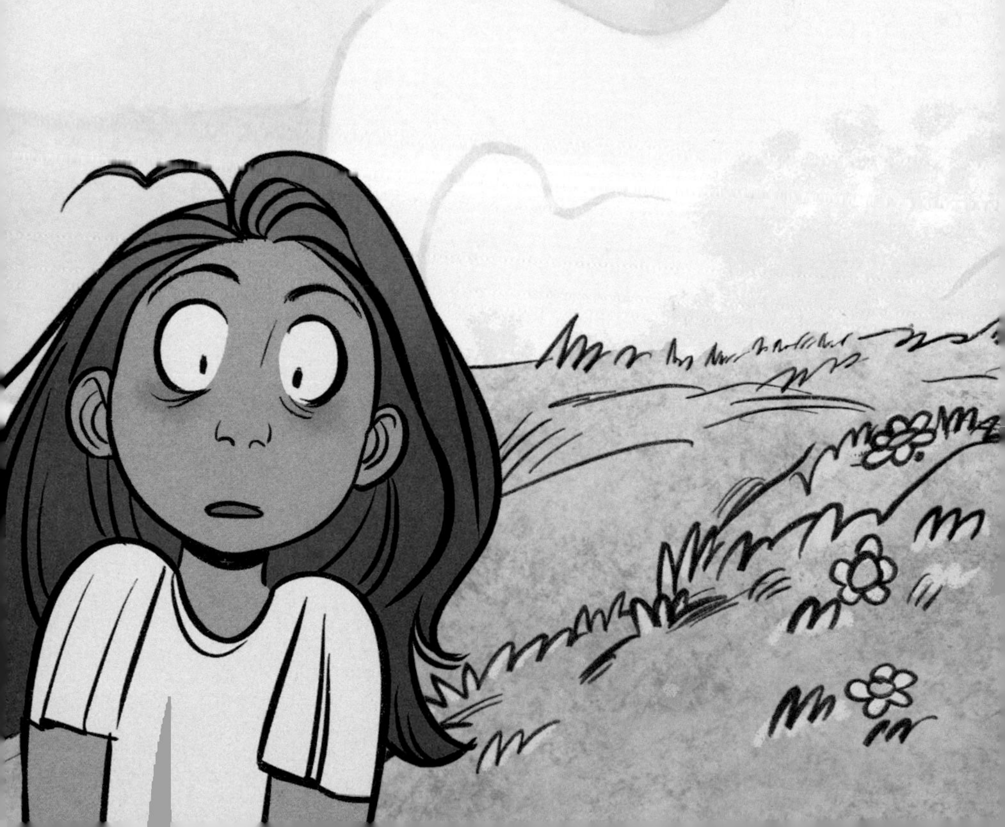

CHAPTER ONE

NUBIA

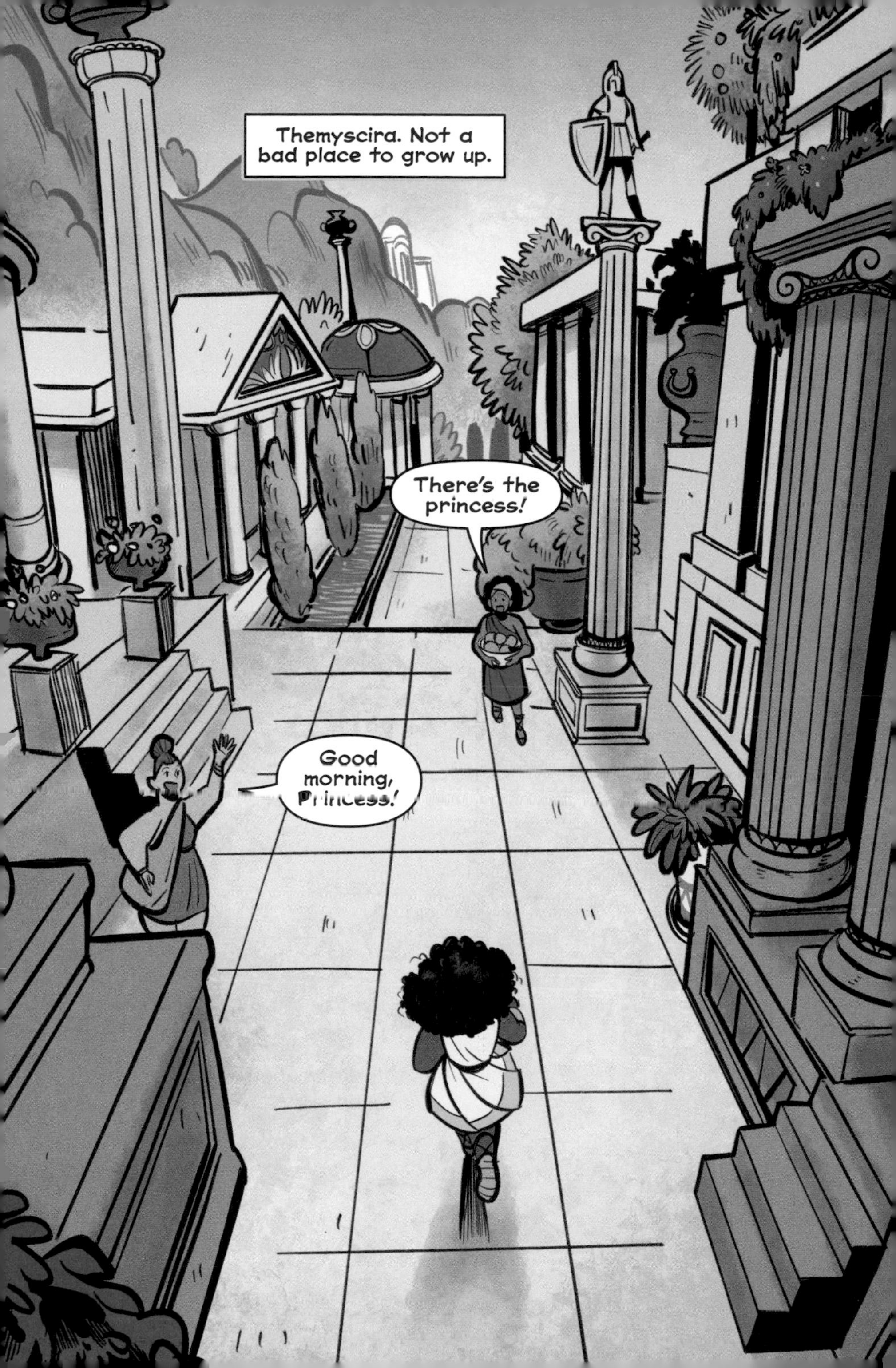
Themyscira. Not a bad place to grow up.
There's the princess!
Good morning, Princess!

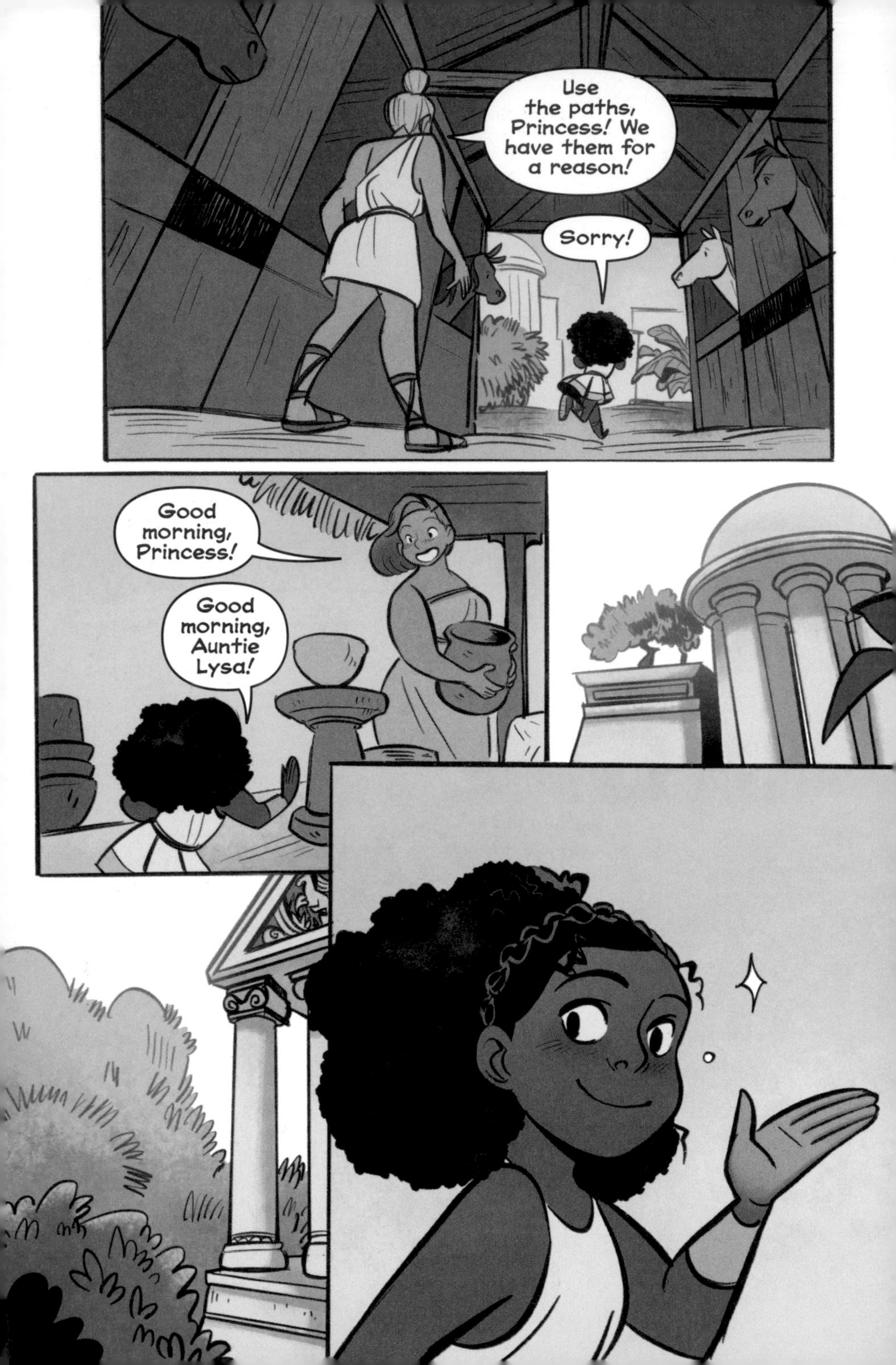
Use the paths, Princess! We have them for a reason!
Sorry!
Good morning, Princess!
Good morning, Auntie Lysa!

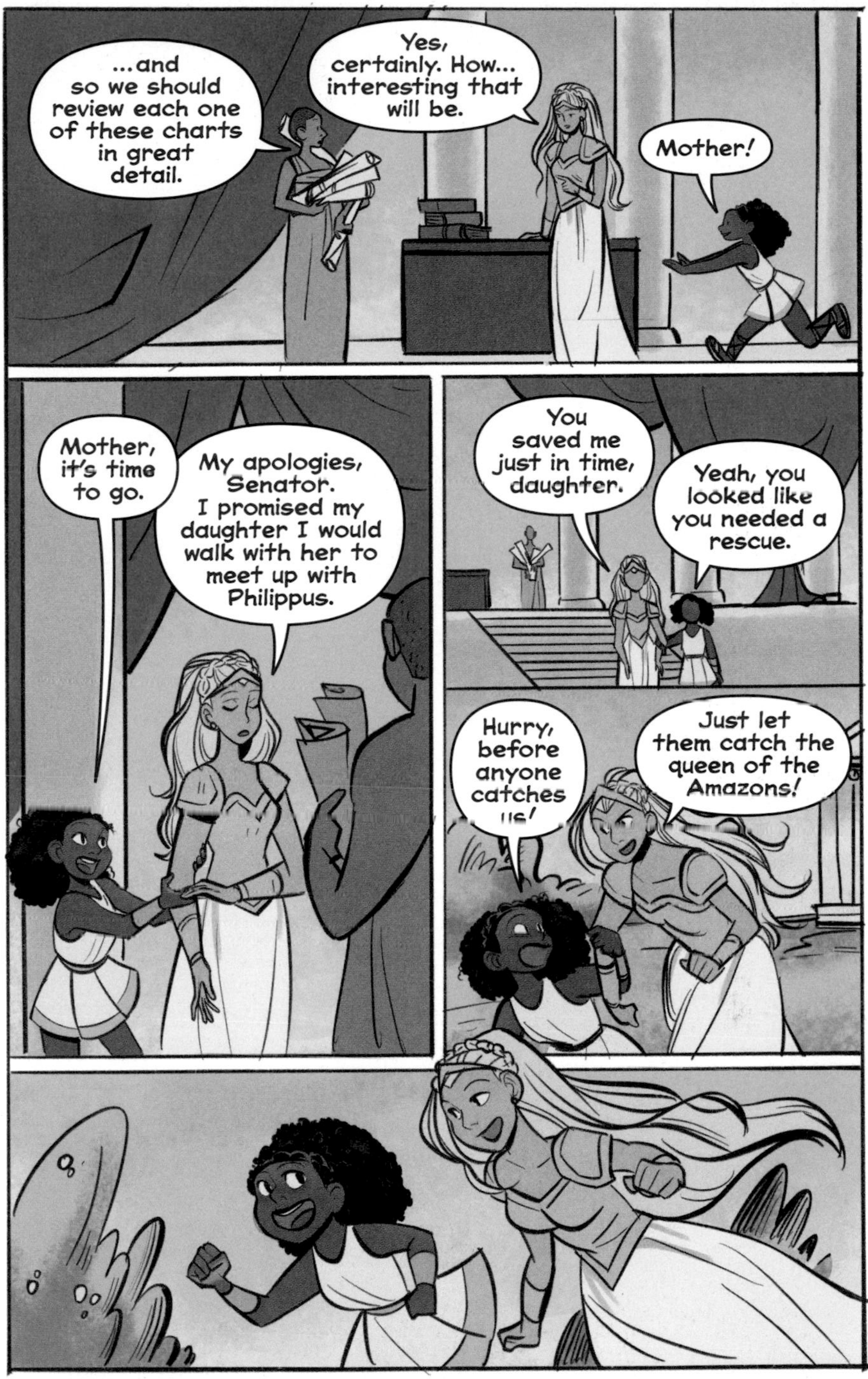
...and so we should review each one of these charts in great detail.
Yes, certainly. How... interesting that will be.
Mother!
Mother, it's time to go.
My apologies, Senator. I promised my daughter I would walk with her to meet up with Philippus.
You saved me just in time, daughter.
Yeah, you looked like you needed a rescue.
Hurry, before anyone catches us!
Just let them catch the queen of the Amazons!

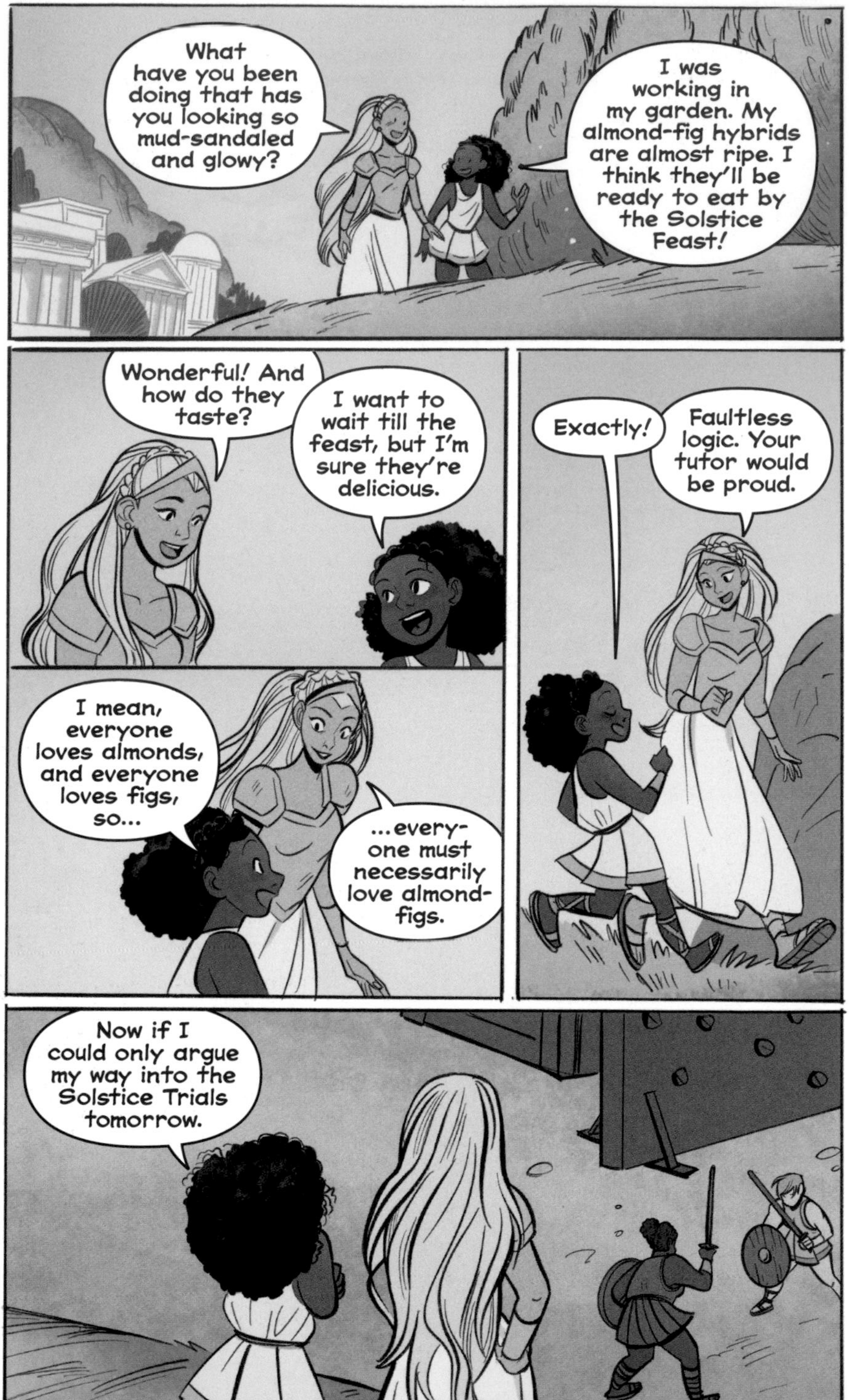
What have you been doing that has you looking so mud-sandaled and glowy?
I was working in my garden. My almond-fig hybrids are almost ripe. I think they'll be ready to eat by the Solstice Feast!
Wonderful! And how do they taste?
I want to wait till the feast, but I'm sure they're delicious.
I mean, everyone loves almonds, and everyone loves figs, so...
...every-one must necessarily love almond-figs.
Exactly!
Faultless logic. Your tutor would be proud.
Now if I could only argue my way into the Solstice Trials tomorrow.

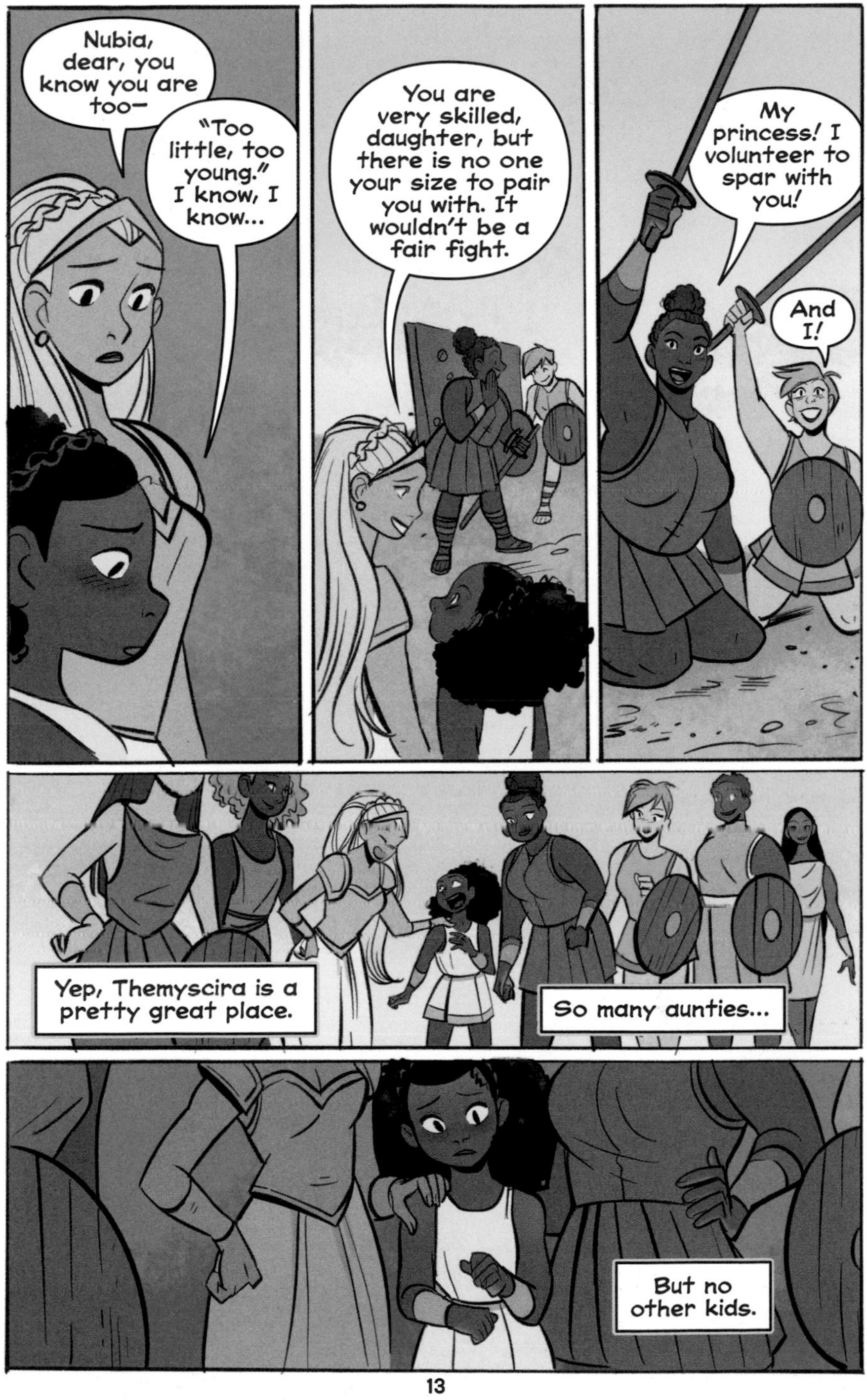
Nubia, dear, you know you are too—
"Too little, too young." I know, I know...
You are very skilled, daughter, but there is no one your size to pair you with. It wouldn't be a fair fight.
My princess! I volunteer to spar with you!
And I!
Yep, Themyscira is a pretty great place.
So many aunties...
But no other kids.

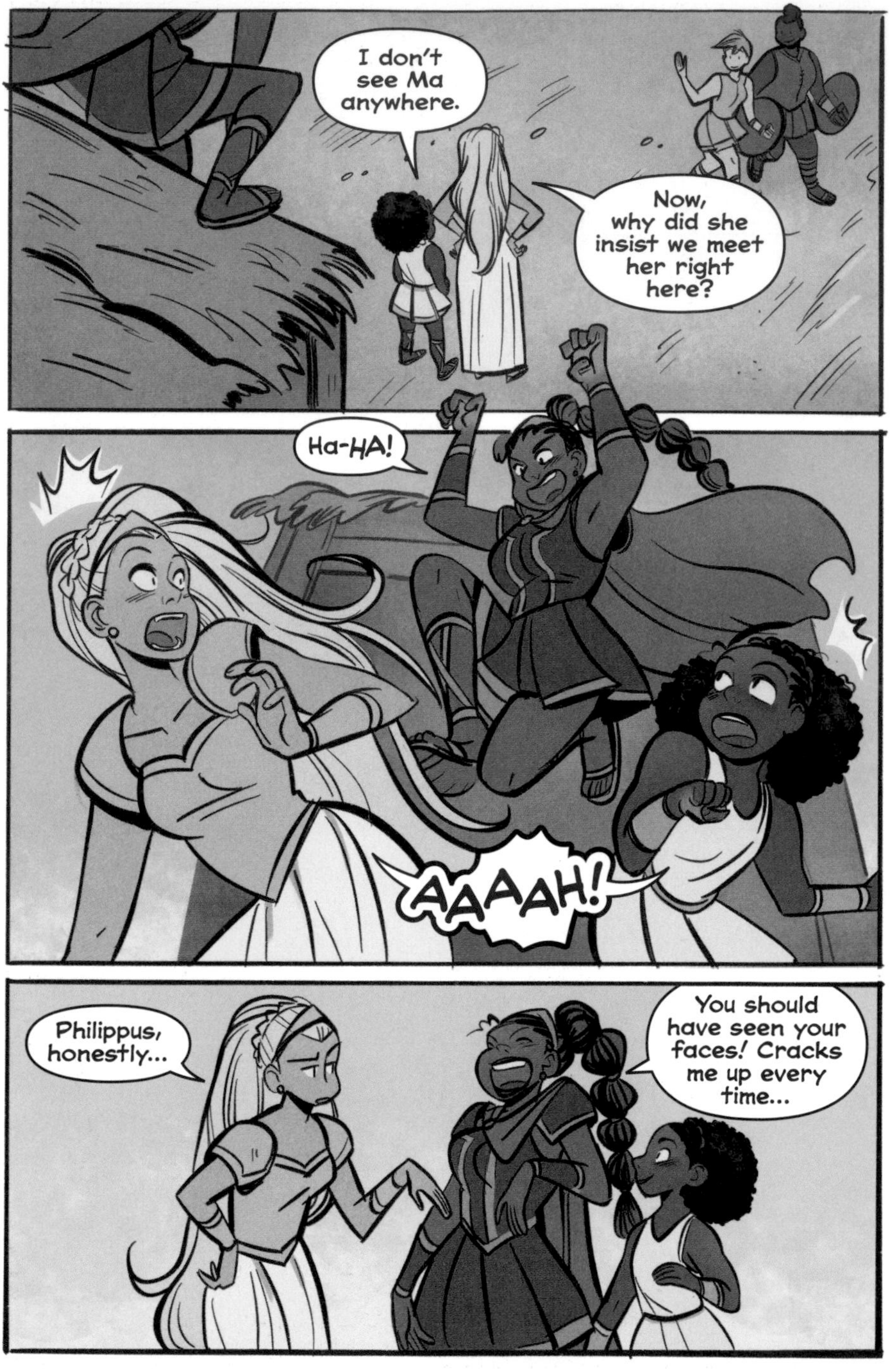
I don't see Ma anywhere.
Now, why did she insist we meet her right here?
Ha-HA!
AAAAH!
Philippus, honestly...
You should have seen your faces! Cracks me up every time...

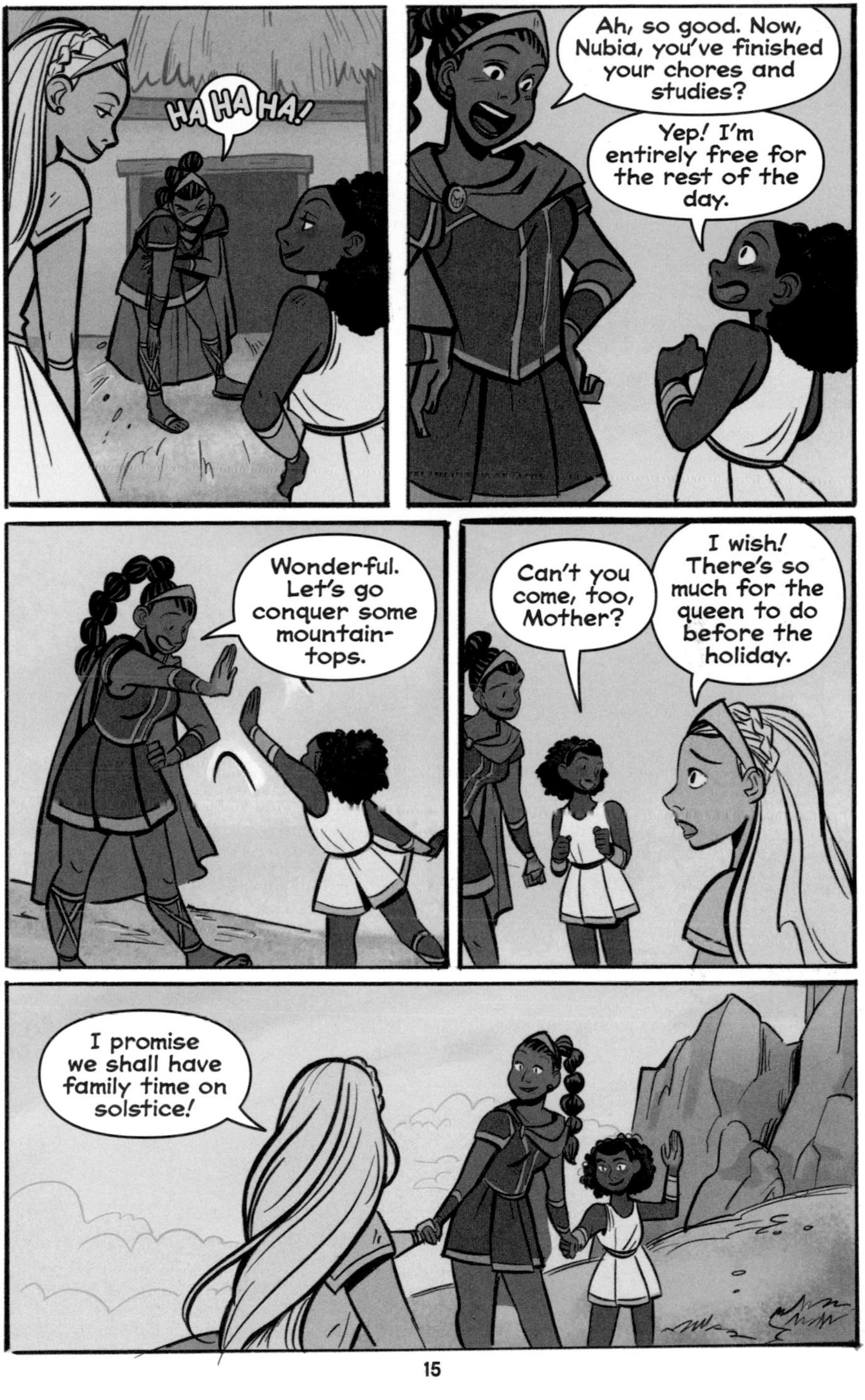
HA HA HA!
Ah, so good. Now, Nubia, you've finished your chores and studies?
Yep! I'm entirely free for the rest of the day.
Wonderful. Let's go conquer some mountain-tops.
Can't you come, too, Mother?
I wish! There's so much for the queen to do before the holiday.
I promise we shall have family time on solstice!

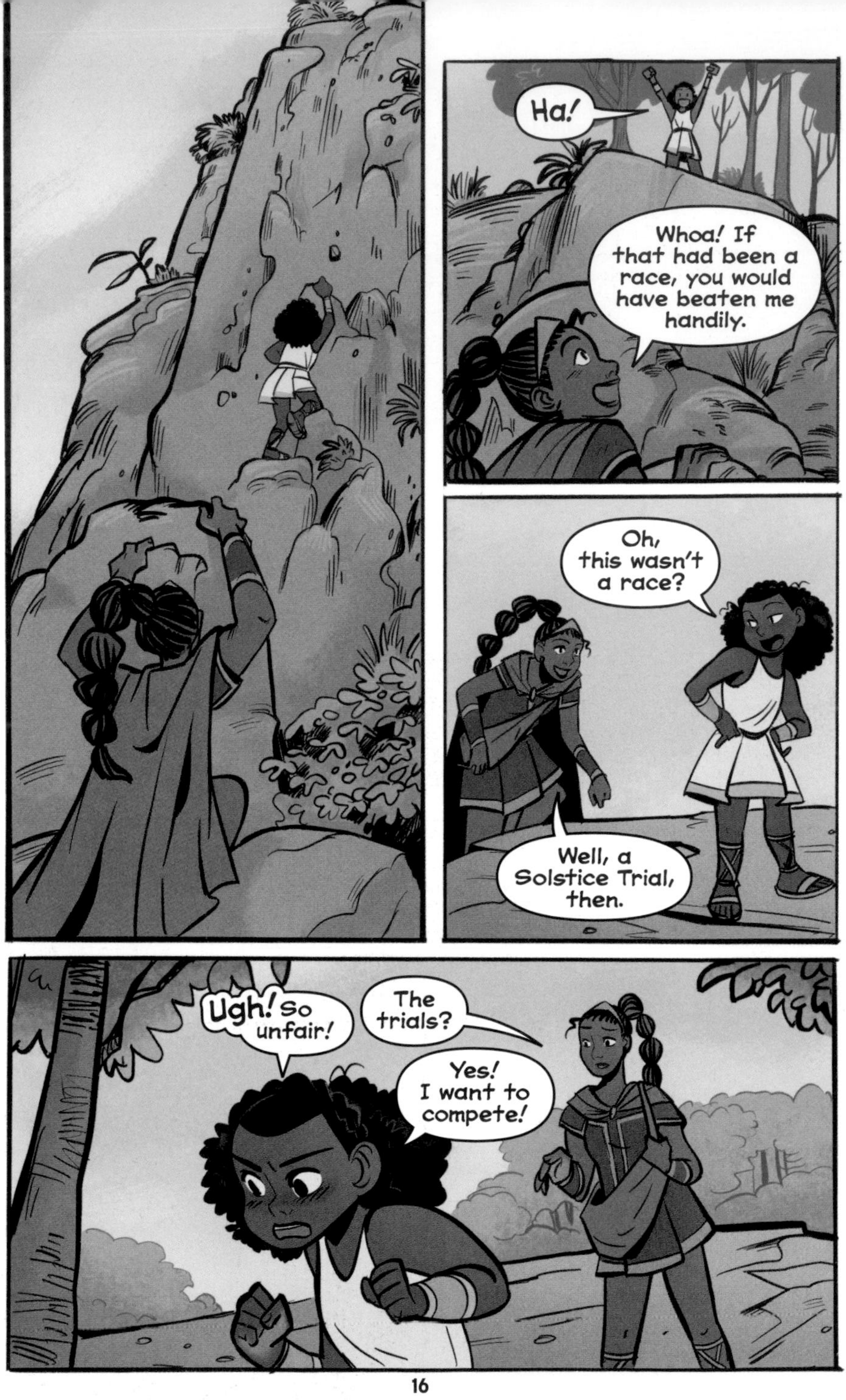
Ha!
Whoa! If that had been a race, you would have beaten me handily.
Oh, this wasn't a race?
Well, a Solstice Trial, then.
Ugh! So unfair!
The trials?
Yes! I want to compete!

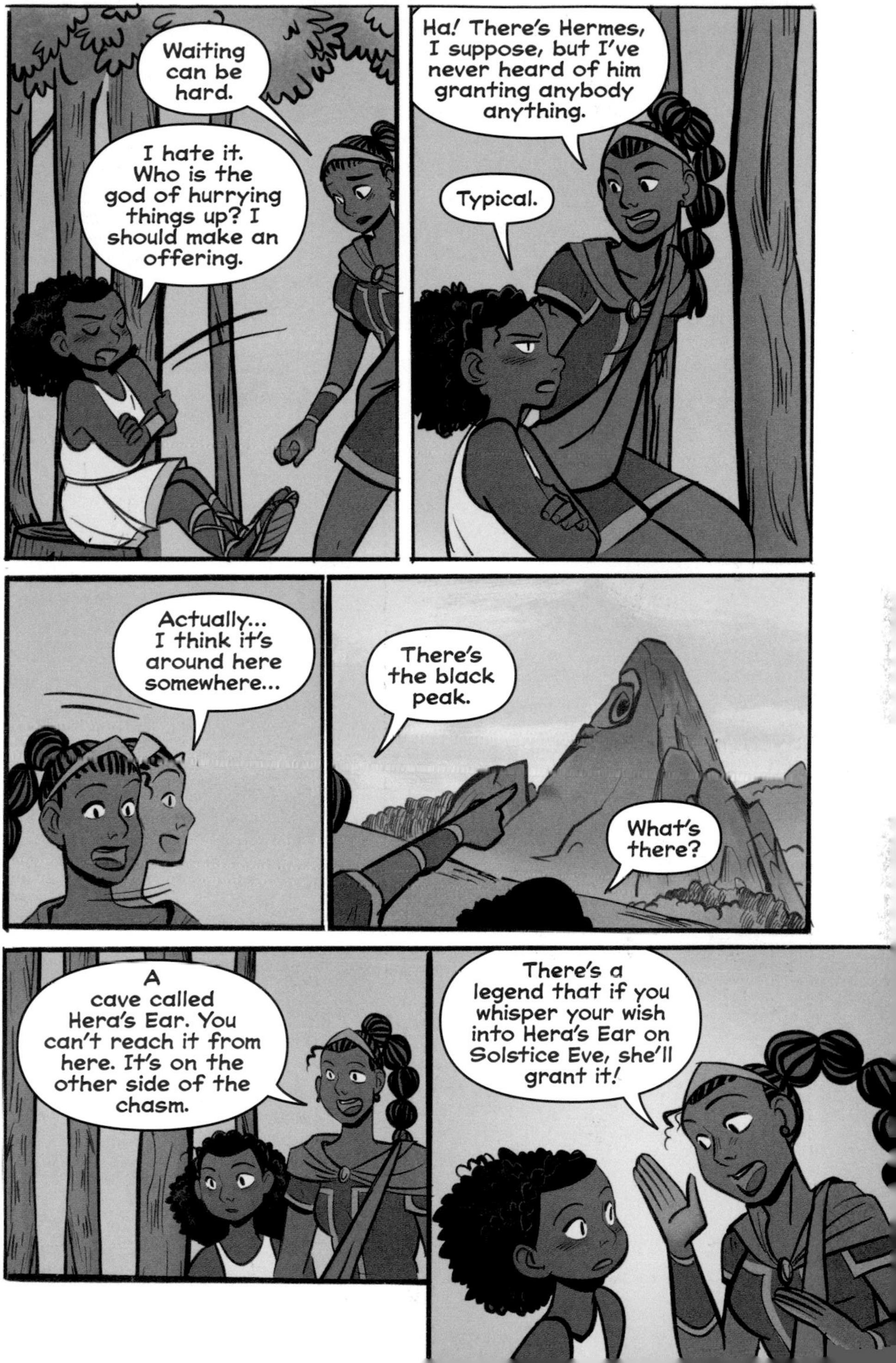
Waiting can be hard.
I hate it. Who is the god of hurrying things up? I should make an offering.
Ha! There's Hermes, I suppose, but I've never heard of him granting anybody anything.
Typical.
Actually... I think it's around here somewhere...
There's the black peak.
What's there?
A cave called Hera's Ear. You can't reach it from here. It's on the other side of the chasm.
There's a legend that if you whisper your wish into Hera's Ear on Solstice Eve, she'll grant it!

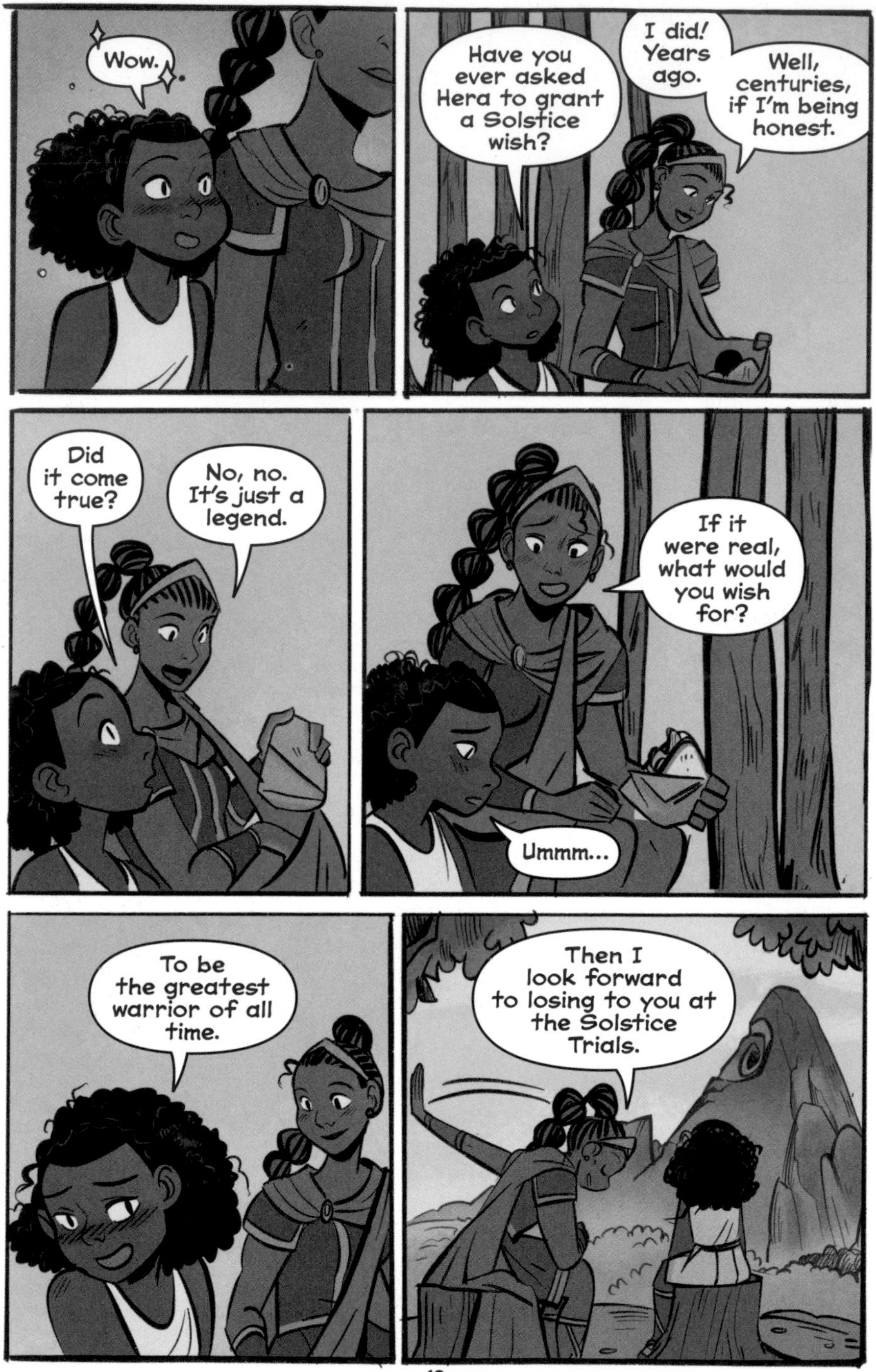
Wow.
Have you ever asked Hera to grant a Solstice wish?
I did! Years ago.
Well, centuries, if I'm being honest.
Did it come true?
No, no. It's just a legend.
If it were real, what would you wish for?
Ummm...
To be the greatest warrior of all time.
Then I look forward to losing to you at the Solstice Trials.

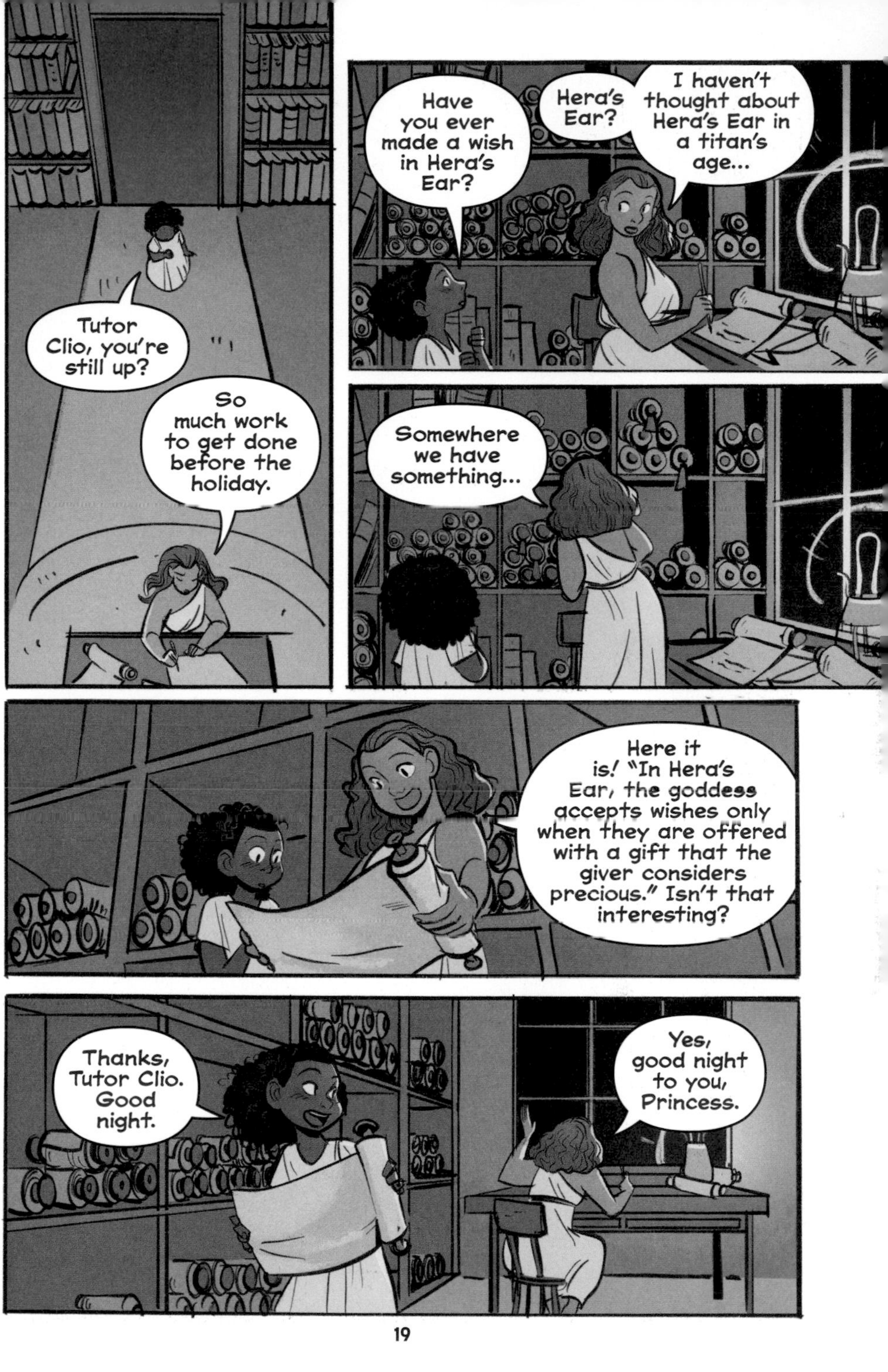
Tutor Clio, you're still up?
So much work to get done before the holiday.
Have you ever made a wish in Hera's Ear?
Hera's Ear?
I haven't thought about Hera's Ear in a titan's age...
Somewhere we have something...
Here it is! "In Hera's Ear, the goddess accepts wishes only when they are offered with a gift that the giver considers precious." Isn't that interesting?
Thanks, Tutor Clio. Good night.
Yes, good night to you, Princess.

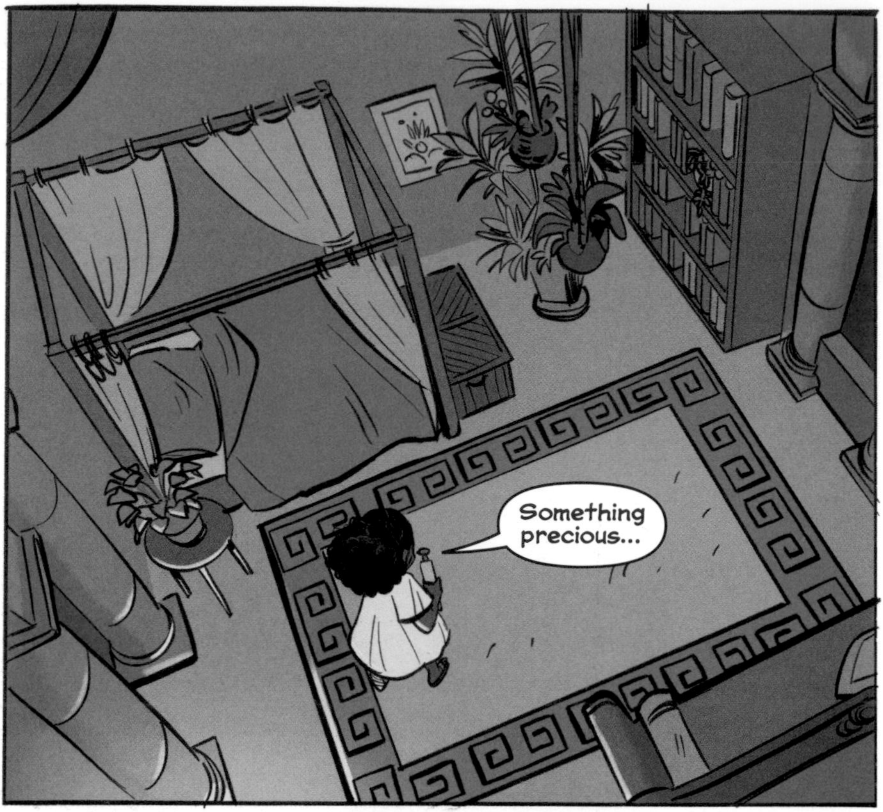
Something precious...

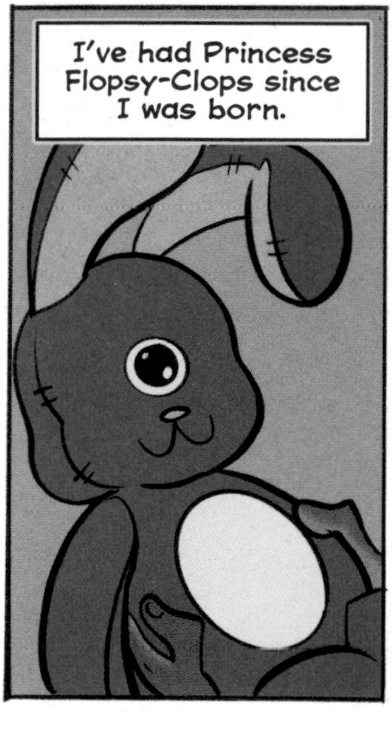
I've had Princess Flopsy-Clops since I was born.

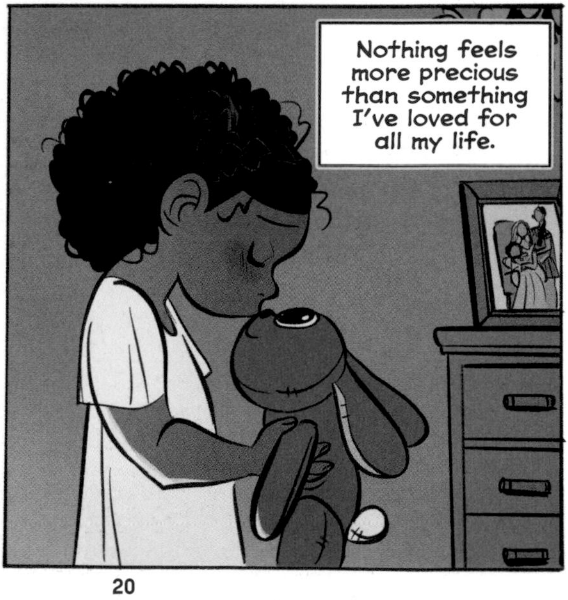
Nothing feels more precious than something I've loved for all my life.

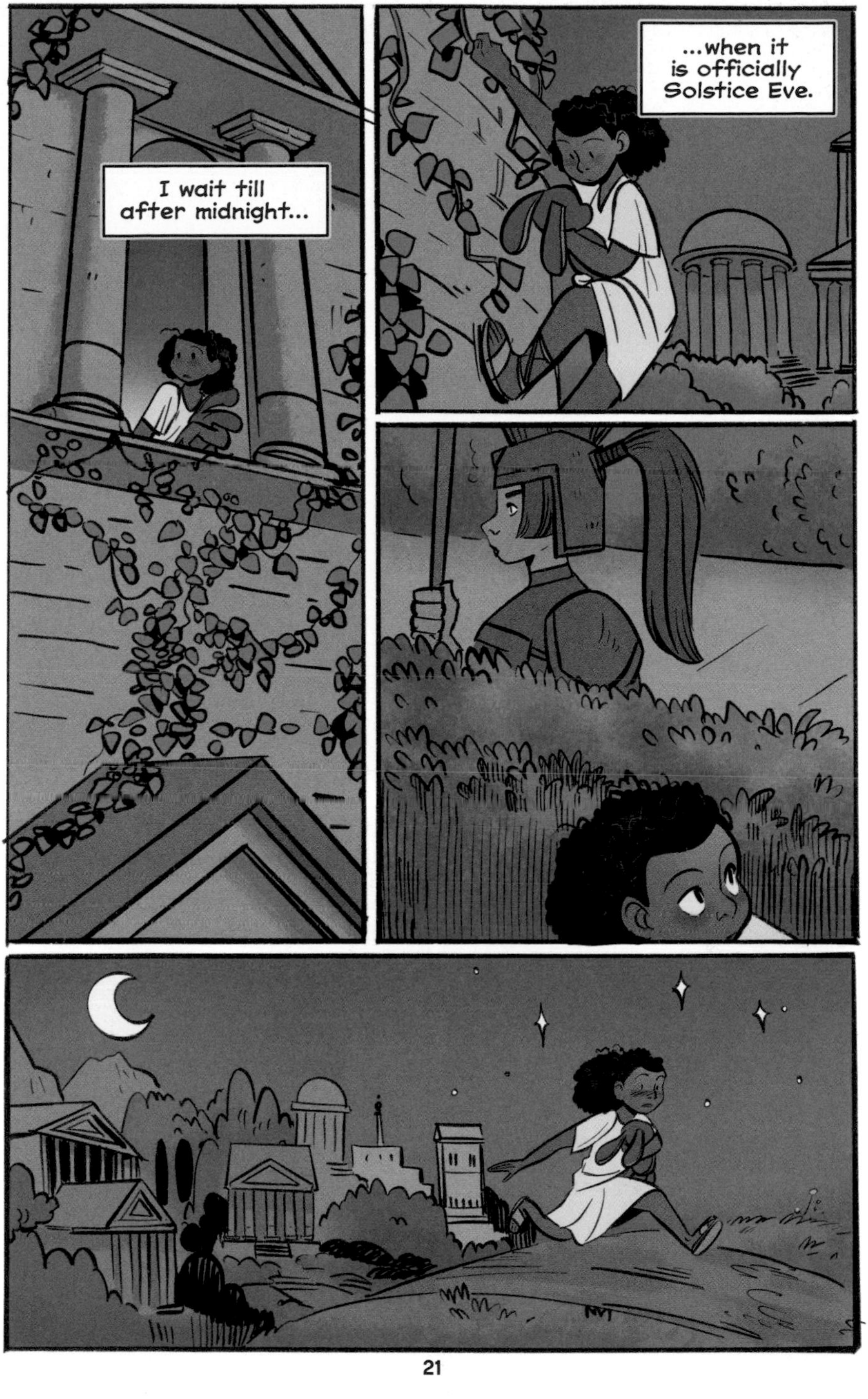
I wait till after midnight...
...when it is officially Solstice Eve.

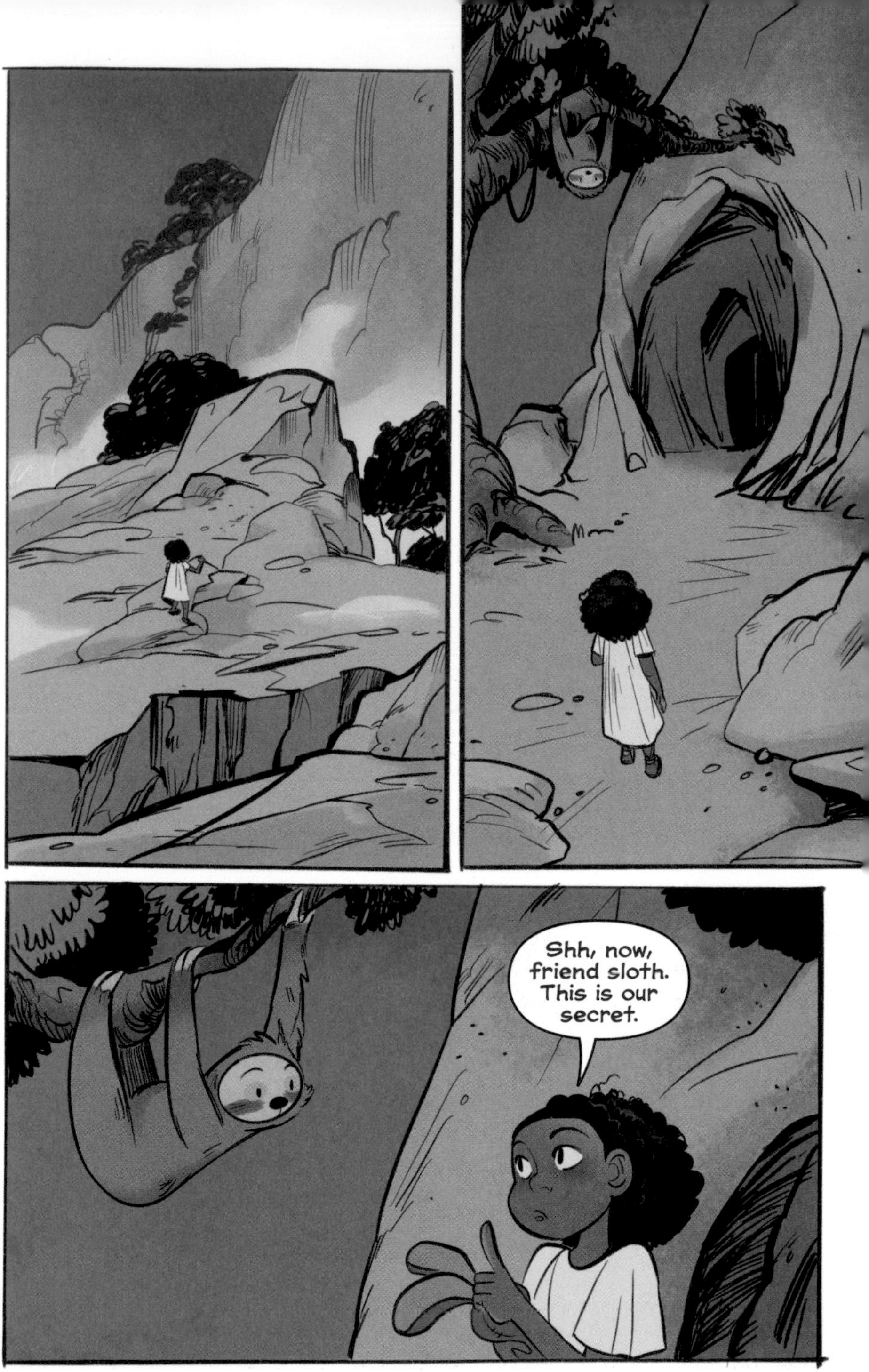
Shh, now, friend sloth. This is our secret.

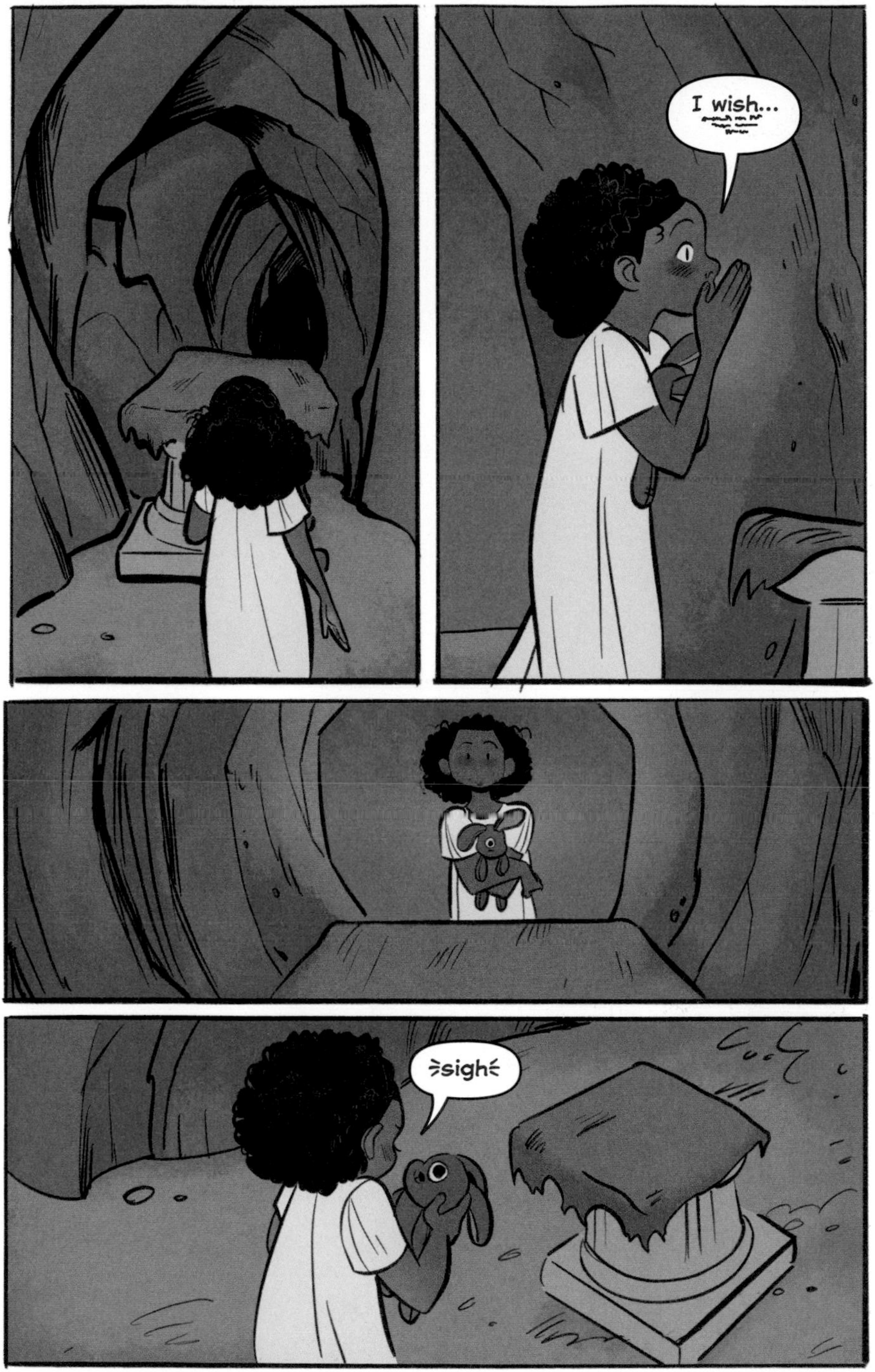
I wish...
sigh

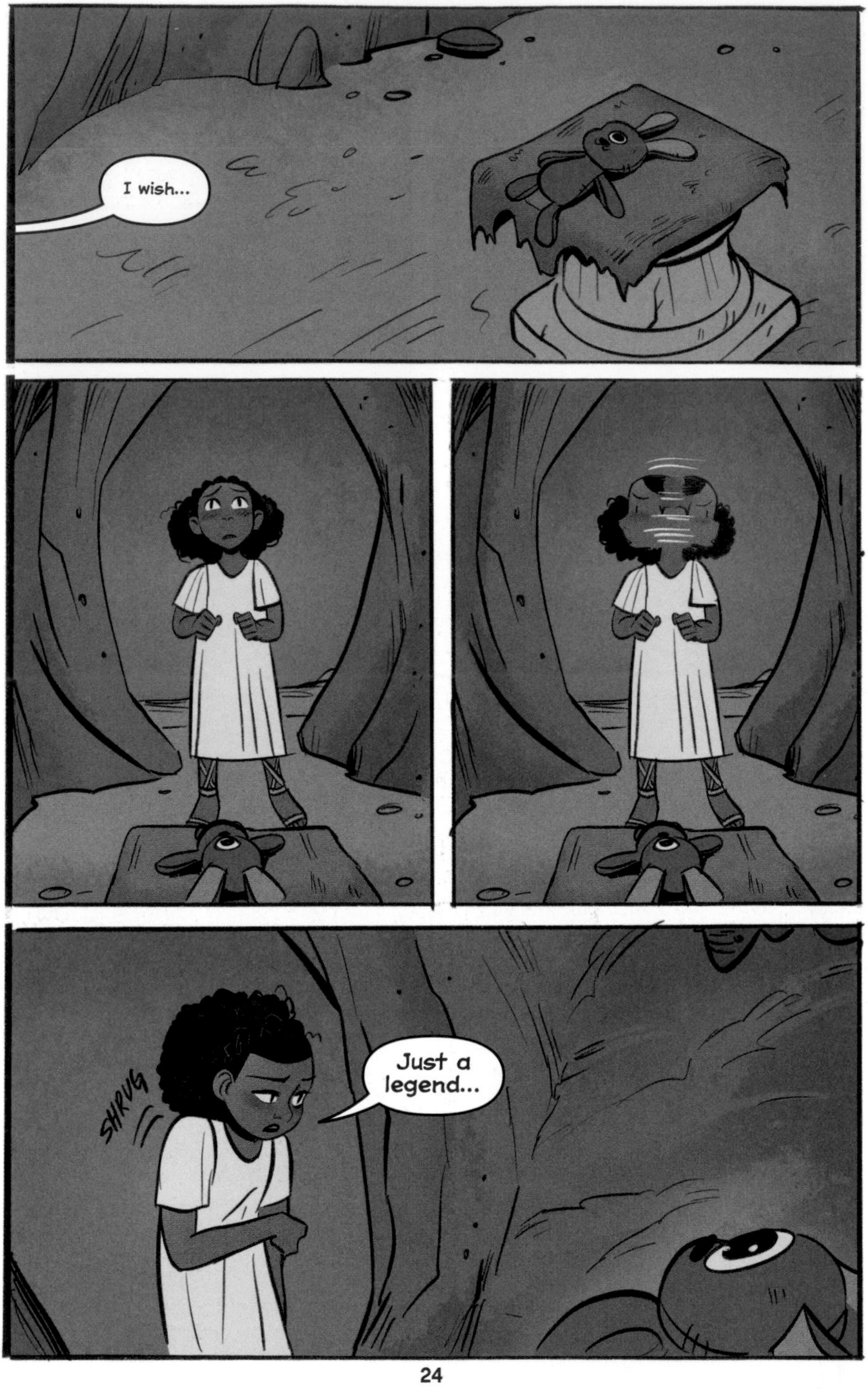
I wish...
SHRUG
Just a legend...

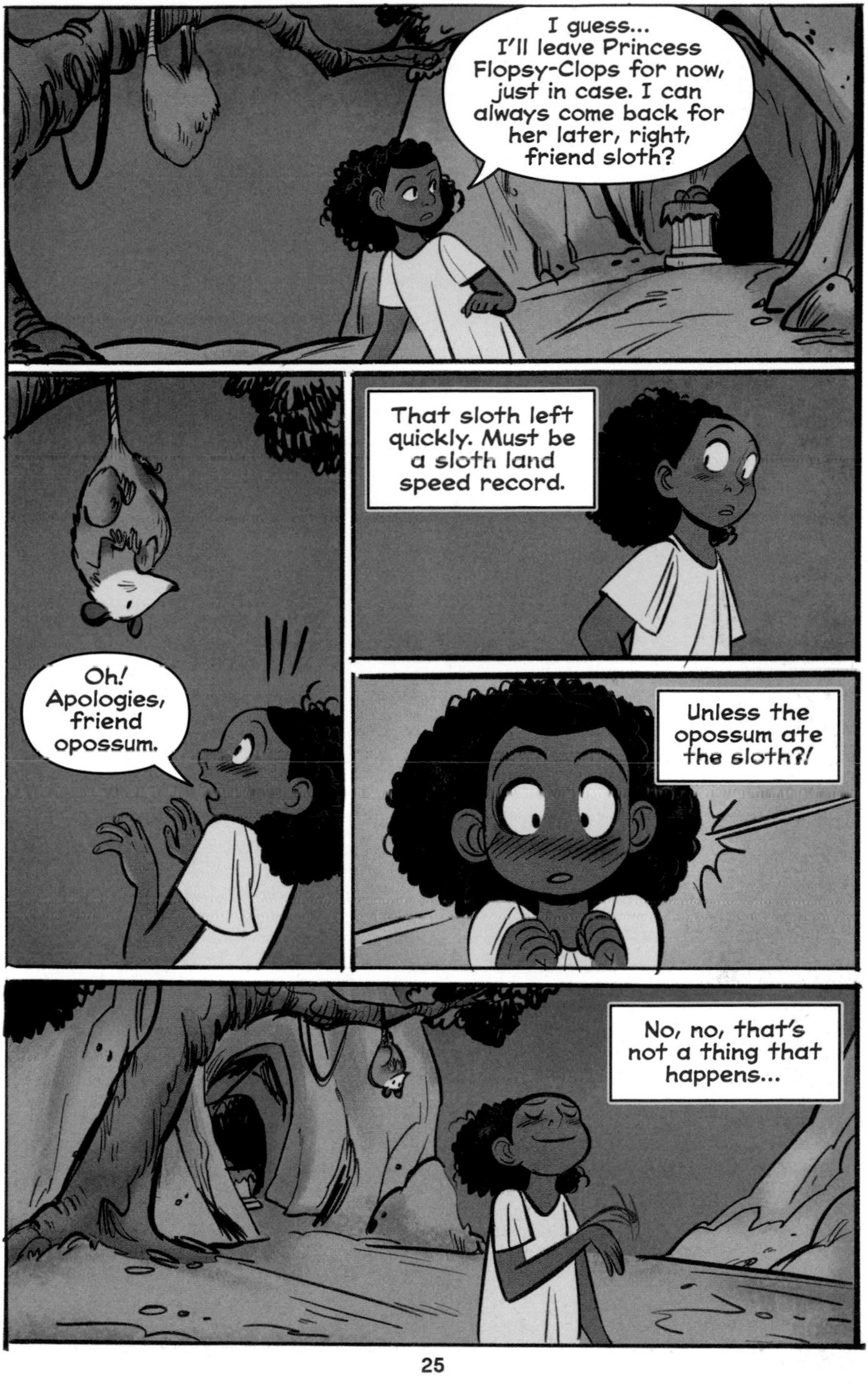
I guess... I'll leave Princess Flopsy-Clops for now, just in case. I can always come back for her later, right, friend sloth?
That sloth left quickly. Must be a sloth land speed record.
Oh! Apologies, friend opossum.
Unless the opossum ate the sloth?!
No, no, that's not a thing that happens...

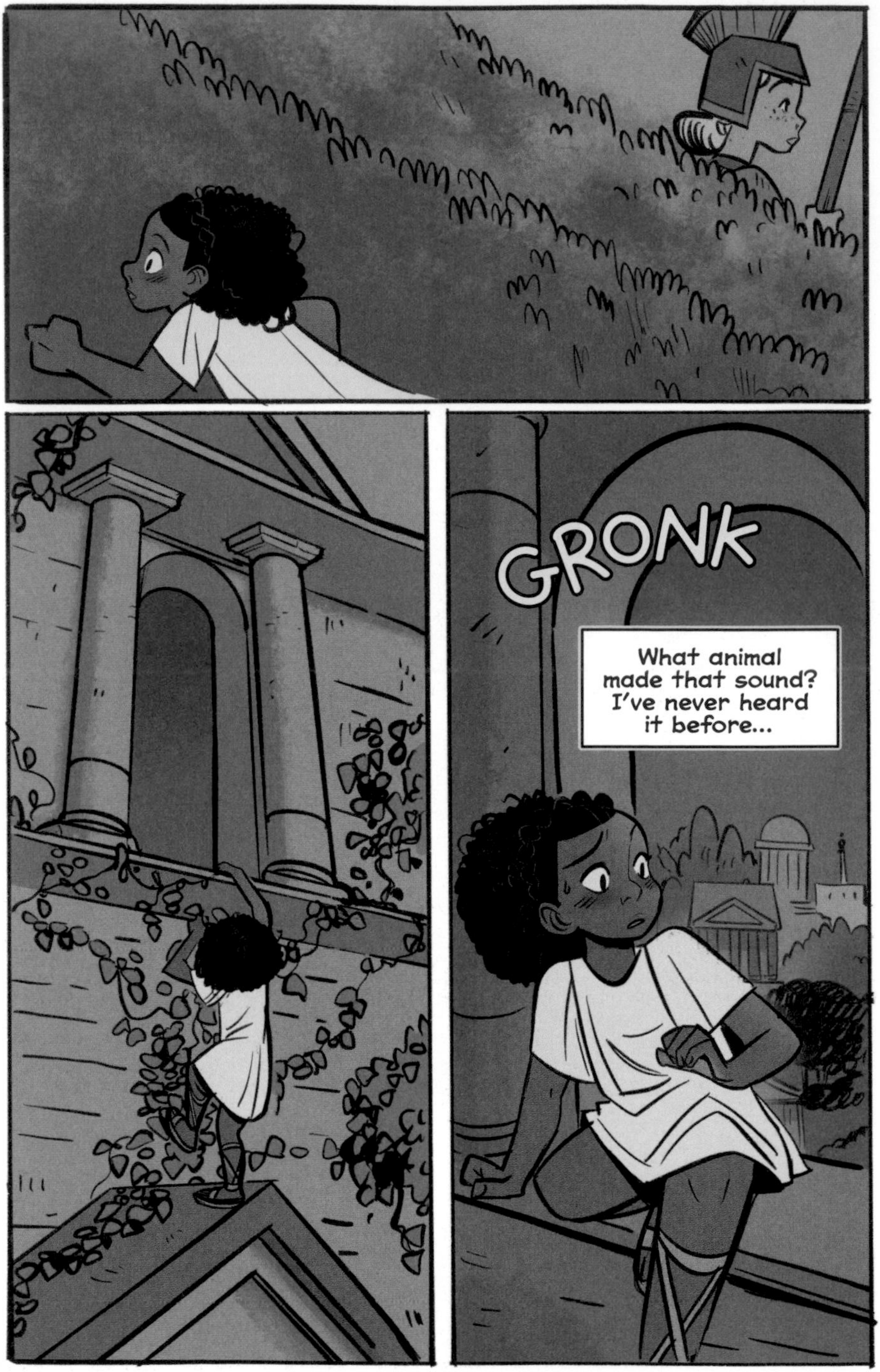
GRONK
What animal made that sound? I've never heard it before...

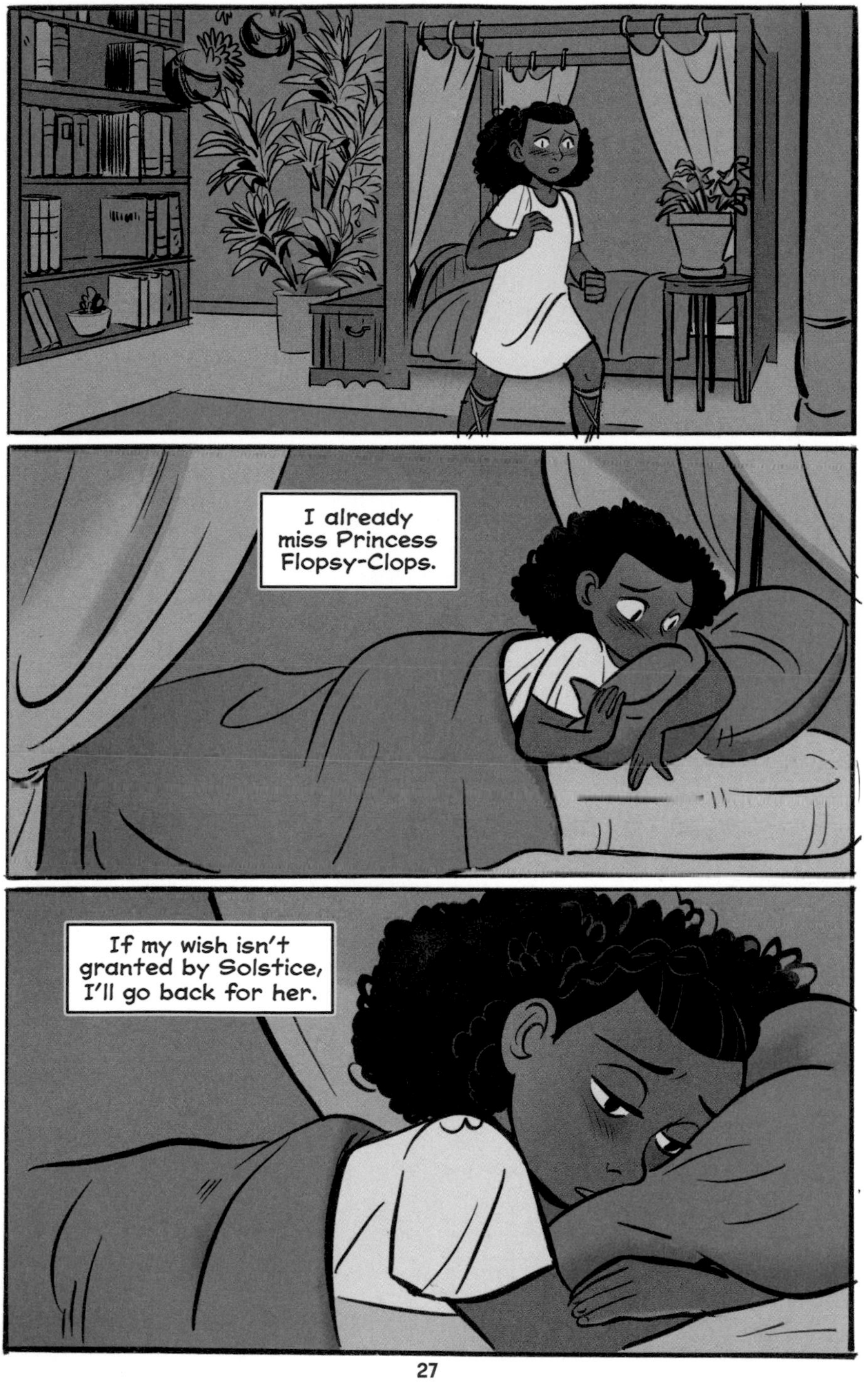
I already miss Princess Flopsy-Clops.
If my wish isn't granted by Solstice, I'll go back for her.

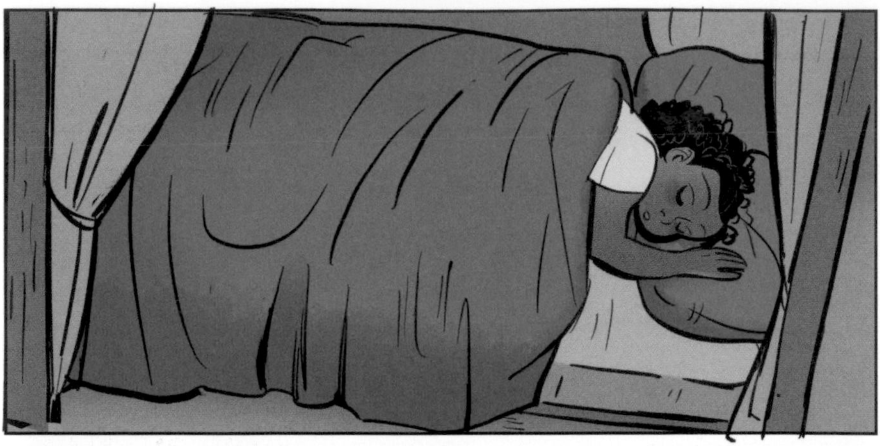

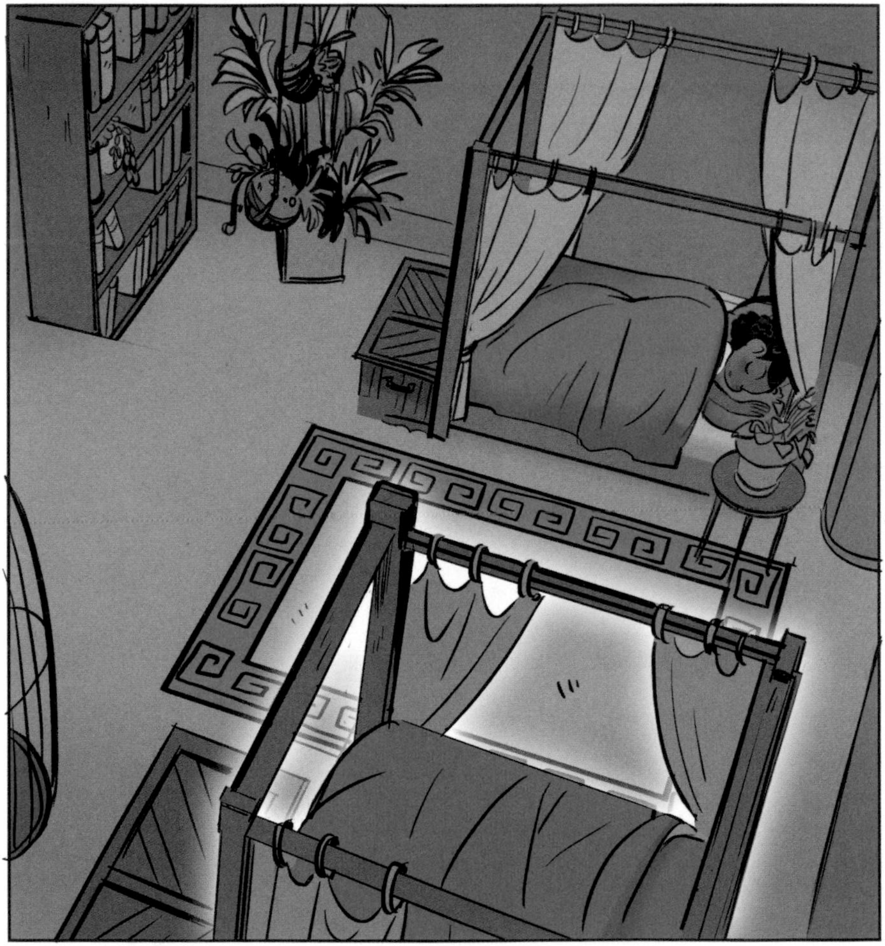

CHAPTER TWO

DIANA

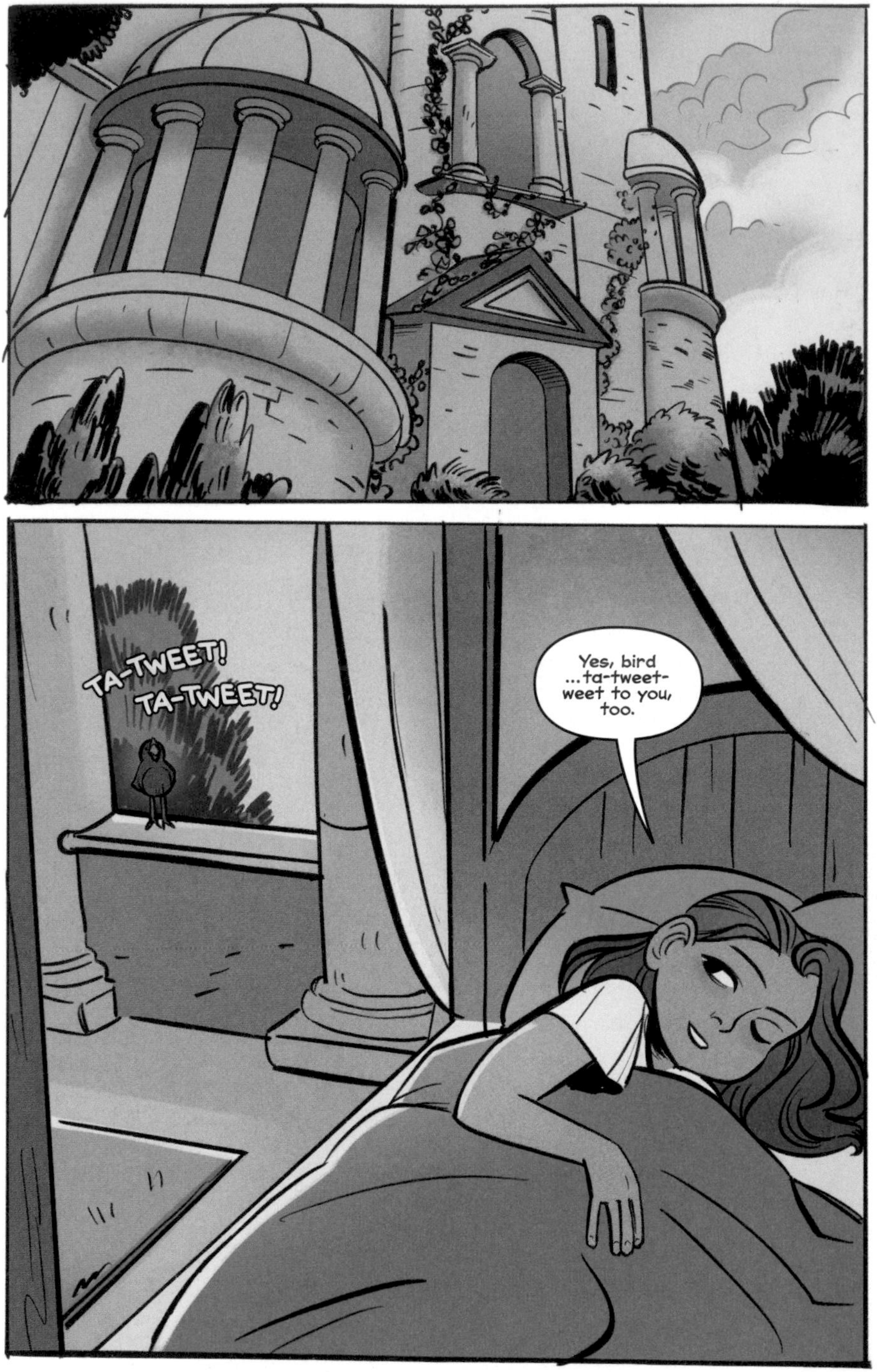
TA-TWEET!
TA-TWEET!
Yes, bird ...ta-tweet-weet to you, too.

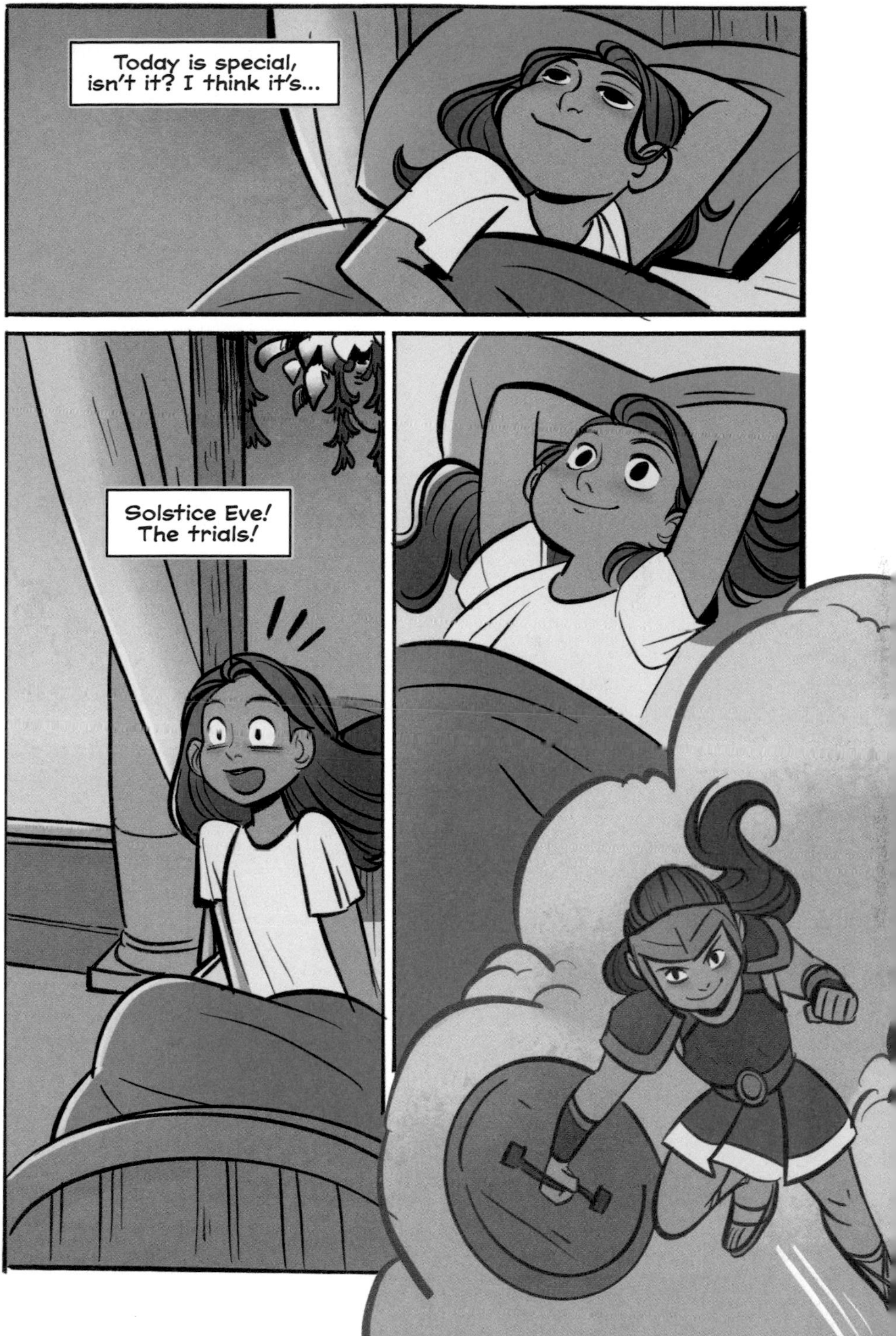
Today is special, isn't it? I think it's...
Solstice Eve! The trials!

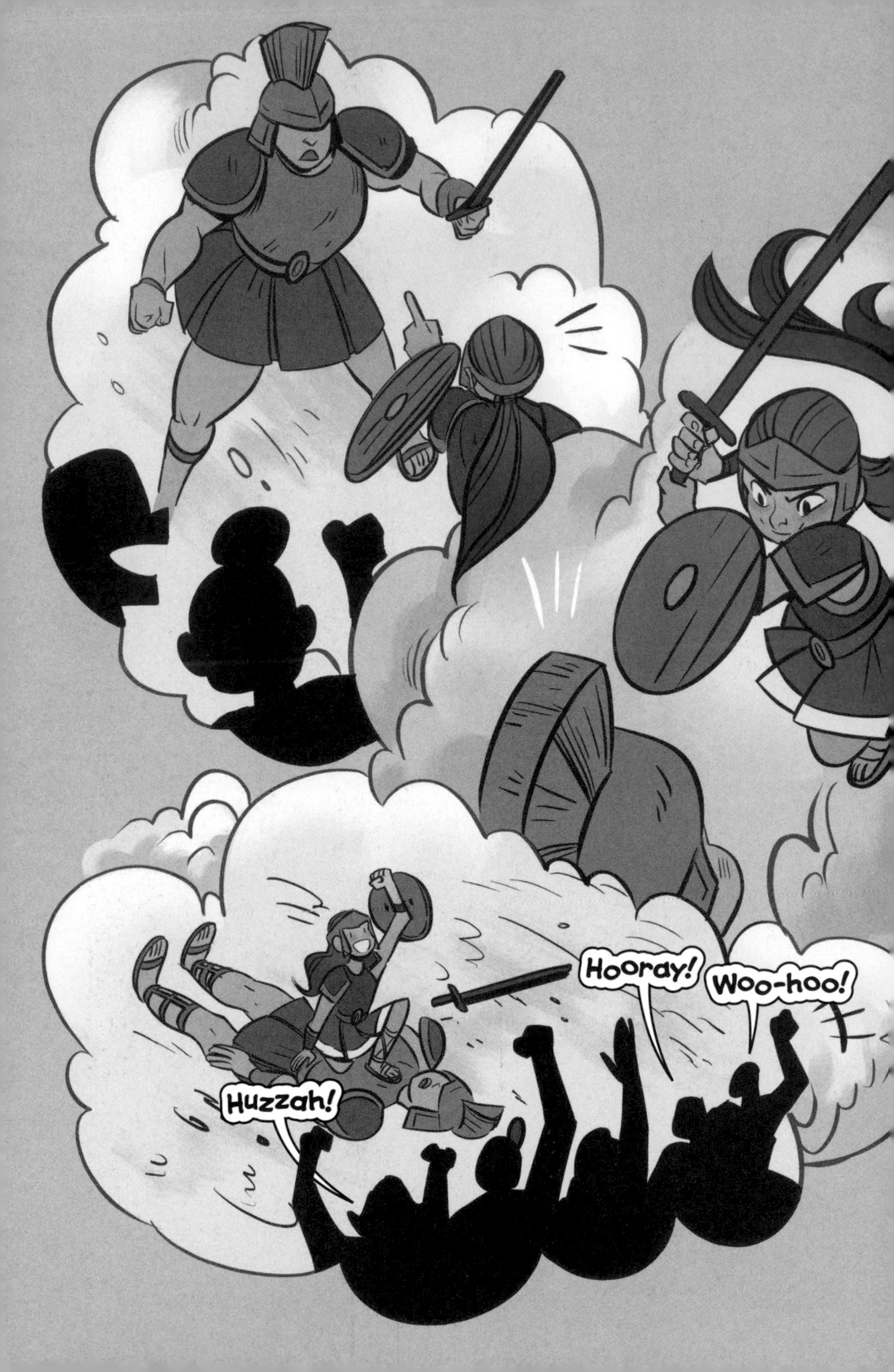
Huzzah!
Hooray!
Woo-hoo!

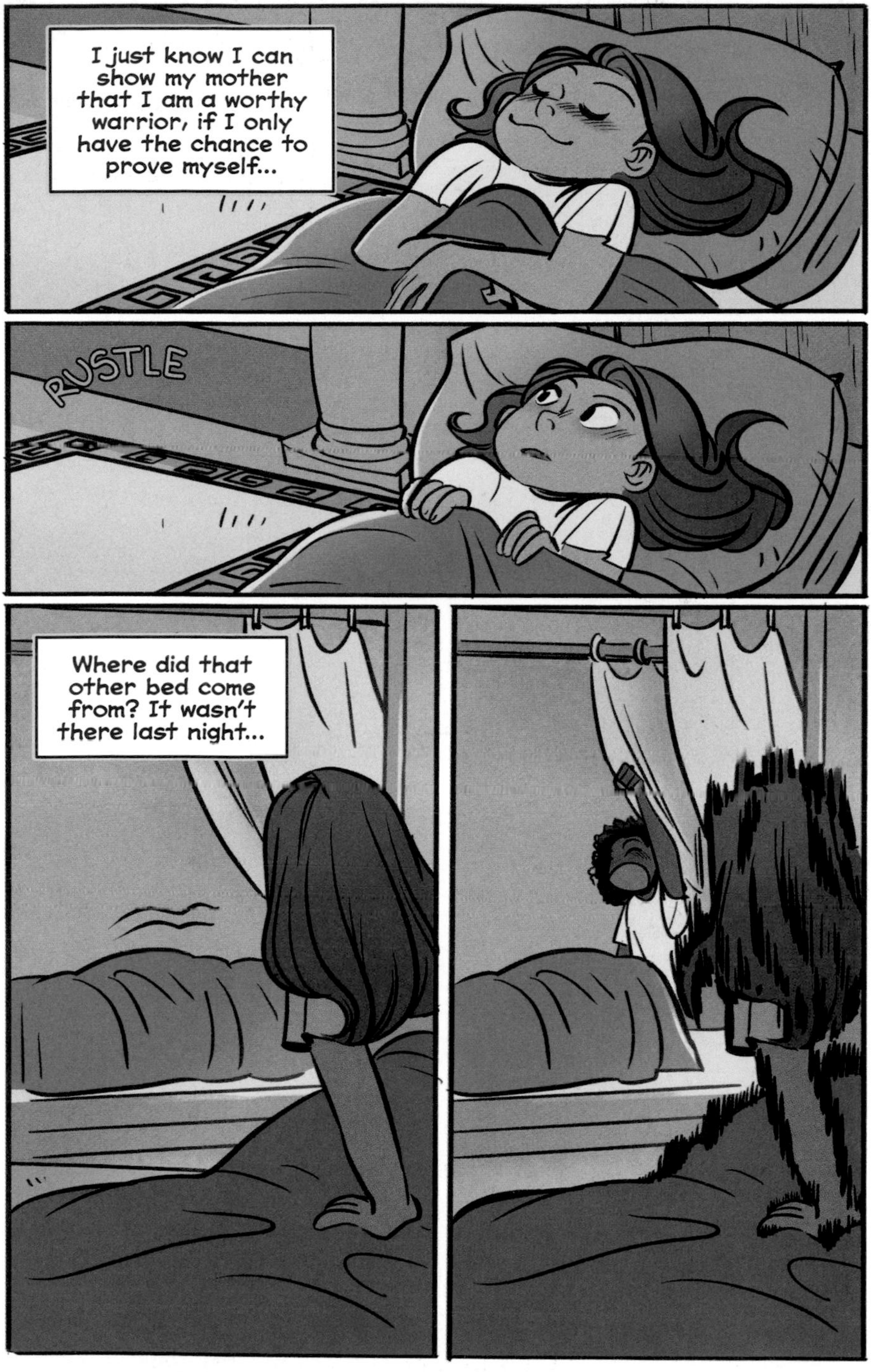
I just know I can show my mother that I am a worthy warrior, if I only have the chance to prove myself...
RUSTLE
Where did that other bed come from? It wasn't there last night...

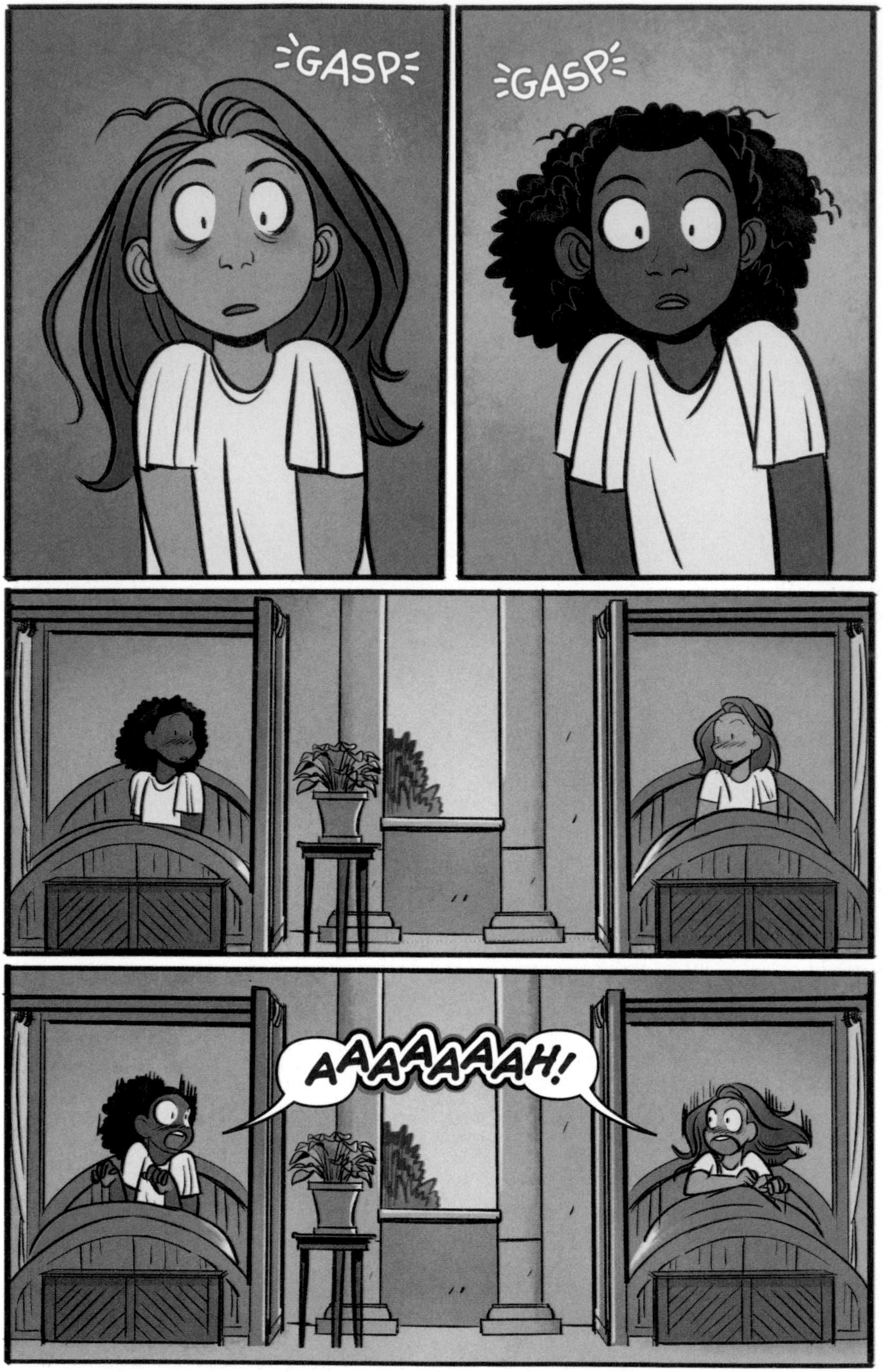
GASP
GASP
AAAAAAAH!

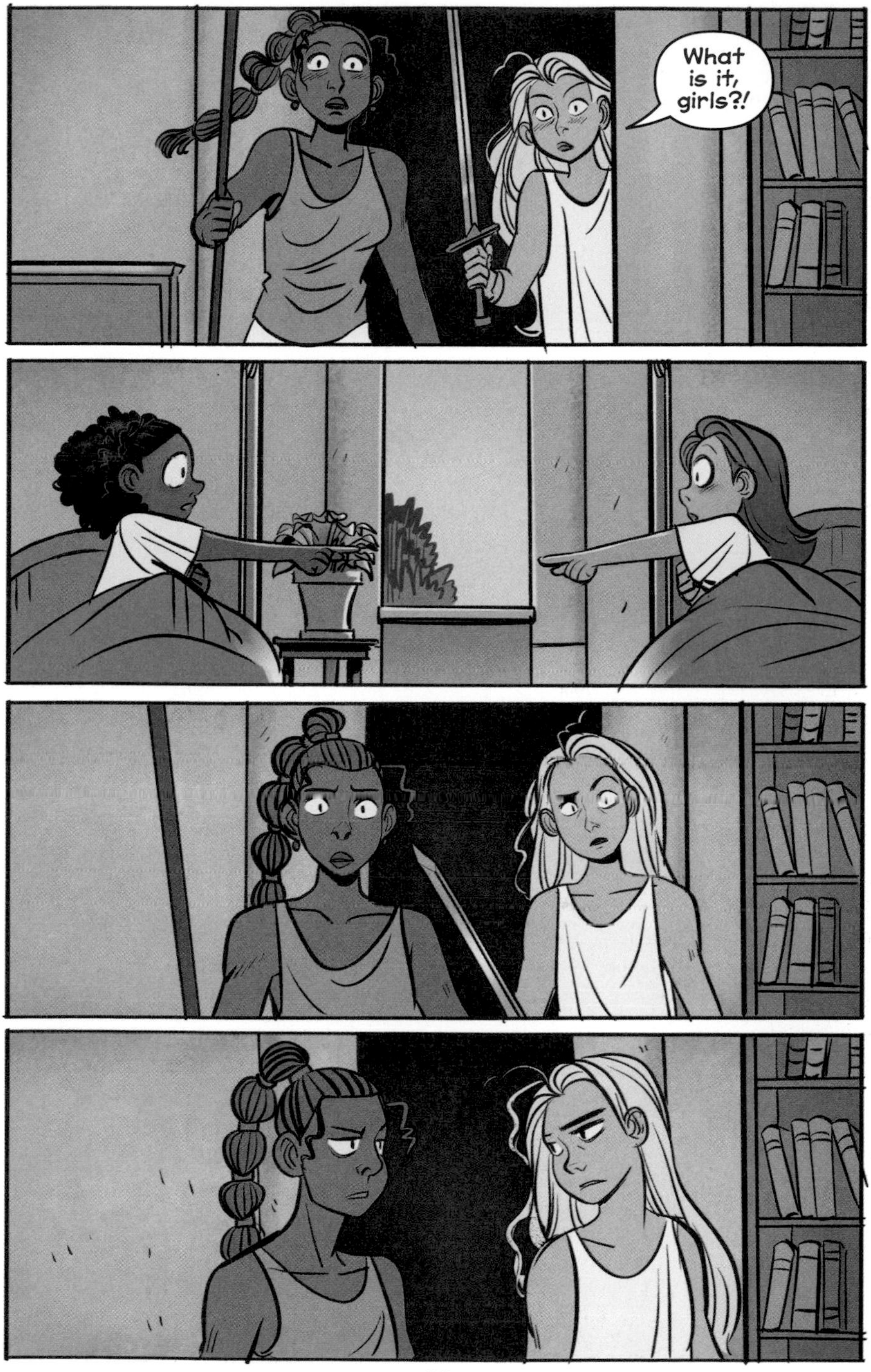
What is it, girls?!

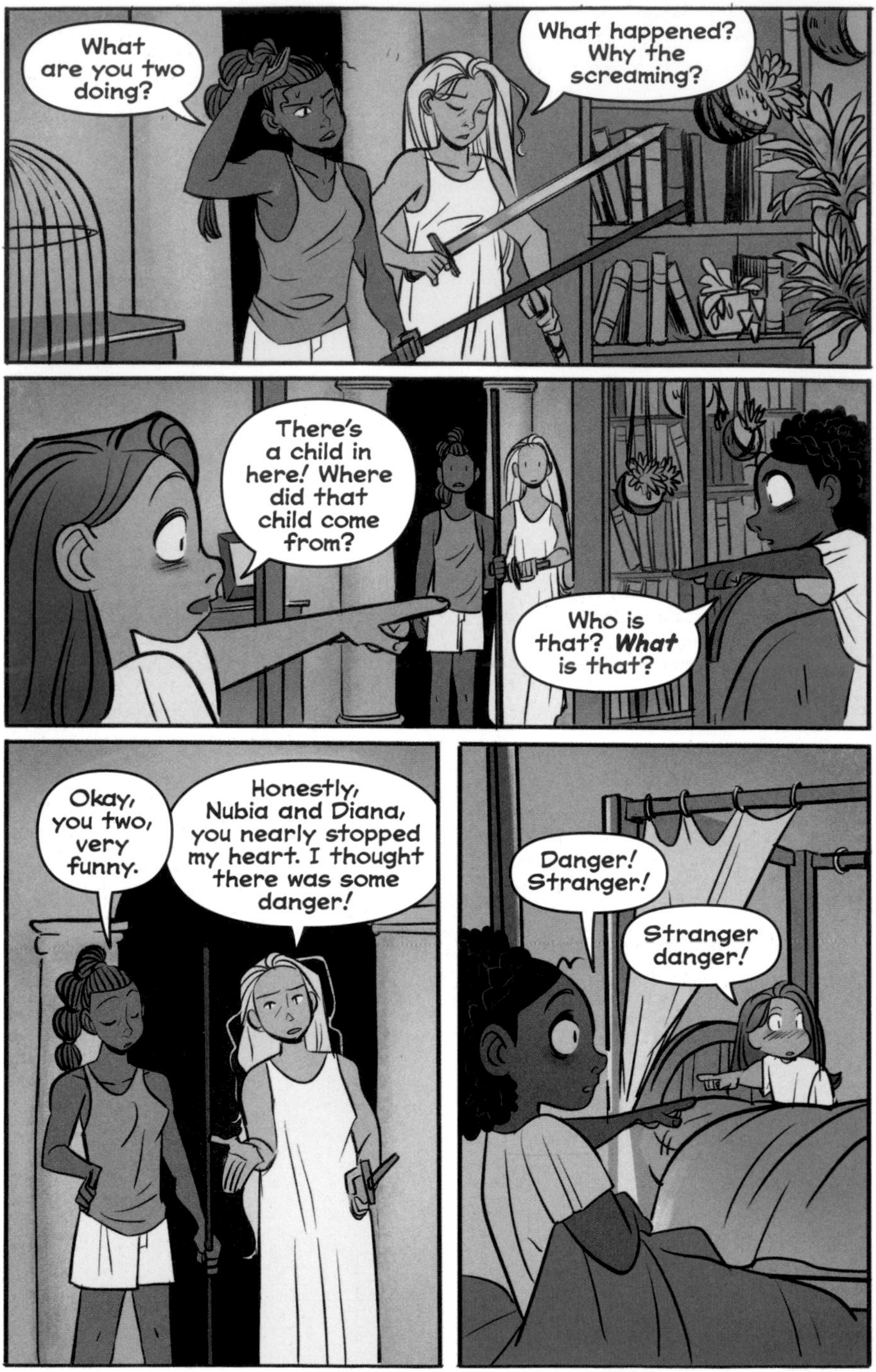
What are you two doing?
What happened? Why the screaming?
There's a child in here! Where did that child come from?
Who is that? *What* is that?
Okay, you two, very funny.
Honestly, Nubia and Diana, you nearly stopped my heart. I thought there was some danger!
Danger! Stranger!
Stranger danger!

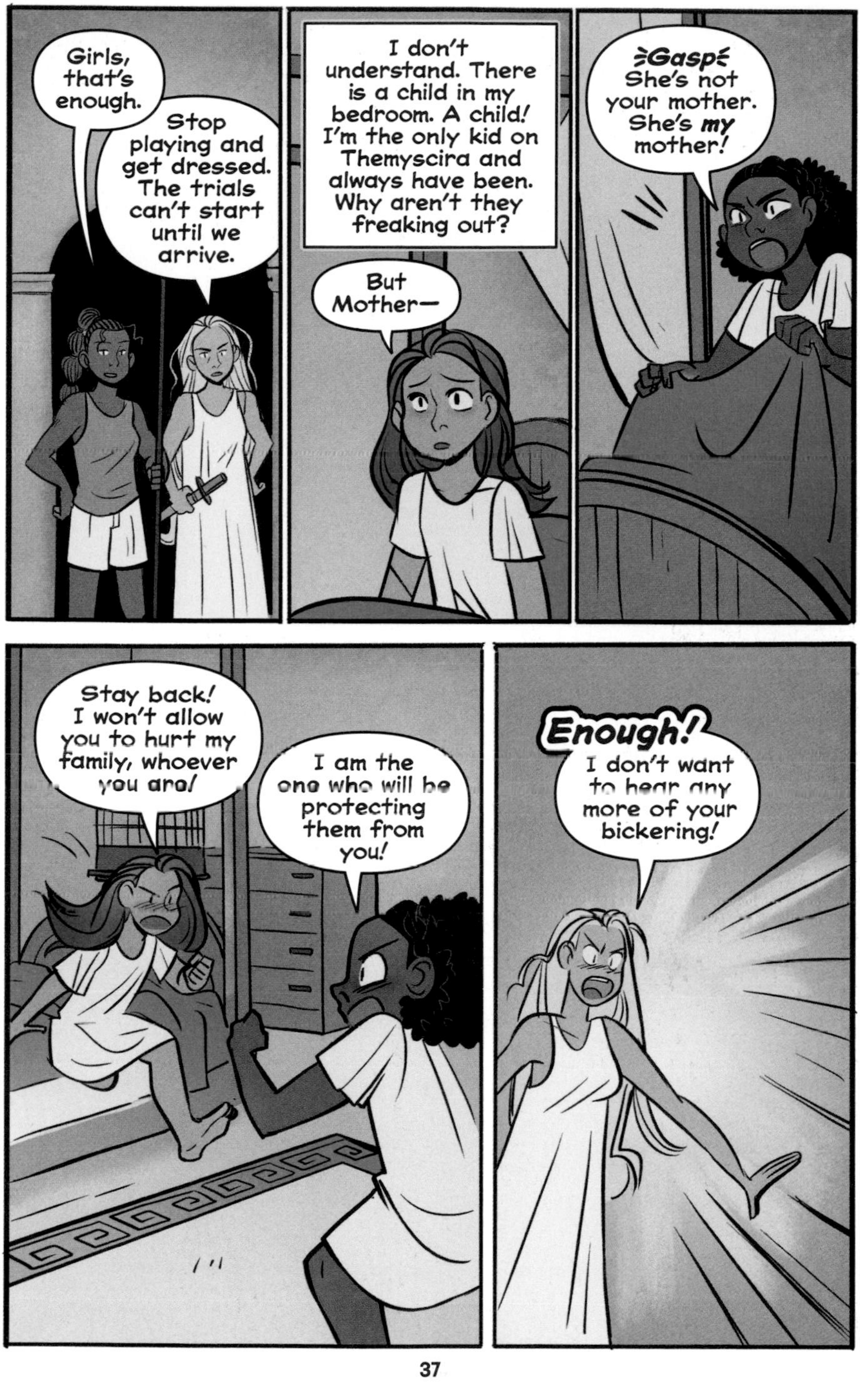

Girls, that's enough.
Stop playing and get dressed. The trials can't start until we arrive.
I don't understand. There is a child in my bedroom. A child! I'm the only kid on Themyscira and always have been. Why aren't they freaking out?
But Mother—
Gasp
She's not your mother. She's *my* mother!
Stay back! I won't allow you to hurt my family, whoever you are!
I am the one who will be protecting them from you!
Enough!
I don't want to hear any more of your bickering!

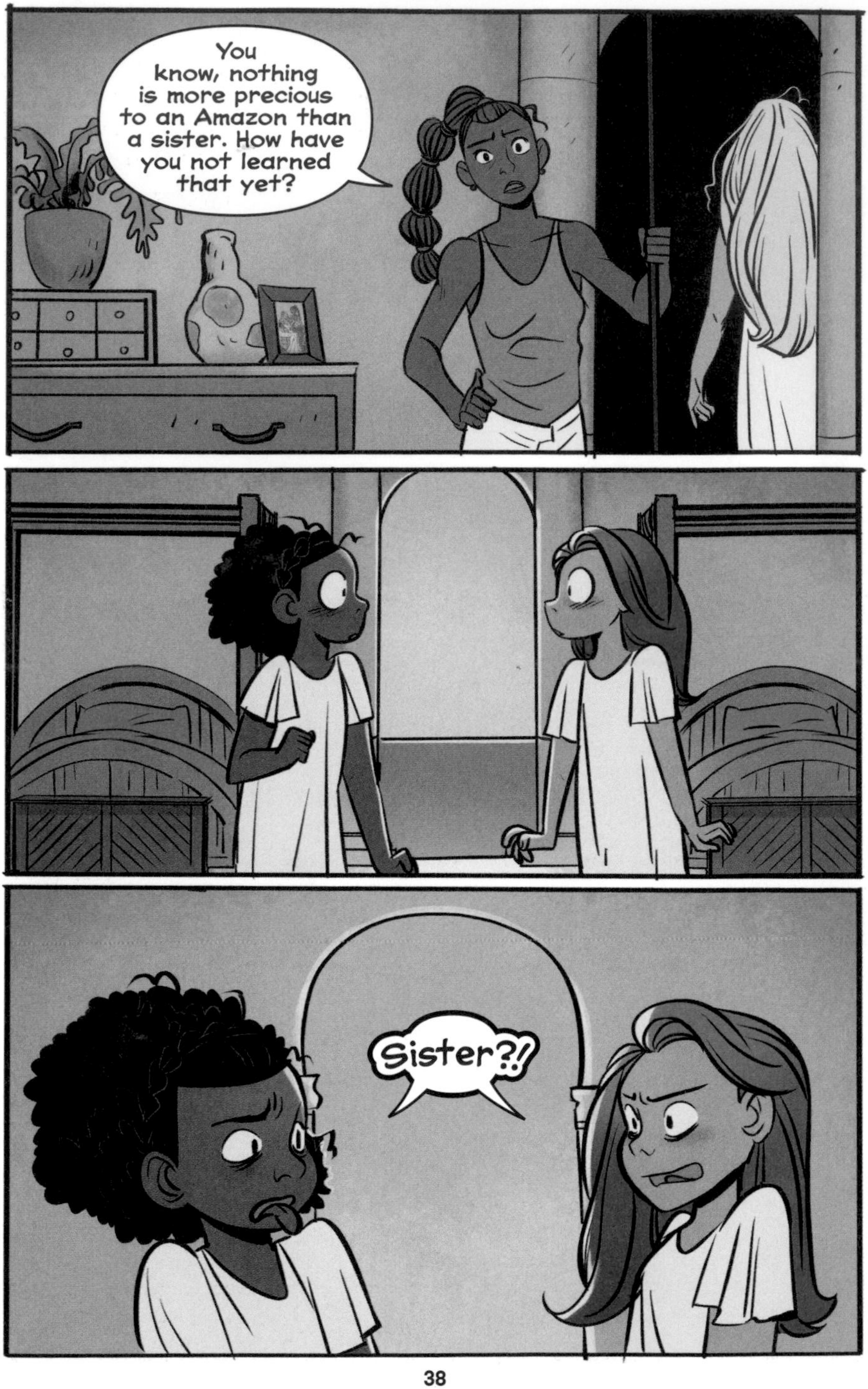
You know, nothing is more precious to an Amazon than a sister. How have you not learned that yet?
Sister?!

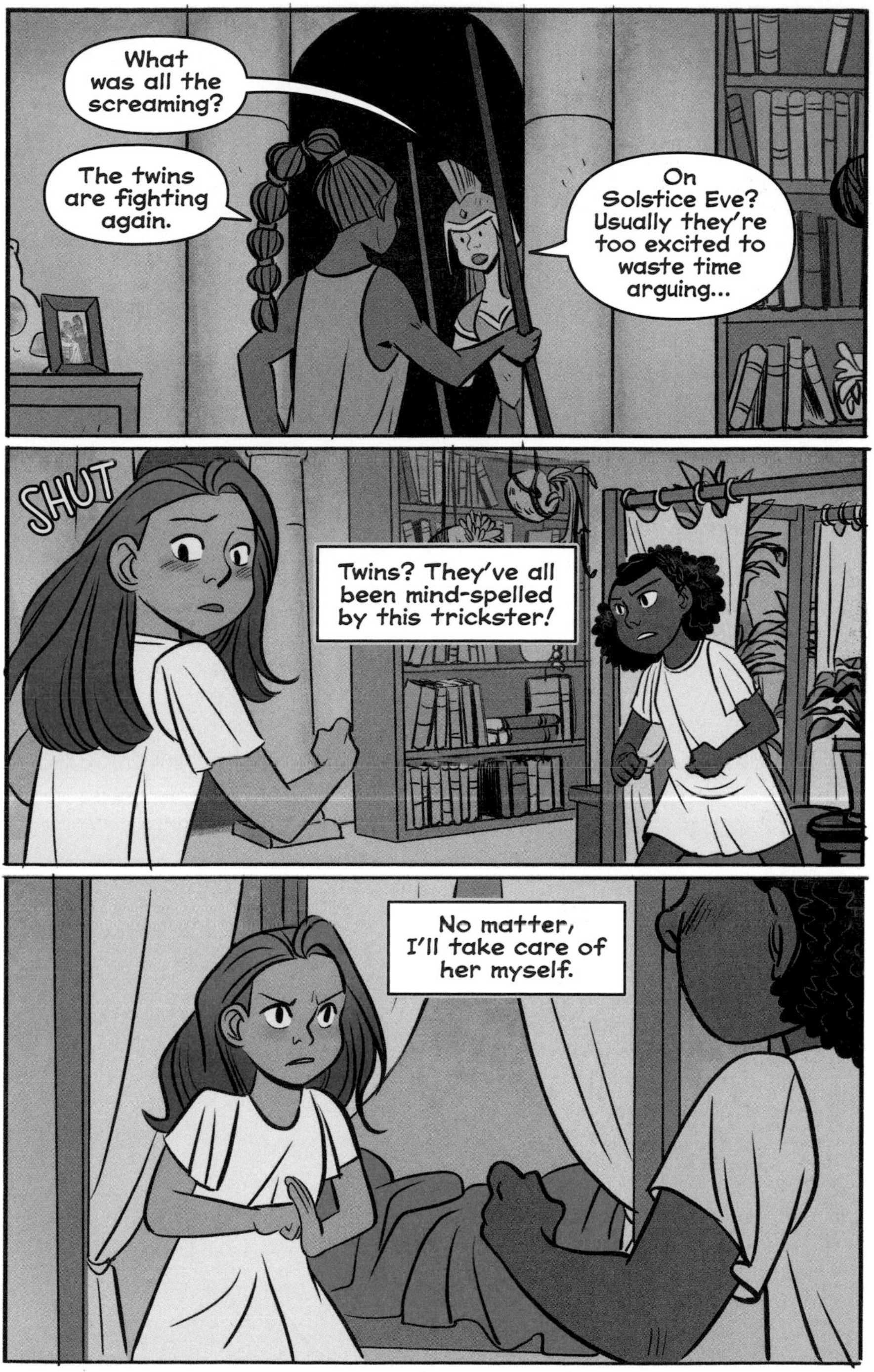
What was all the screaming?
The twins are fighting again.
On Solstice Eve? Usually they're too excited to waste time arguing...
SHUT
Twins? They've all been mind-spelled by this trickster!
No matter, I'll take care of her myself.

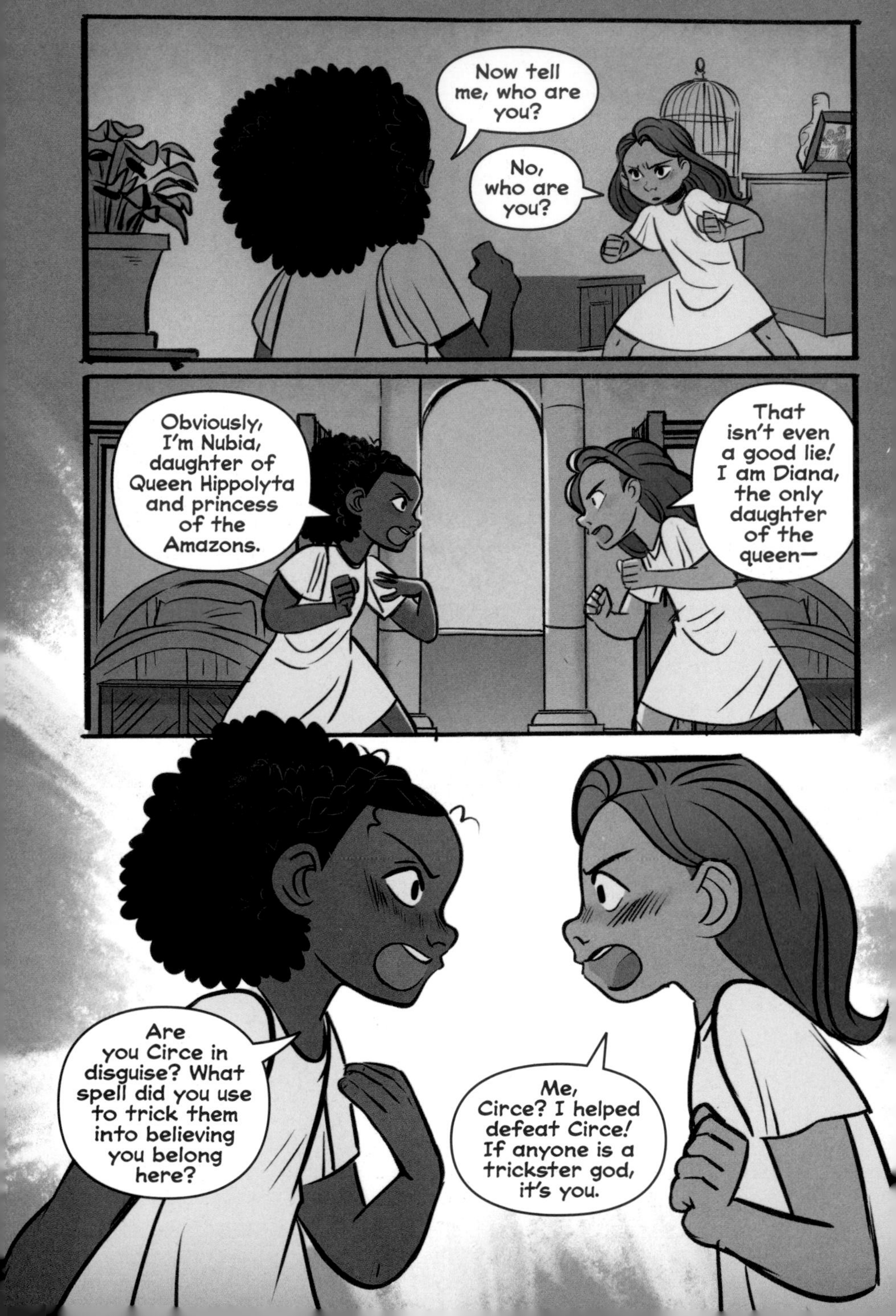
Now tell me, who are you?
No, who are you?
Obviously, I'm Nubia, daughter of Queen Hippolyta and princess of the Amazons.
That isn't even a good lie! I am Diana, the only daughter of the queen—
Are you Circe in disguise? What spell did you use to trick them into believing you belong here?
Me, Circe? I helped defeat Circe! If anyone is a trickster god, it's you.

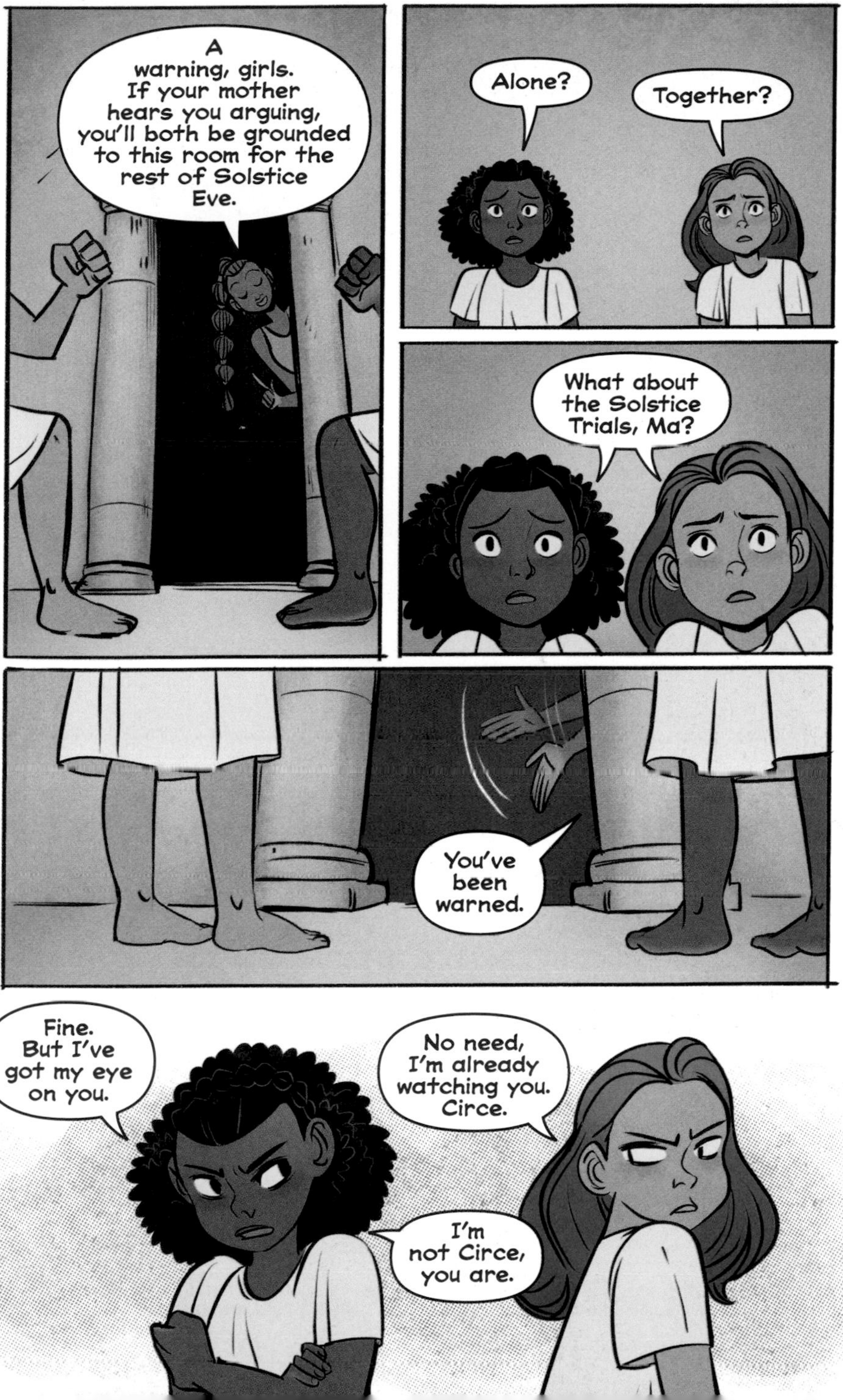
A warning, girls. If your mother hears you arguing, you'll both be grounded to this room for the rest of Solstice Eve.
Alone?
Together?
What about the Solstice Trials, Ma?
You've been warned.
Fine. But I've got my eye on you.
No need, I'm already watching you. Circe.
I'm not Circe, you are.

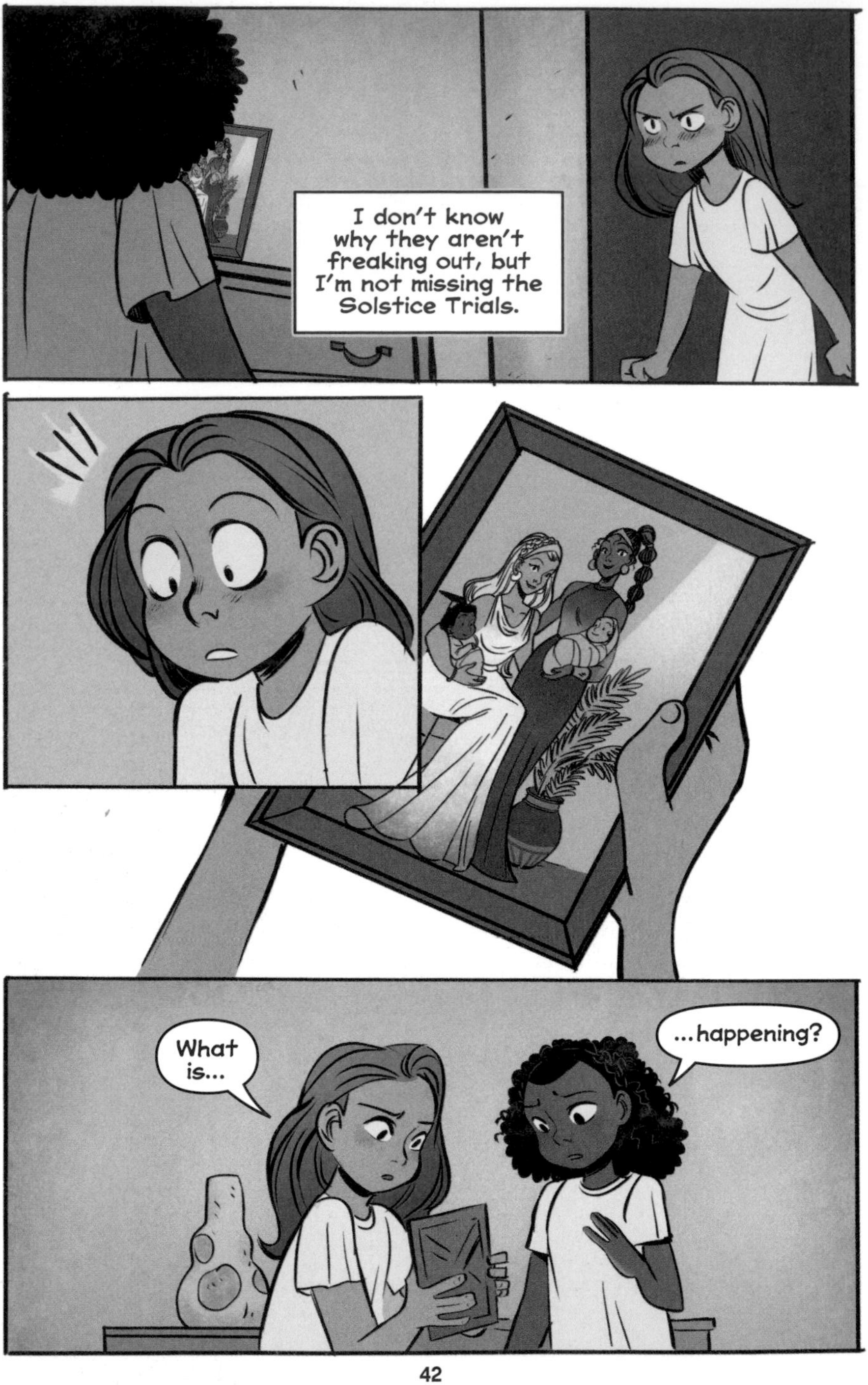
I don't know why they aren't freaking out, but I'm not missing the Solstice Trials.
What is...
...happening?

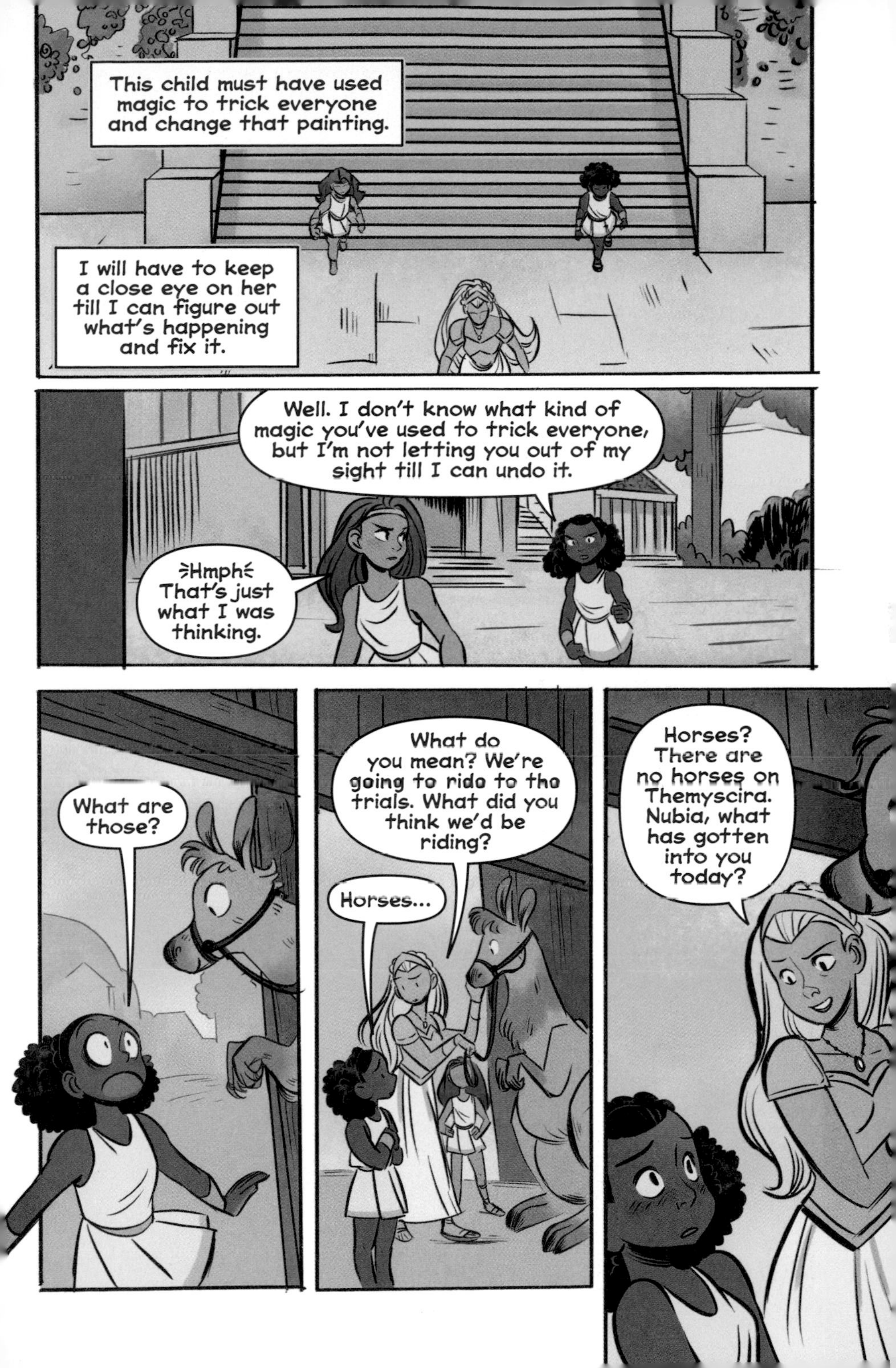
This child must have used magic to trick everyone and change that painting.
I will have to keep a close eye on her till I can figure out what's happening and fix it.
Well. I don't know what kind of magic you've used to trick everyone, but I'm not letting you out of my sight till I can undo it.
Hmph That's just what I was thinking.
What are those?
What do you mean? We're going to ride to the trials. What did you think we'd be riding?
Horses...
Horses? There are no horses on Themyscira. Nubia, what has gotten into you today?

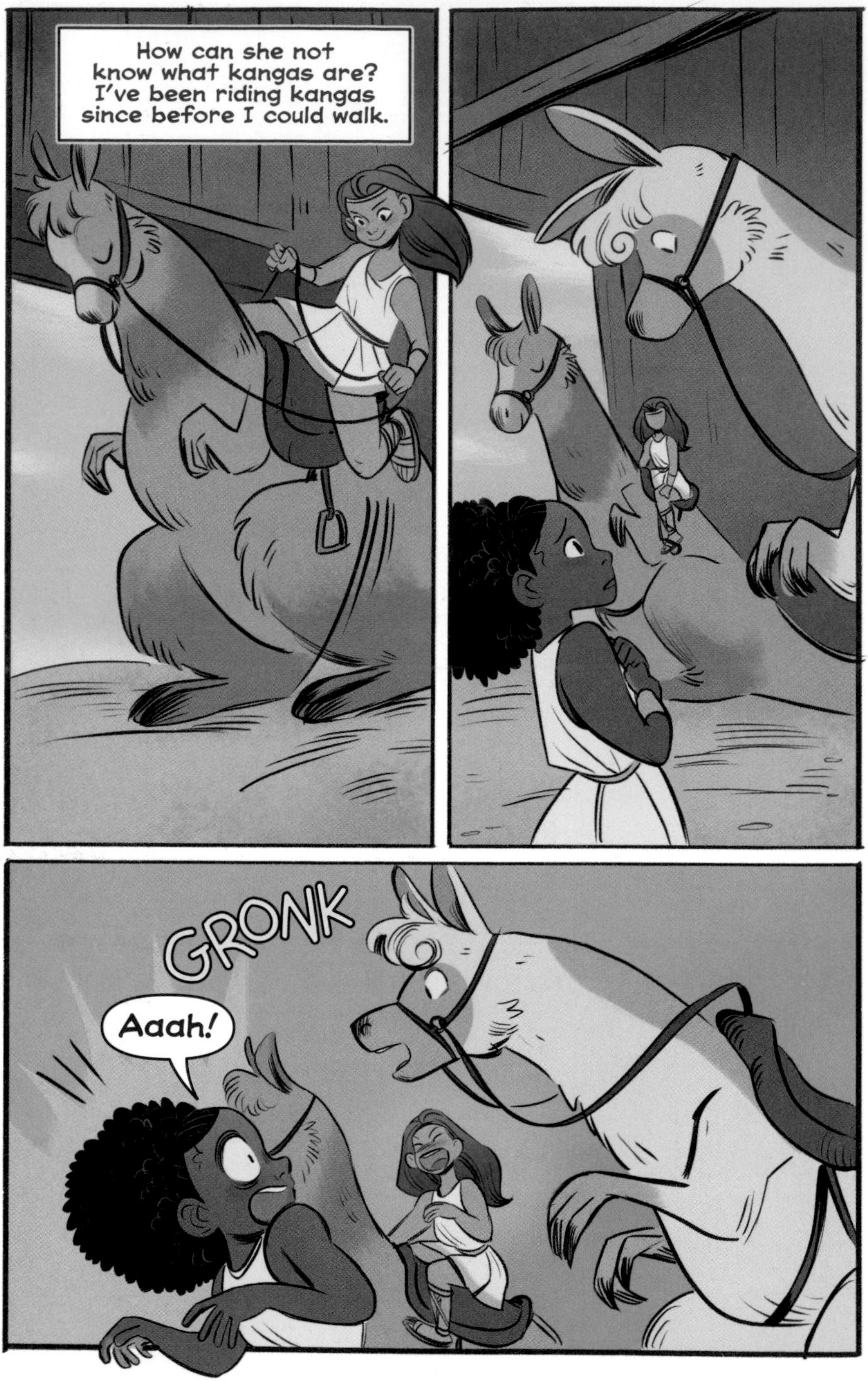
How can she not know what kangas are? I've been riding kangas since before I could walk.
GRONK
Aaah!

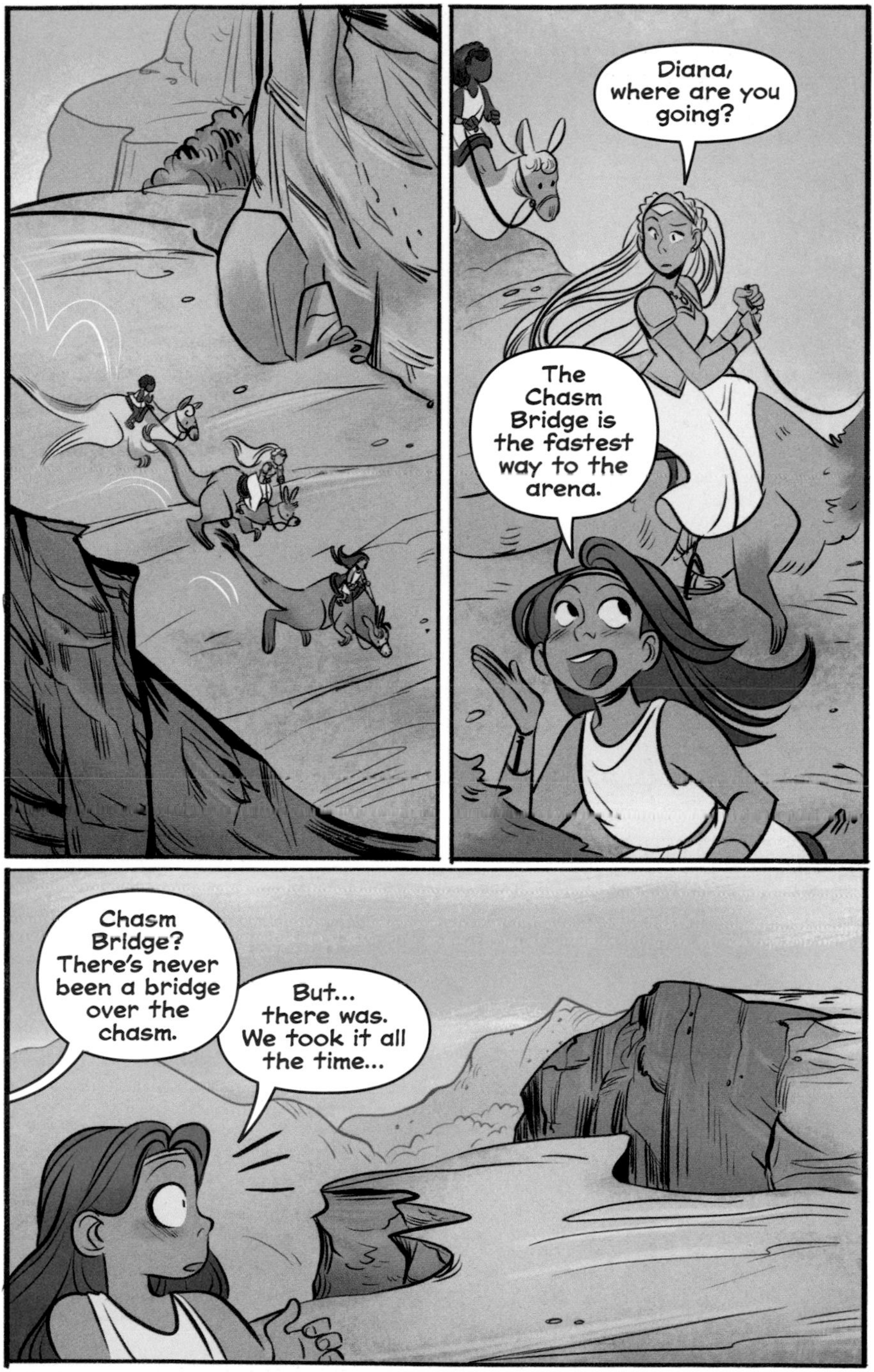
Diana, where are you going?
The Chasm Bridge is the fastest way to the arena.
Chasm Bridge? There's never been a bridge over the chasm.
But... there was. We took it all the time...

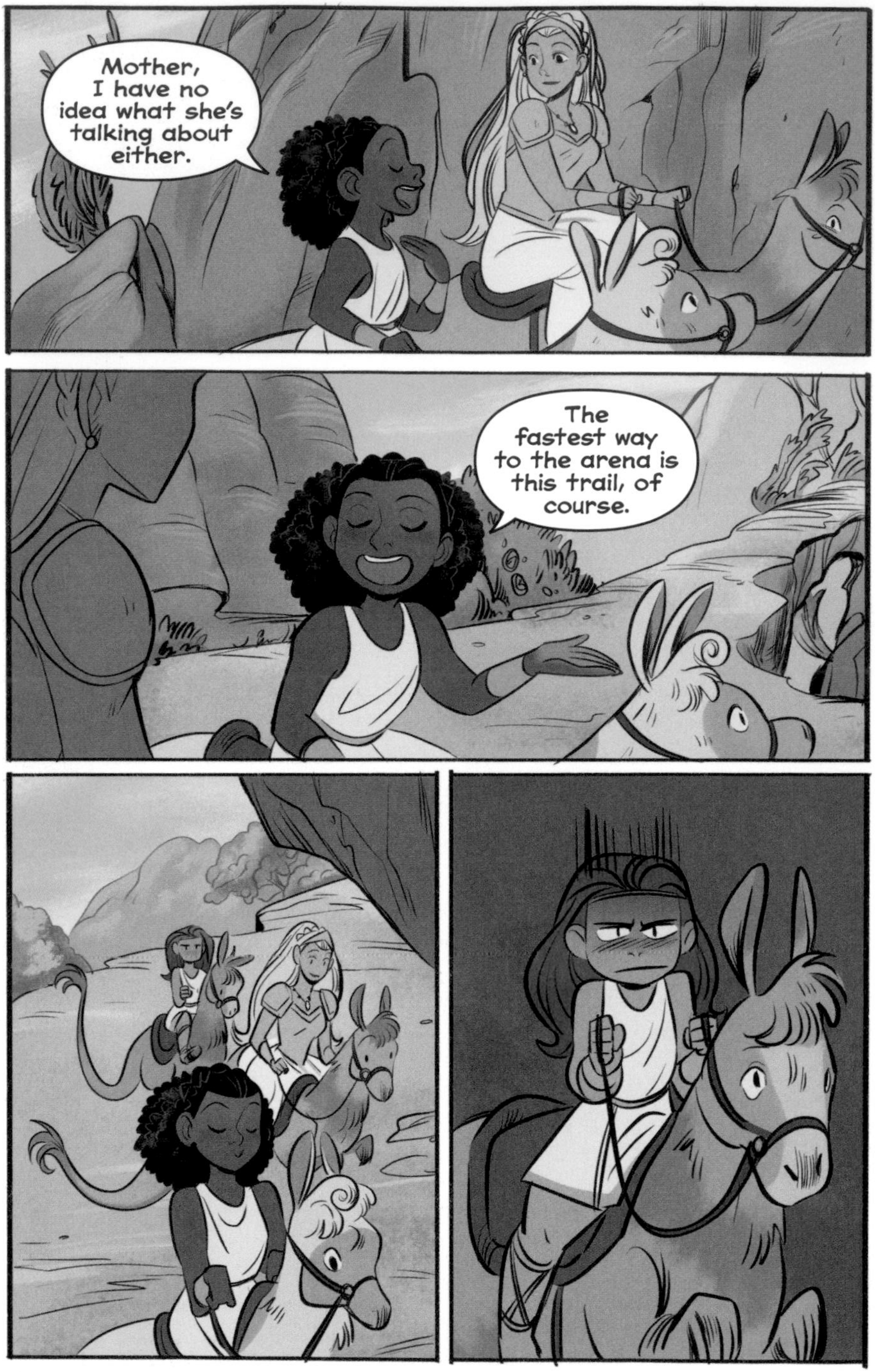
Mother, I have no idea what she's talking about either.
The fastest way to the arena is this trail, of course.

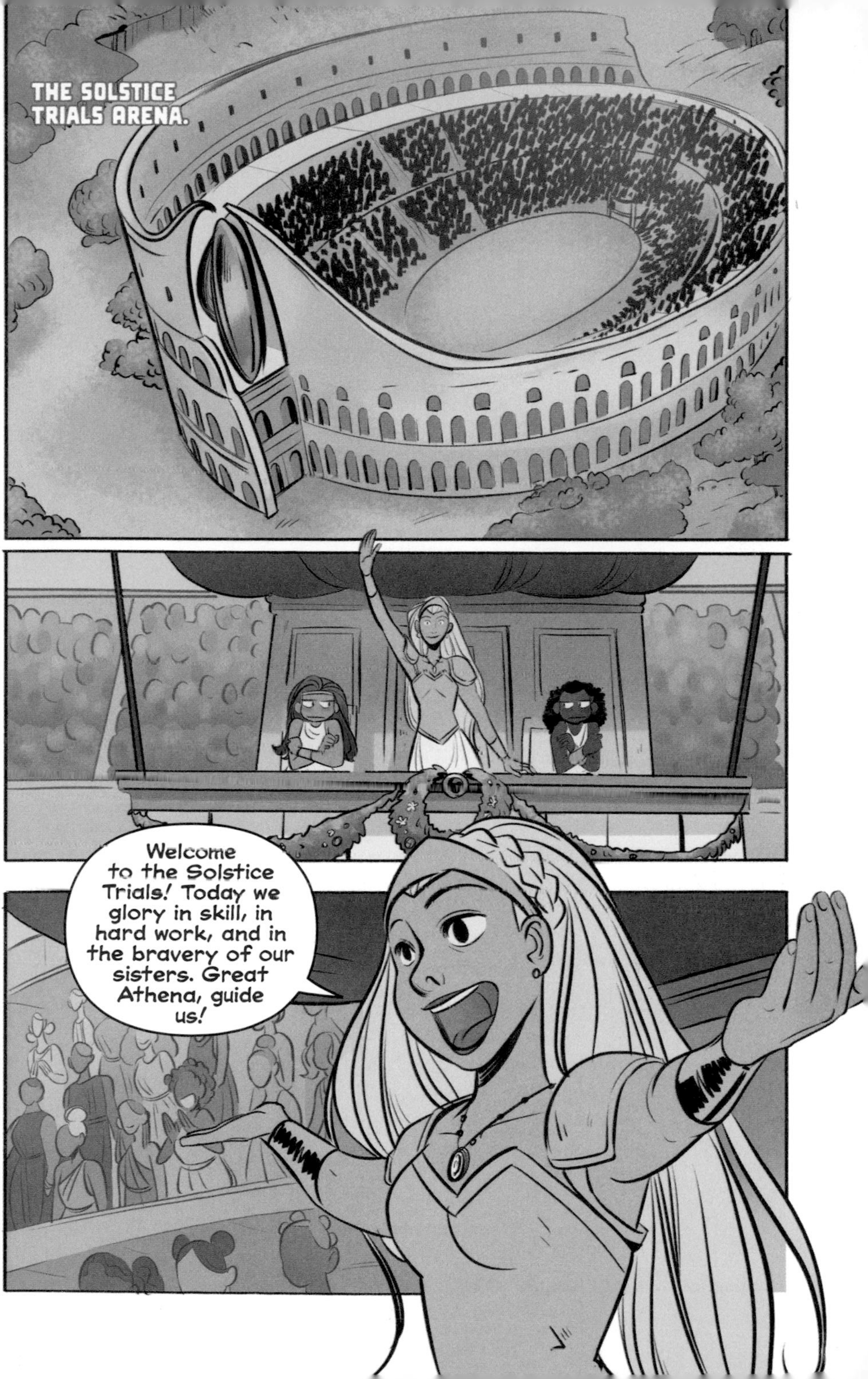
THE SOLSTICE TRIALS ARENA.
Welcome to the Solstice Trials! Today we glory in skill, in hard work, and in the bravery of our sisters. Great Athena, guide us!

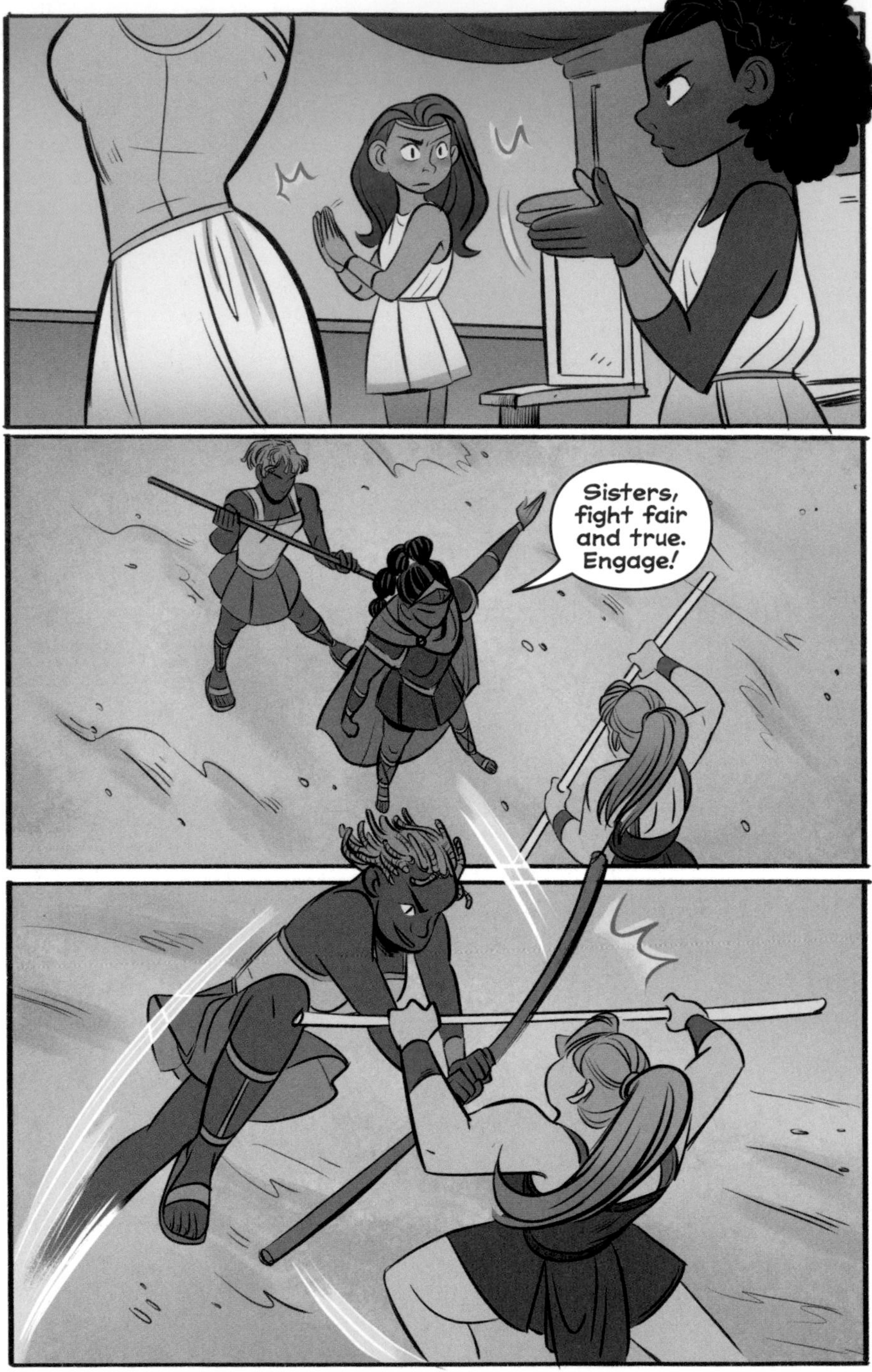
Sisters, fight fair and true. Engage!

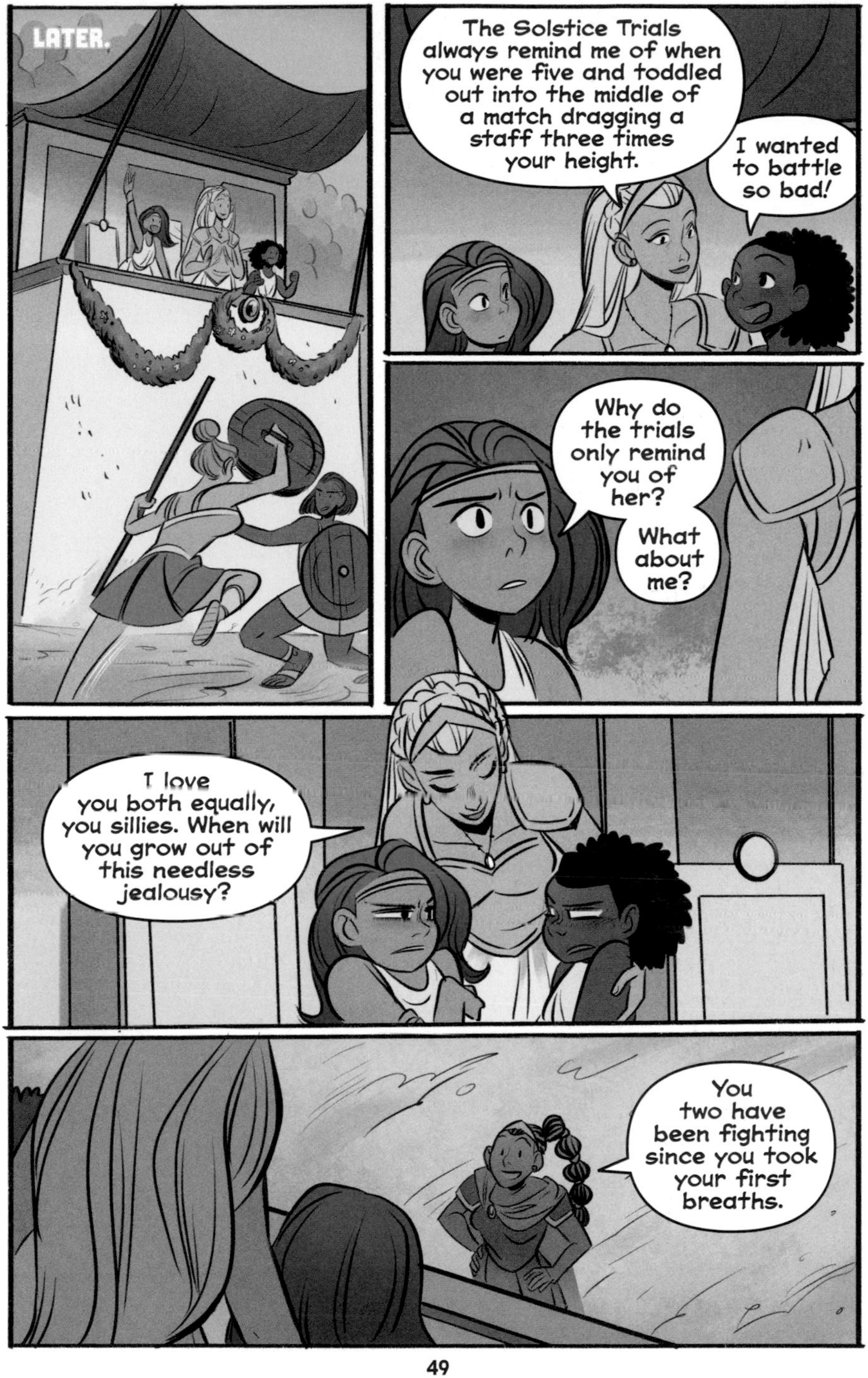
LATER.
The Solstice Trials always remind me of when you were five and toddled out into the middle of a match dragging a staff three times your height.
I wanted to battle so bad!
Why do the trials only remind you of her?
What about me?
I love you both equally, you sillies. When will you grow out of this needless jealousy?
You two have been fighting since you took your first breaths.

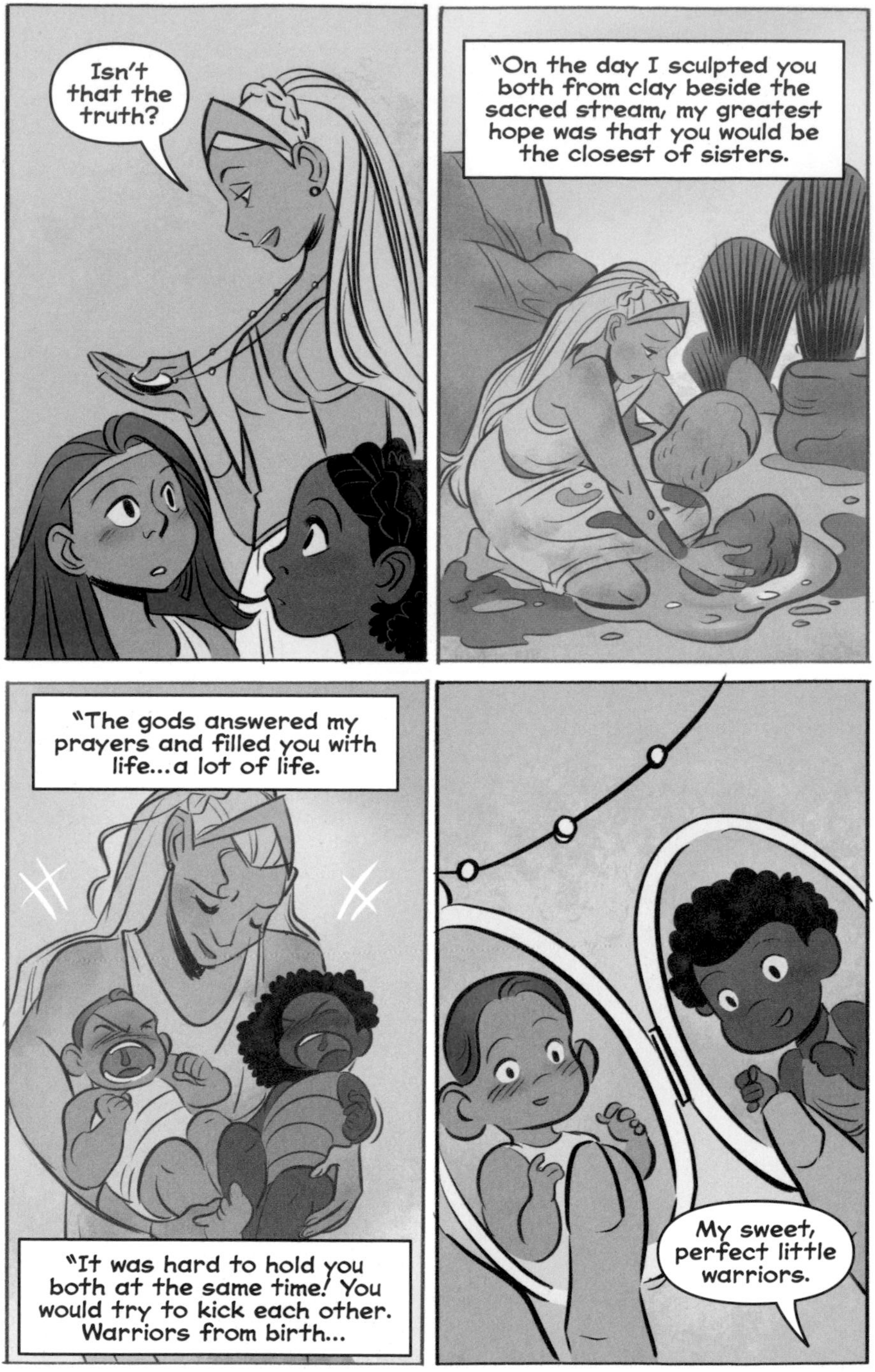
Isn't that the truth?
"On the day I sculpted you both from clay beside the sacred stream, my greatest hope was that you would be the closest of sisters.
"The gods answered my prayers and filled you with life...a lot of life.
"It was hard to hold you both at the same time! You would try to kick each other. Warriors from birth...
My sweet, perfect little warriors.

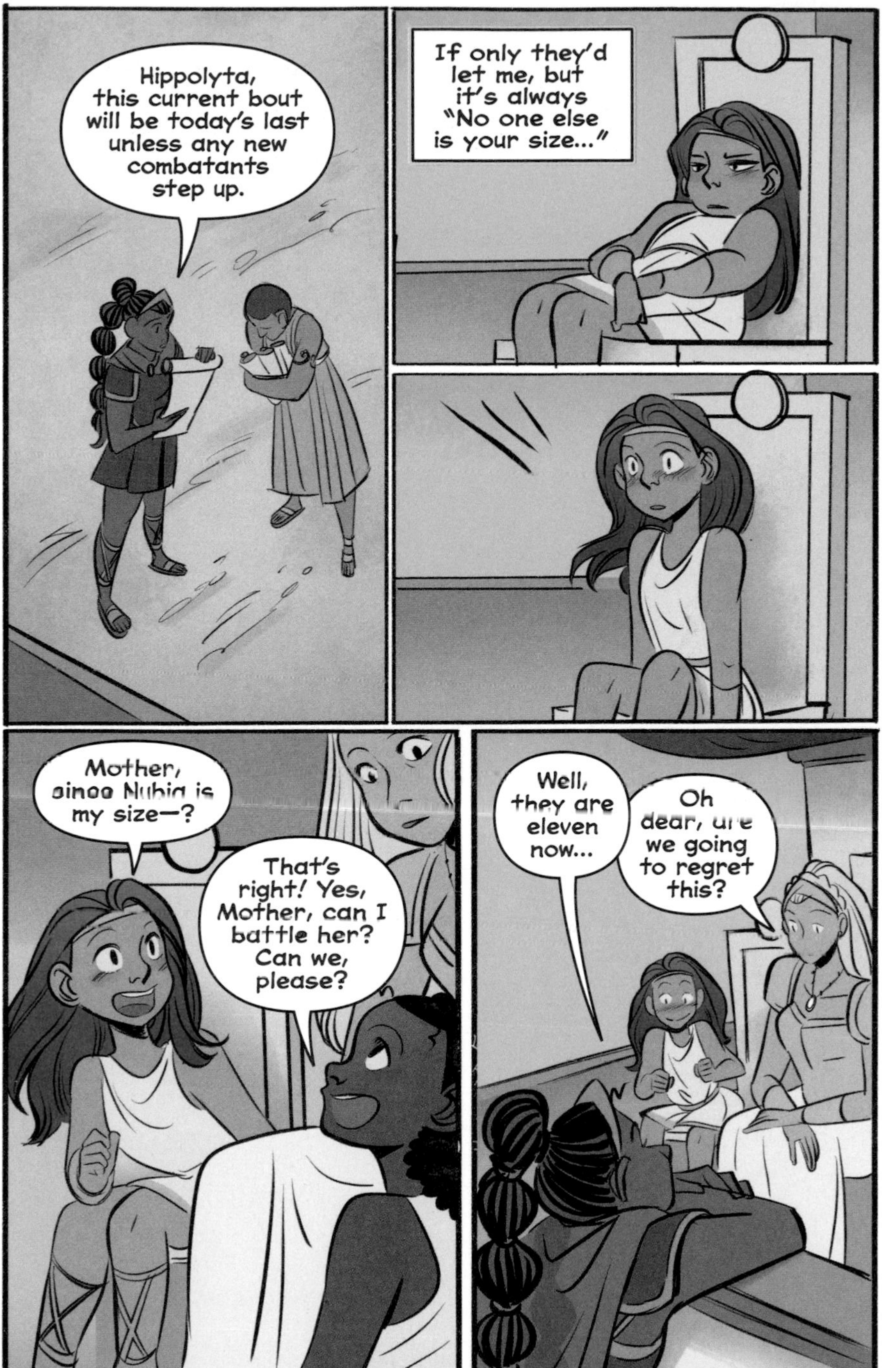
Hippolyta, this current bout will be today's last unless any new combatants step up.
If only they'd let me, but it's always "No one else is your size..."
Mother, since Nubia is my size—?
That's right! Yes, Mother, can I battle her? Can we, please?
Well, they are eleven now...
Oh dear, are we going to regret this?

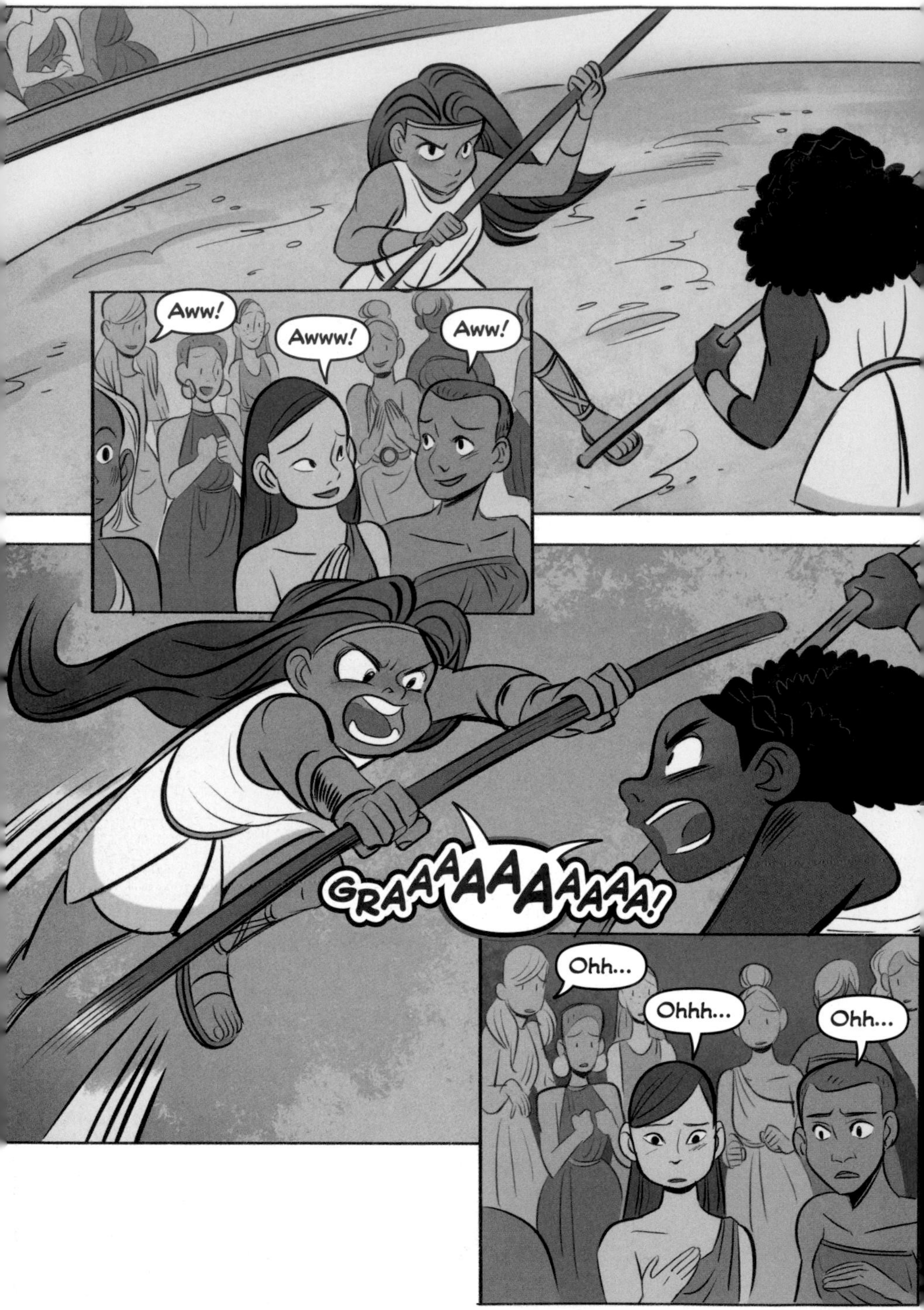
Aww!
Awww!
Aww!
GRAAAAAAAAAA!
Ohh...
Ohhh...
Ohh...

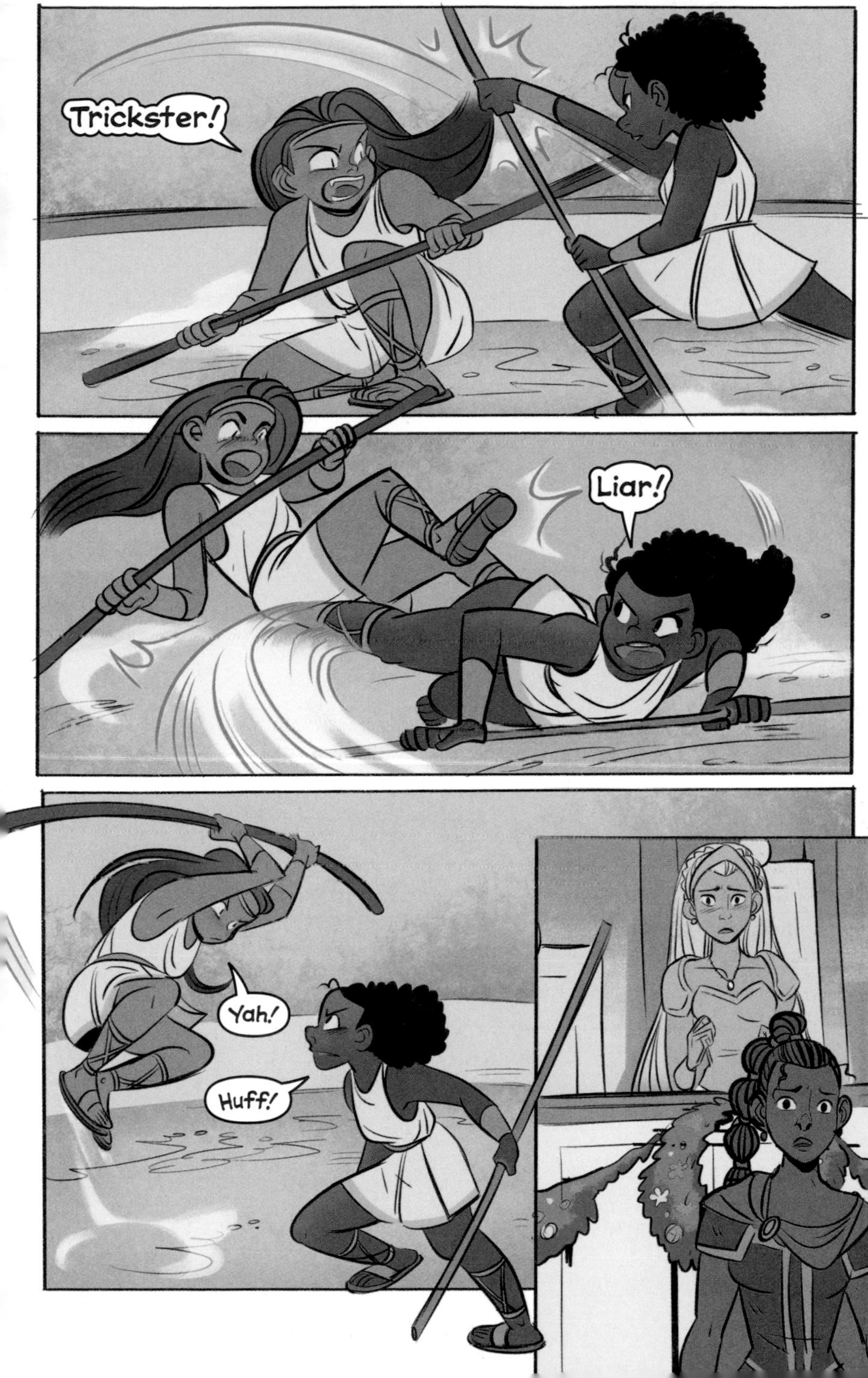
Trickster!
Liar!
Yah!
Huff!

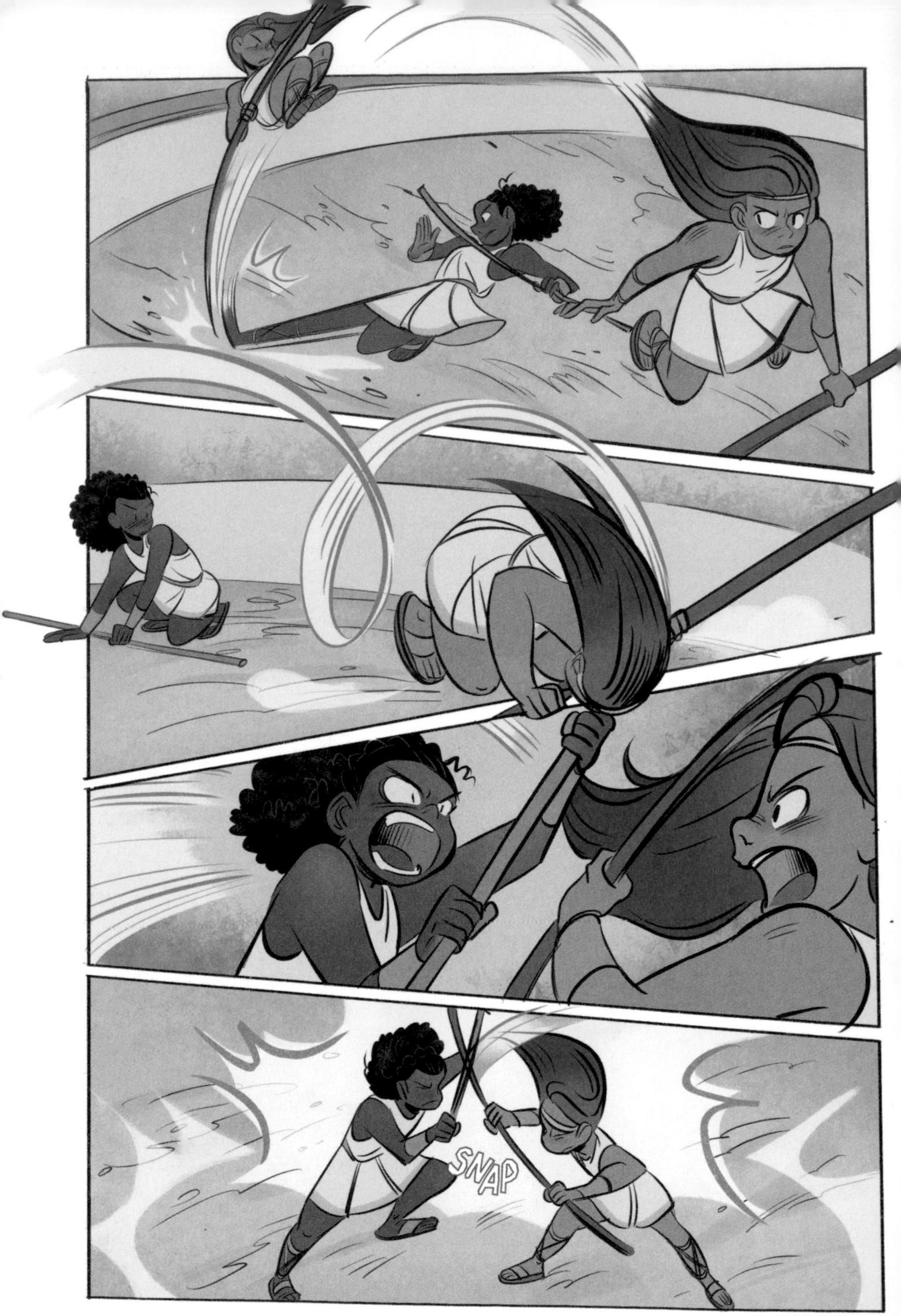
SNAP

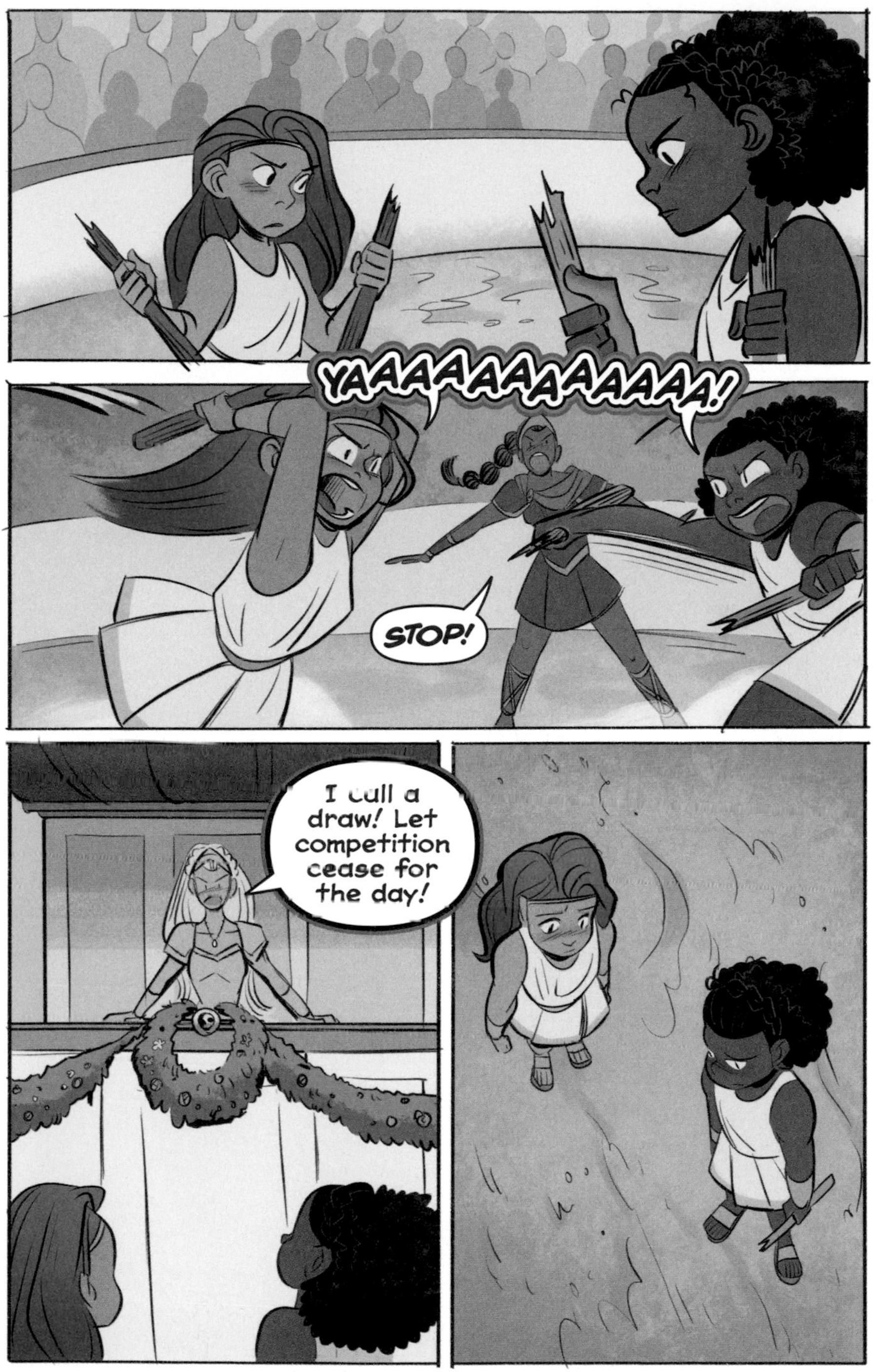
YAAAAAAAAAAAA!
STOP!
I call a draw! Let competition cease for the day!

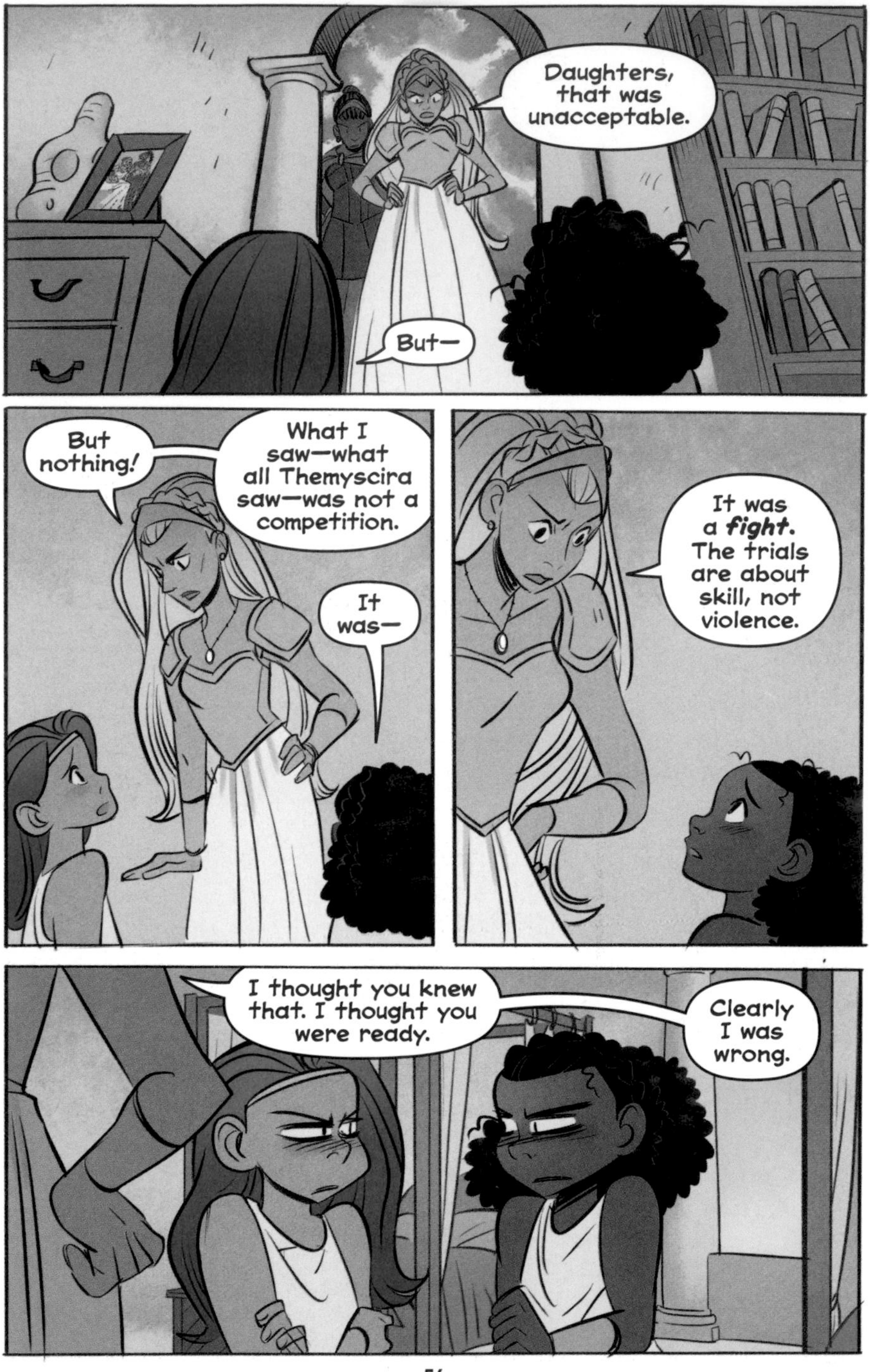
Daughters, that was unacceptable.
But—
But nothing!
What I saw—what all Themyscira saw—was not a competition.
It was—
It was a ***fight***. The trials are about skill, not violence.
I thought you knew that. I thought you were ready.
Clearly I was wrong.

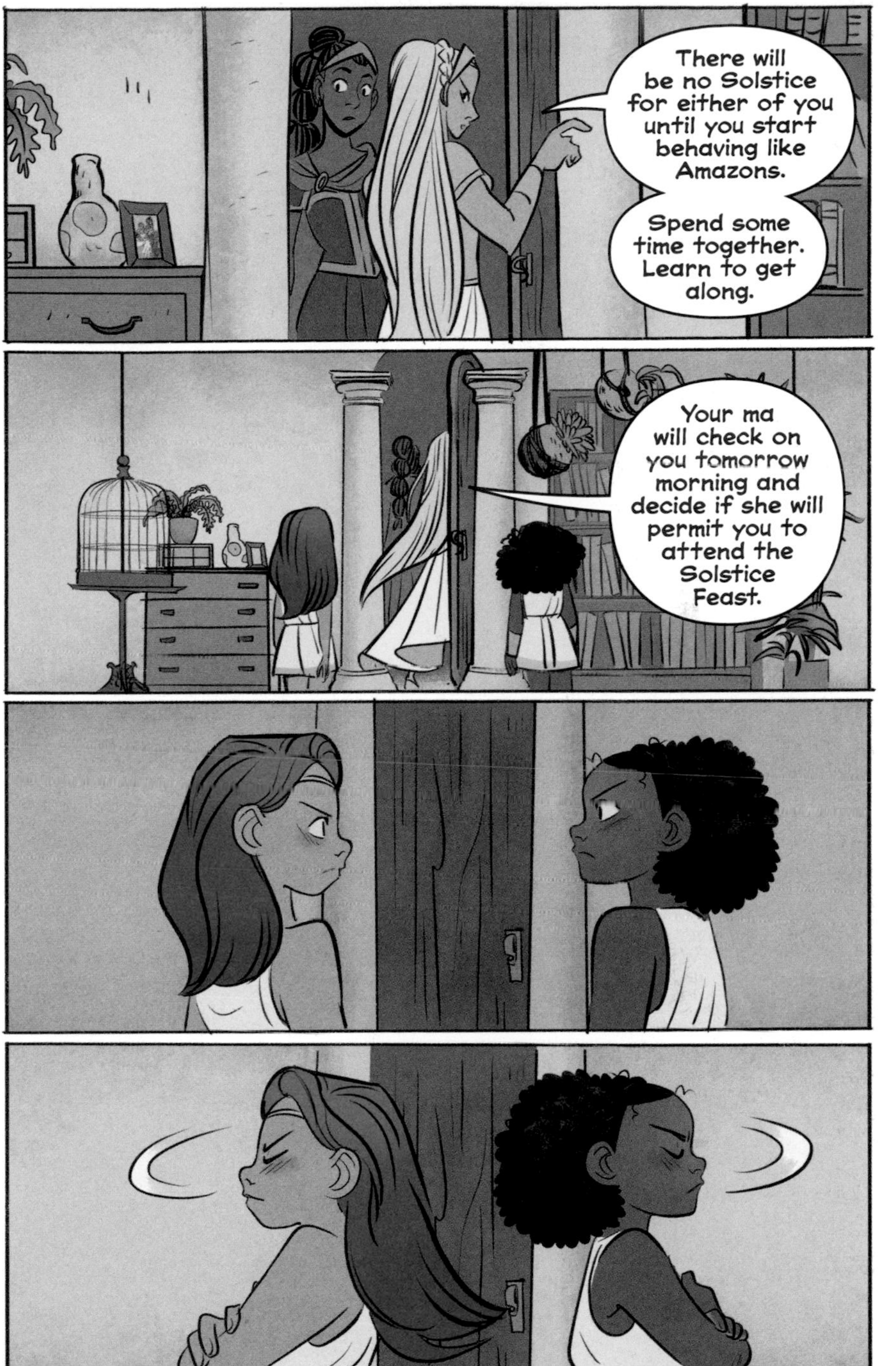
There will be no Solstice for either of you until you start behaving like Amazons.
Spend some time together. Learn to get along.
Your ma will check on you tomorrow morning and decide if she will permit you to attend the Solstice Feast.

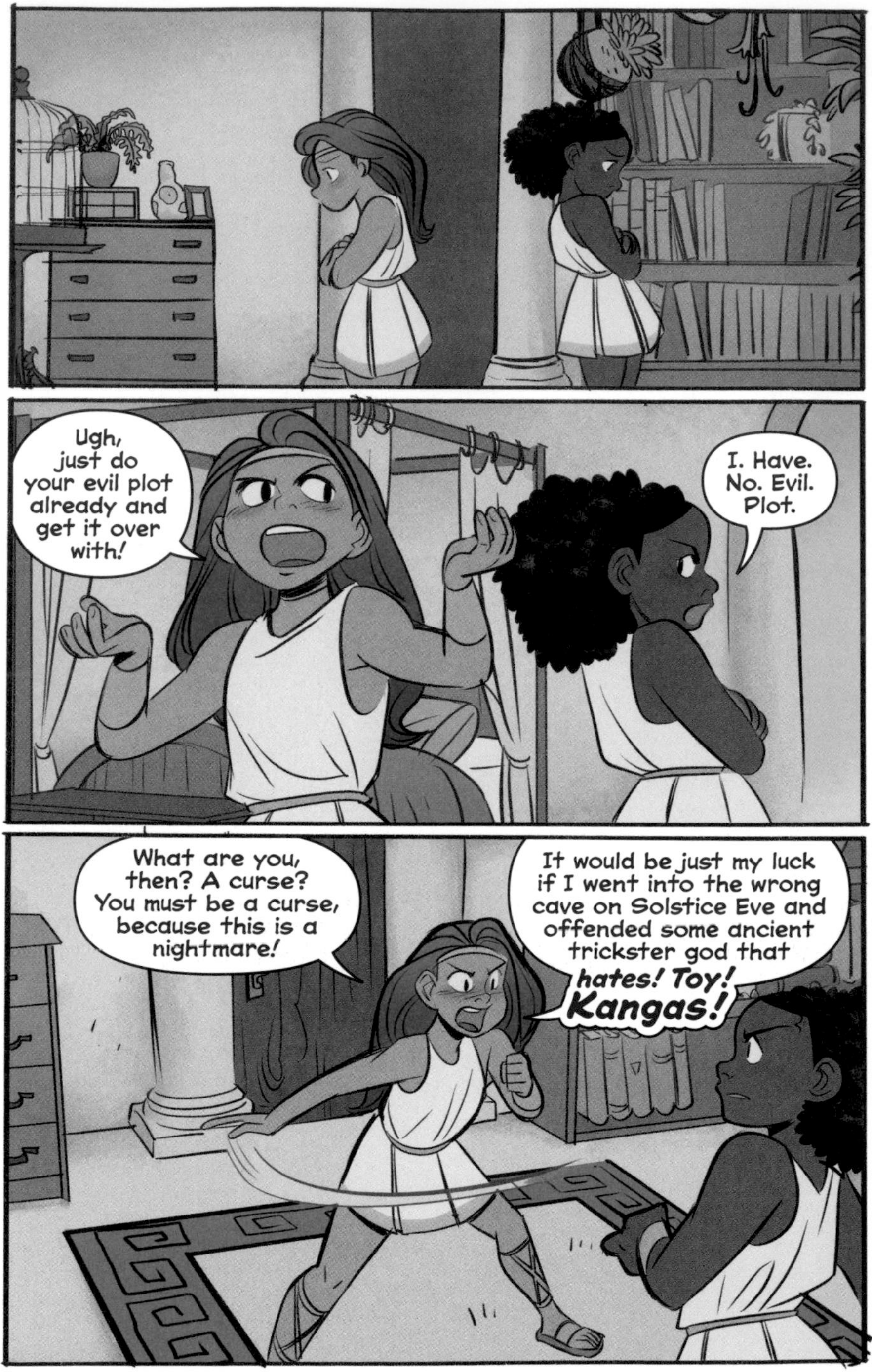
Ugh, just do your evil plot already and get it over with!
I. Have. No. Evil. Plot.
What are you, then? A curse? You must be a curse, because this is a nightmare!
It would be just my luck if I went into the wrong cave on Solstice Eve and offended some ancient trickster god that hates! Toy! Kangas!

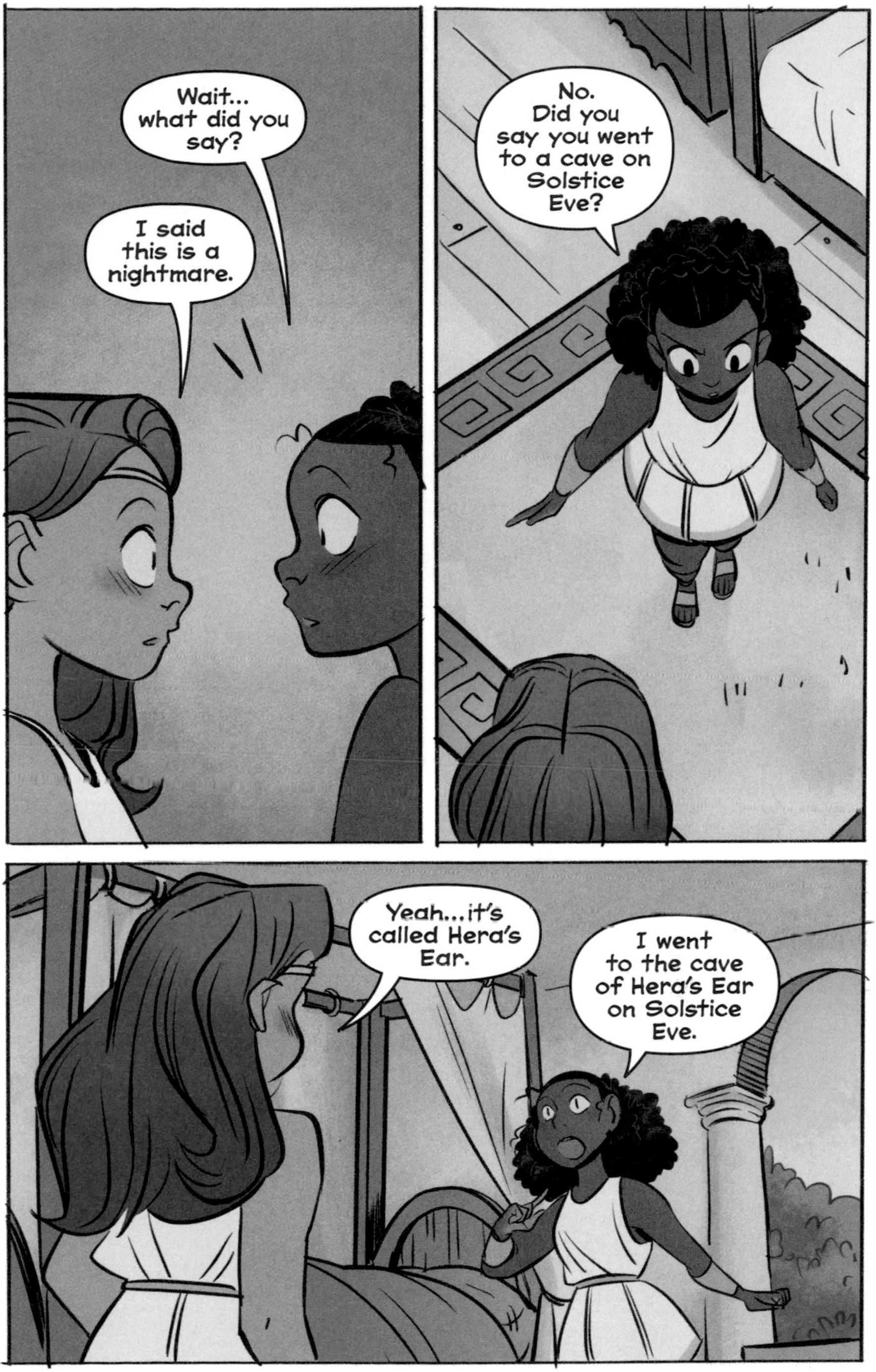
Wait... what did you say?
I said this is a nightmare.
No. Did you say you went to a cave on Solstice Eve?
Yeah...it's called Hera's Ear.
I went to the cave of Hera's Ear on Solstice Eve.

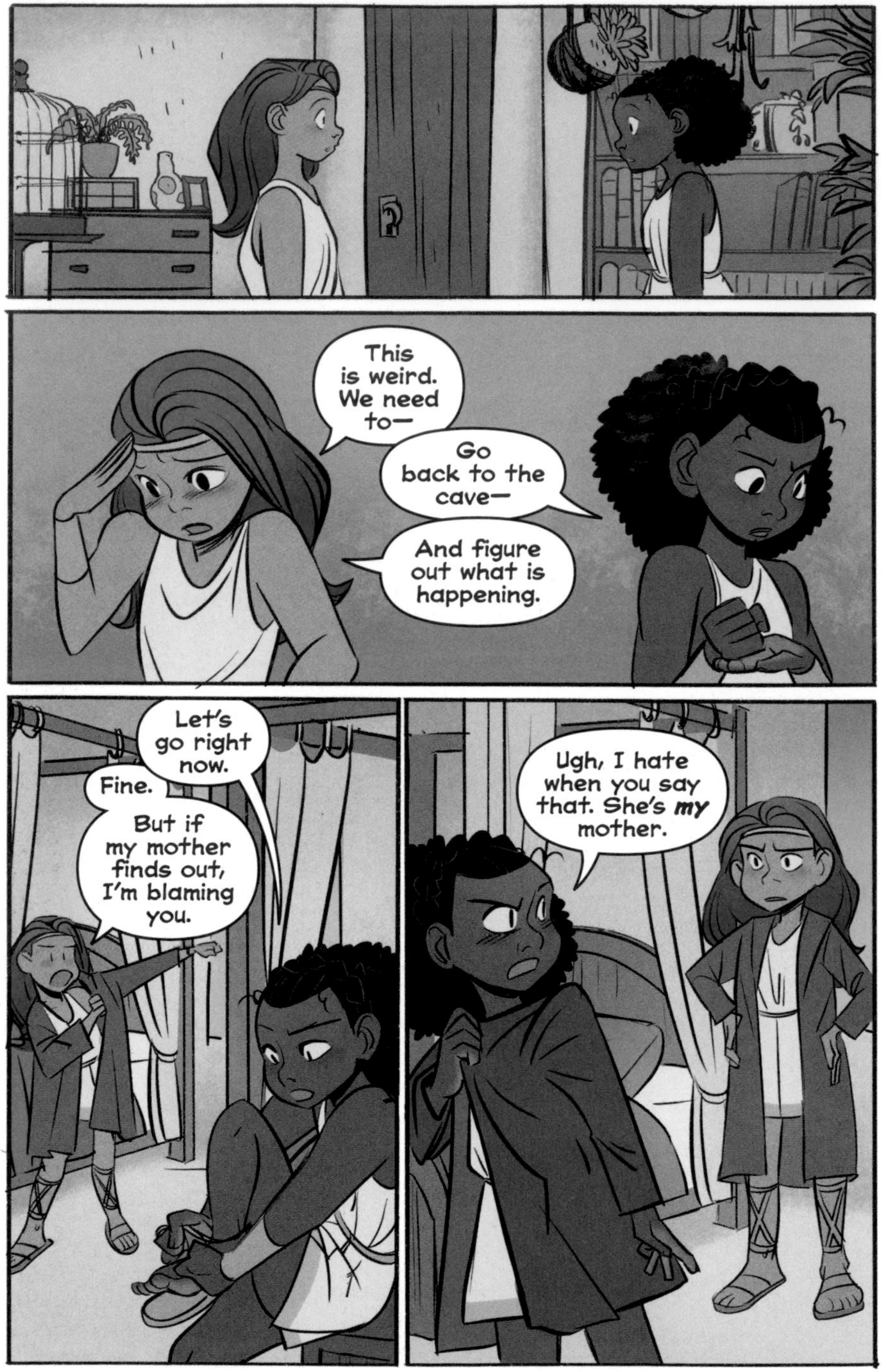
This is weird. We need to—
Go back to the cave—
And figure out what is happening.
Let's go right now.
Fine.
But if my mother finds out, I'm blaming you.
Ugh, I hate when you say that. She's *my* mother.

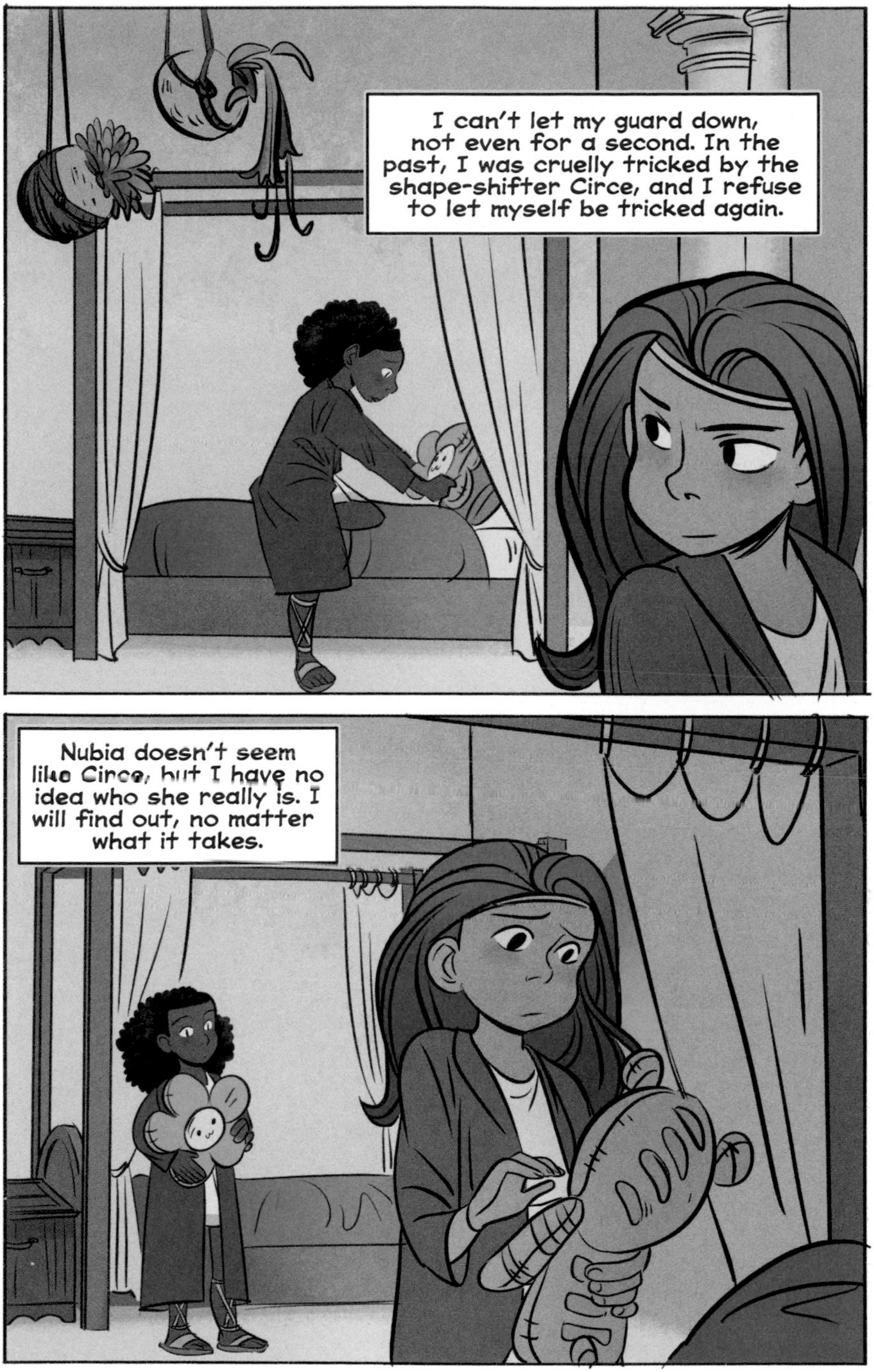
I can't let my guard down, not even for a second. In the past, I was cruelly tricked by the shape-shifter Circe, and I refuse to let myself be tricked again.
Nubia doesn't seem like Circe, but I have no idea who she really is. I will find out, no matter what it takes.

CHAPTER THREE

NUBIA

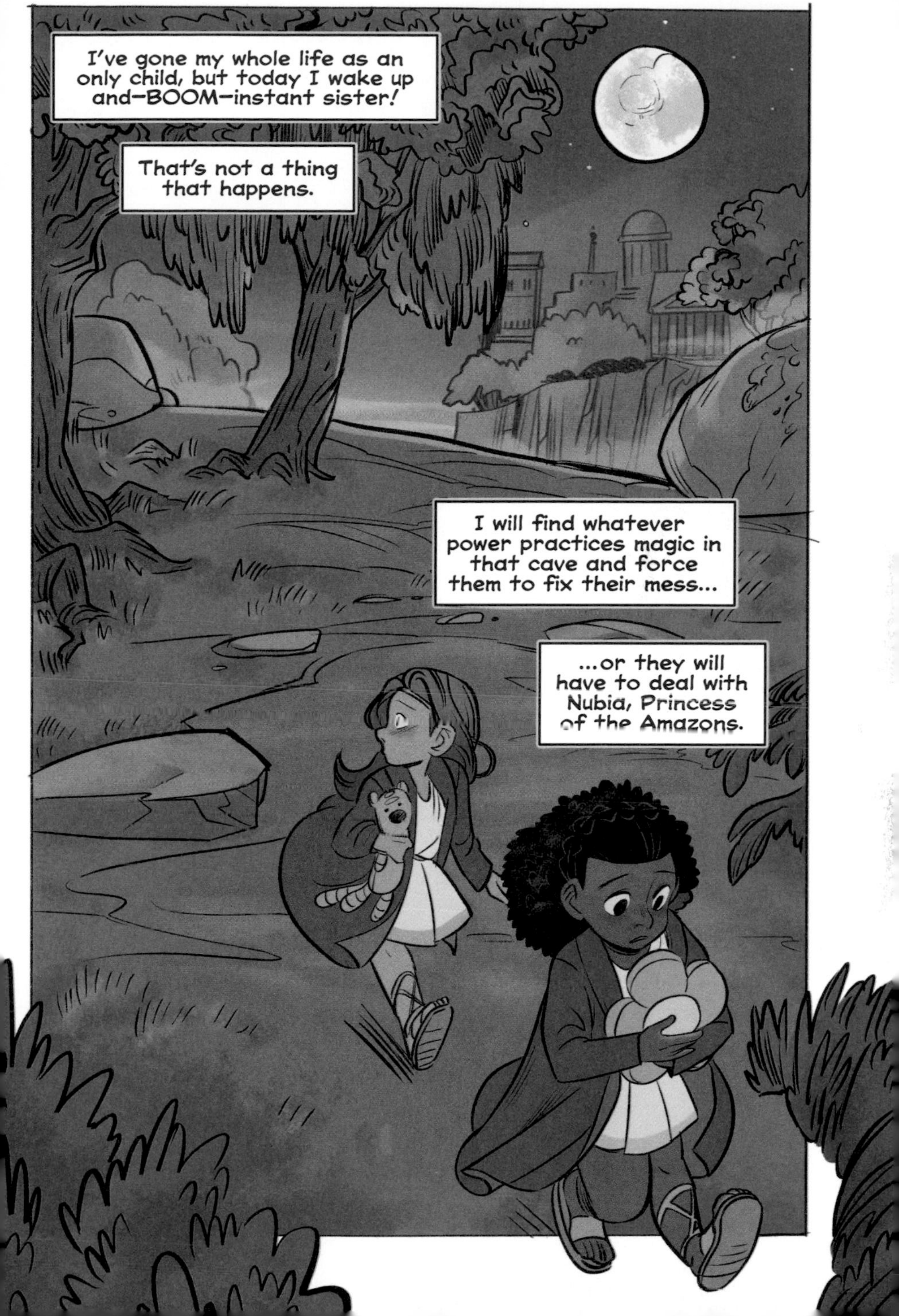
I've gone my whole life as an only child, but today I wake up and—BOOM—instant sister!
That's not a thing that happens.
I will find whatever power practices magic in that cave and force them to fix their mess...
...or they will have to deal with Nubia, Princess of the Amazons.

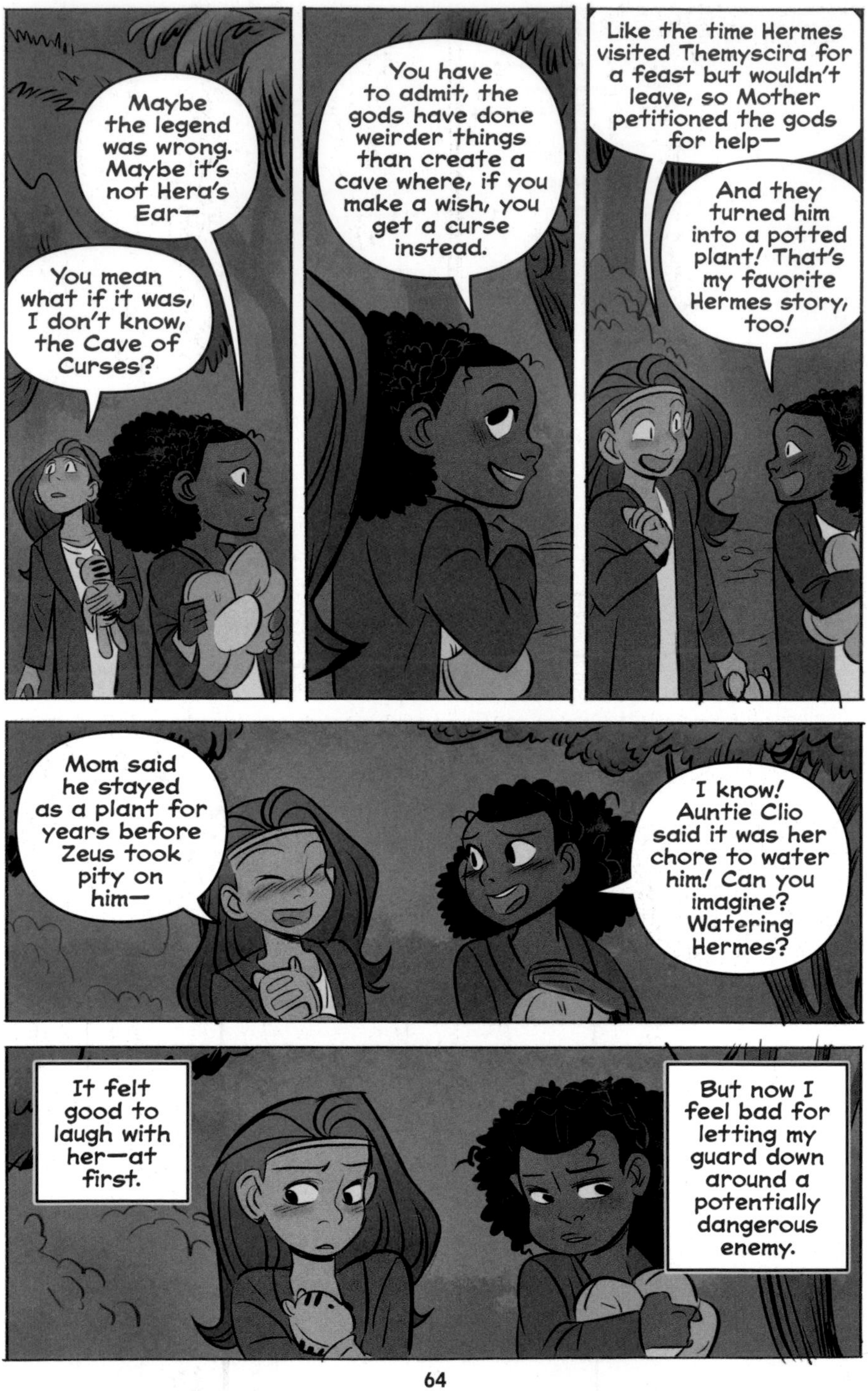
Maybe the legend was wrong. Maybe it's not Hera's Ear—
You mean what if it was, I don't know, the Cave of Curses?
You have to admit, the gods have done weirder things than create a cave where, if you make a wish, you get a curse instead.
Like the time Hermes visited Themyscira for a feast but wouldn't leave, so Mother petitioned the gods for help—
And they turned him into a potted plant! That's my favorite Hermes story, too!
Mom said he stayed as a plant for years before Zeus took pity on him—
I know! Auntie Clio said it was her chore to water him! Can you imagine? Watering Hermes?
It felt good to laugh with her—at first.
But now I feel bad for letting my guard down around a potentially dangerous enemy.

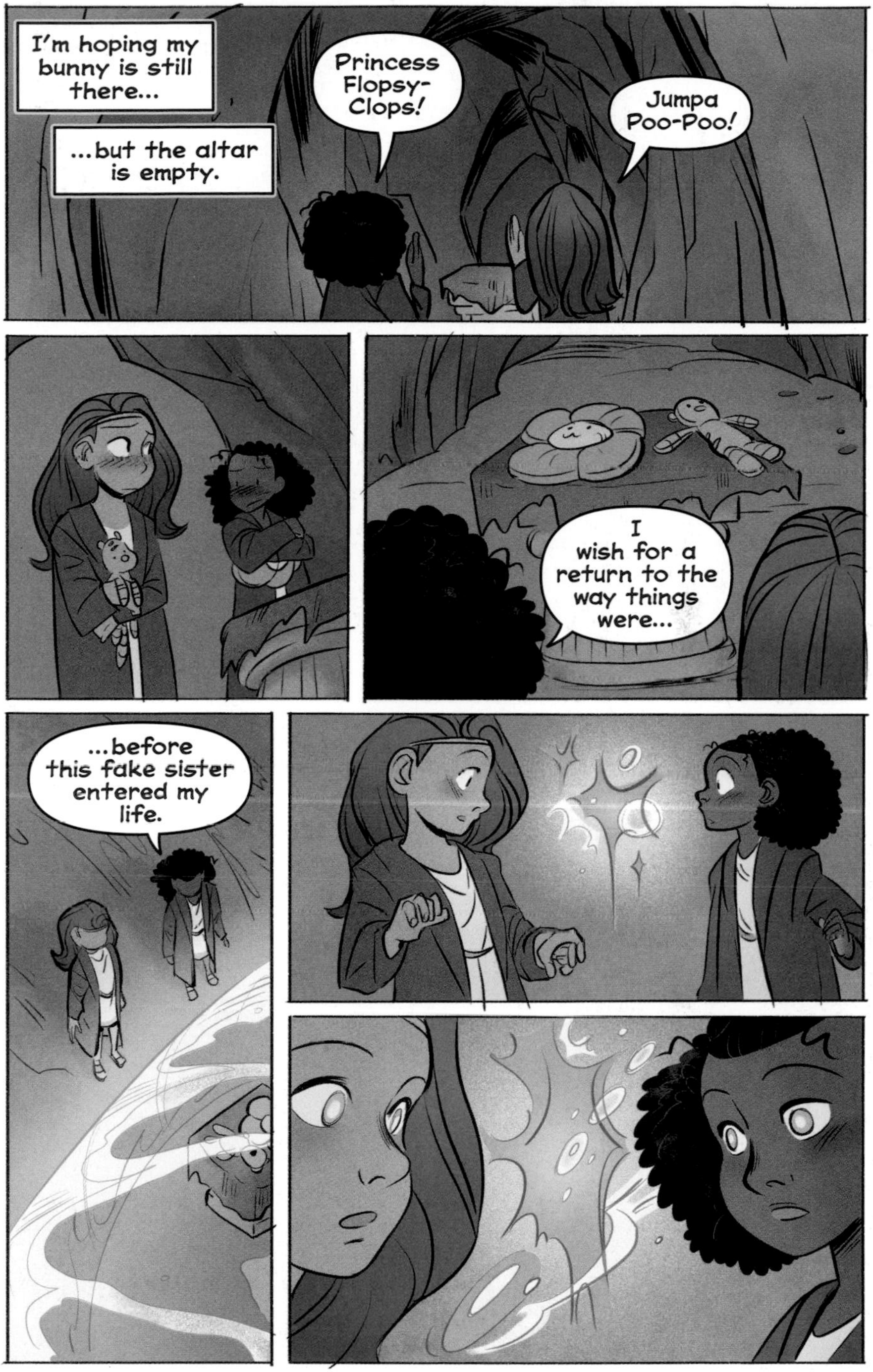
I'm hoping my bunny is still there...
...but the altar is empty.
Princess Flopsy-Clops!
Jumpa Poo-Poo!
I wish for a return to the way things were...
...before this fake sister entered my life.

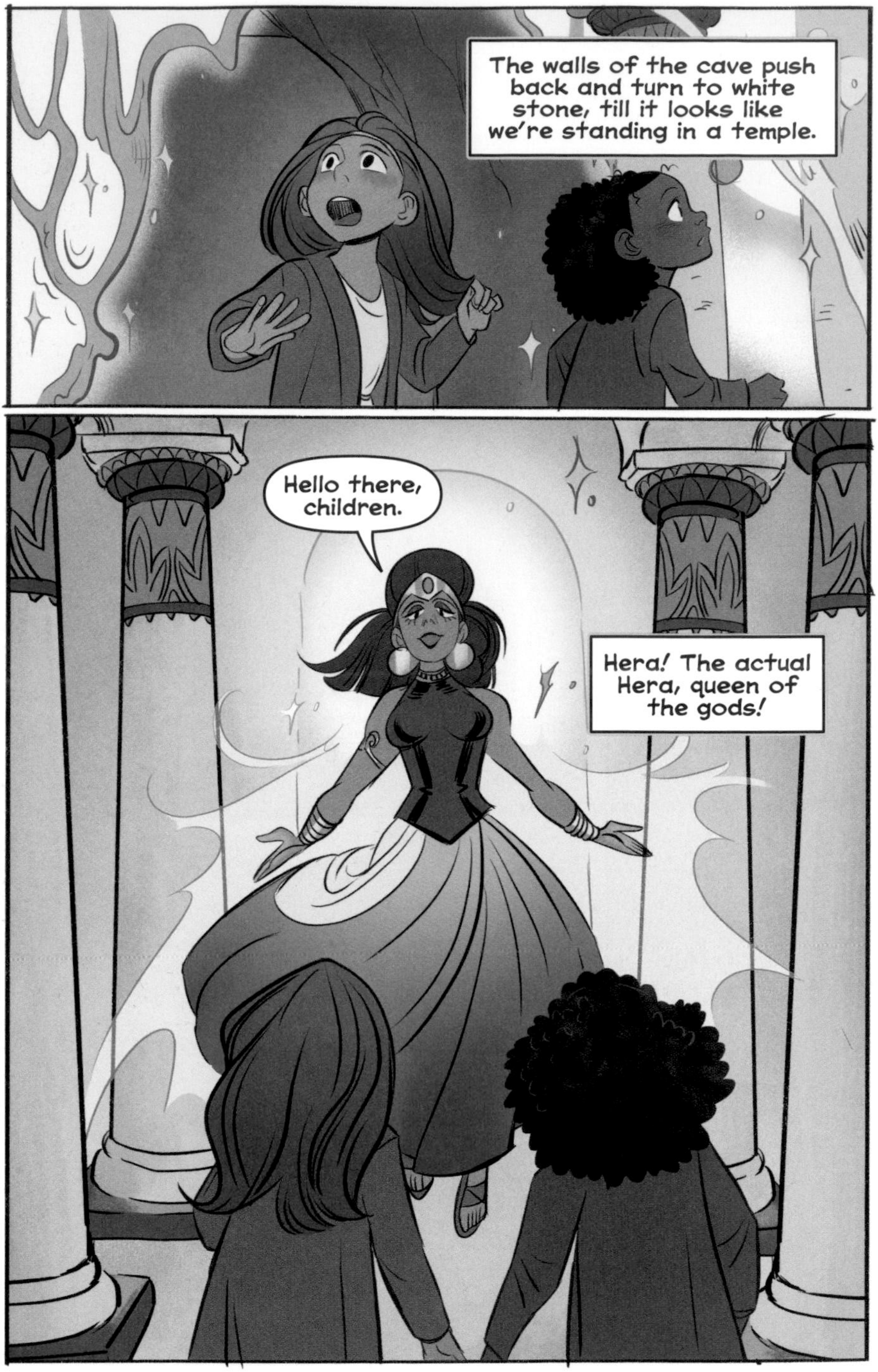
The walls of the cave push back and turn to white stone, till it looks like we're standing in a temple.
Hello there, children.
Hera! The actual Hera, queen of the gods!

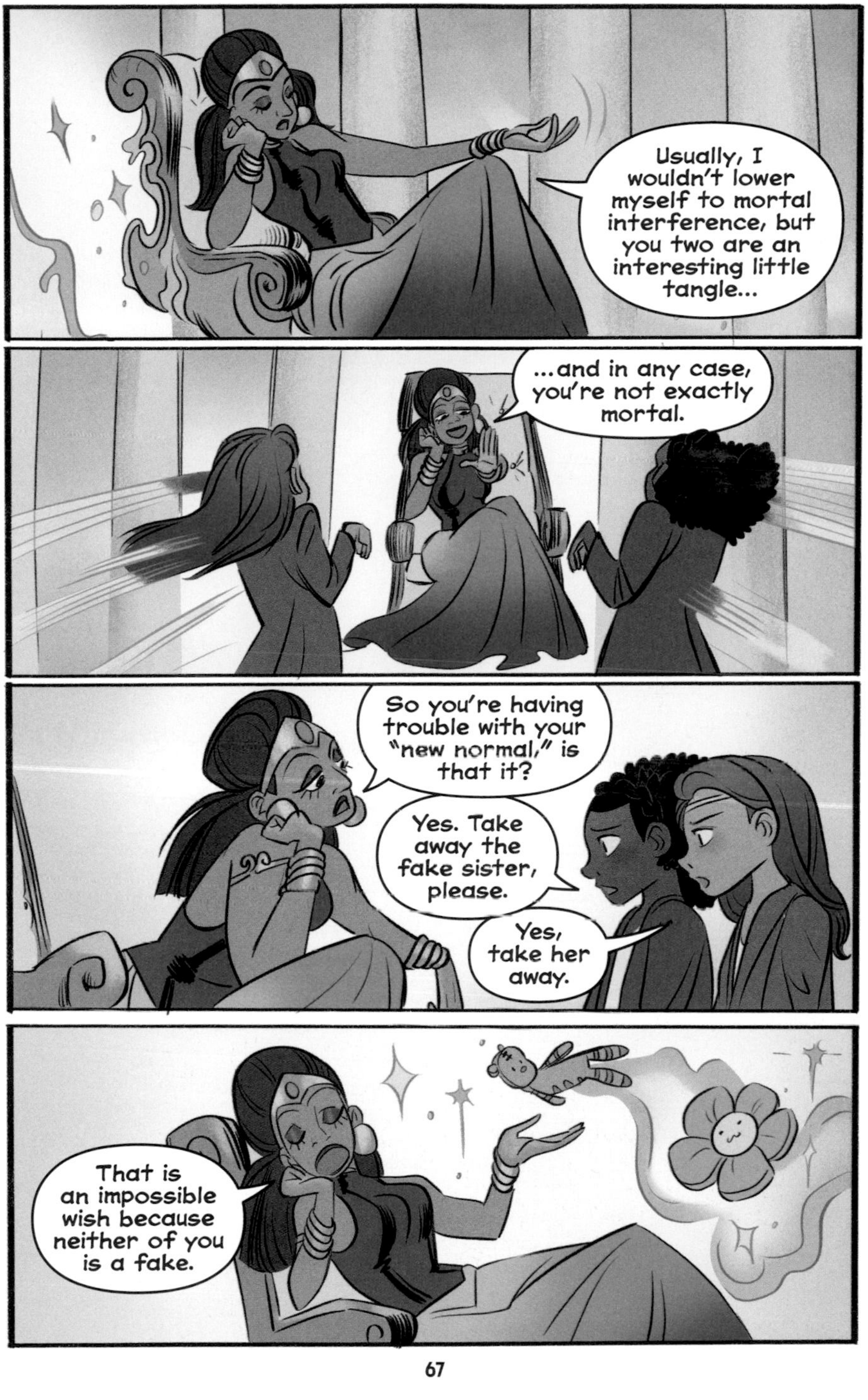
Usually, I wouldn't lower myself to mortal interference, but you two are an interesting little tangle...
...and in any case, you're not exactly mortal.
So you're having trouble with your "new normal," is that it?
Yes. Take away the fake sister, please.
Yes, take her away.
That is an impossible wish because neither of you is a fake.

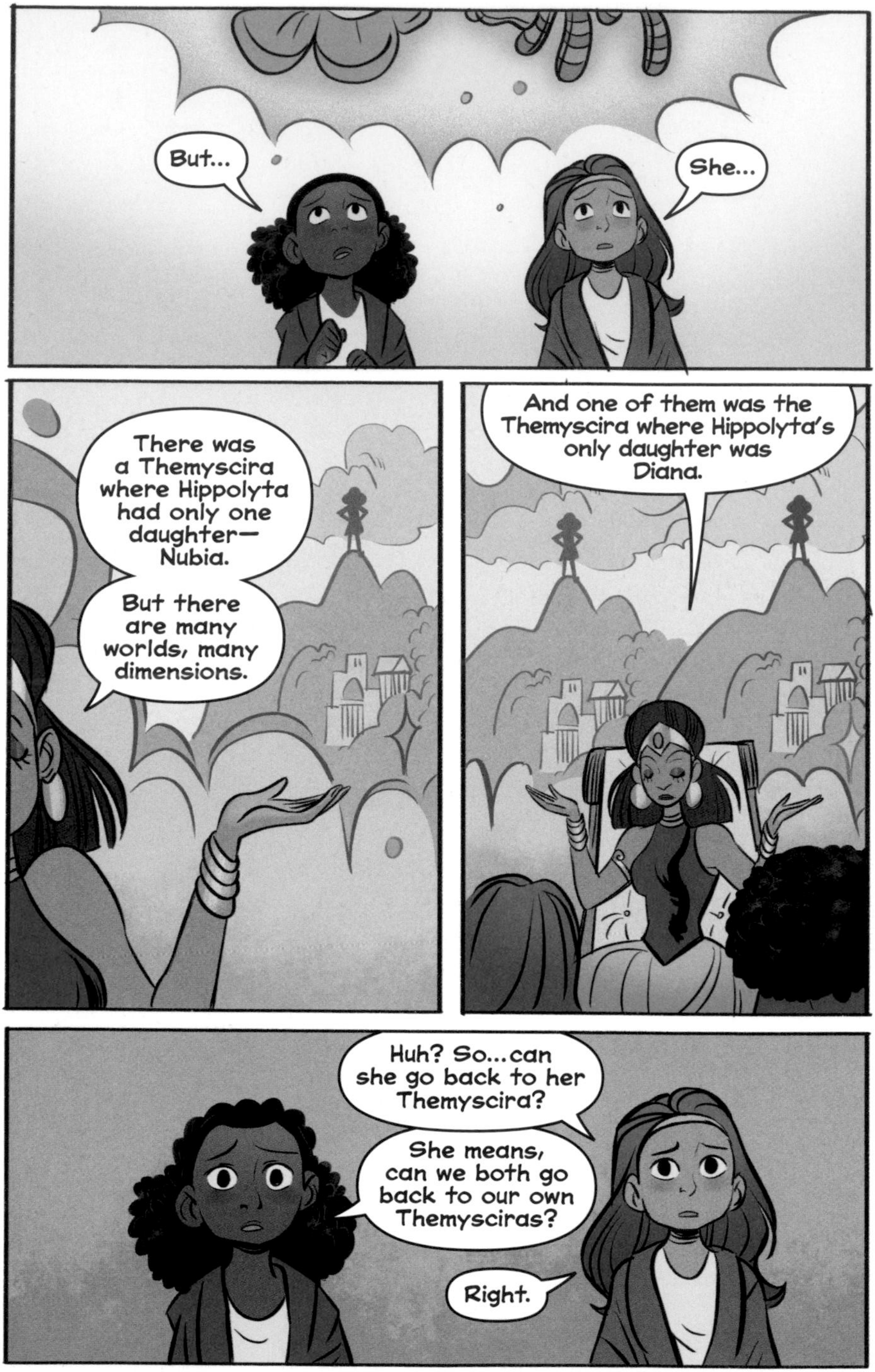

But...
She...
There was a Themyscira where Hippolyta had only one daughter—Nubia.
But there are many worlds, many dimensions.
And one of them was the Themyscira where Hippolyta's only daughter was Diana.
Huh? So...can she go back to her Themyscira?
She means, can we both go back to our own Themysciras?
Right.

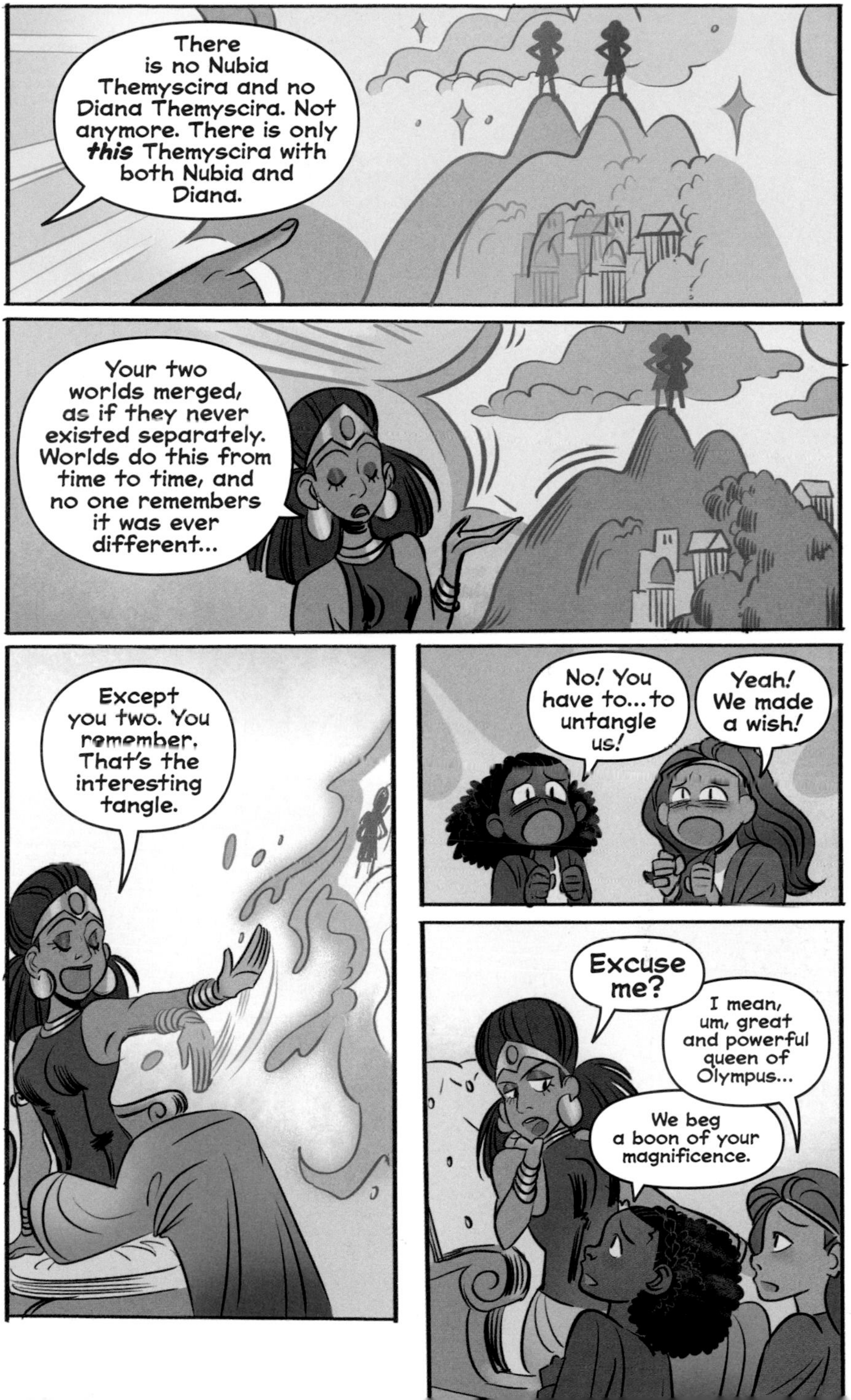
There is no Nubia Themyscira and no Diana Themyscira. Not anymore. There is only *this* Themyscira with both Nubia and Diana.
Your two worlds merged, as if they never existed separately. Worlds do this from time to time, and no one remembers it was ever different...
Except you two. You remember. That's the interesting tangle.
No! You have to...to untangle us!
Yeah! We made a wish!
Excuse me?
I mean, um, great and powerful queen of Olympus...
We beg a boon of your magnificence.

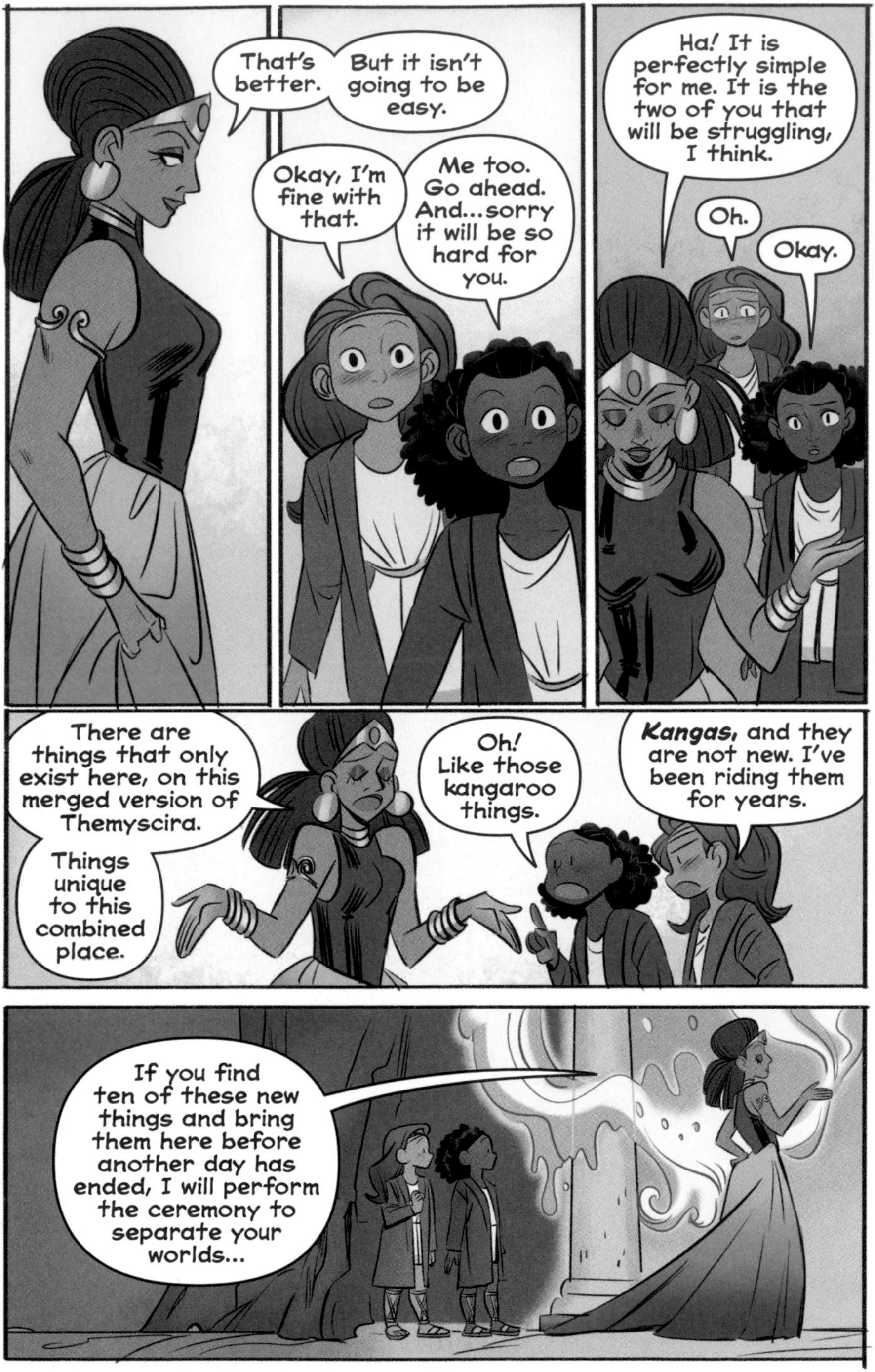
That's better.
But it isn't going to be easy.
Okay, I'm fine with that.
Me too. Go ahead. And...sorry it will be so hard for you.
Ha! It is perfectly simple for me. It is the two of you that will be struggling, I think.
Oh.
Okay.
There are things that only exist here, on this merged version of Themyscira.
Things unique to this combined place.
Oh! Like those kangaroo things.
Kangas, and they are not new. I've been riding them for years.
If you find ten of these new things and bring them here before another day has ended, I will perform the ceremony to separate your worlds...

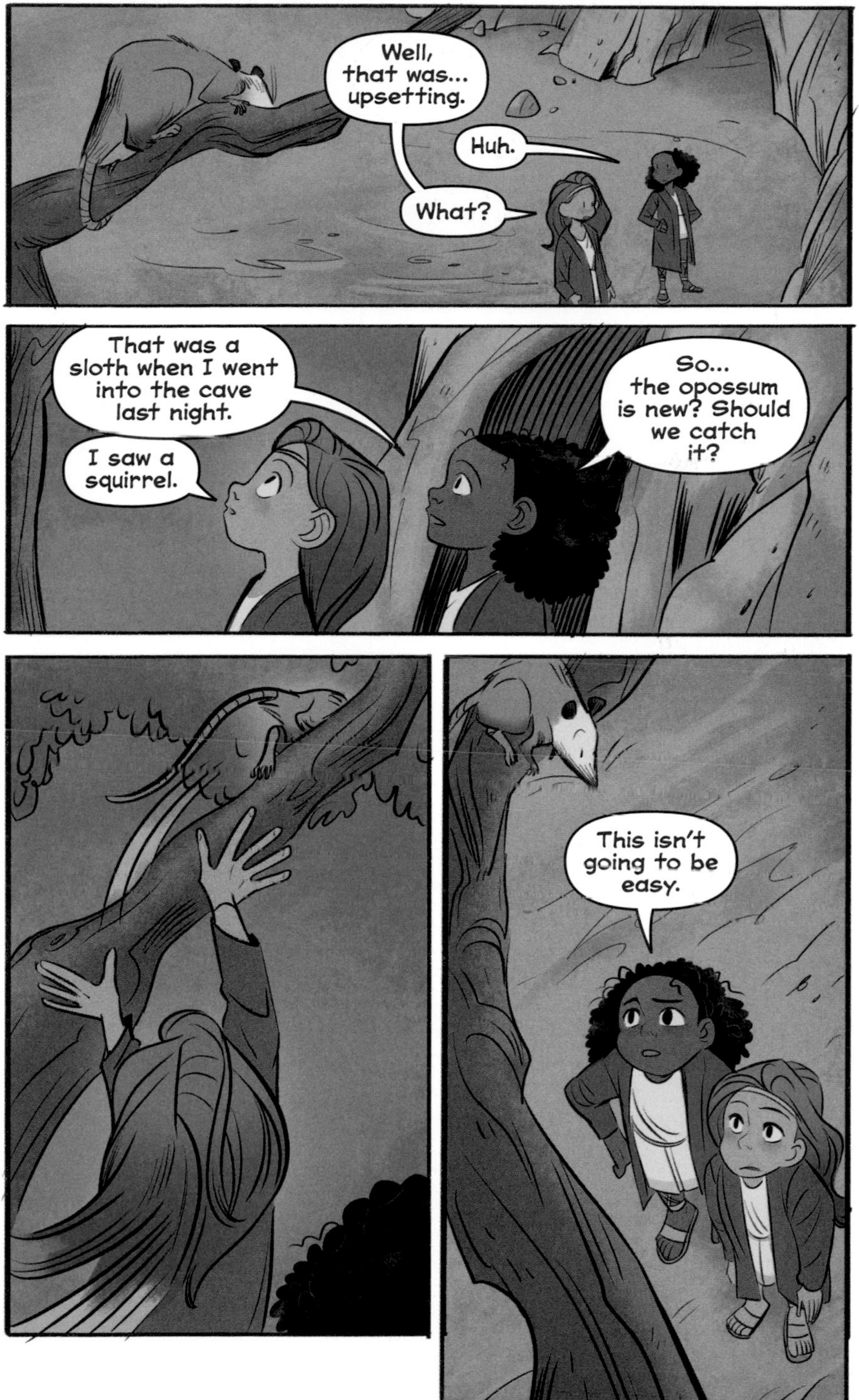
Well, that was... upsetting.
Huh.
What?
That was a sloth when I went into the cave last night.
I saw a squirrel.
So... the opossum is new? Should we catch it?
This isn't going to be easy.

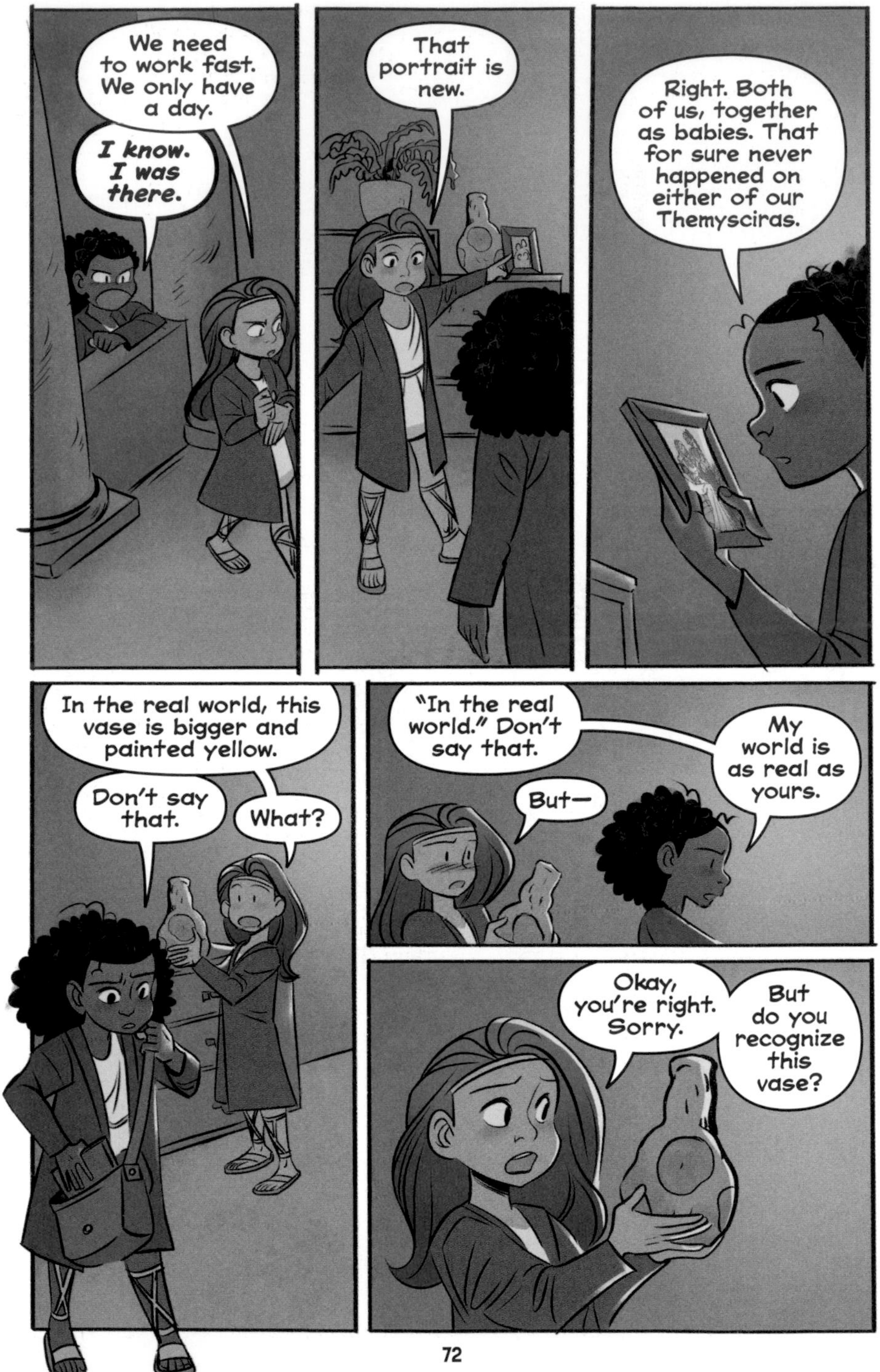

We need to work fast. We only have a day.
I know. I was there.
That portrait is new.
Right. Both of us, together as babies. That for sure never happened on either of our Themysciras.
In the real world, this vase is bigger and painted yellow.
Don't say that.
What?
"In the real world." Don't say that.
My world is as real as yours.
But—
Okay, you're right. Sorry.
But do you recognize this vase?

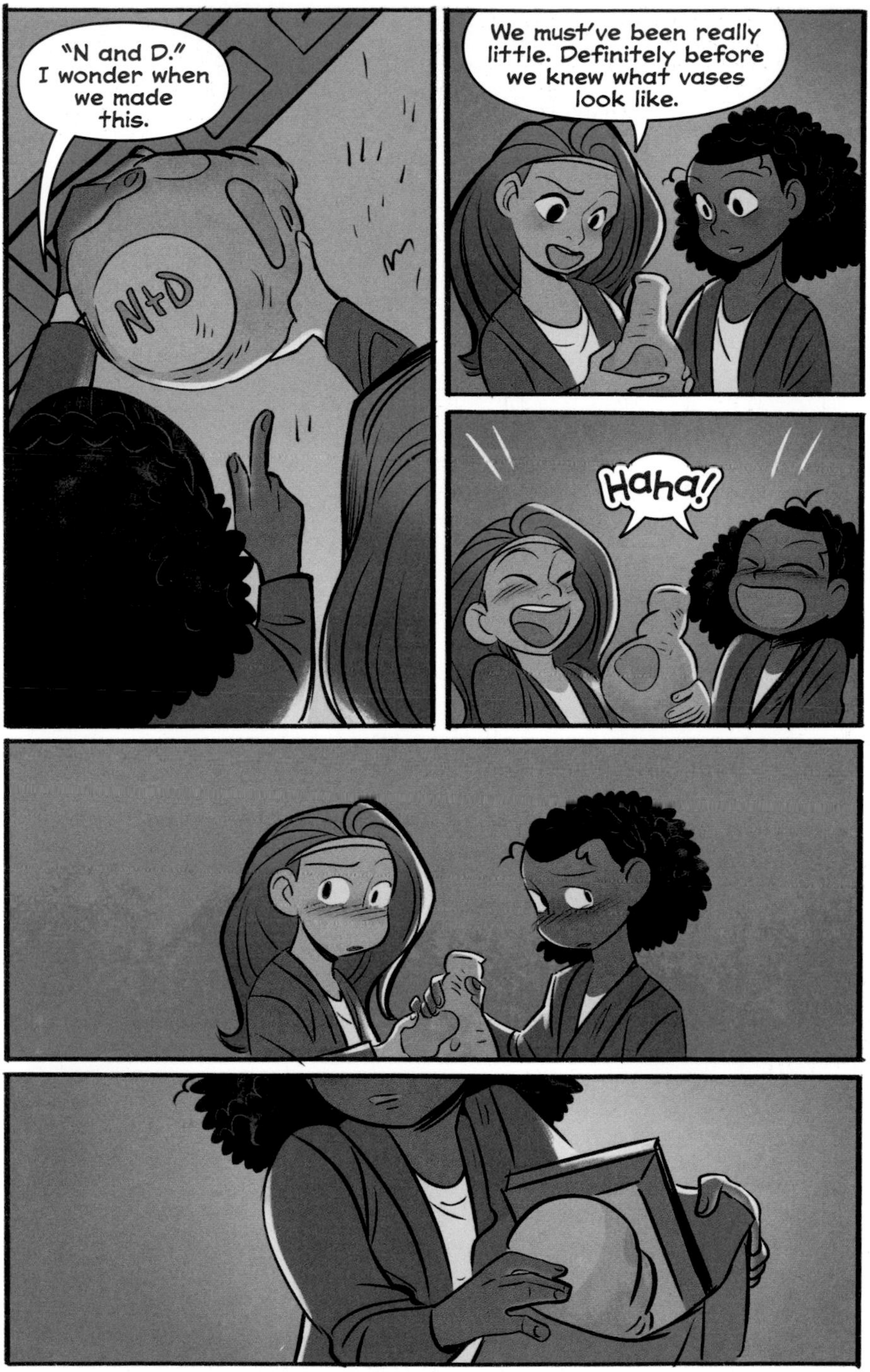
"N and D." I wonder when we made this.
N+D
We must've been really little. Definitely before we knew what vases look like.
Haha!

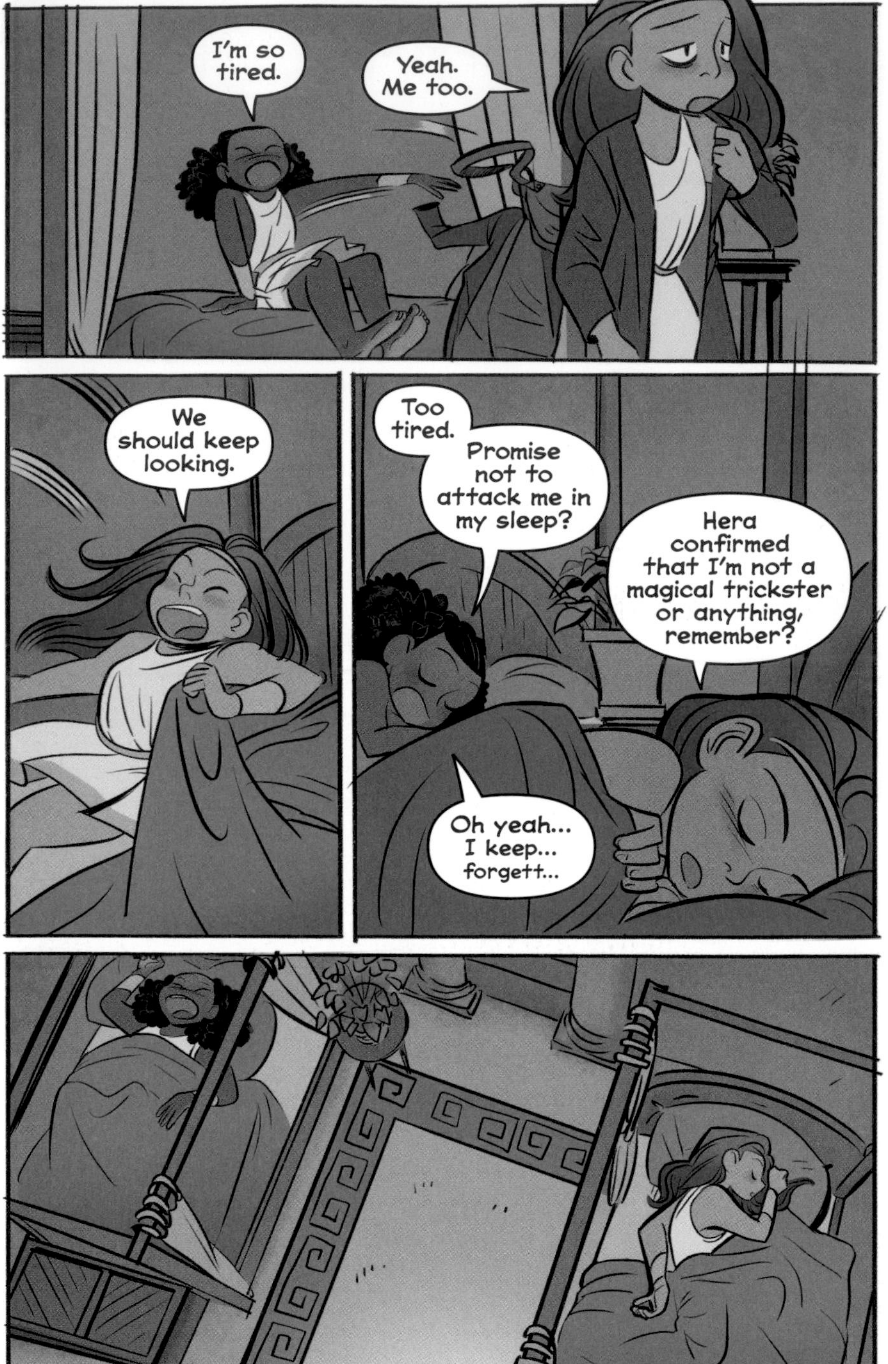
I'm so tired.
Yeah. Me too.
We should keep looking.
Too tired.
Promise not to attack me in my sleep?
Hera confirmed that I'm not a magical trickster or anything, remember?
Oh yeah... I keep... forgett...

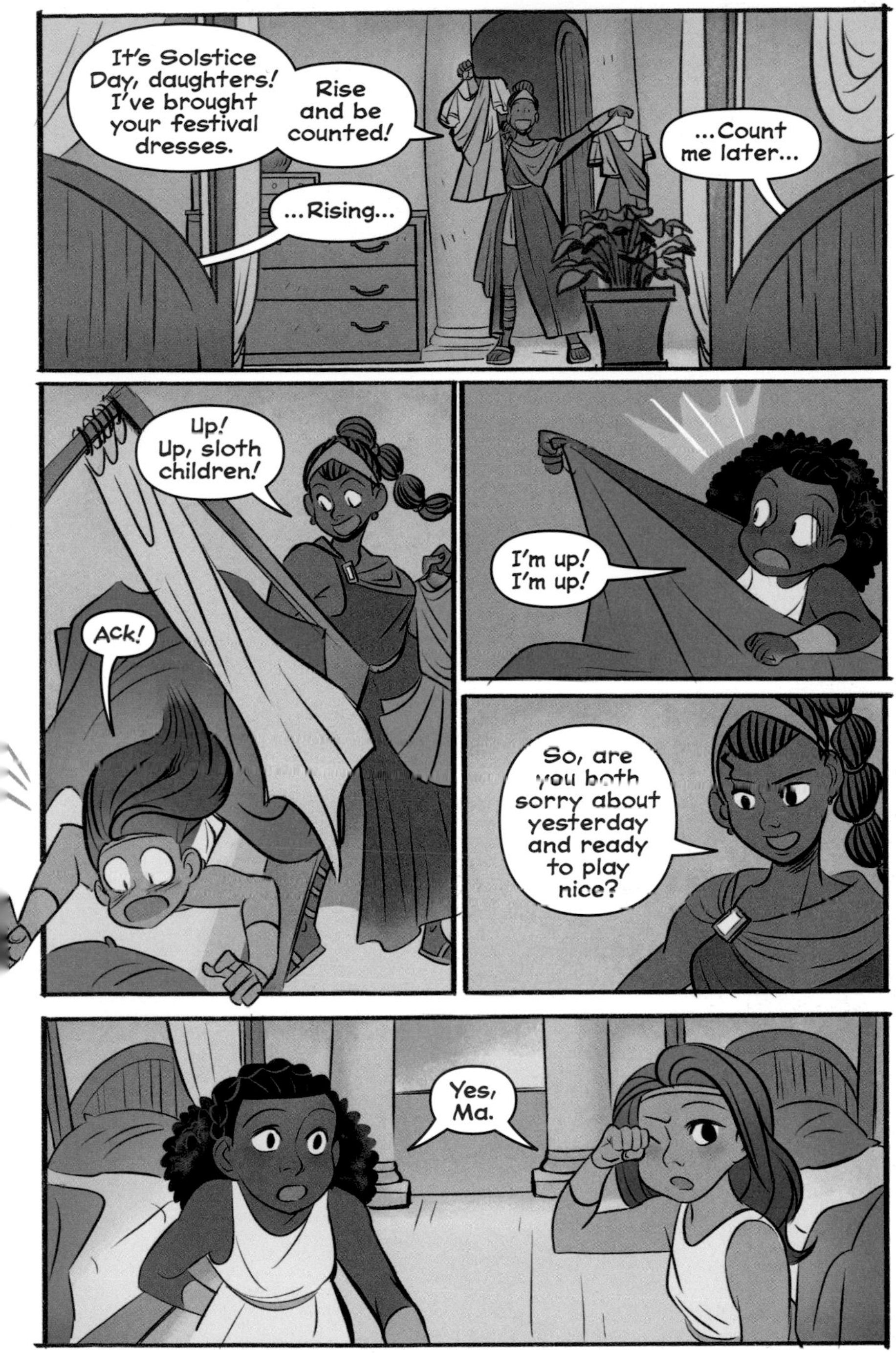
It's Solstice Day, daughters! I've brought your festival dresses.
Rise and be counted!
...Count me later...
...Rising...
Up! Up, sloth children!
Ack!
I'm up! I'm up!
So, are you both sorry about yesterday and ready to play nice?
Yes, Ma.

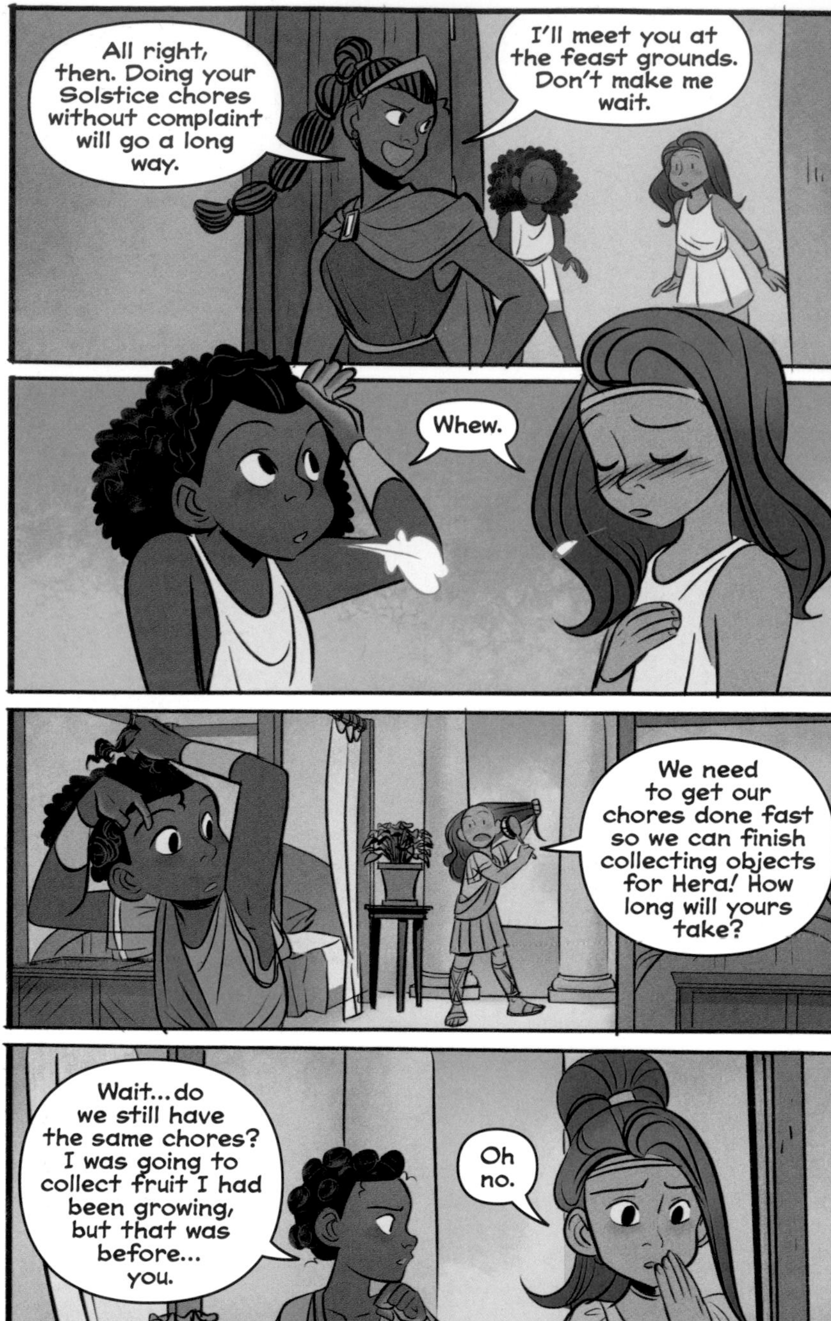
All right, then. Doing your Solstice chores without complaint will go a long way.
I'll meet you at the feast grounds. Don't make me wait.
Whew.
We need to get our chores done fast so we can finish collecting objects for Hera! How long will yours take?
Wait...do we still have the same chores? I was going to collect fruit I had been growing, but that was before... you.
Oh no.

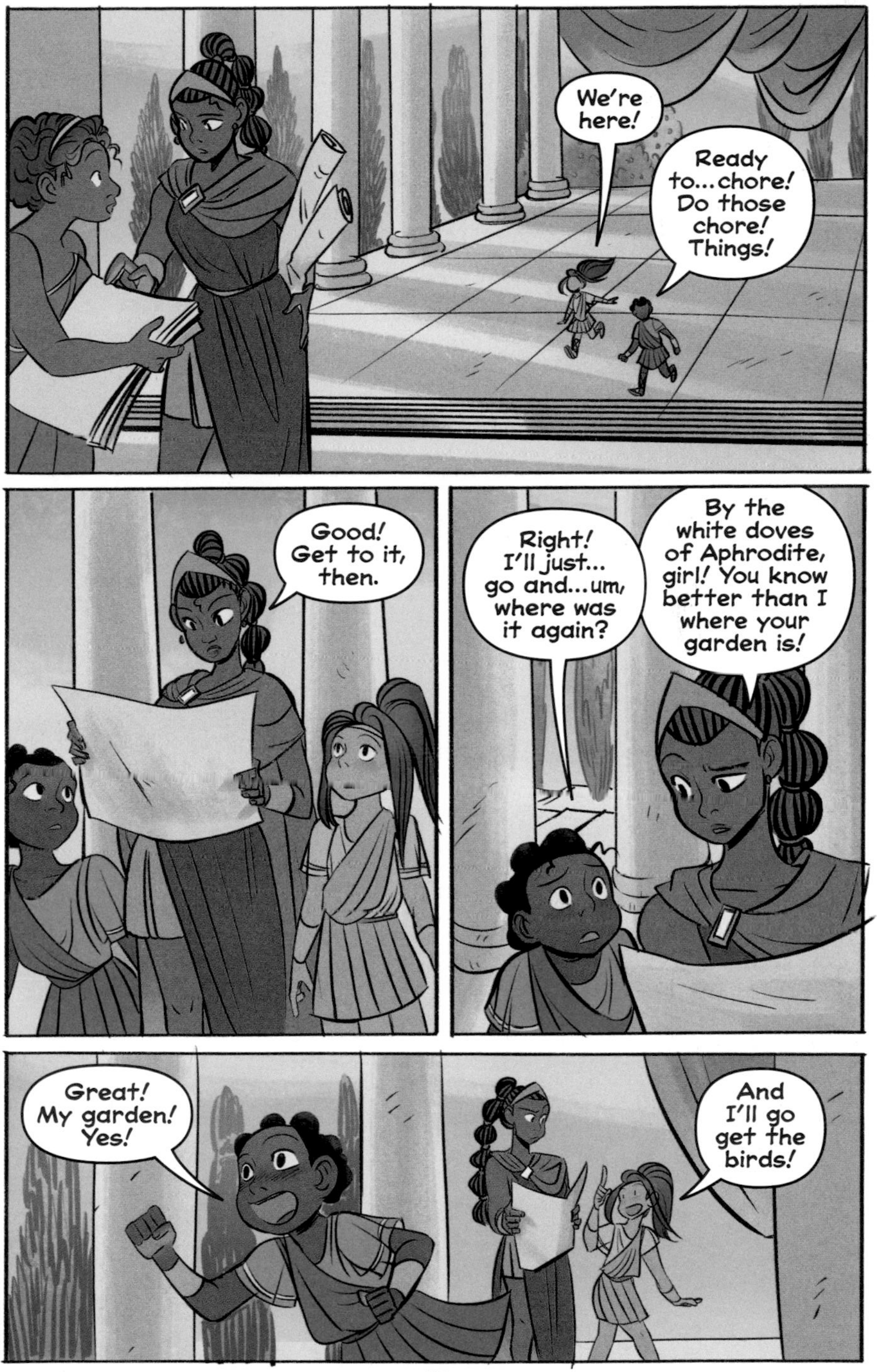
We're here!
Ready to...chore! Do those chore! Things!
Good! Get to it, then.
Right! I'll just... go and...um, where was it again?
By the white doves of Aphrodite, girl! You know better than I where your garden is!
Great! My garden! Yes!
And I'll go get the birds!

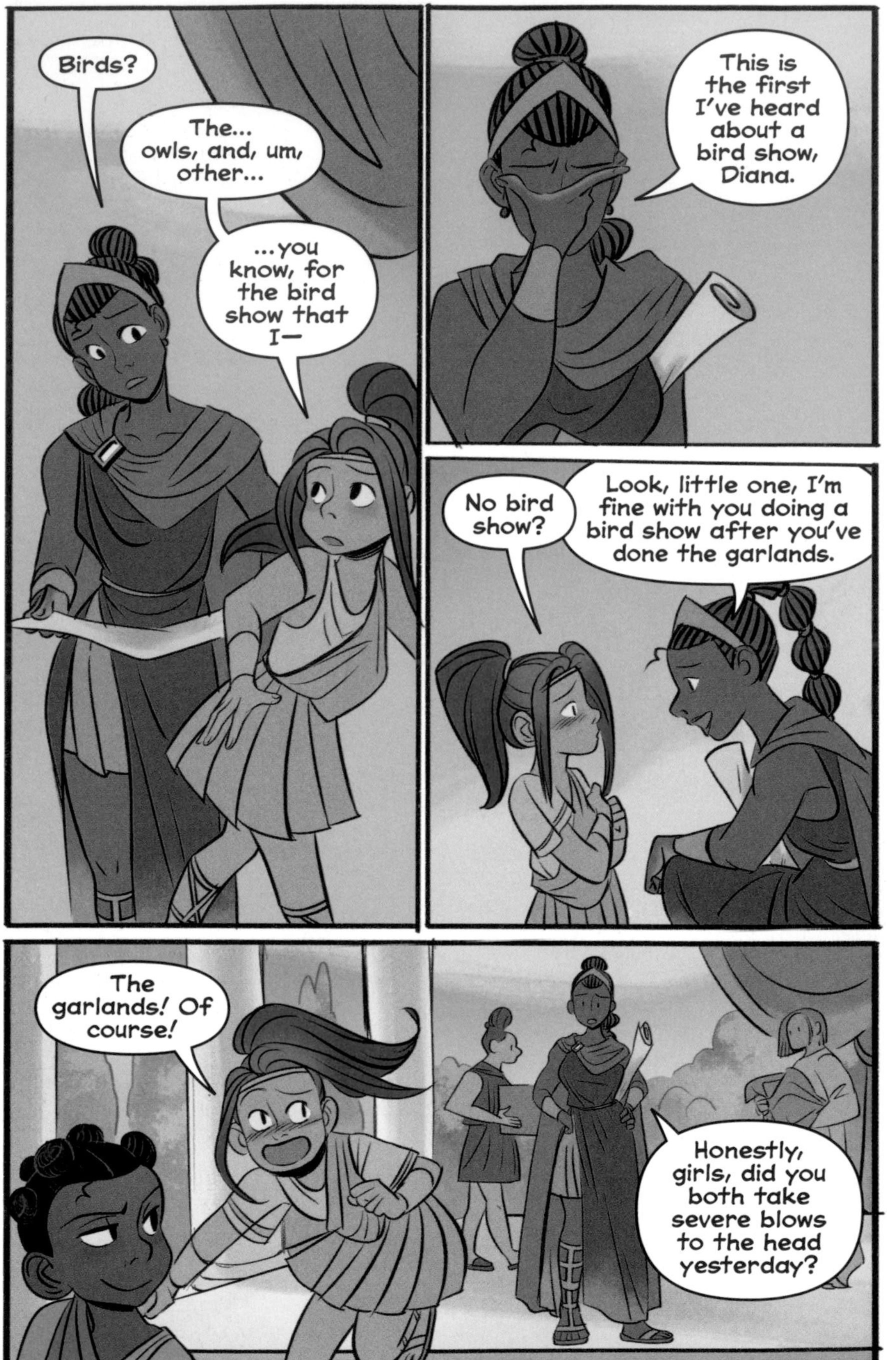
Birds?
The... owls, and, um, other...
...you know, for the bird show that I—
This is the first I've heard about a bird show, Diana.
No bird show?
Look, little one, I'm fine with you doing a bird show after you've done the garlands.
The garlands! Of course!
Honestly, girls, did you both take severe blows to the head yesterday?

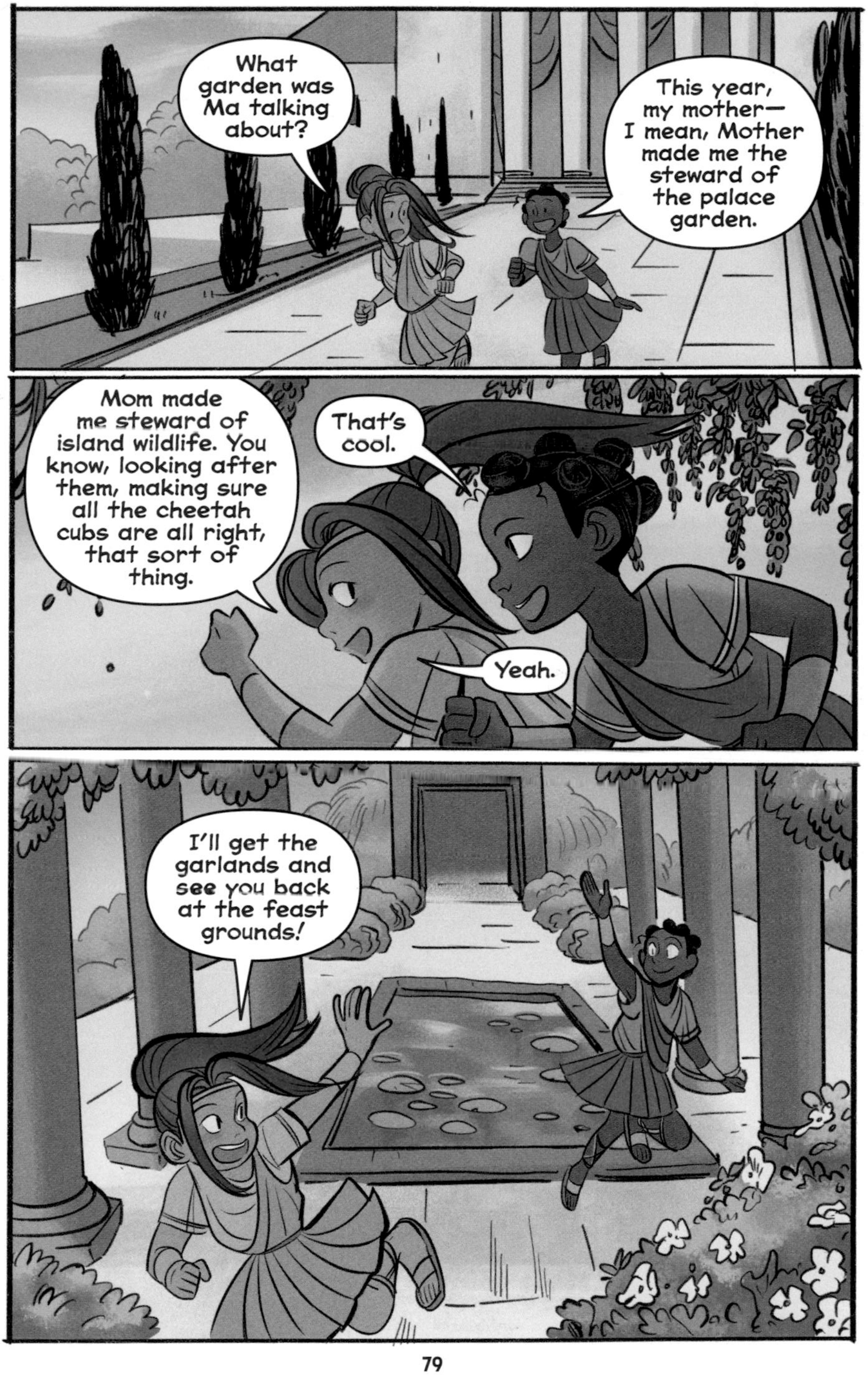
What garden was Ma talking about?
This year, my mother— I mean, Mother made me the steward of the palace garden.
Mom made me steward of island wildlife. You know, looking after them, making sure all the cheetah cubs are all right, that sort of thing.
That's cool.
Yeah.
I'll get the garlands and see you back at the feast grounds!

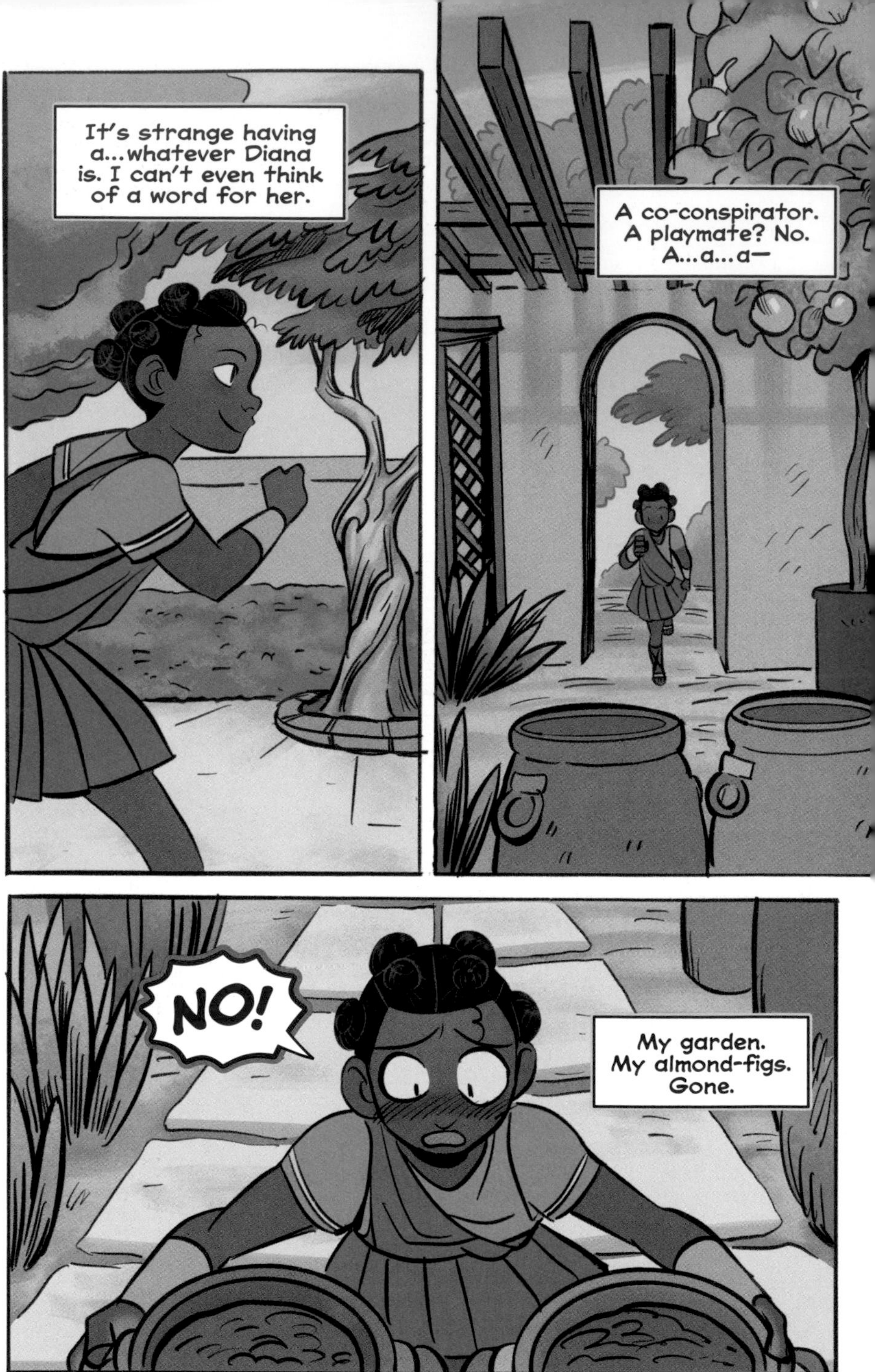
It's strange having a...whatever Diana is. I can't even think of a word for her.
A co-conspirator. A playmate? No. A...a...a—
NO!
My garden. My almond-figs. Gone.

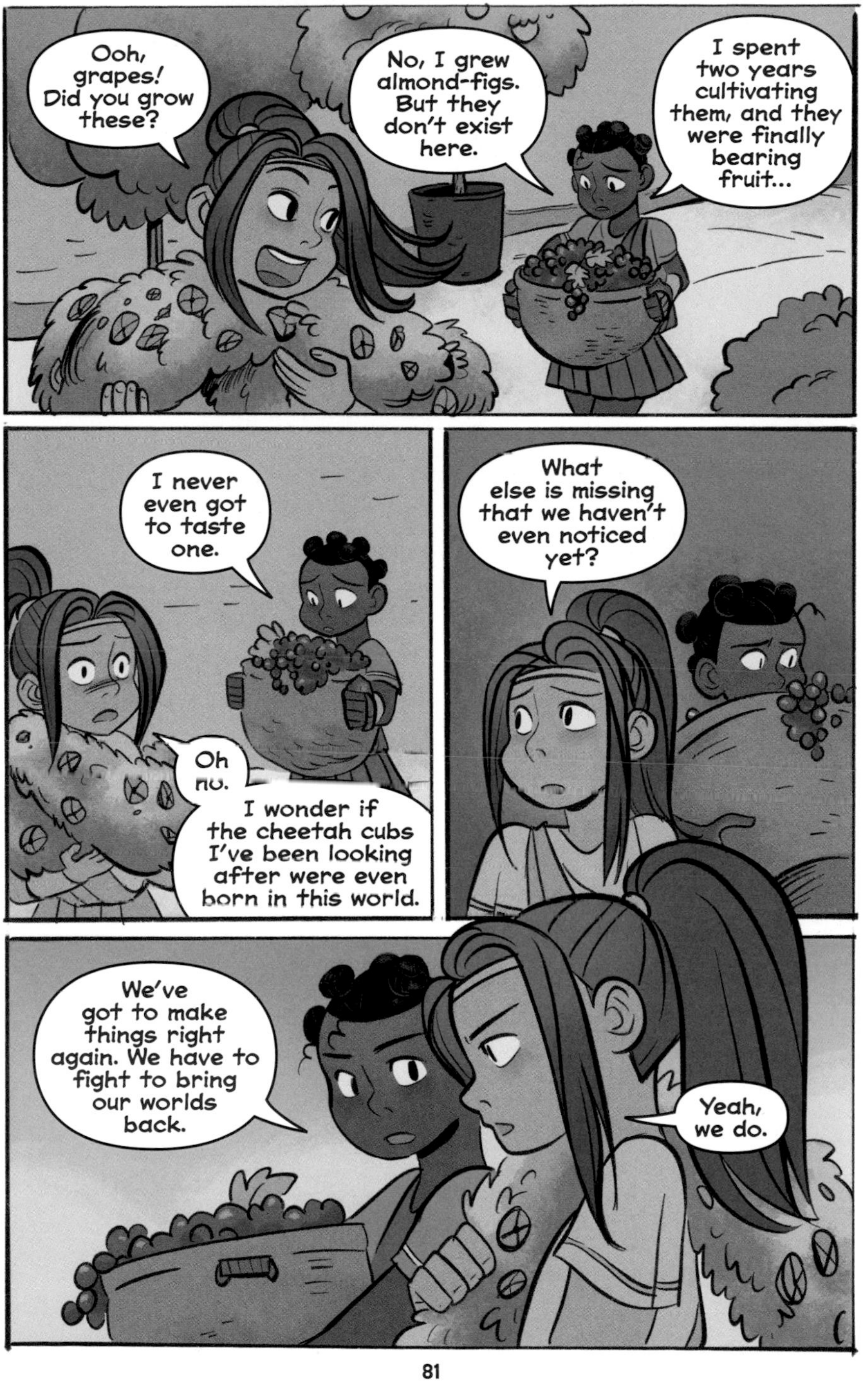
Ooh, grapes! Did you grow these?
No, I grew almond-figs. But they don't exist here.
I spent two years cultivating them, and they were finally bearing fruit...
I never even got to taste one.
Oh no.
I wonder if the cheetah cubs I've been looking after were even born in this world.
What else is missing that we haven't even noticed yet?
We've got to make things right again. We have to fight to bring our worlds back.
Yeah, we do.

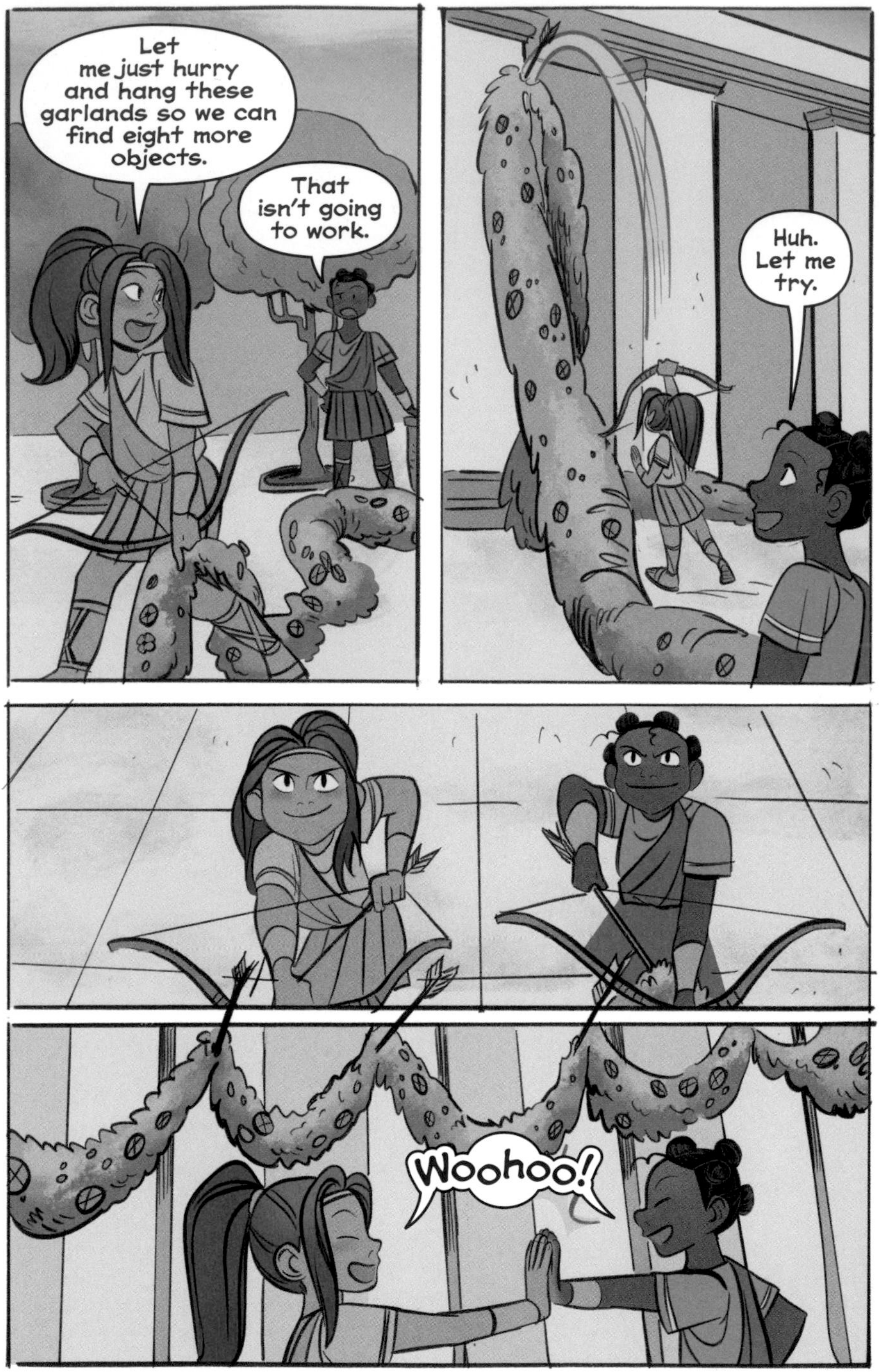
Let me just hurry and hang these garlands so we can find eight more objects.
That isn't going to work.
Huh. Let me try.
Woohoo!

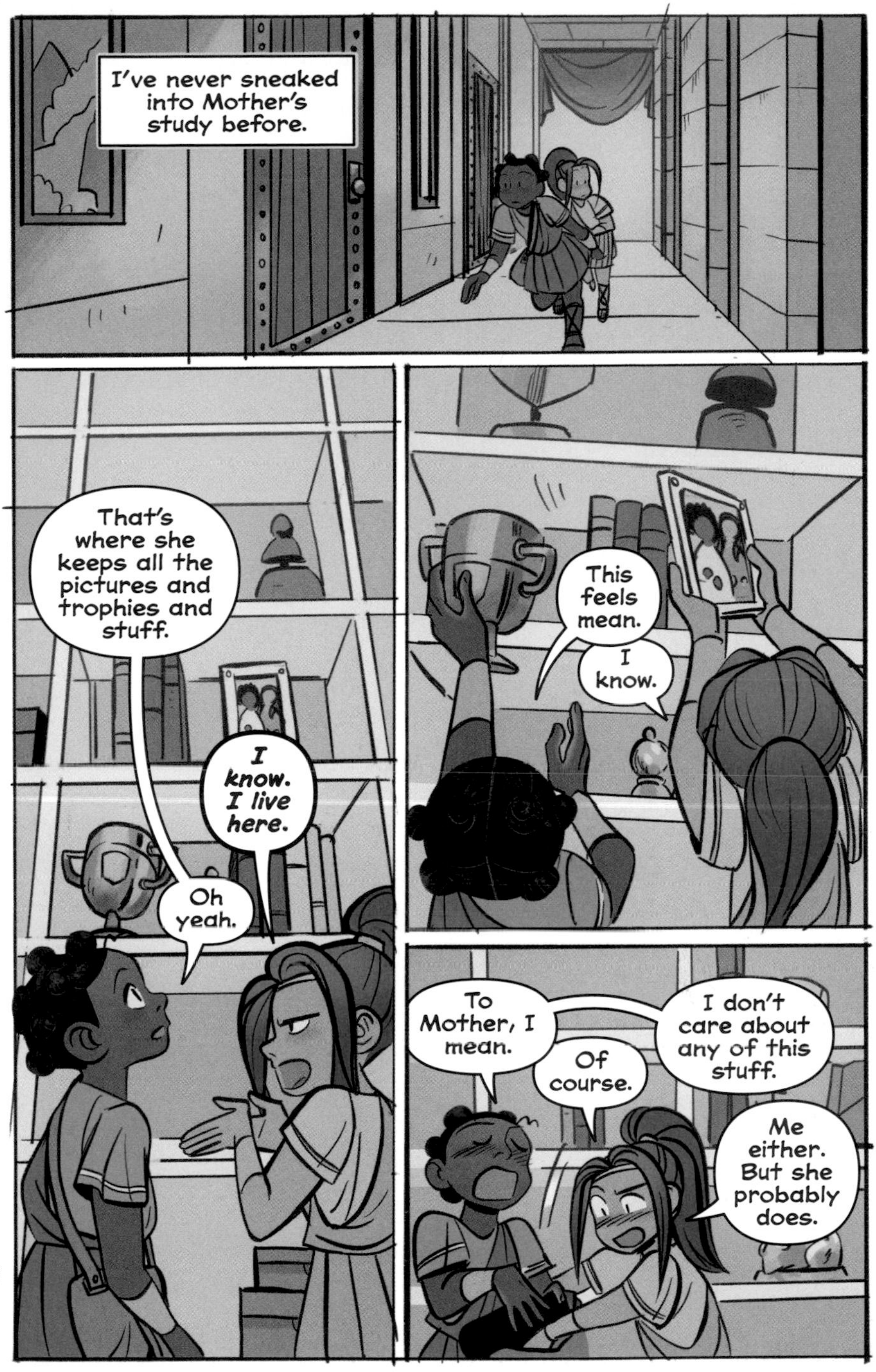
I've never sneaked into Mother's study before.
That's where she keeps all the pictures and trophies and stuff.
I know. I live here.
Oh yeah.
This feels mean.
I know.
To Mother, I mean.
Of course.
I don't care about any of this stuff.
Me either. But she probably does.

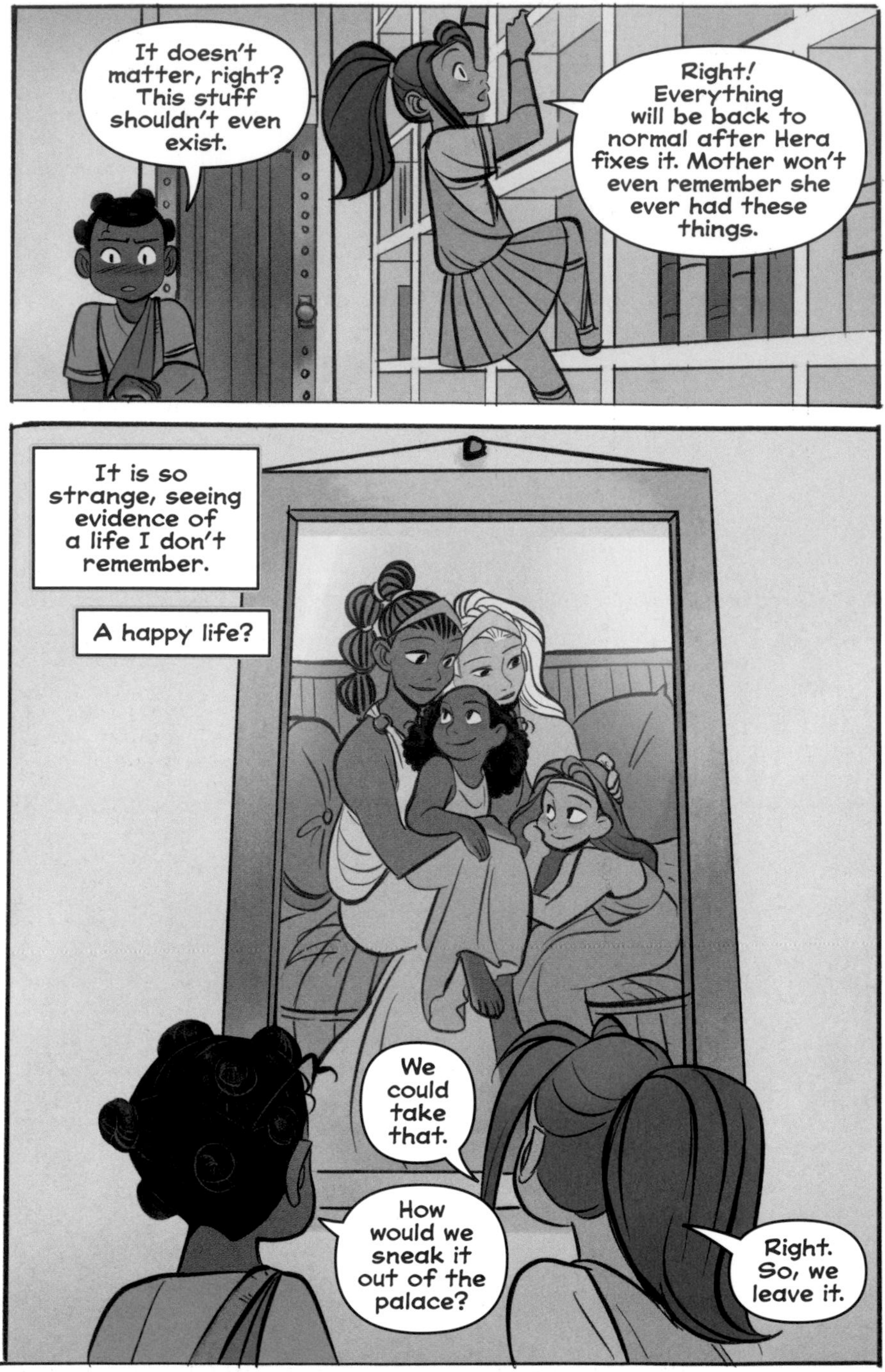
It doesn't matter, right? This stuff shouldn't even exist.
Right! Everything will be back to normal after Hera fixes it. Mother won't even remember she ever had these things.
It is so strange, seeing evidence of a life I don't remember.
A happy life?
We could take that.
How would we sneak it out of the palace?
Right. So, we leave it.

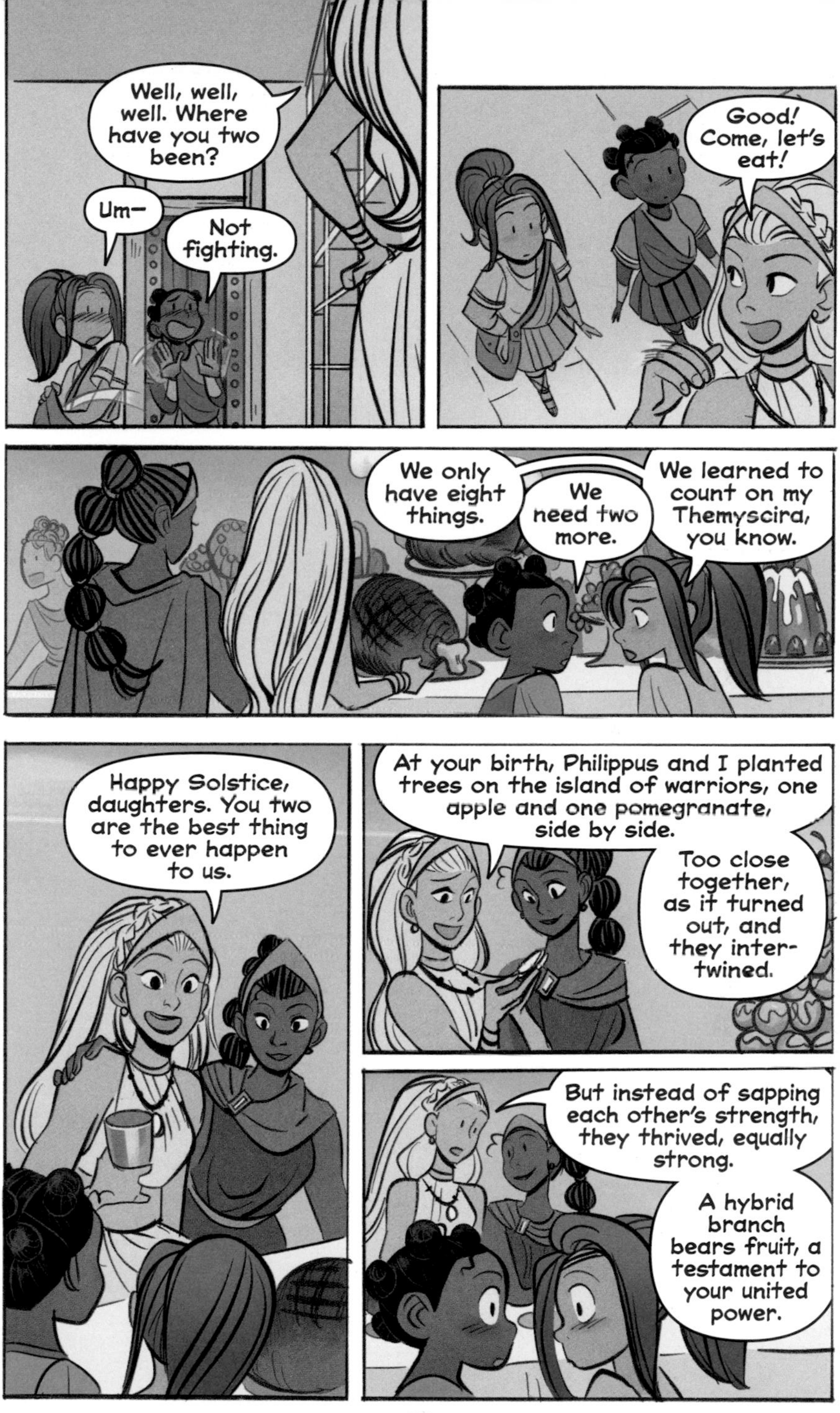
Well, well, well. Where have you two been?
Um—
Not fighting.
Good! Come, let's eat!
We only have eight things.
We need two more.
We learned to count on my Themyscira, you know.
Happy Solstice, daughters. You two are the best thing to ever happen to us.
At your birth, Philippus and I planted trees on the island of warriors, one apple and one pomegranate, side by side.
Too close together, as it turned out, and they inter-twined.
But instead of sapping each other's strength, they thrived, equally strong.
A hybrid branch bears fruit, a testament to your united power.

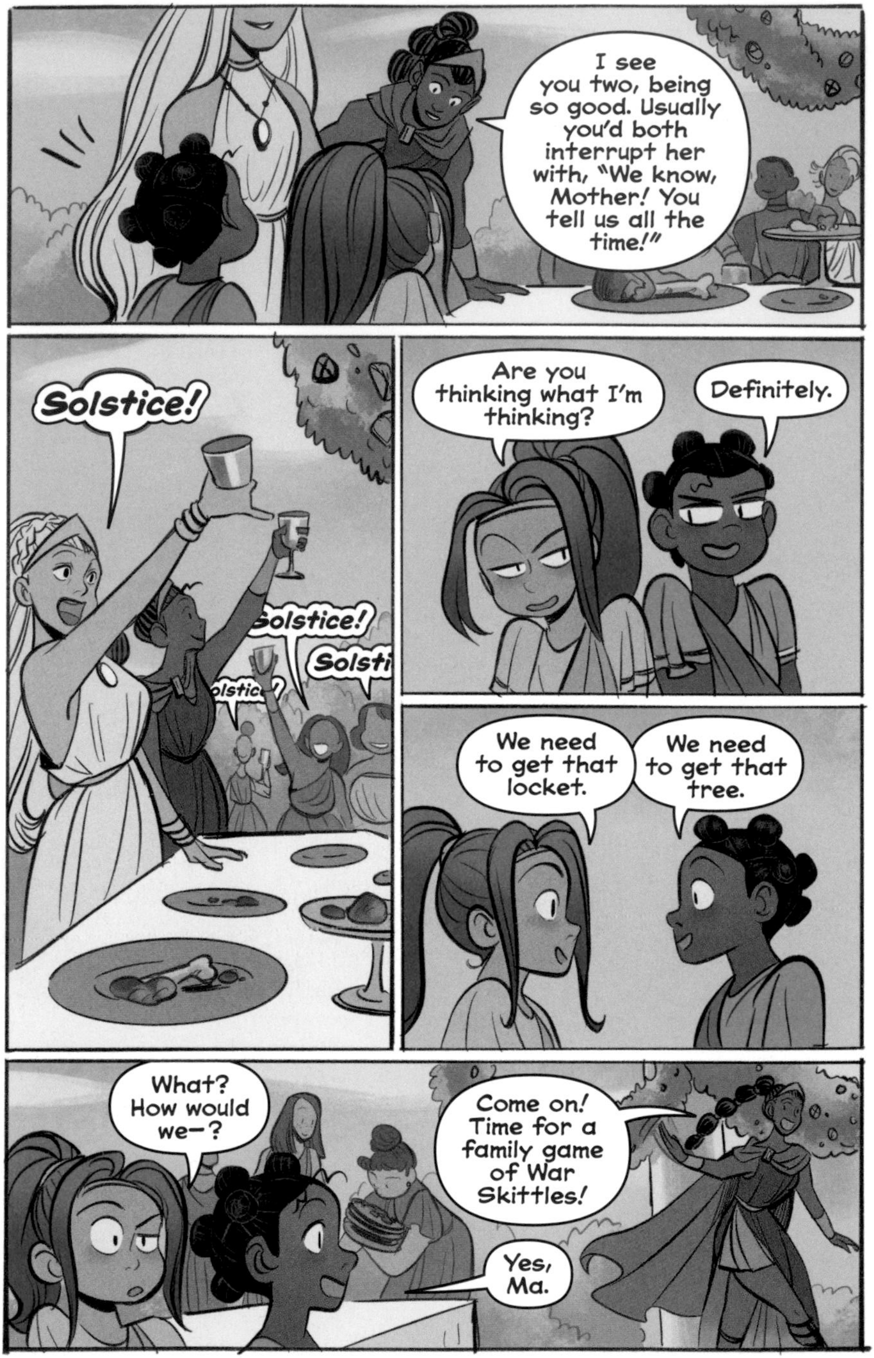
I see you two, being so good. Usually you'd both interrupt her with, "We know, Mother! You tell us all the time!"
Solstice!
Solstice!
Are you thinking what I'm thinking?
Definitely.
We need to get that locket.
We need to get that tree.
What? How would we–?
Come on! Time for a family game of War Skittles!
Yes, Ma.

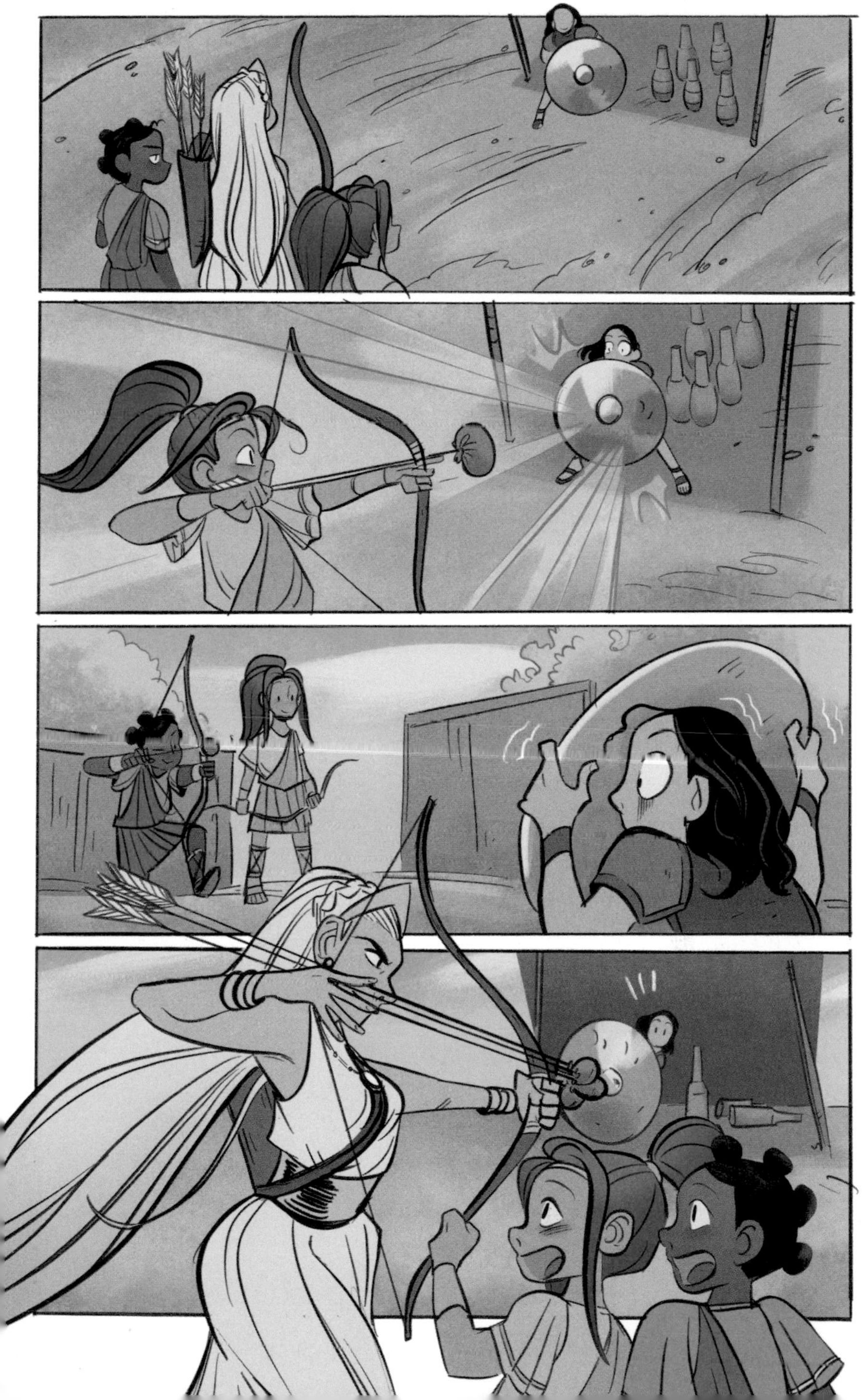

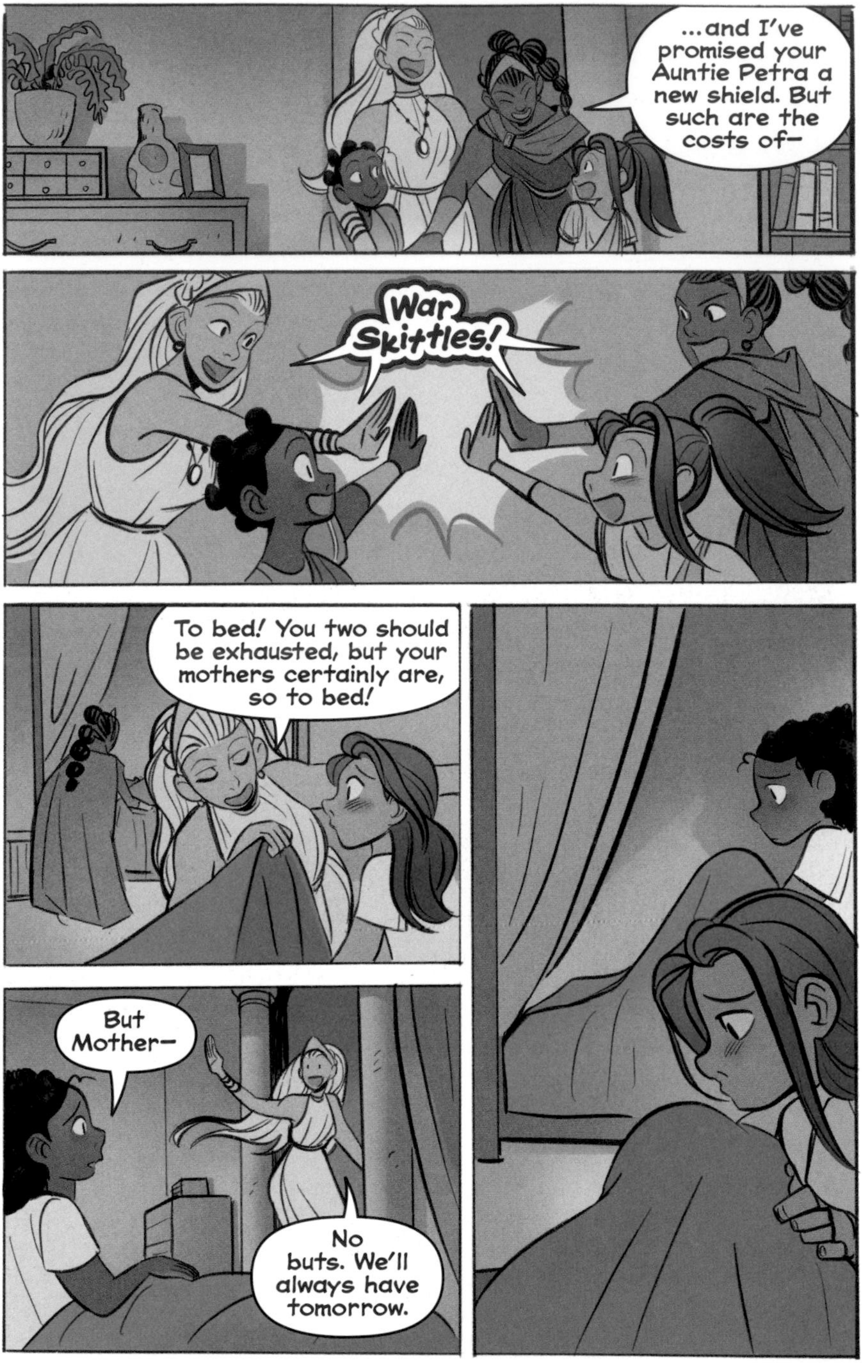
...and I've promised your Auntie Petra a new shield. But such are the costs of–
War Skittles!
To bed! You two should be exhausted, but your mothers certainly are, so to bed!
But Mother–
No buts. We'll always have tomorrow.

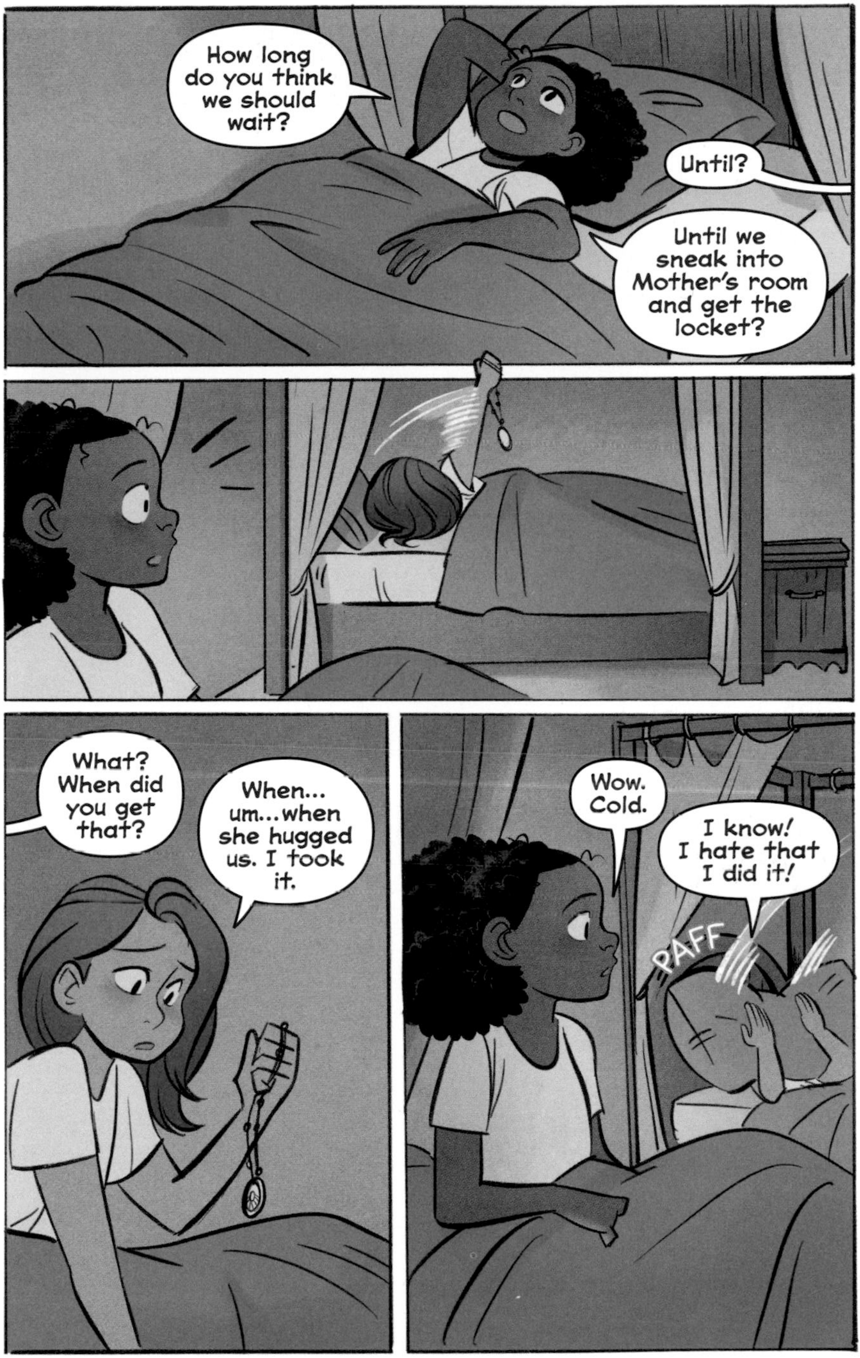
How long do you think we should wait?
Until?
Until we sneak into Mother's room and get the locket?
What? When did you get that?
When... um...when she hugged us. I took it.
Wow. Cold.
I know! I hate that I did it!
PAFF

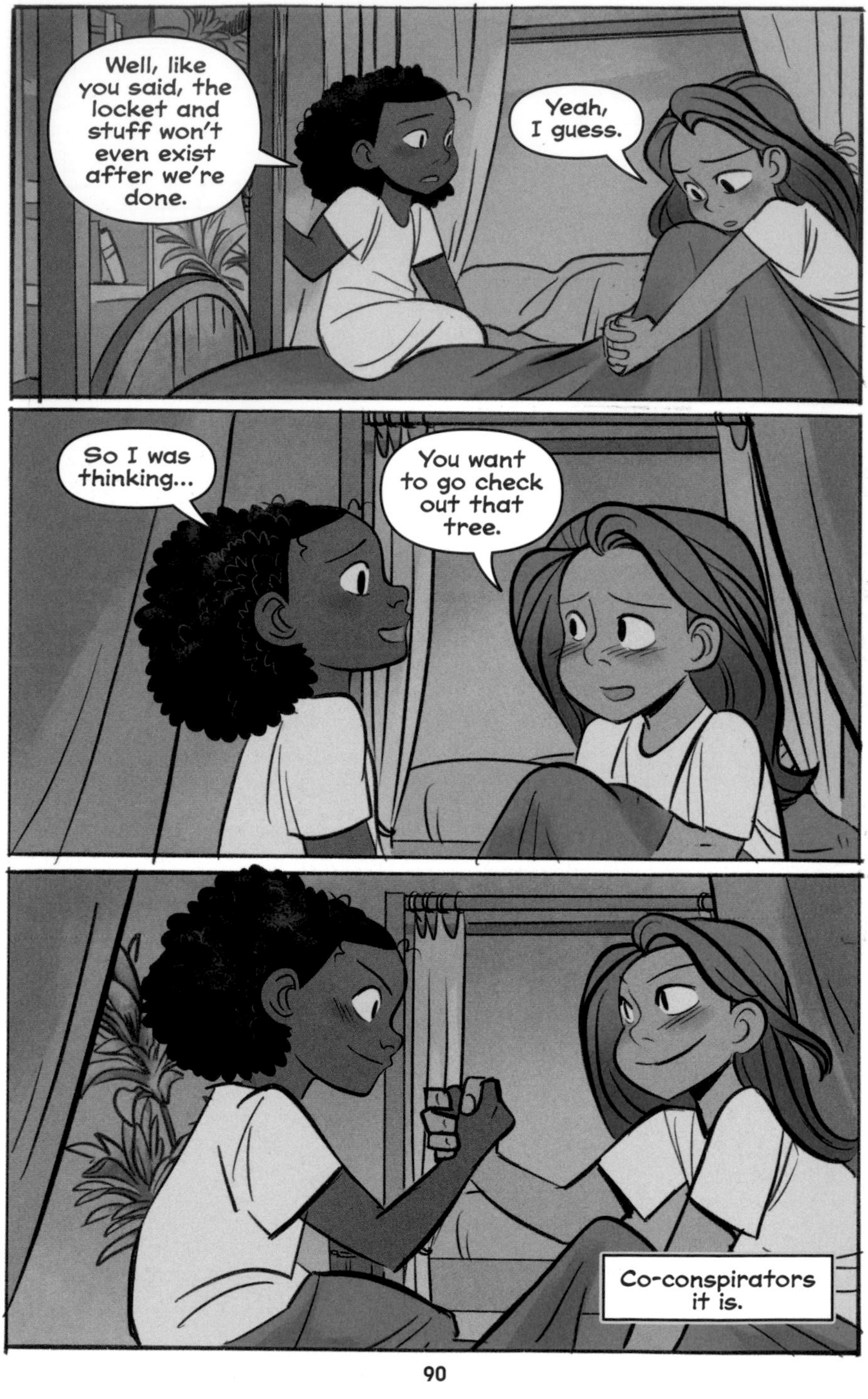
Well, like you said, the locket and stuff won't even exist after we're done.
Yeah, I guess.
So I was thinking...
You want to go check out that tree.
Co-conspirators it is.

CHAPTER FOUR

DIANA

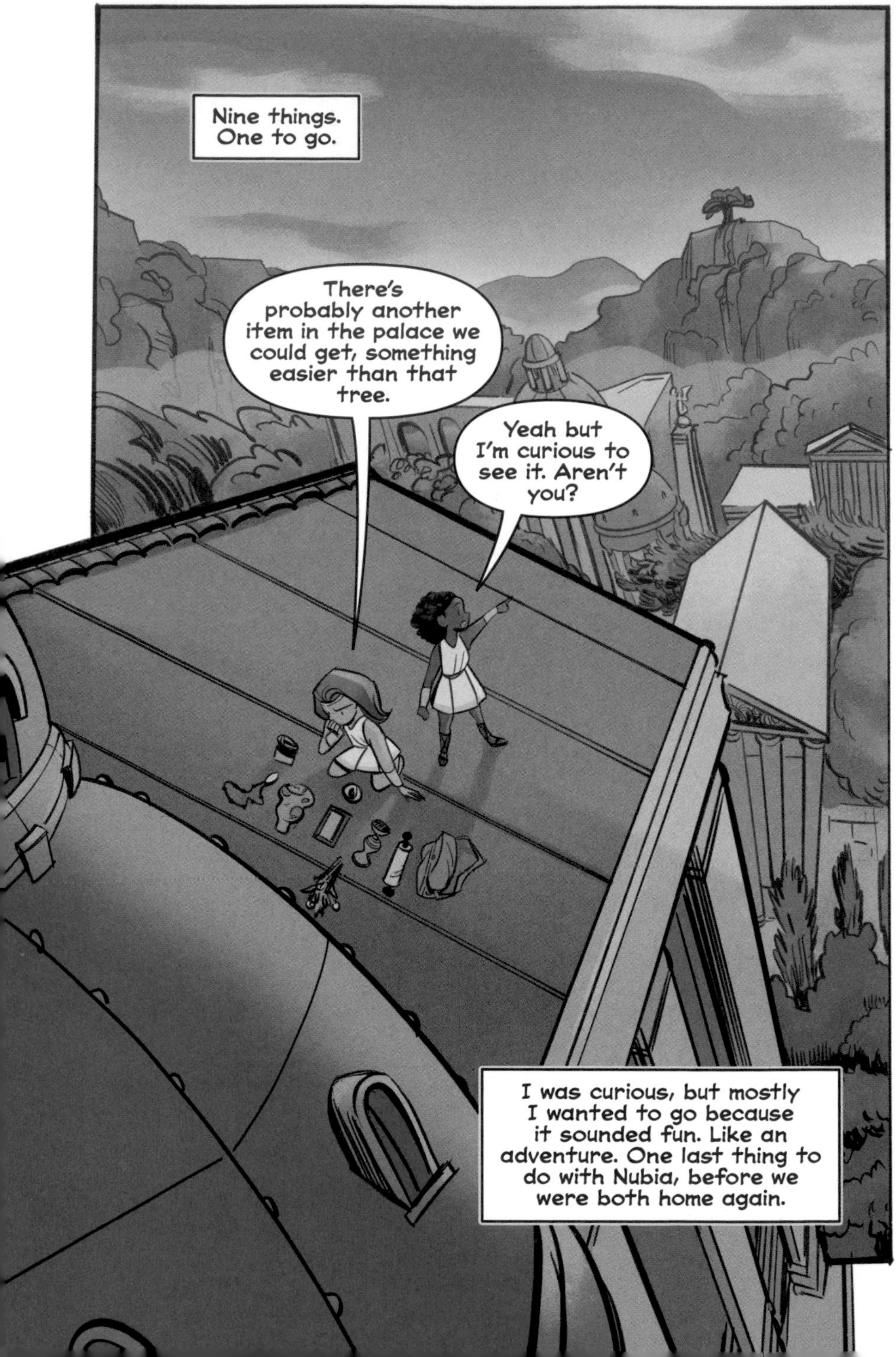
Nine things.
One to go.
There's probably another item in the palace we could get, something easier than that tree.
Yeah but I'm curious to see it. Aren't you?
I was curious, but mostly I wanted to go because it sounded fun. Like an adventure. One last thing to do with Nubia, before we were both home again.

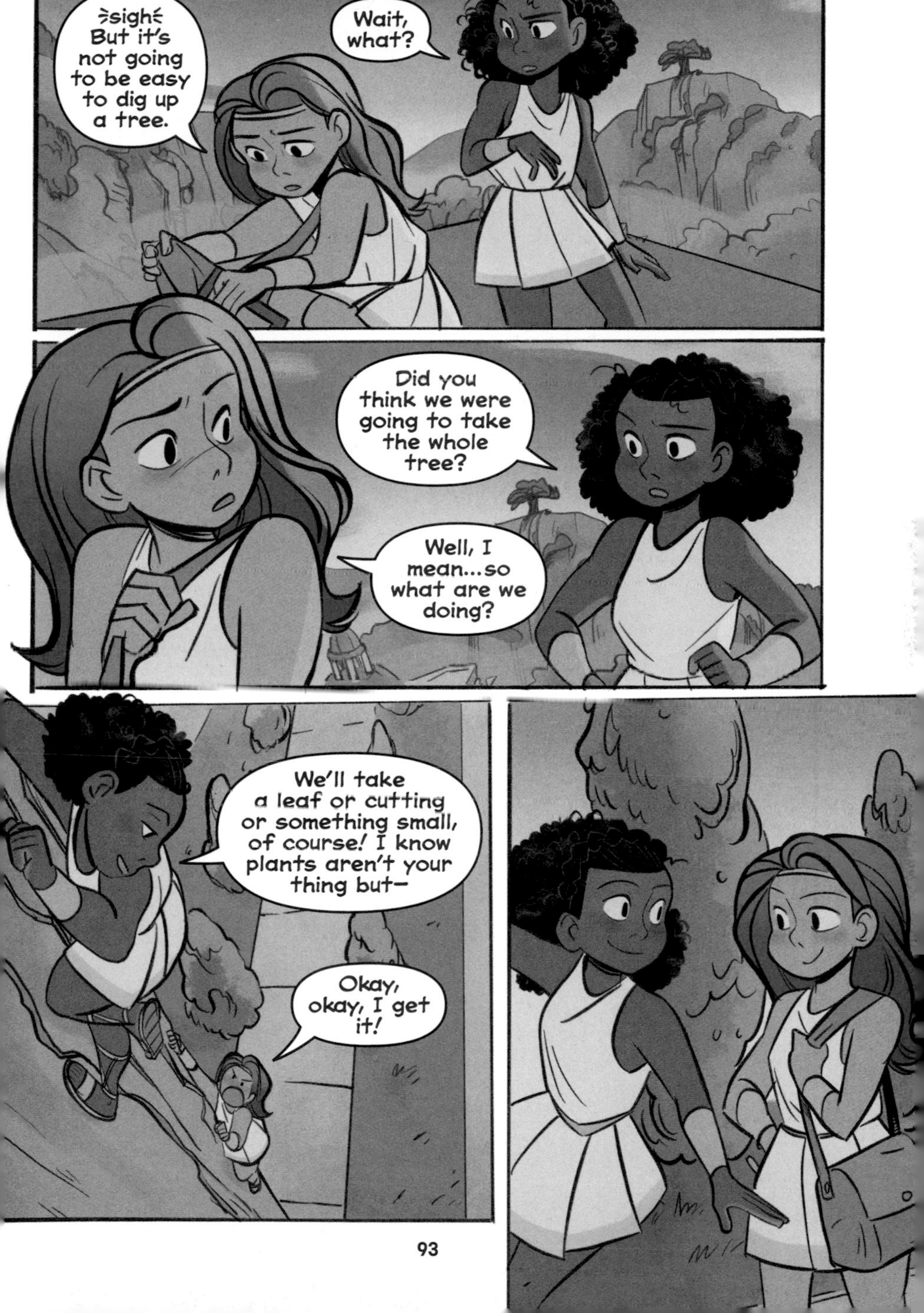

>sigh< But it's not going to be easy to dig up a tree.
Wait, what?
Did you think we were going to take the whole tree?
Well, I mean...so what are we doing?
We'll take a leaf or cutting or something small, of course! I know plants aren't your thing but—
Okay, okay, I get it!

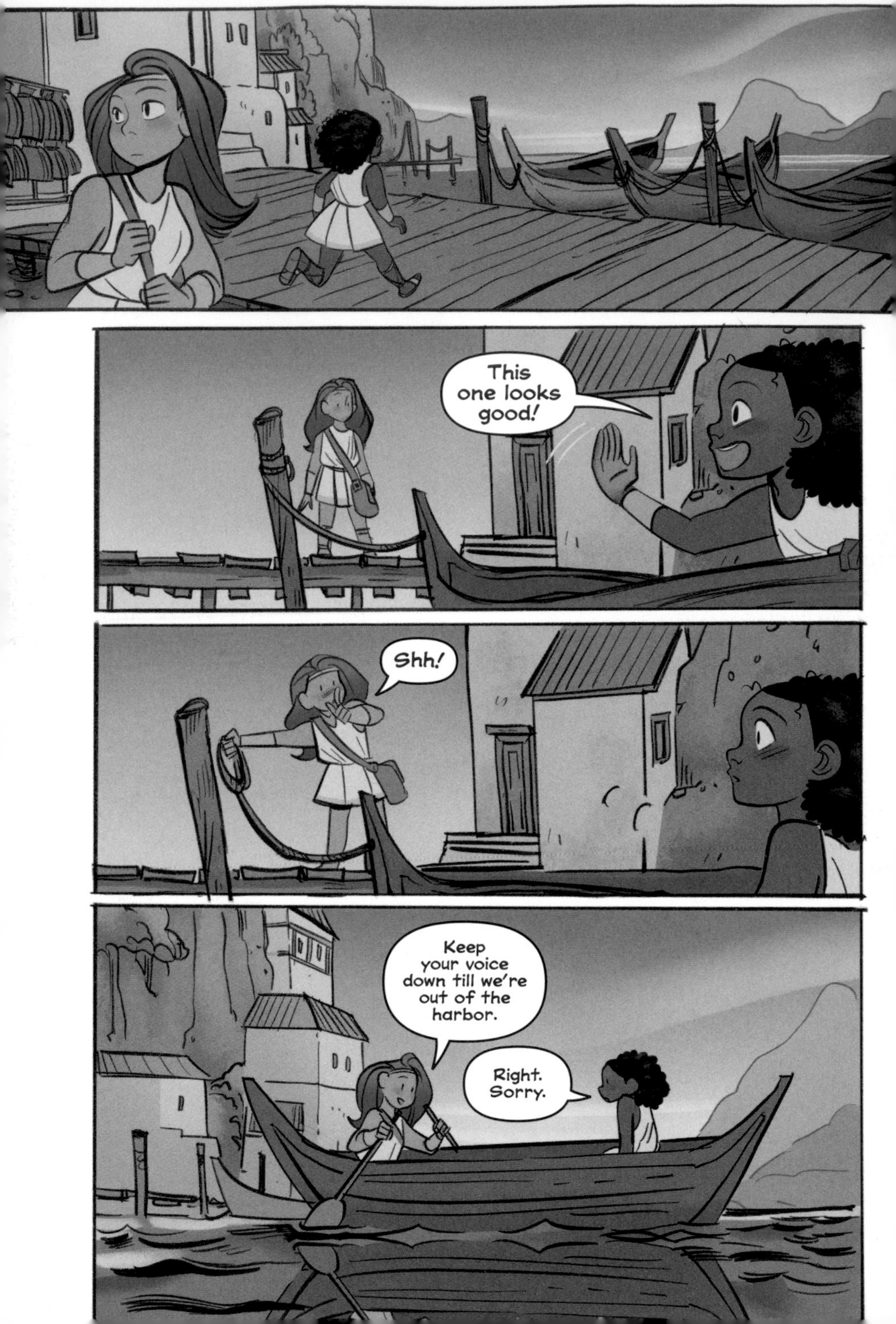
This one looks good!
Shh!
Keep your voice down till we're out of the harbor.
Right. Sorry.

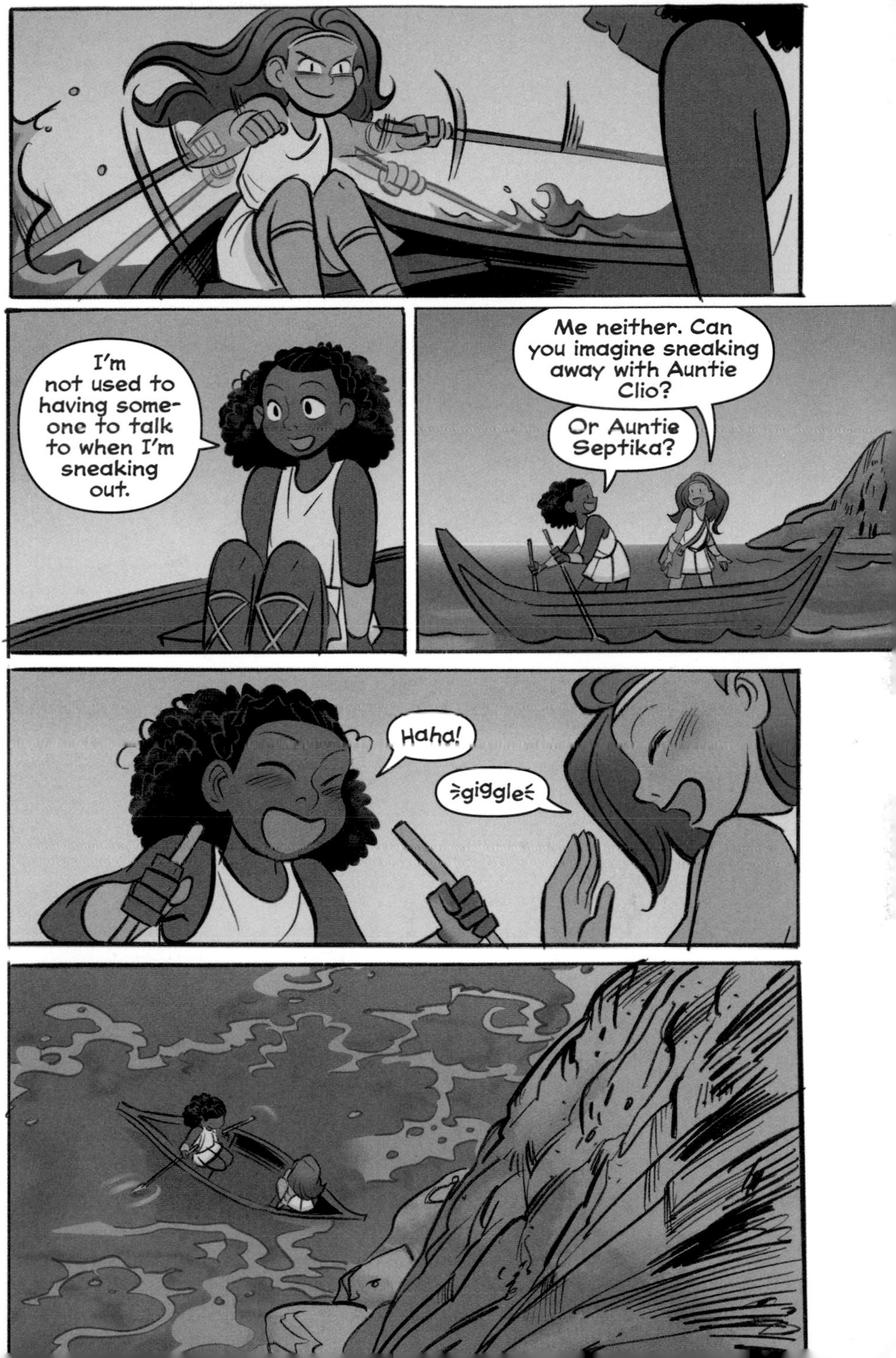
I'm not used to having some-one to talk to when I'm sneaking out.
Me neither. Can you imagine sneaking away with Auntie Clio?
Or Auntie Septika?
Haha!
≥giggle≤

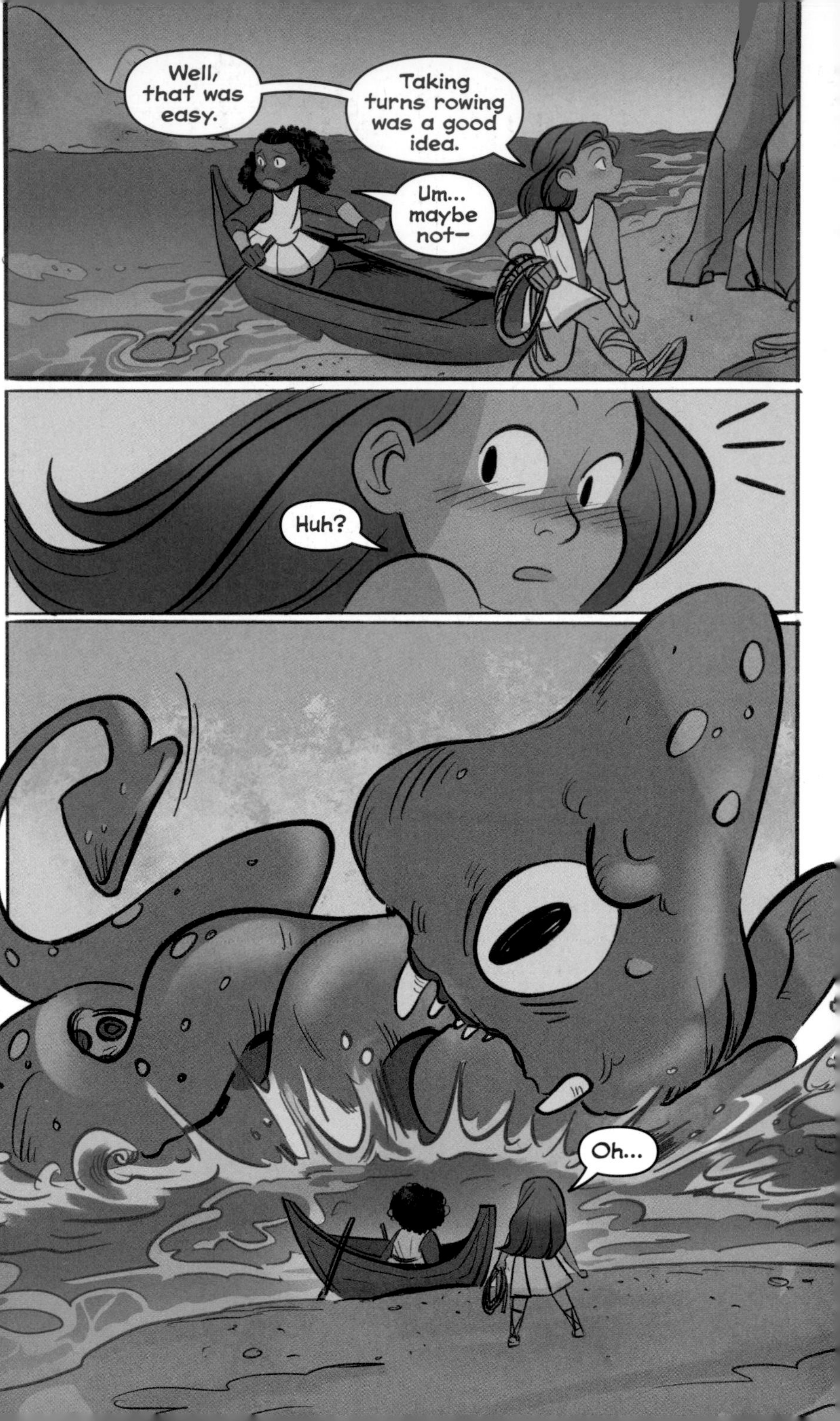
Well, that was easy.
Taking turns rowing was a good idea.
Um... maybe not—
Huh?
Oh...

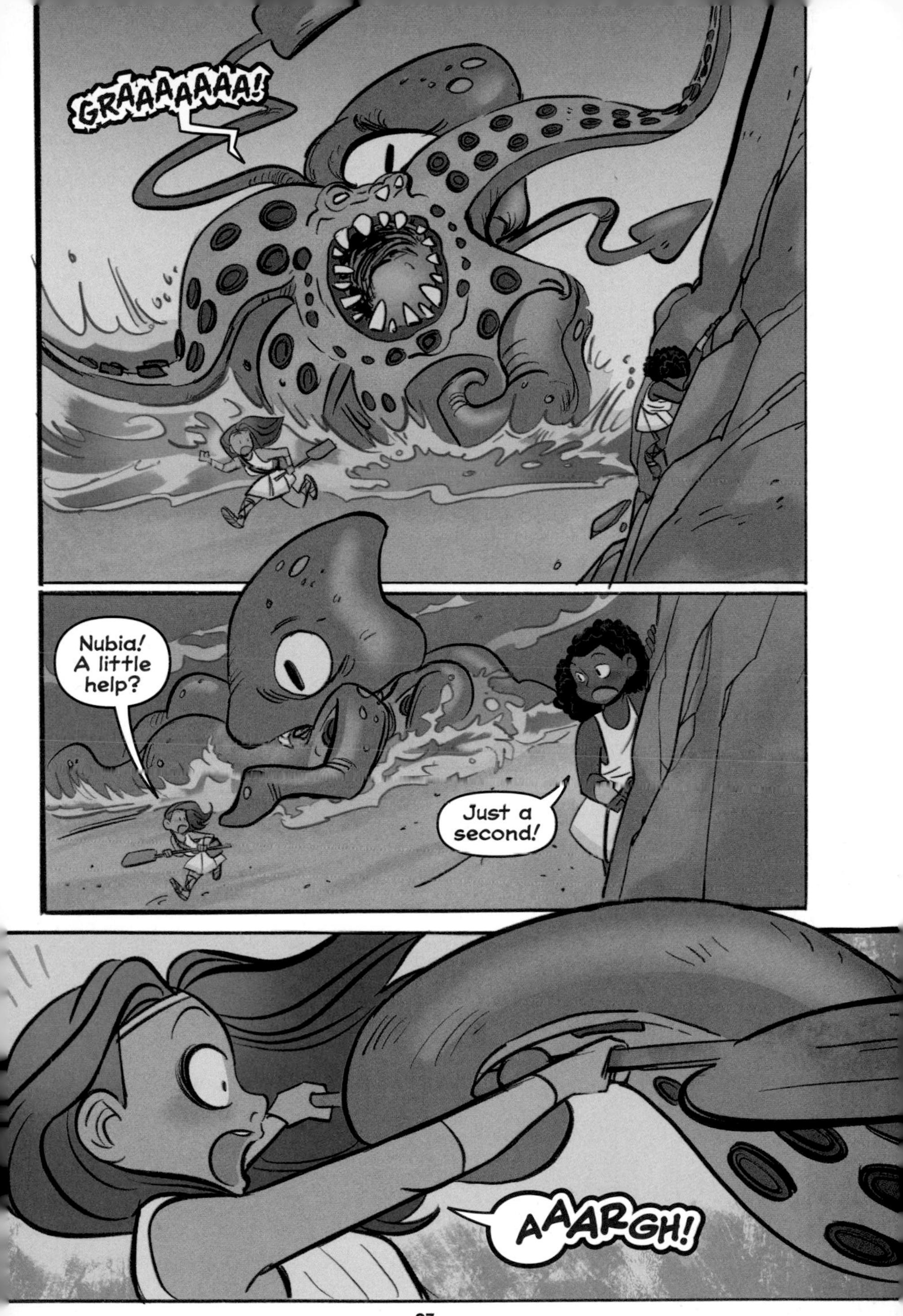
GRAAAAAAA!
Nubia! A little help?
Just a second!
AAARGH!

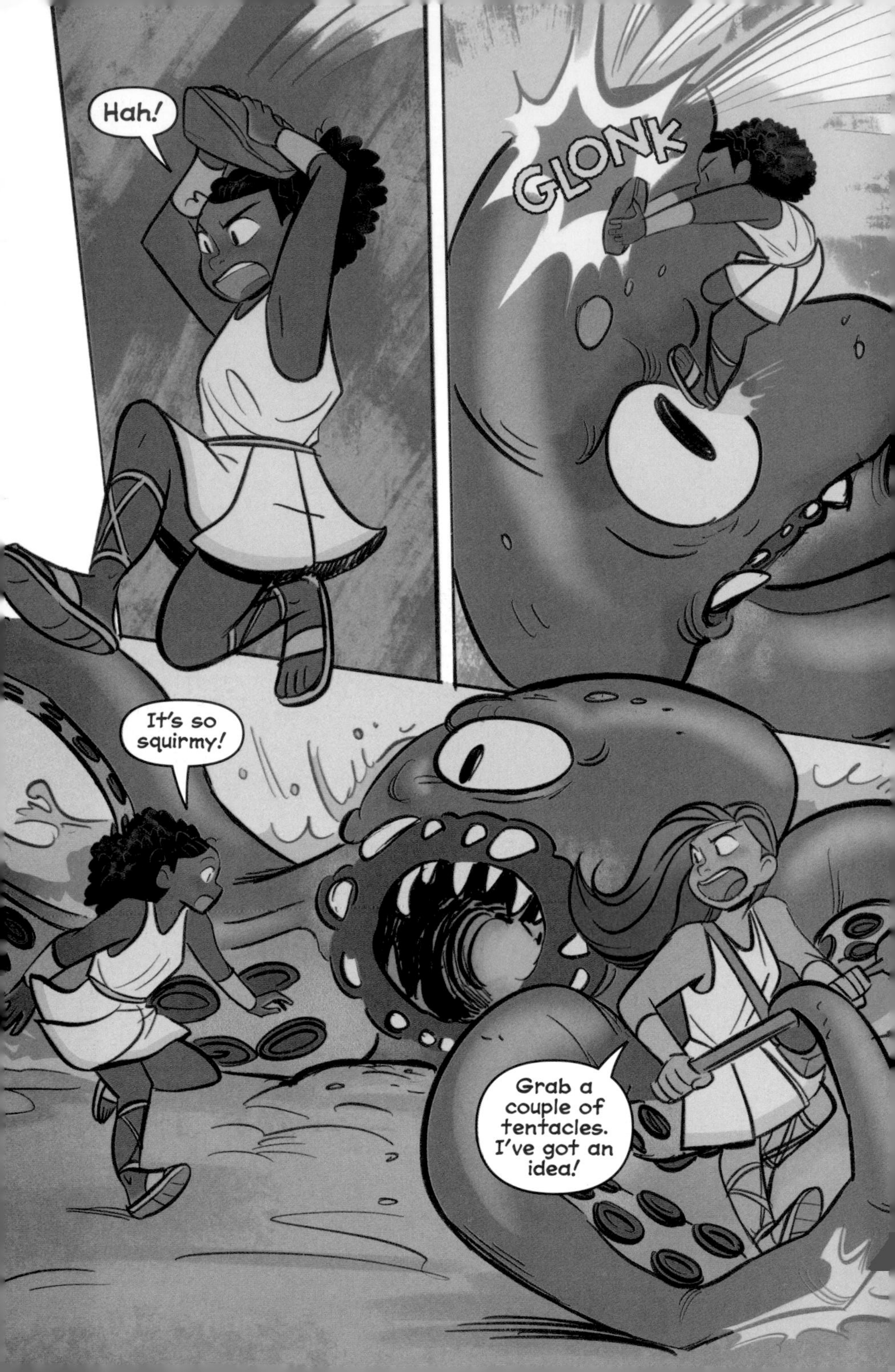
Hah!
GLONK
It's so squirmy!
Grab a couple of tentacles. I've got an idea!

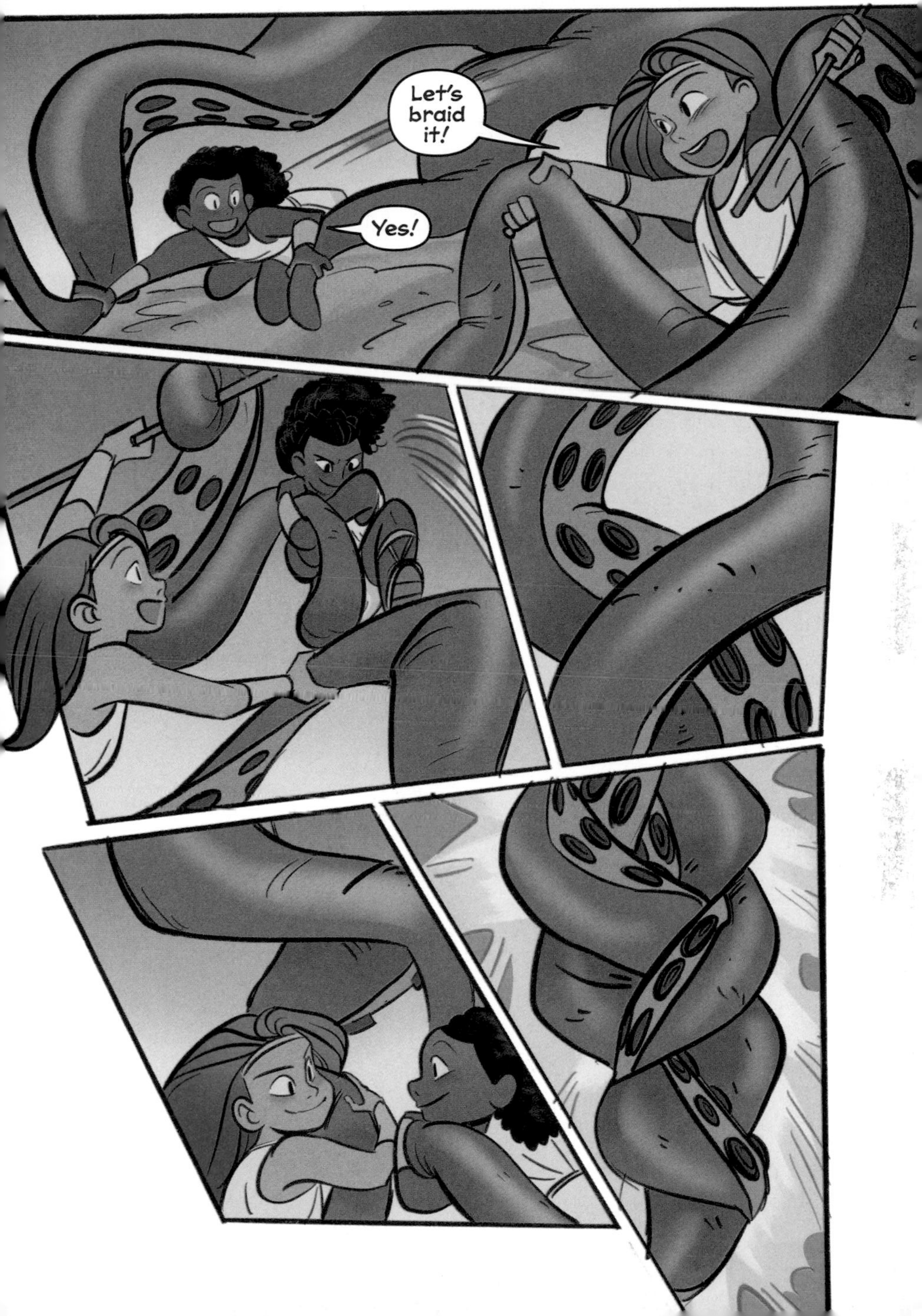
Let's braid it!
Yes!

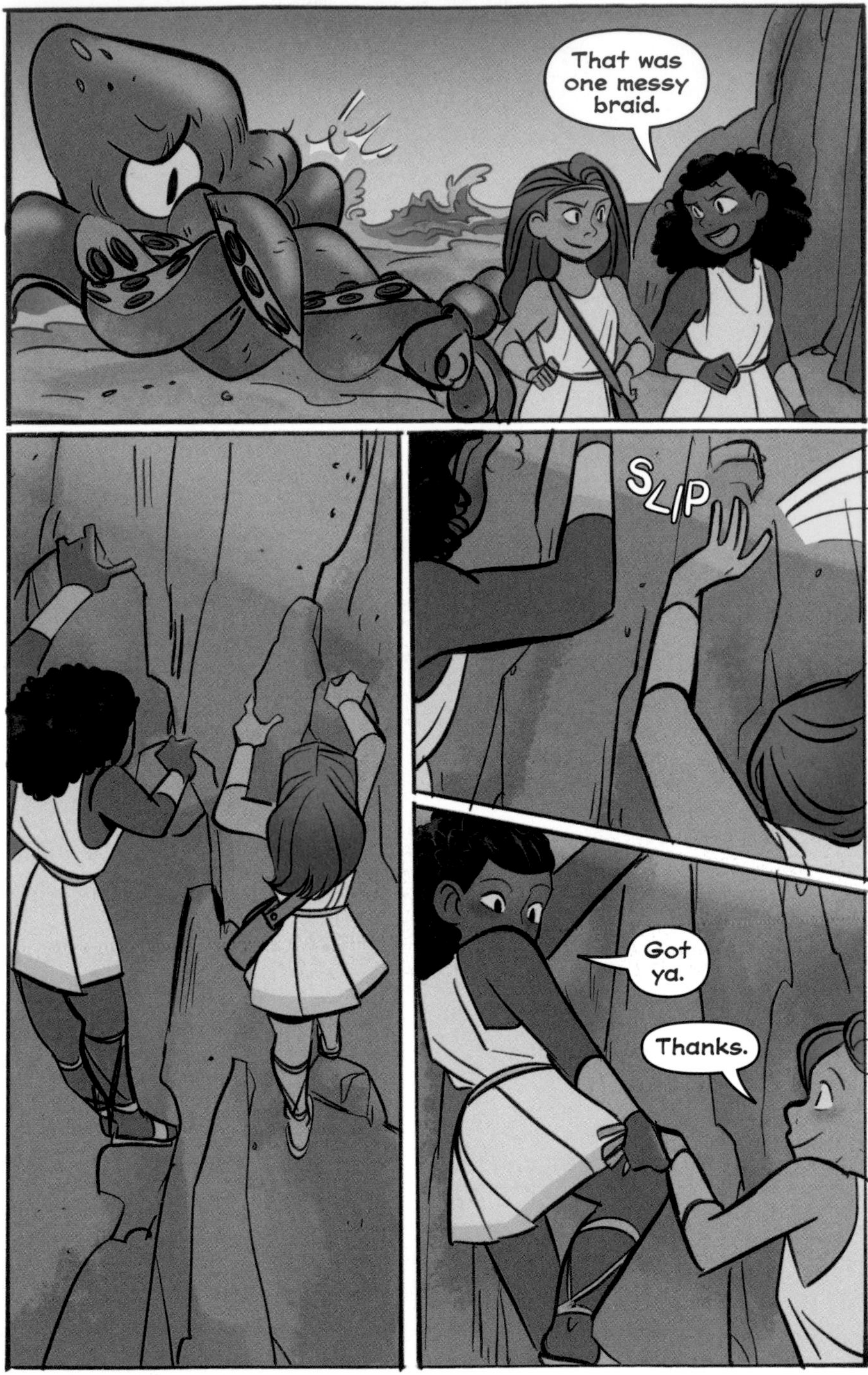
That was one messy braid.
SLIP
Got ya.
Thanks.

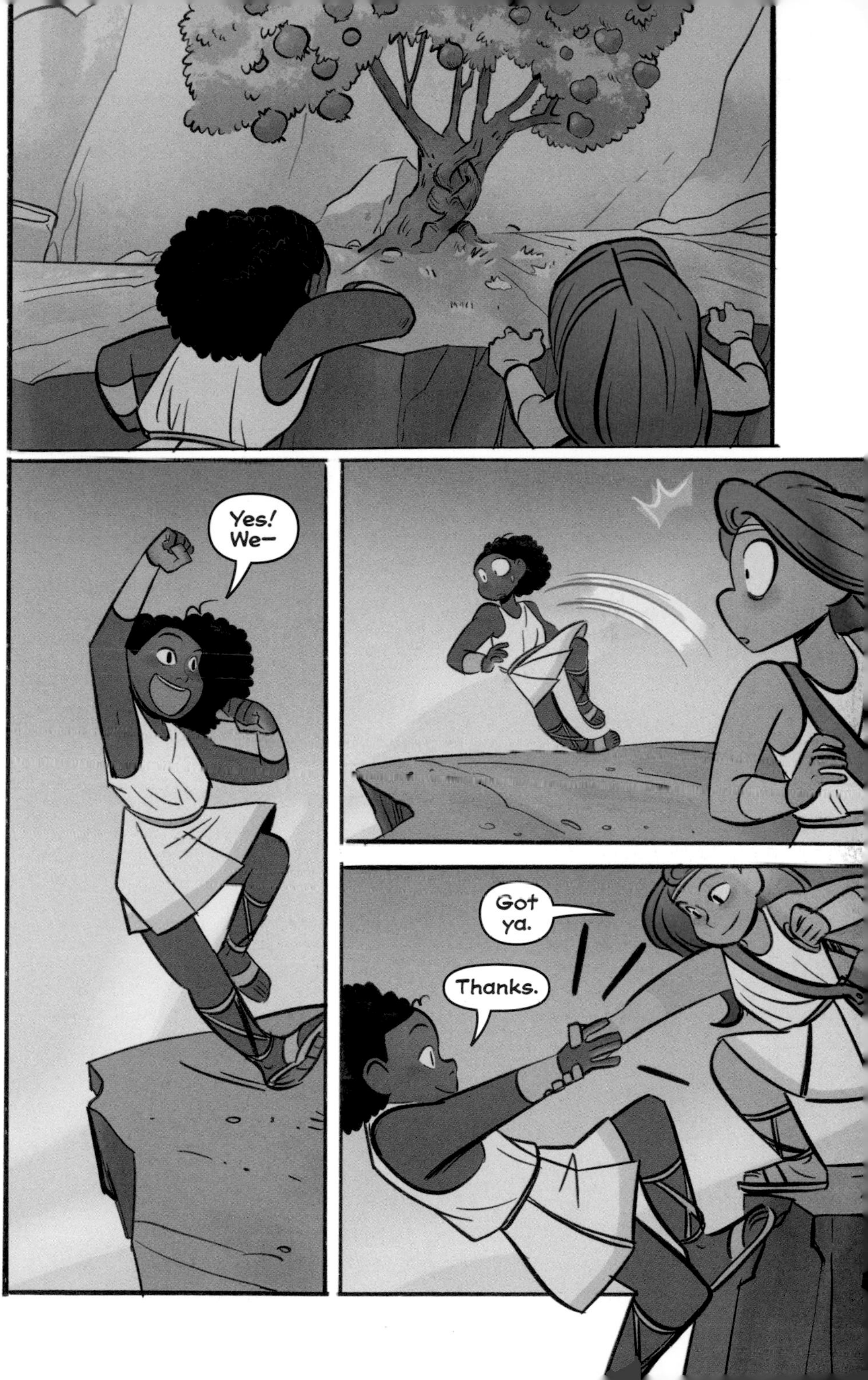
Yes! We—
Got ya.
Thanks.

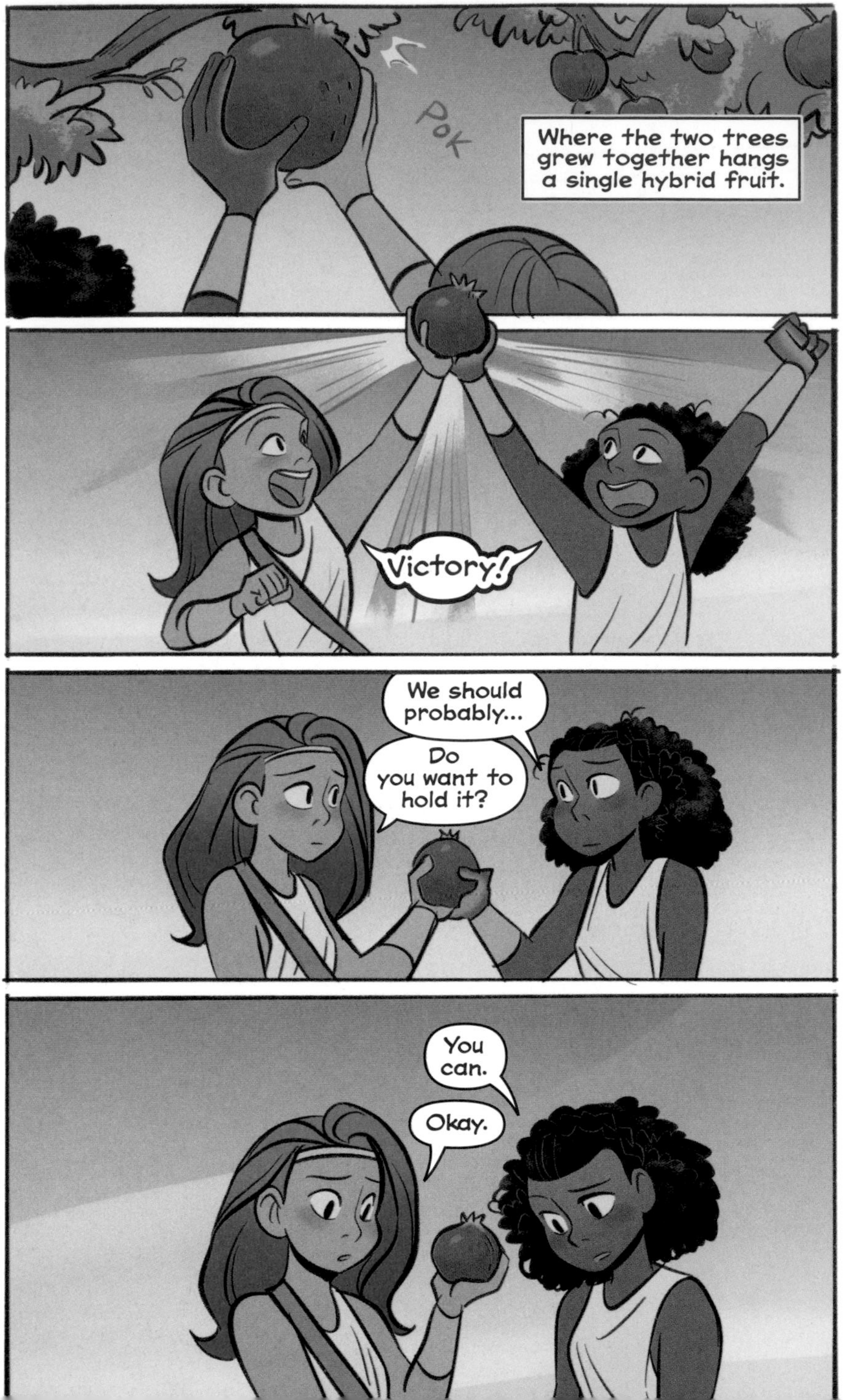
POK
Where the two trees grew together hangs a single hybrid fruit.
Victory!
We should probably...
Do you want to hold it?
You can.
Okay.

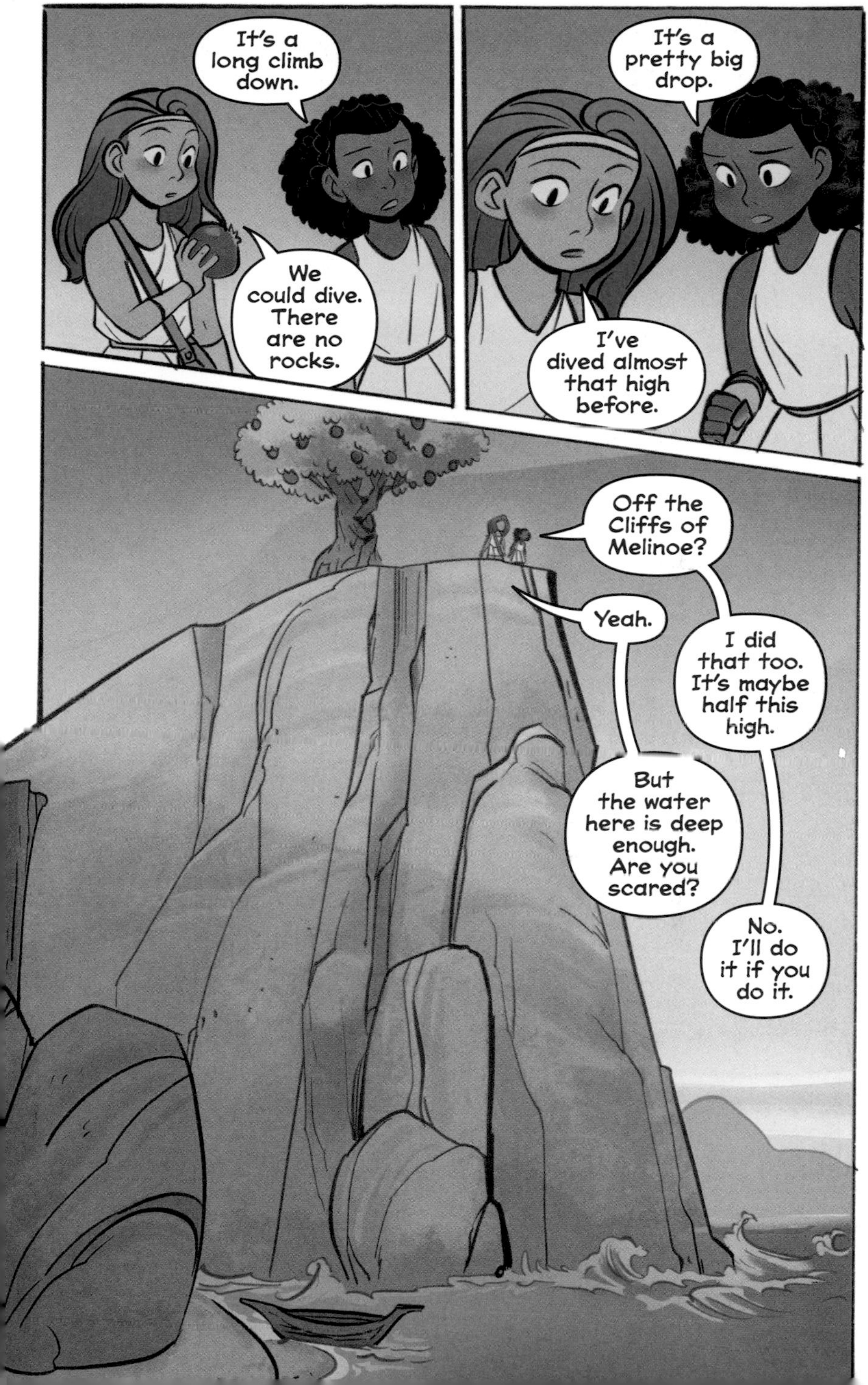
It's a long climb down.
We could dive. There are no rocks.
It's a pretty big drop.
I've dived almost that high before.
Off the Cliffs of Melinoe?
Yeah.
I did that too. It's maybe half this high.
But the water here is deep enough. Are you scared?
No. I'll do it if you do it.

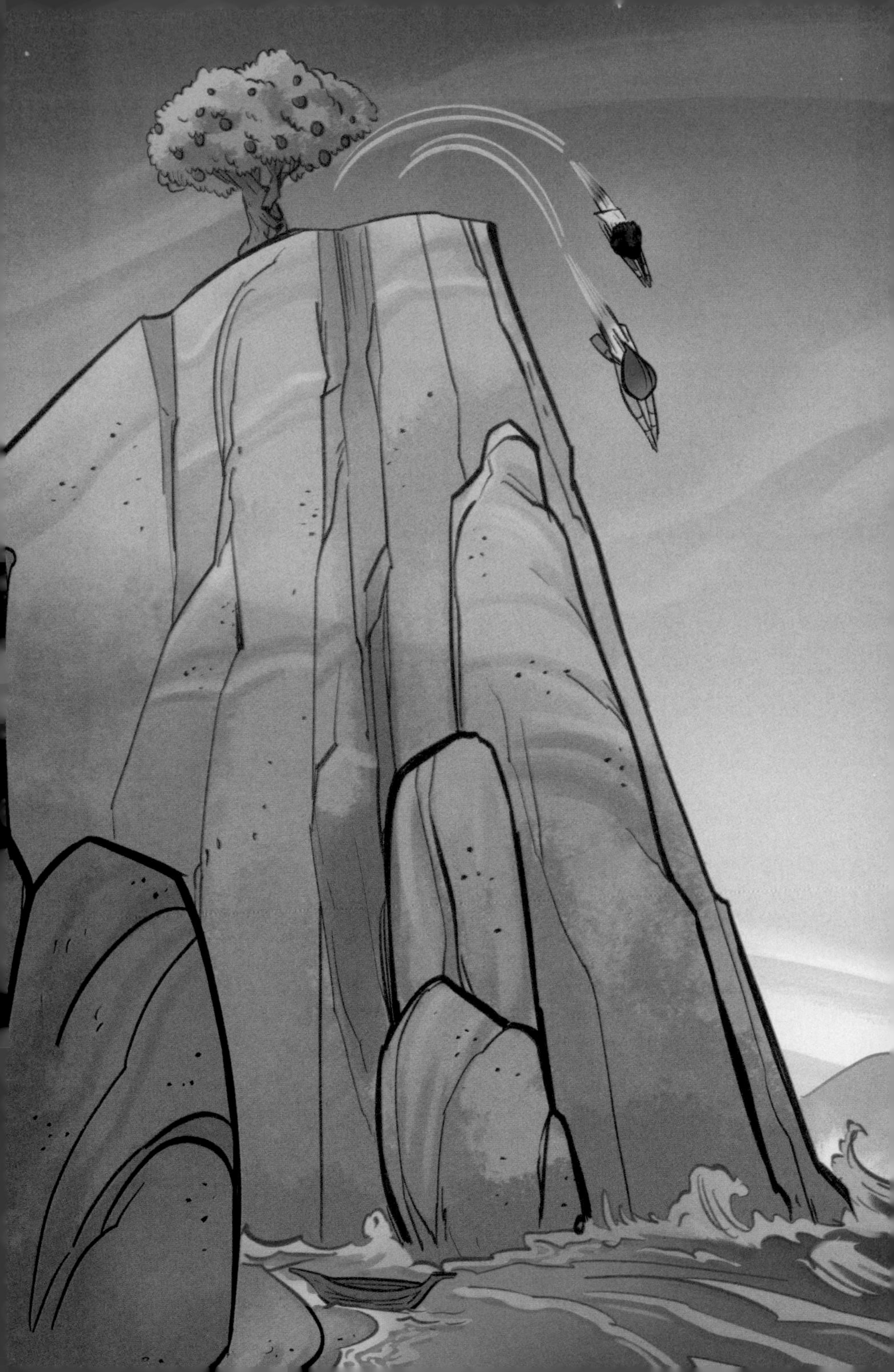

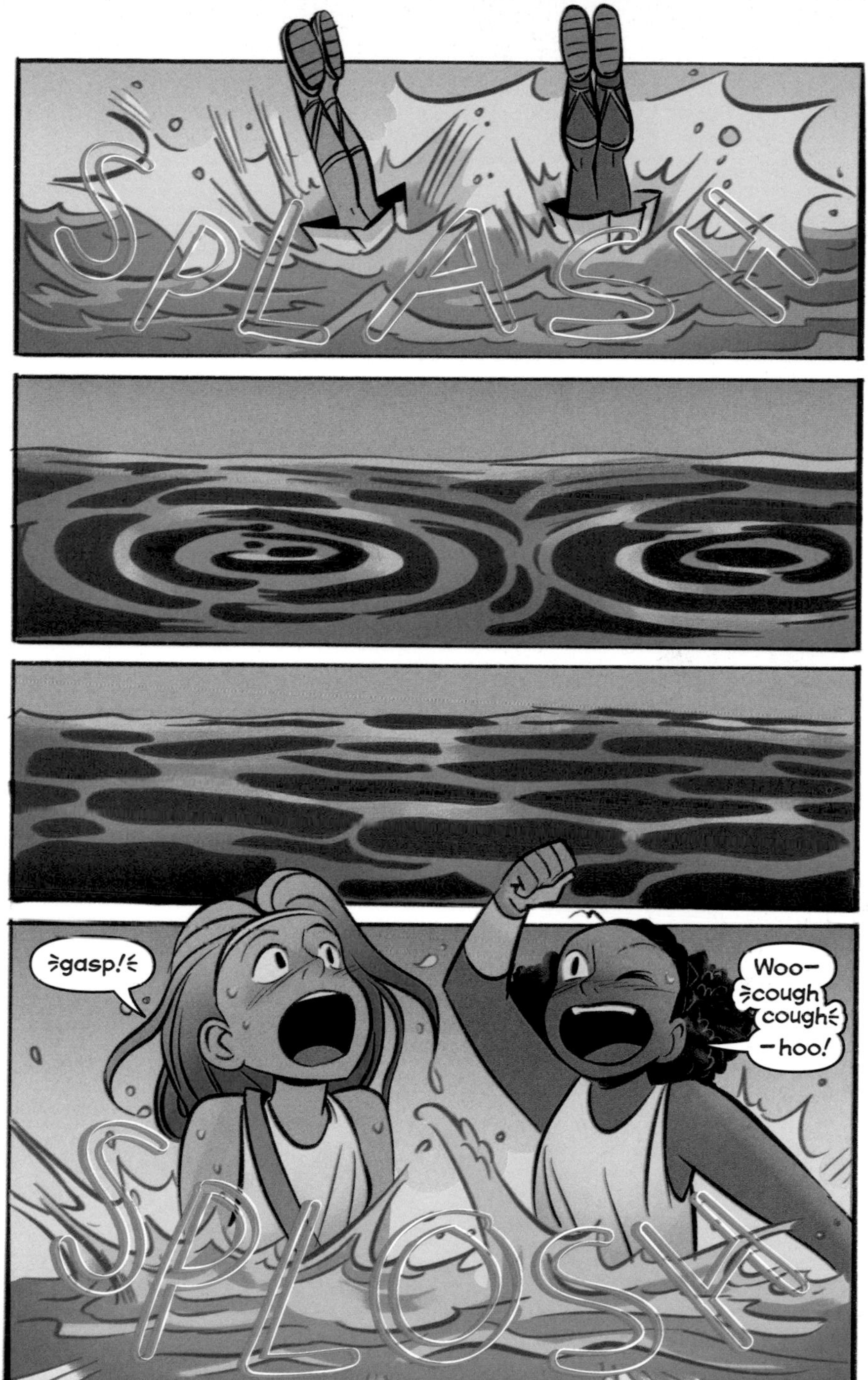
SPLASH
gasp!
Woo- cough cough -hoo!
SPLOSH

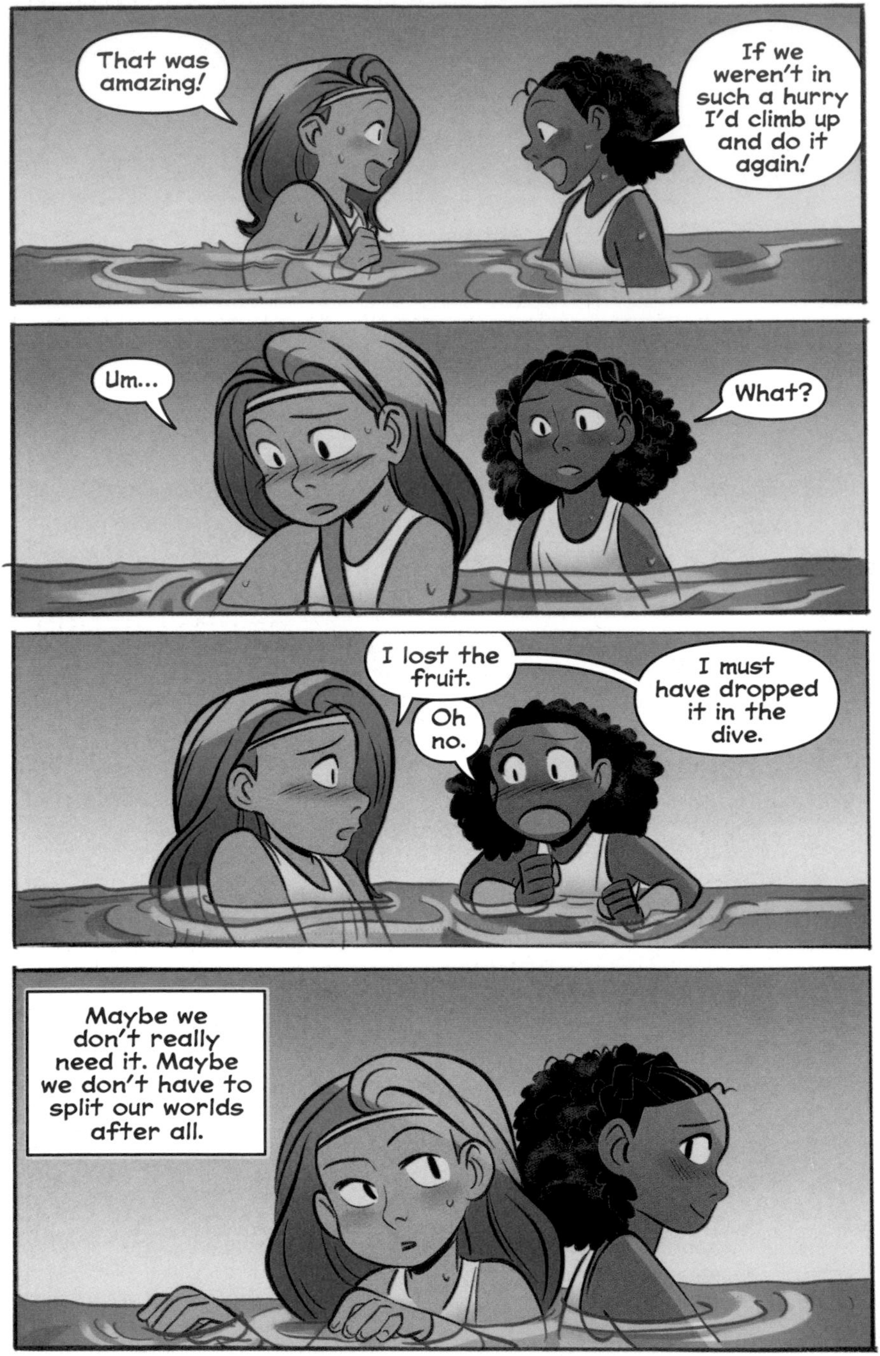
That was amazing!
If we weren't in such a hurry I'd climb up and do it again!
Um...
What?
I lost the fruit.
I must have dropped it in the dive.
Oh no.
Maybe we don't really need it. Maybe we don't have to split our worlds after all.

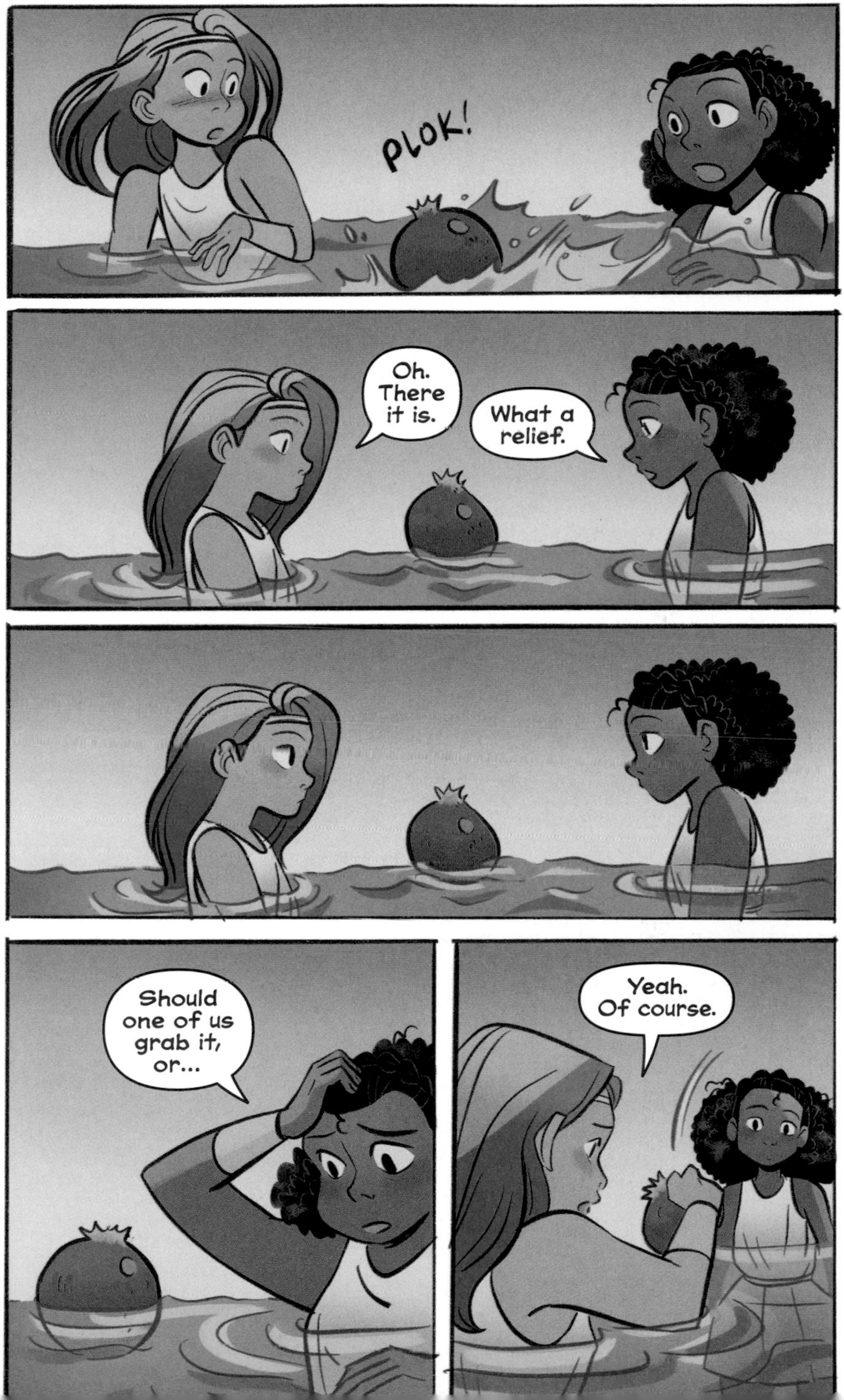
PLOK!
Oh. There it is.
What a relief.
Should one of us grab it, or...
Yeah. Of course.

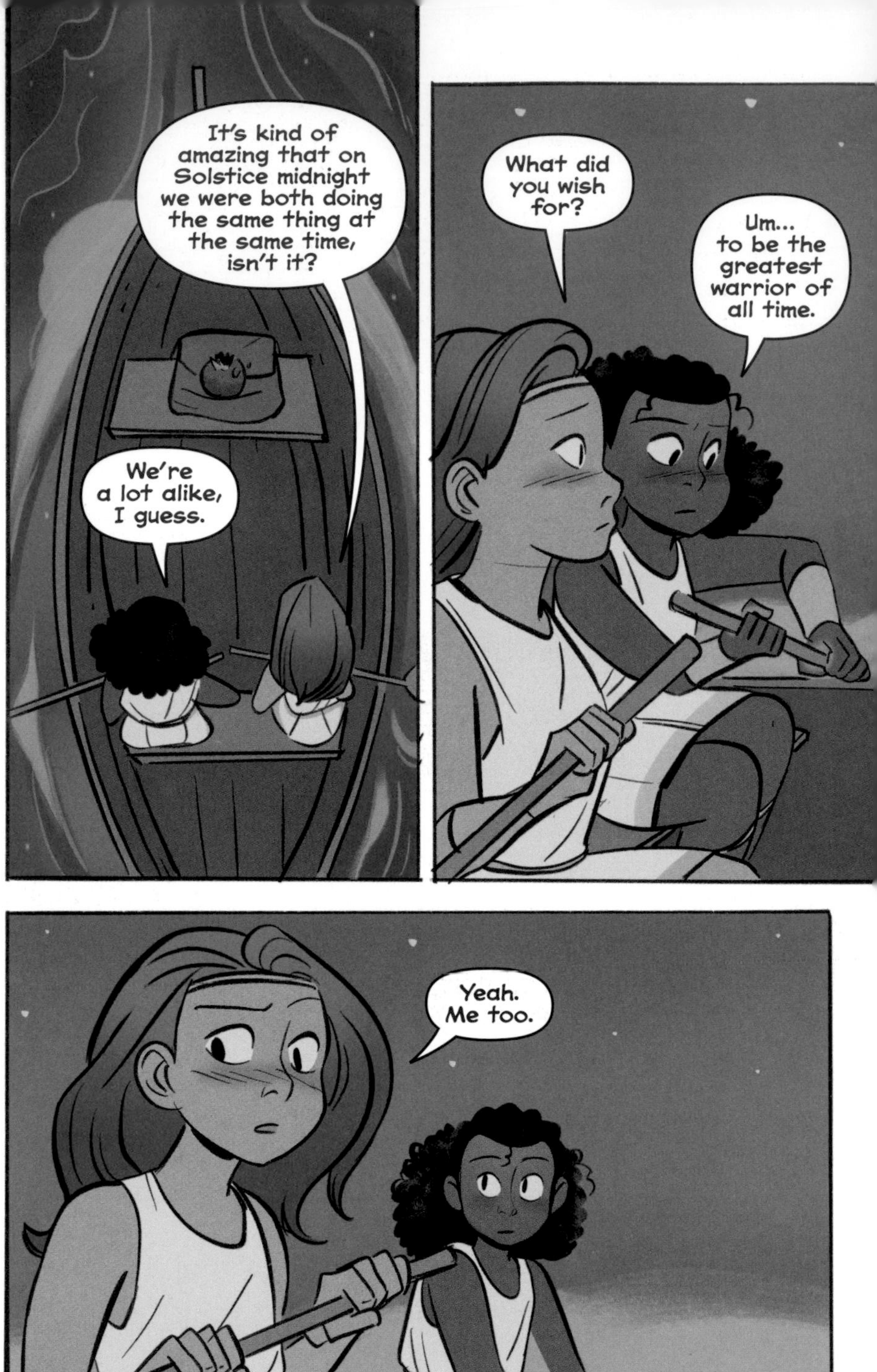
It's kind of amazing that on Solstice midnight we were both doing the same thing at the same time, isn't it?
We're a lot alike, I guess.
What did you wish for?
Um... to be the greatest warrior of all time.
Yeah. Me too.

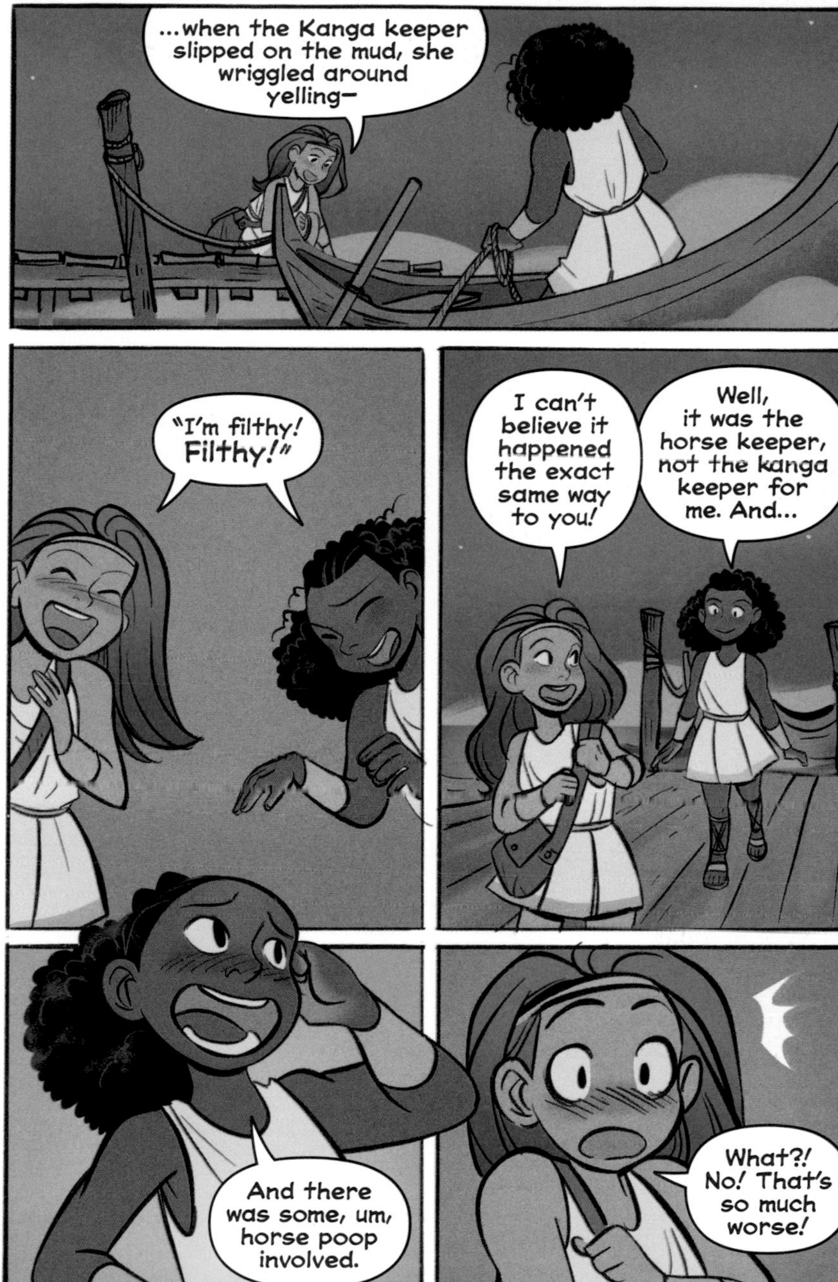
...when the Kanga keeper slipped on the mud, she wriggled around yelling—
"I'm filthy! Filthy!"
I can't believe it happened the exact same way to you!
Well, it was the horse keeper, not the kanga keeper for me. And...
And there was some, um, horse poop involved.
What?! No! That's so much worse!

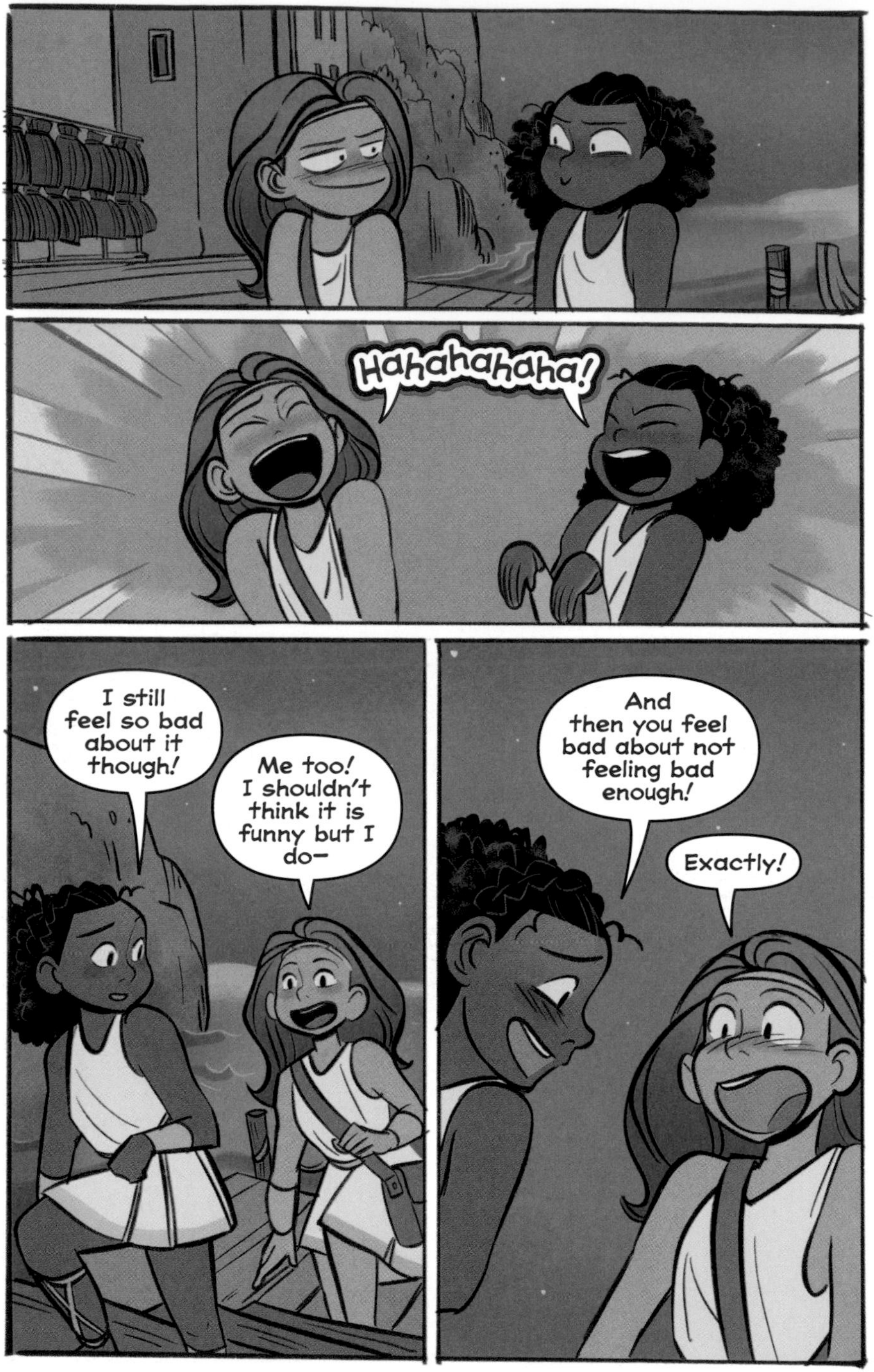
Hahahahaha!
I still feel so bad about it though!
Me too! I shouldn't think it is funny but I do–
And then you feel bad about not feeling bad enough!
Exactly!

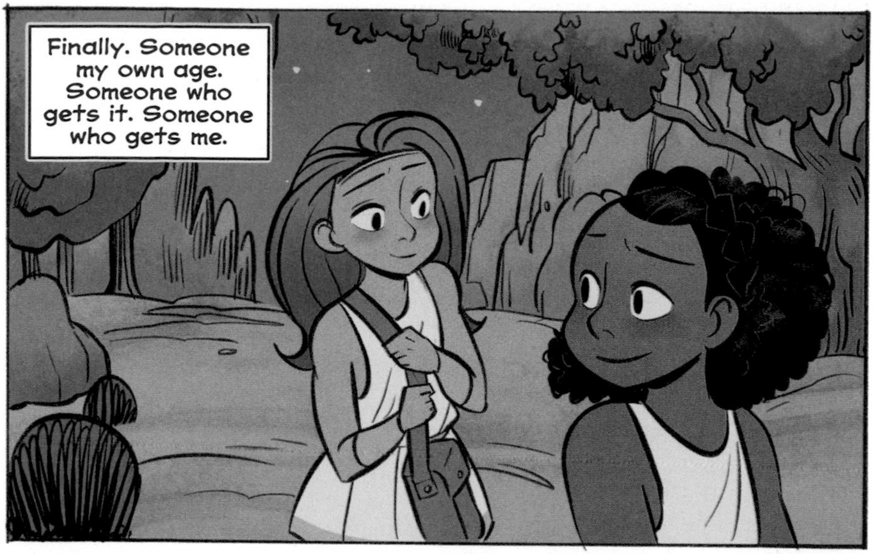
Finally. Someone my own age. Someone who gets it. Someone who gets me.

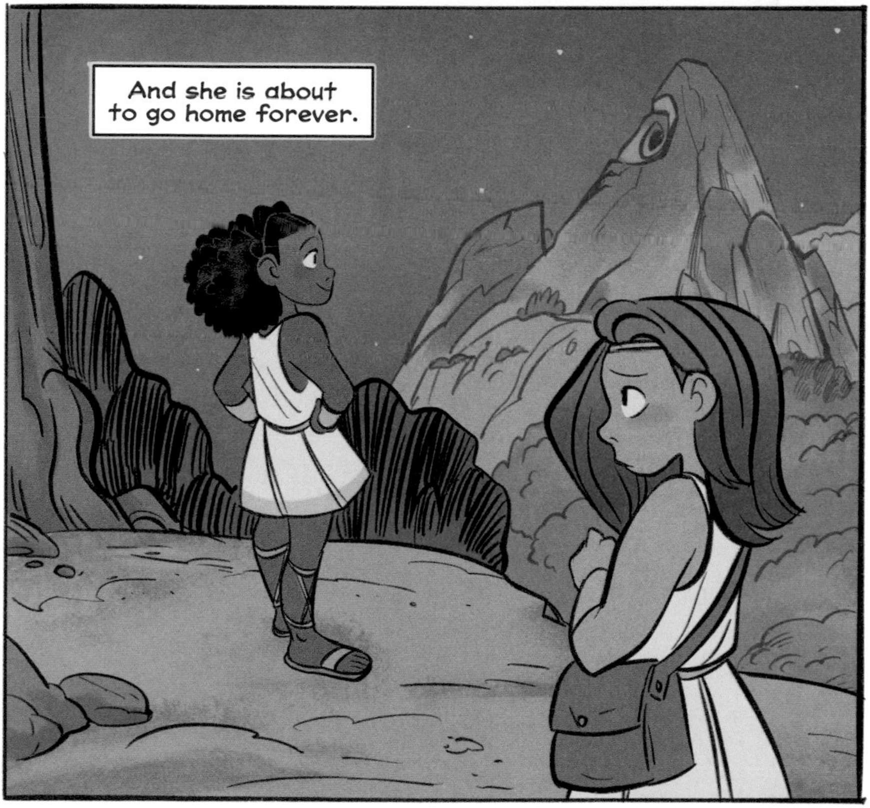
And she is about to go home forever.

CHAPTER FIVE

NUBIA

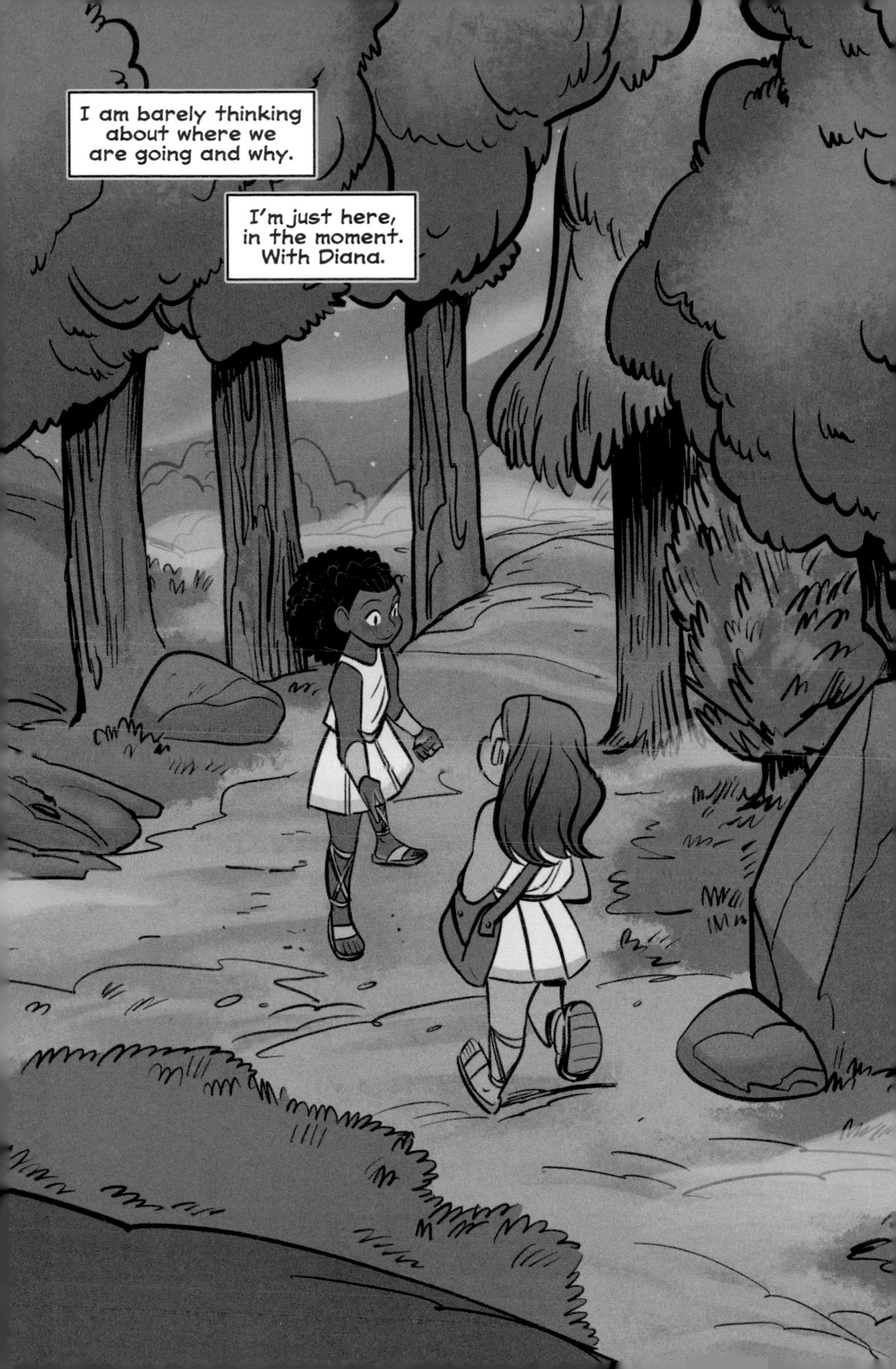
I am barely thinking about where we are going and why.
I'm just here, in the moment. With Diana.

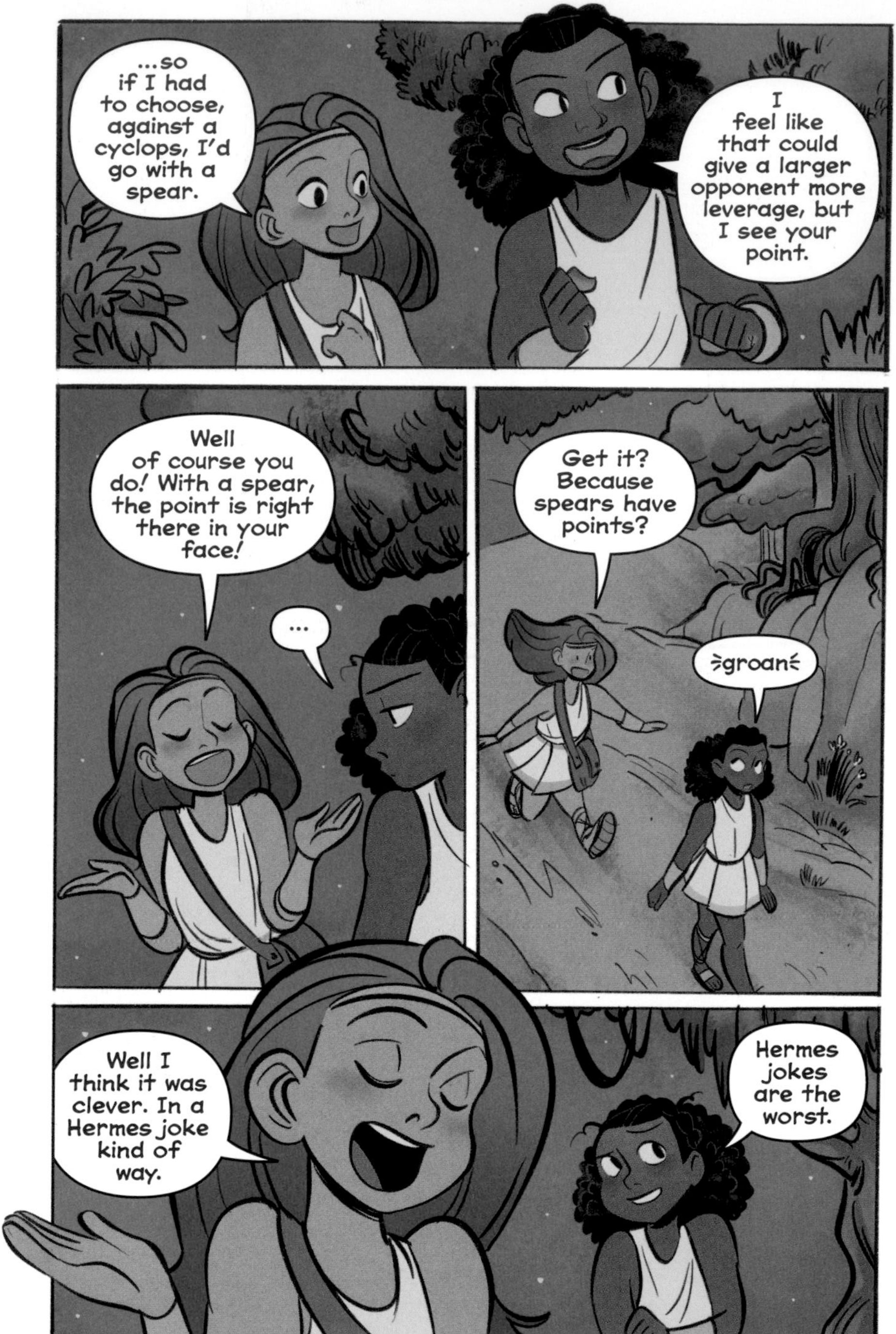
...so if I had to choose, against a cyclops, I'd go with a spear.
I feel like that could give a larger opponent more leverage, but I see your point.
Well of course you do! With a spear, the point is right there in your face!
...
Get it? Because spears have points?
groan
Well I think it was clever. In a Hermes joke kind of way.
Hermes jokes are the worst.

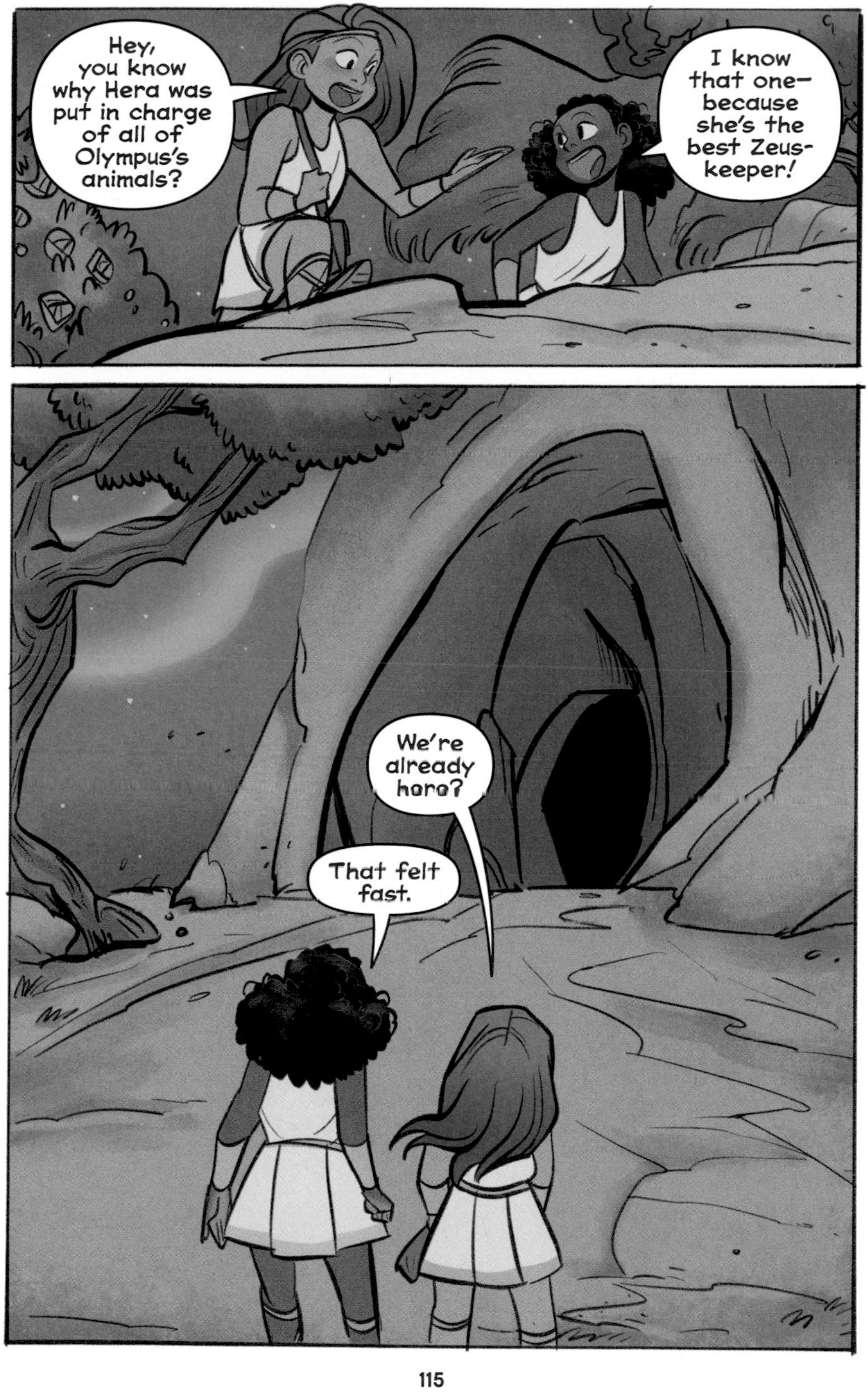
Hey, you know why Hera was put in charge of all of Olympus's animals?
I know that one—because she's the best Zeus-keeper!
We're already here?
That felt fast.

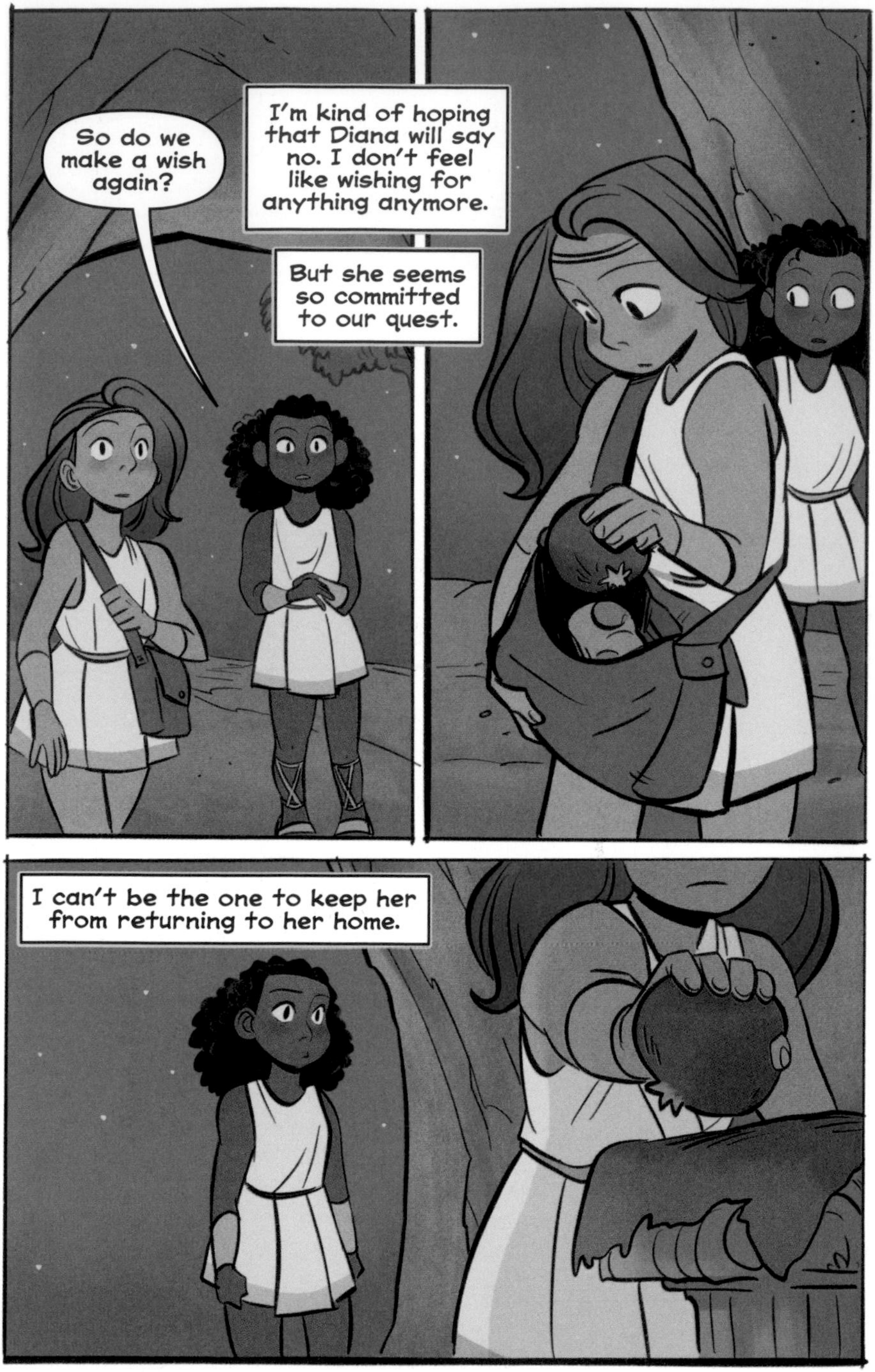
So do we make a wish again?
I'm kind of hoping that Diana will say no. I don't feel like wishing for anything anymore.
But she seems so committed to our quest.
I can't be the one to keep her from returning to her home.

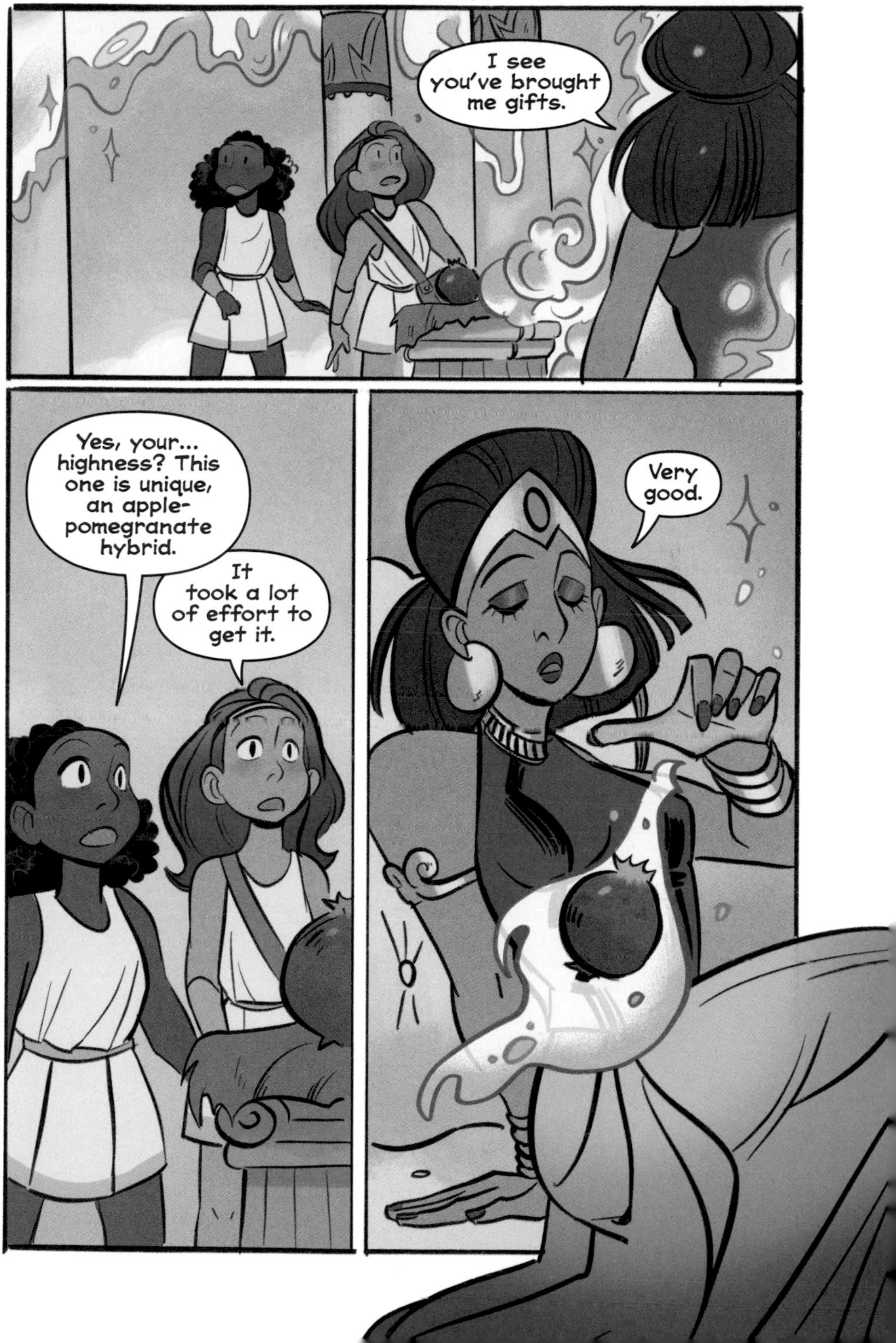
I see you've brought me gifts.
Yes, your... highness? This one is unique, an apple-pomegranate hybrid.
It took a lot of effort to get it.
Very good.

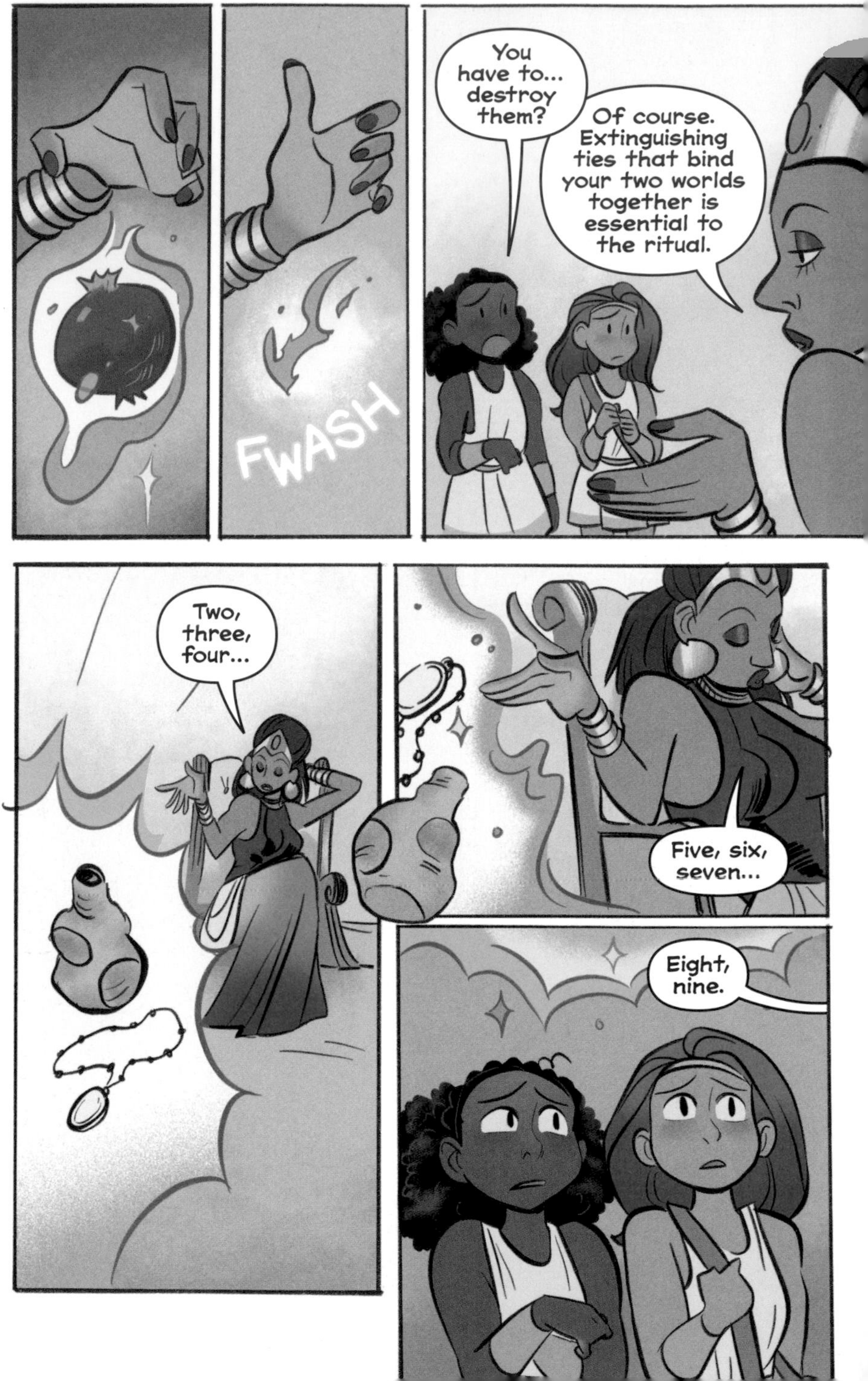
FWASH
You have to... destroy them?
Of course. Extinguishing ties that bind your two worlds together is essential to the ritual.
Two, three, four...
Five, six, seven...
Eight, nine.

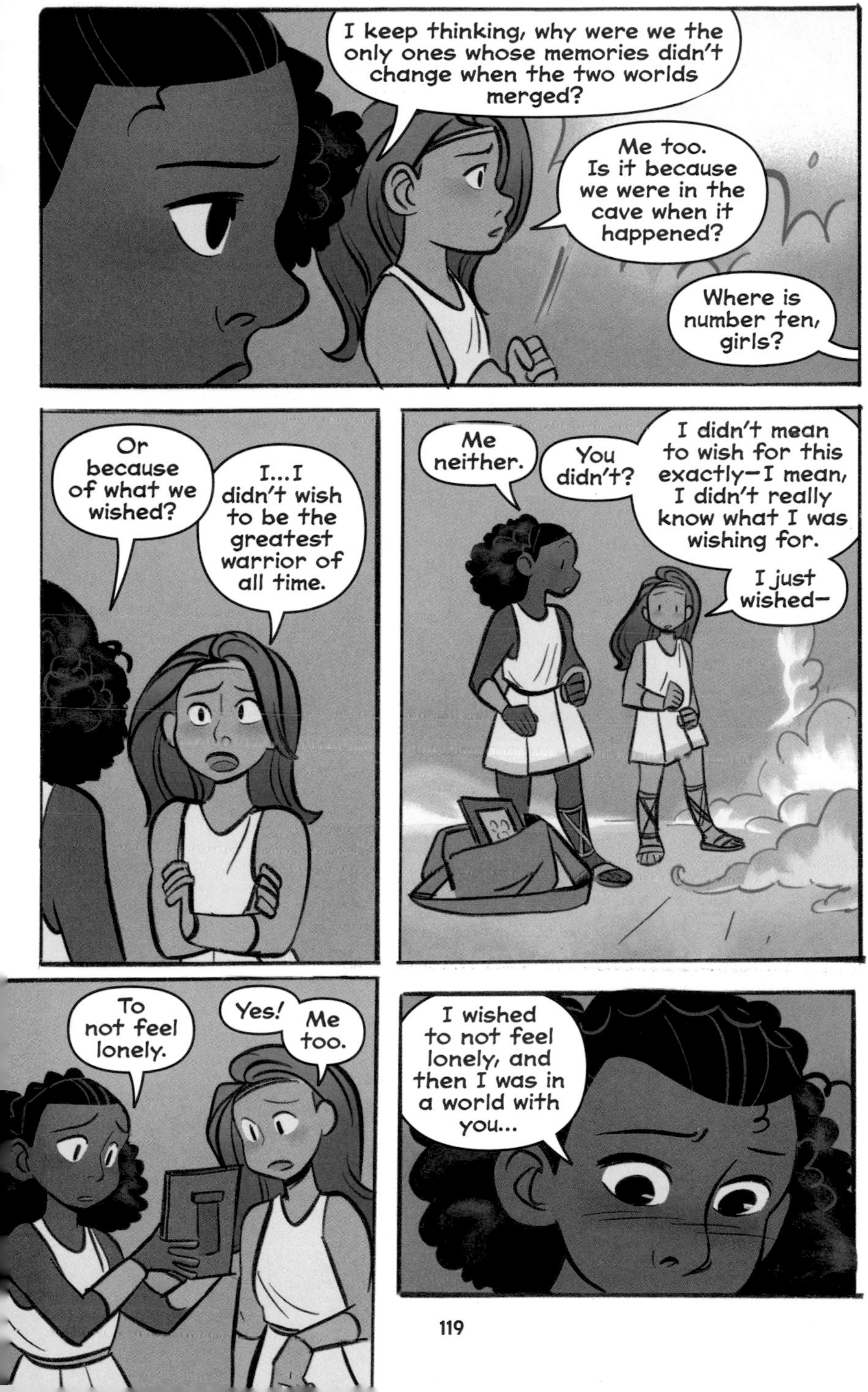
I keep thinking, why were we the only ones whose memories didn't change when the two worlds merged?
Me too. Is it because we were in the cave when it happened?
Where is number ten, girls?
Or because of what we wished?
I...I didn't wish to be the greatest warrior of all time.
Me neither.
You didn't?
I didn't mean to wish for this exactly—I mean, I didn't really know what I was wishing for.
I just wished—
To not feel lonely.
Yes!
Me too.
I wished to not feel lonely, and then I was in a world with you...

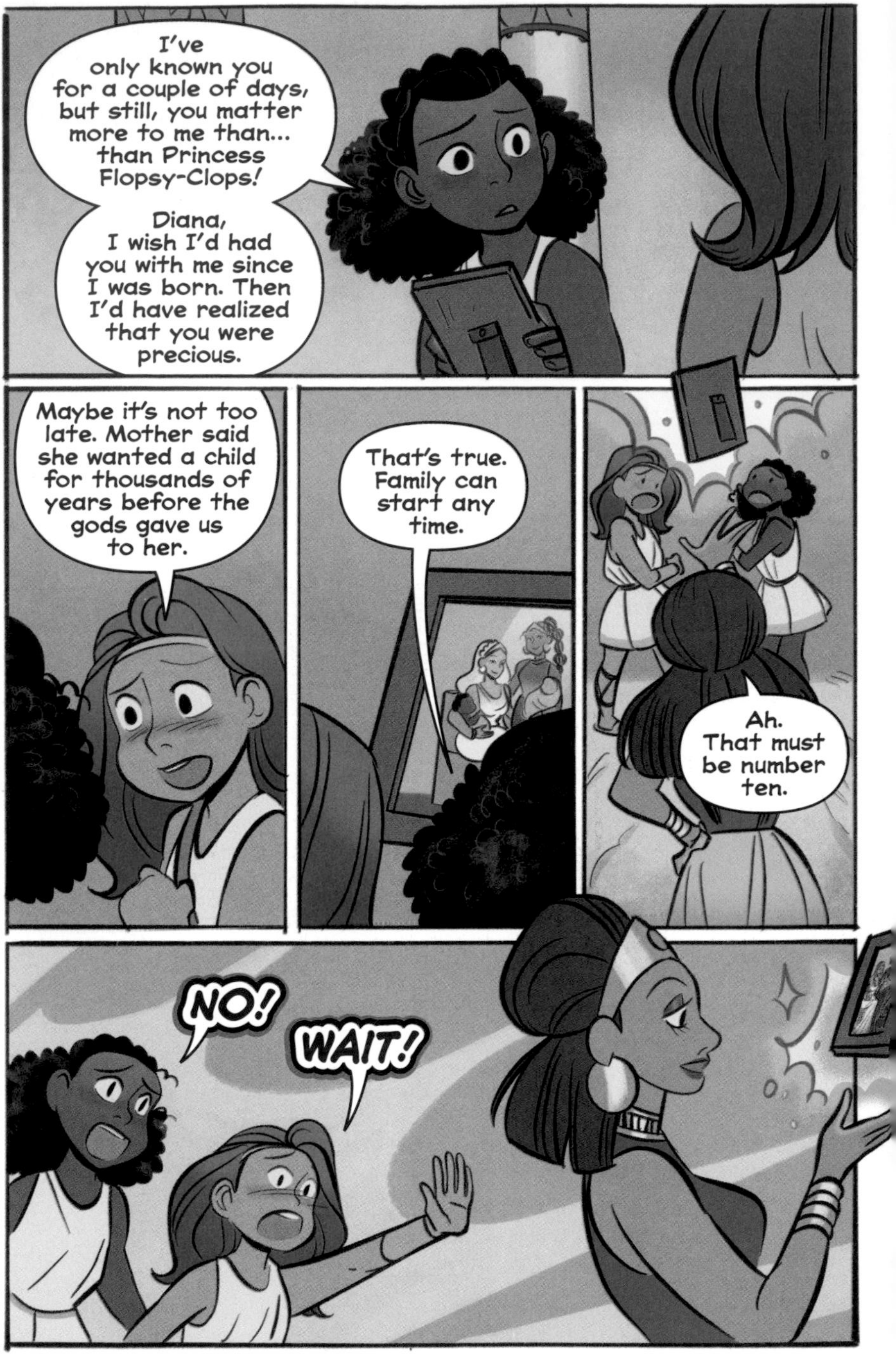

I've only known you for a couple of days, but still, you matter more to me than... than Princess Flopsy-Clops!
Diana, I wish I'd had you with me since I was born. Then I'd have realized that you were precious.
Maybe it's not too late. Mother said she wanted a child for thousands of years before the gods gave us to her.
That's true. Family can start any time.
Ah. That must be number ten.
NO!
WAIT!

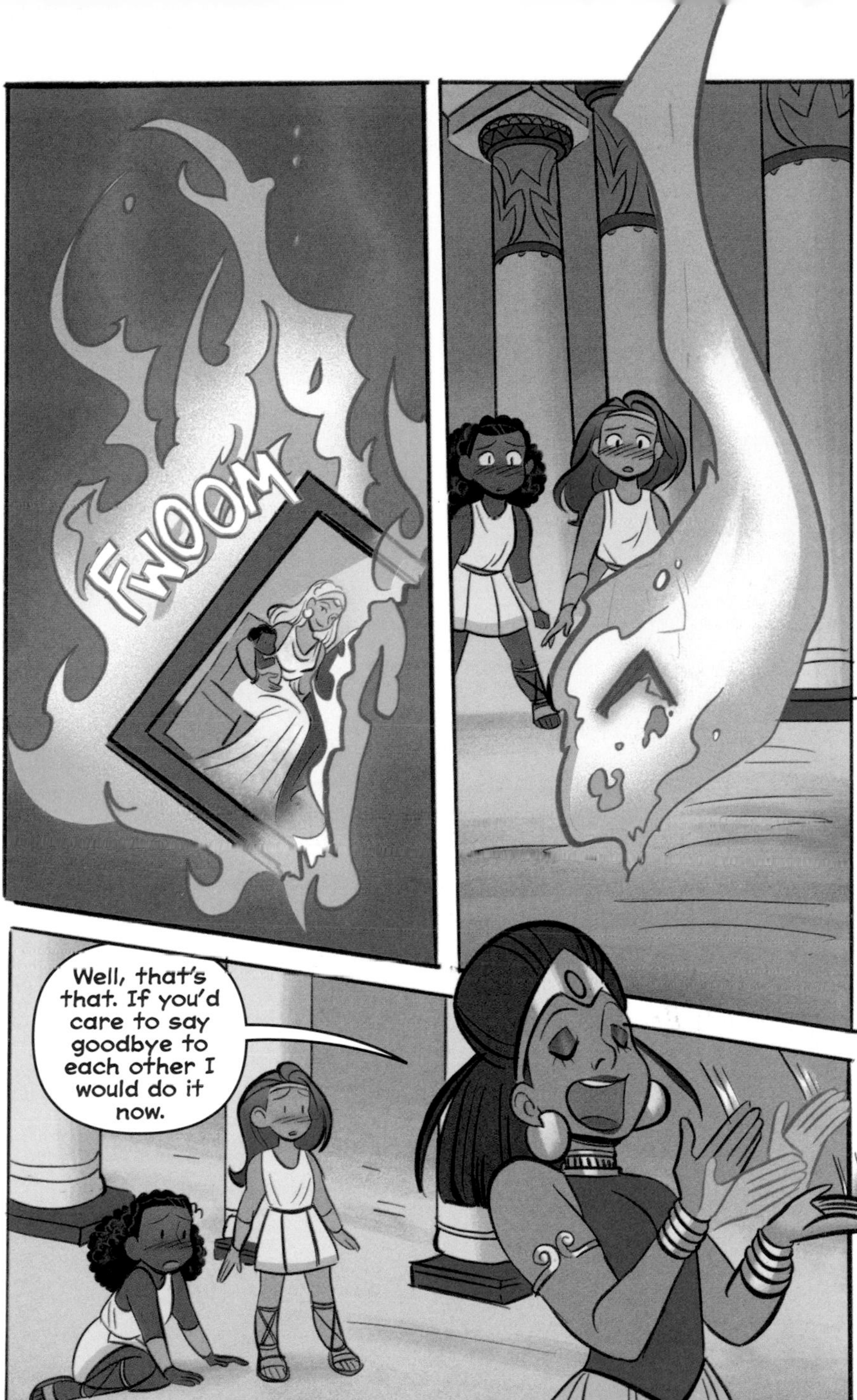
FWOOM
Well, that's that. If you'd care to say goodbye to each other I would do it now.

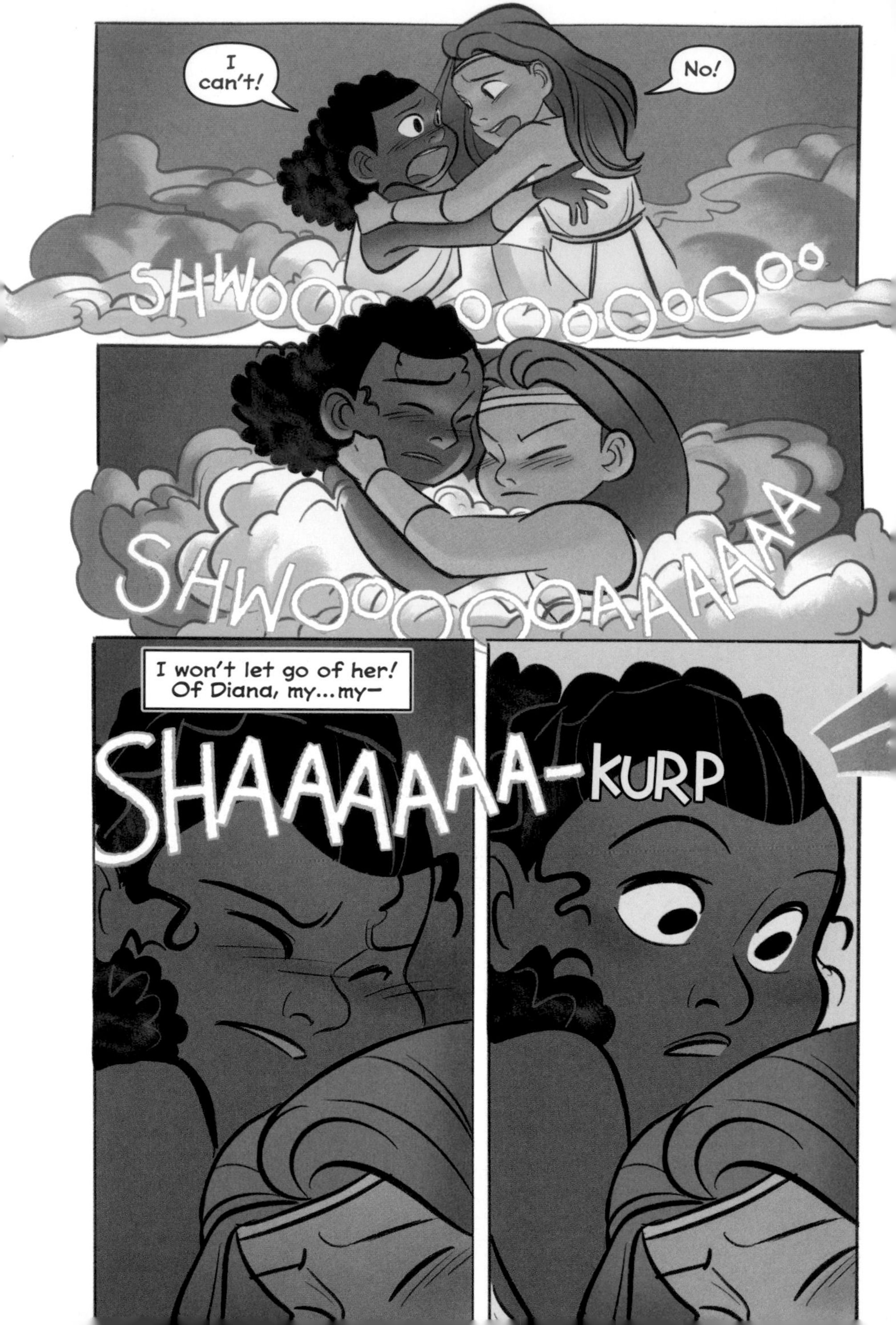
I can't!
No!
SHWOOOOOOOOOOOOO
SHWOOOOOOAAAAAA
I won't let go of her! Of Diana, my...my—
SHAAAAAA-KURP

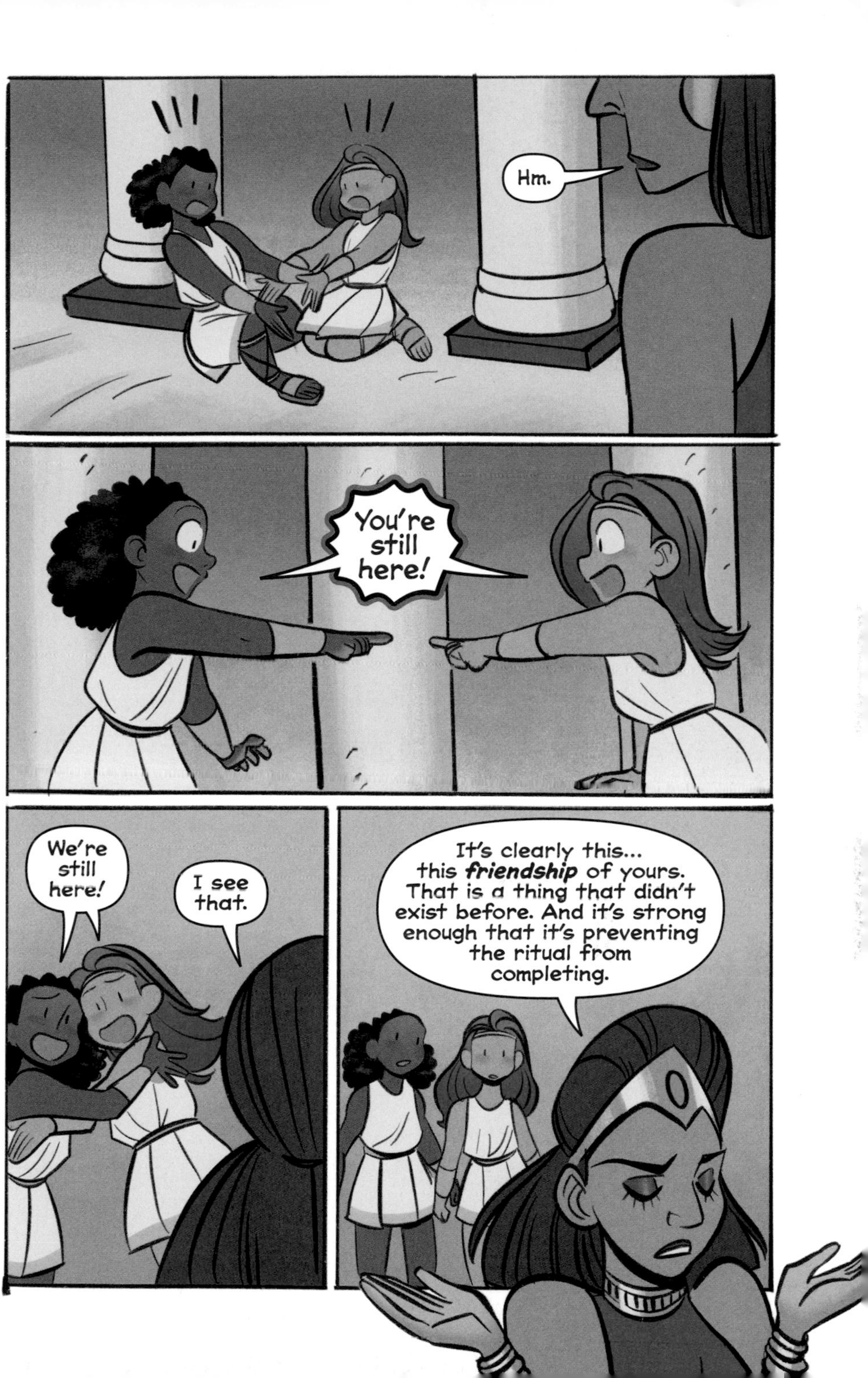
Hm.
You're still here!
We're still here!
I see that.
It's clearly this... this **friendship** of yours. That is a thing that didn't exist before. And it's strong enough that it's preventing the ritual from completing.

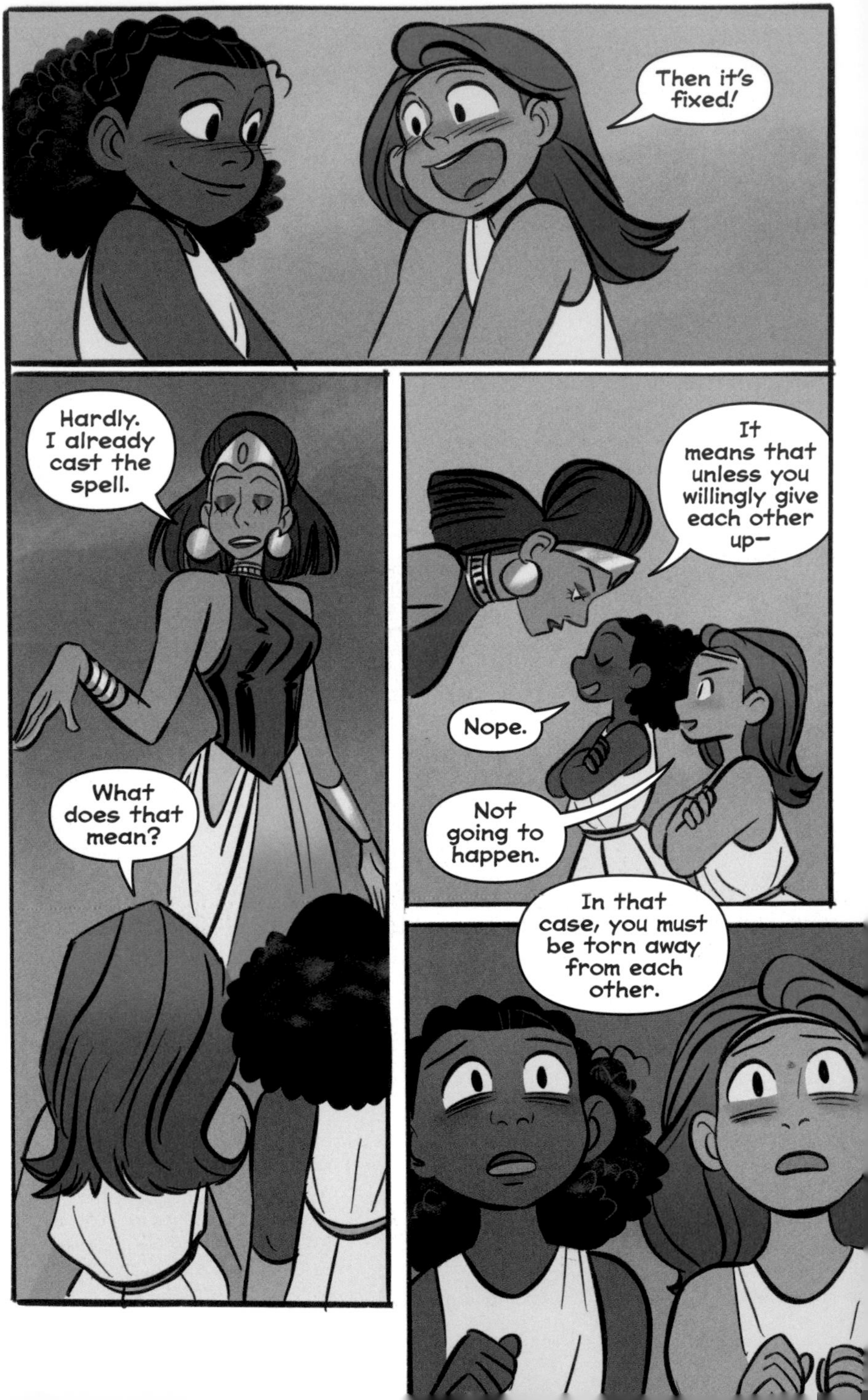
Then it's fixed!
Hardly. I already cast the spell.
What does that mean?
It means that unless you willingly give each other up—
Nope.
Not going to happen.
In that case, you must be torn away from each other.

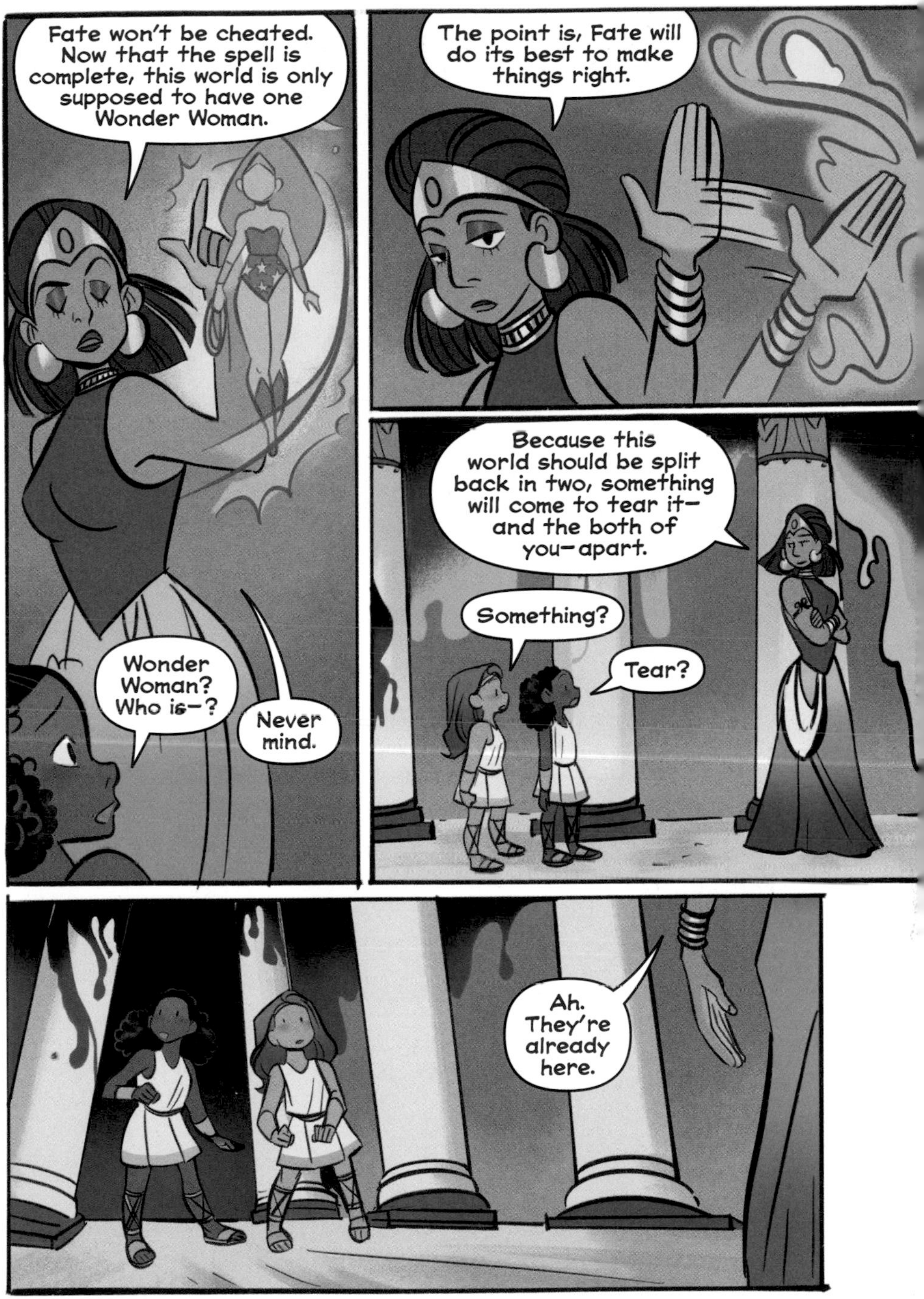
Fate won't be cheated. Now that the spell is complete, this world is only supposed to have one Wonder Woman.
Wonder Woman? Who is—?
Never mind.
The point is, Fate will do its best to make things right.
Because this world should be split back in two, something will come to tear it—and the both of you—apart.
Something?
Tear?
Ah. They're already here.

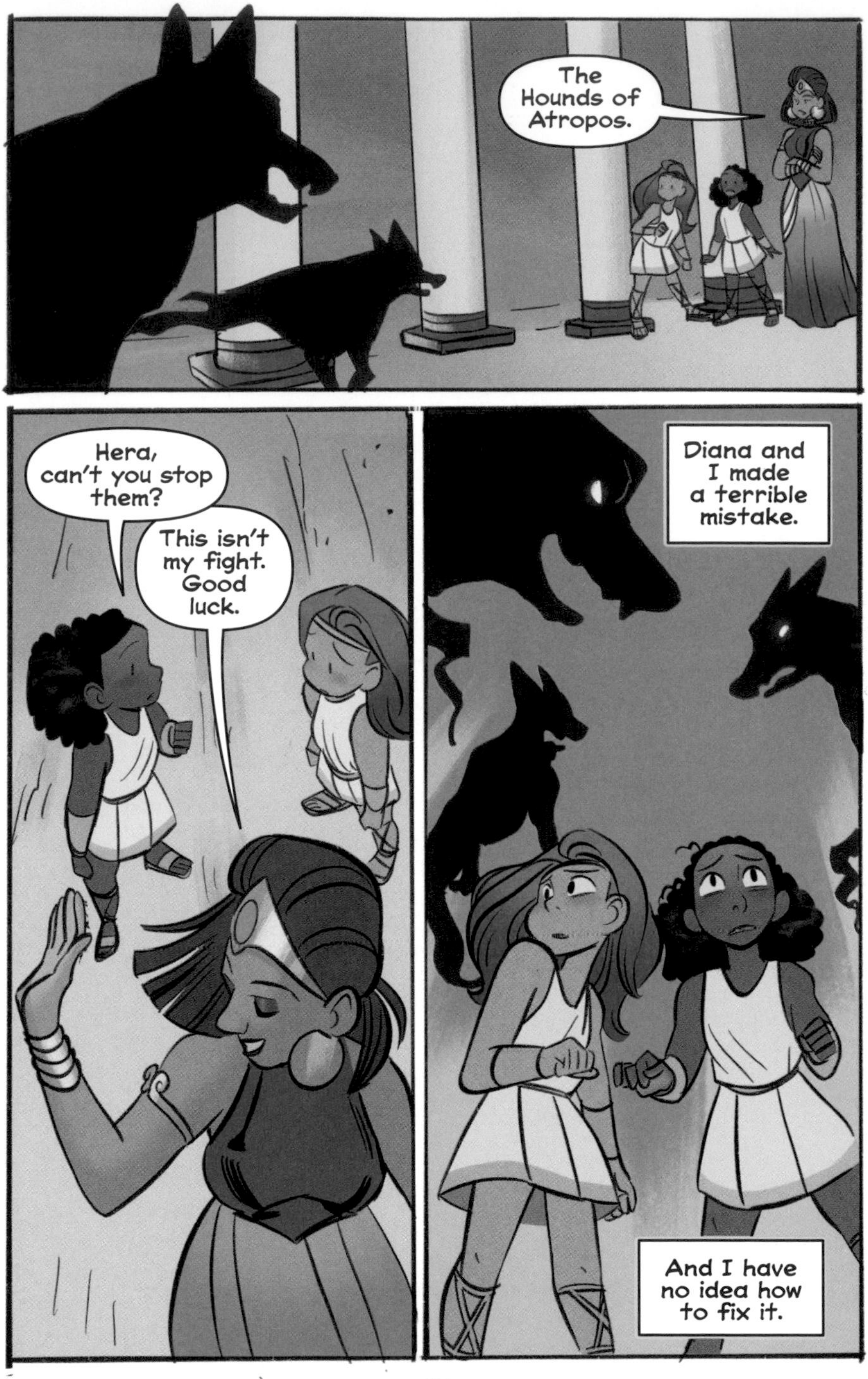
The Hounds of Atropos.
Hera, can't you stop them?
This isn't my fight. Good luck.
Diana and I made a terrible mistake.
And I have no idea how to fix it.

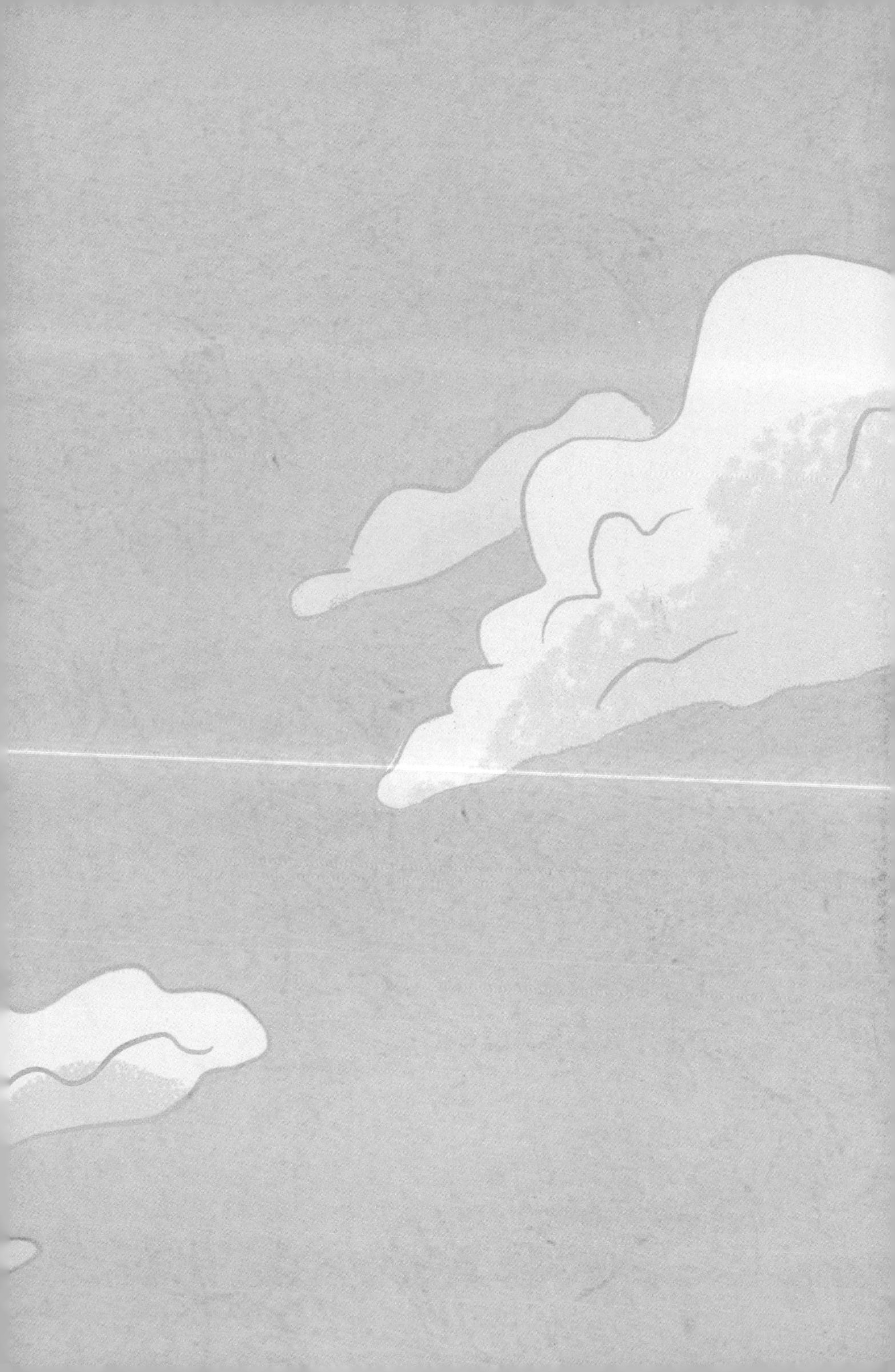

CHAPTER
SIX

DIANA

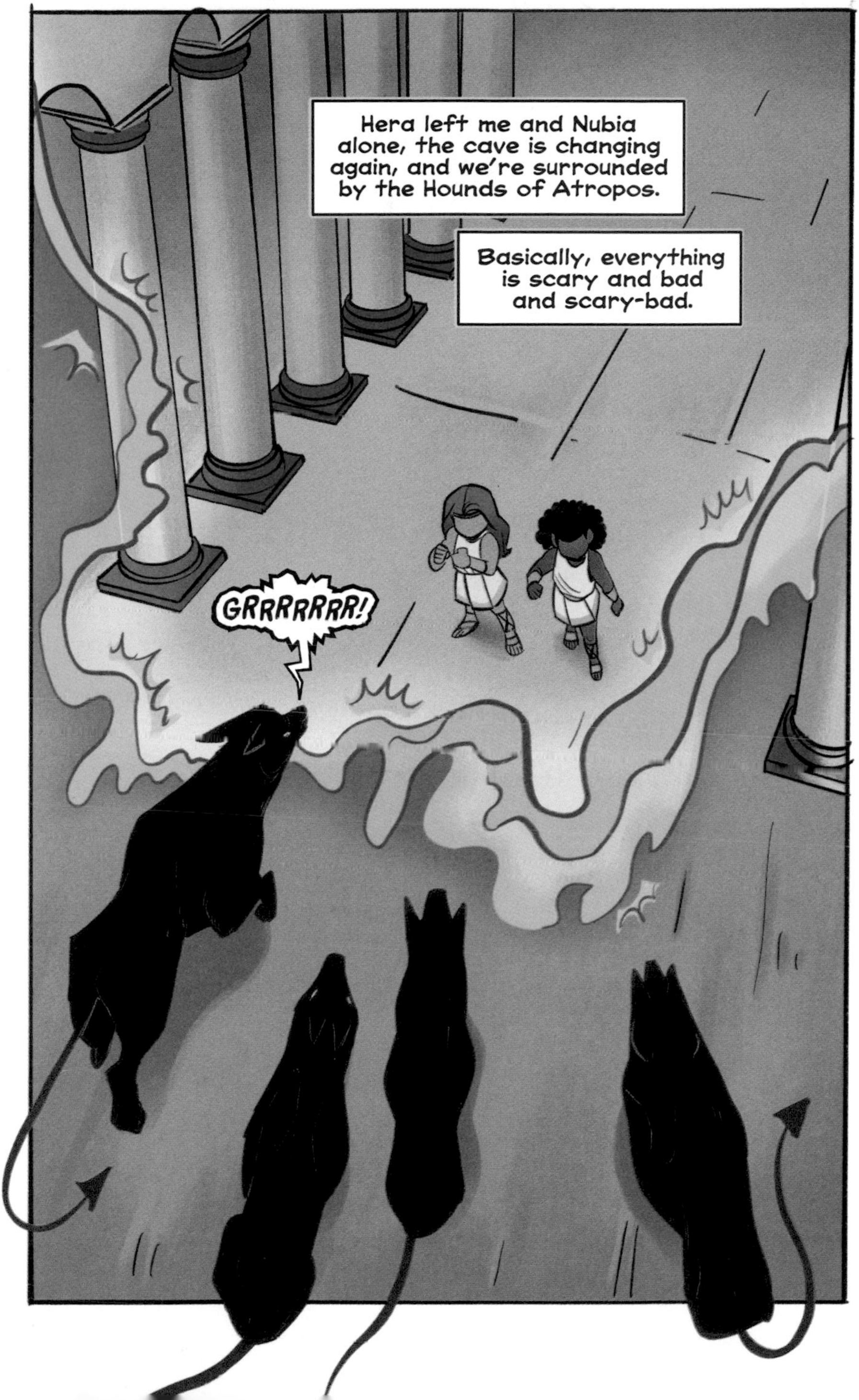

Hera left me and Nubia alone, the cave is changing again, and we're surrounded by the Hounds of Atropos.
Basically, everything is scary and bad and scary-bad.
GRRRRRRR!

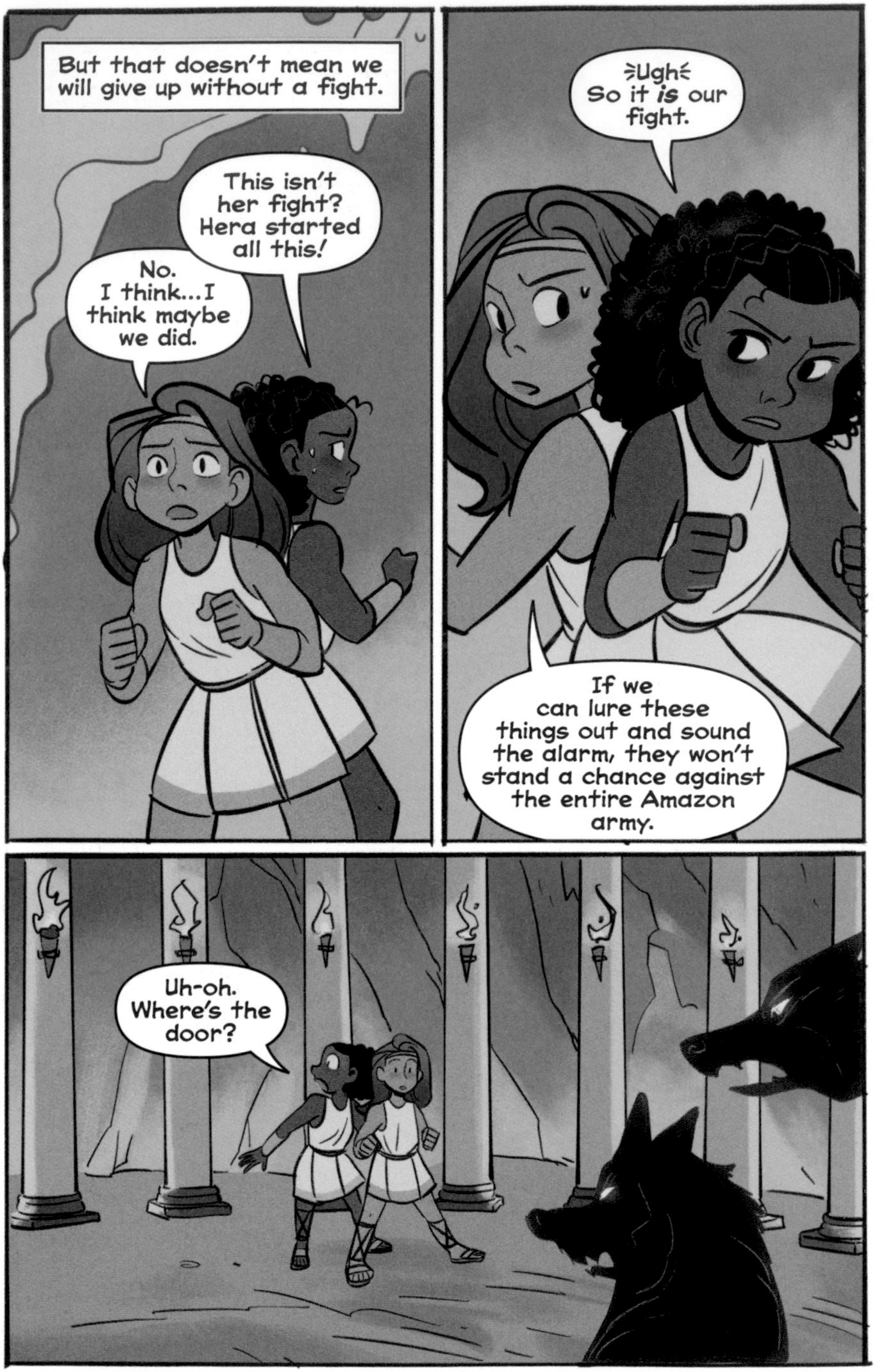
But that doesn't mean we will give up without a fight.
This isn't her fight? Hera started all this!
No. I think...I think maybe we did.
Ugh
So it *is* our fight.
If we can lure these things out and sound the alarm, they won't stand a chance against the entire Amazon army.
Uh-oh. Where's the door?

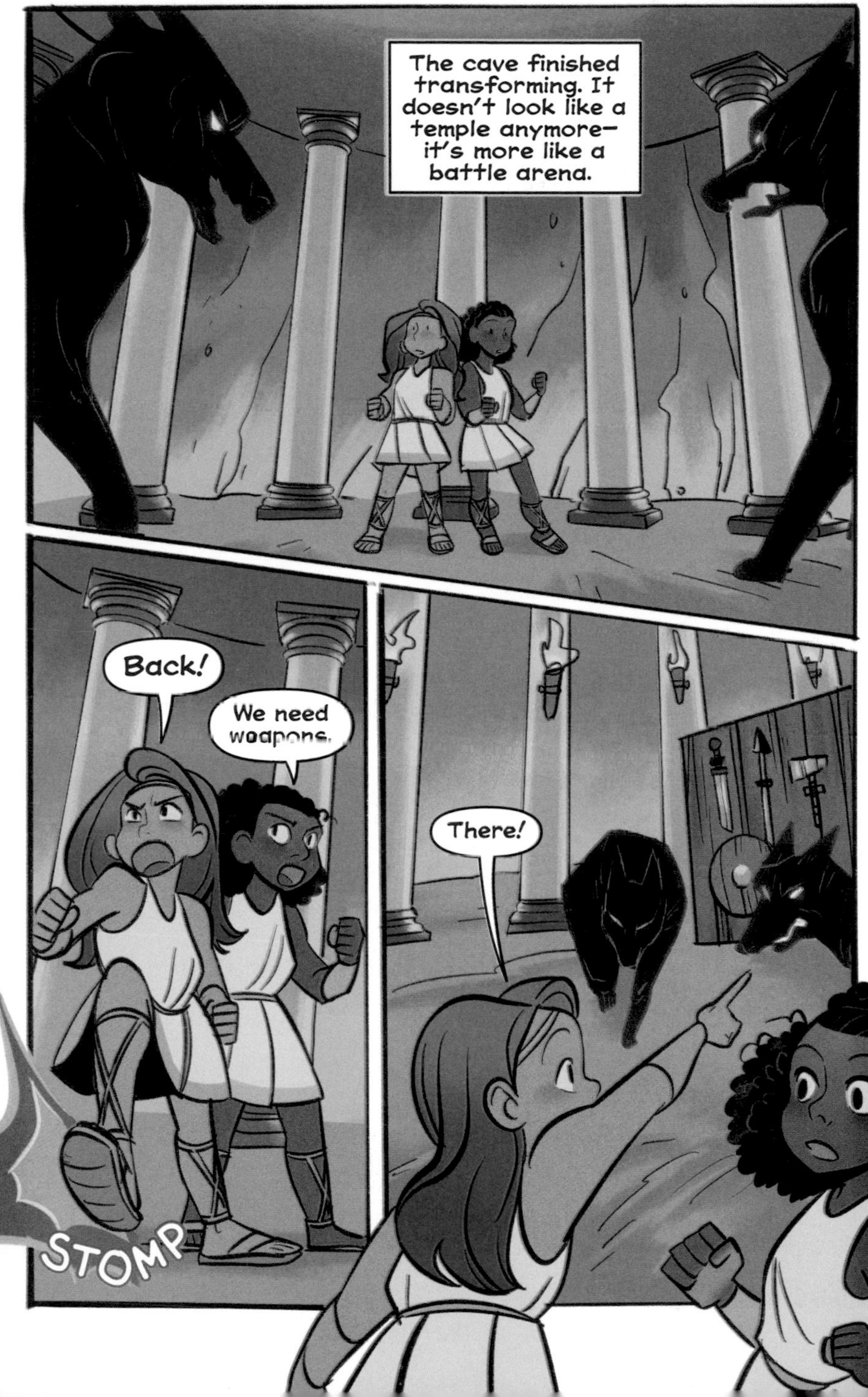
The cave finished transforming. It doesn't look like a temple anymore— it's more like a battle arena.
Back!
We need weapons.
STOMP
There!

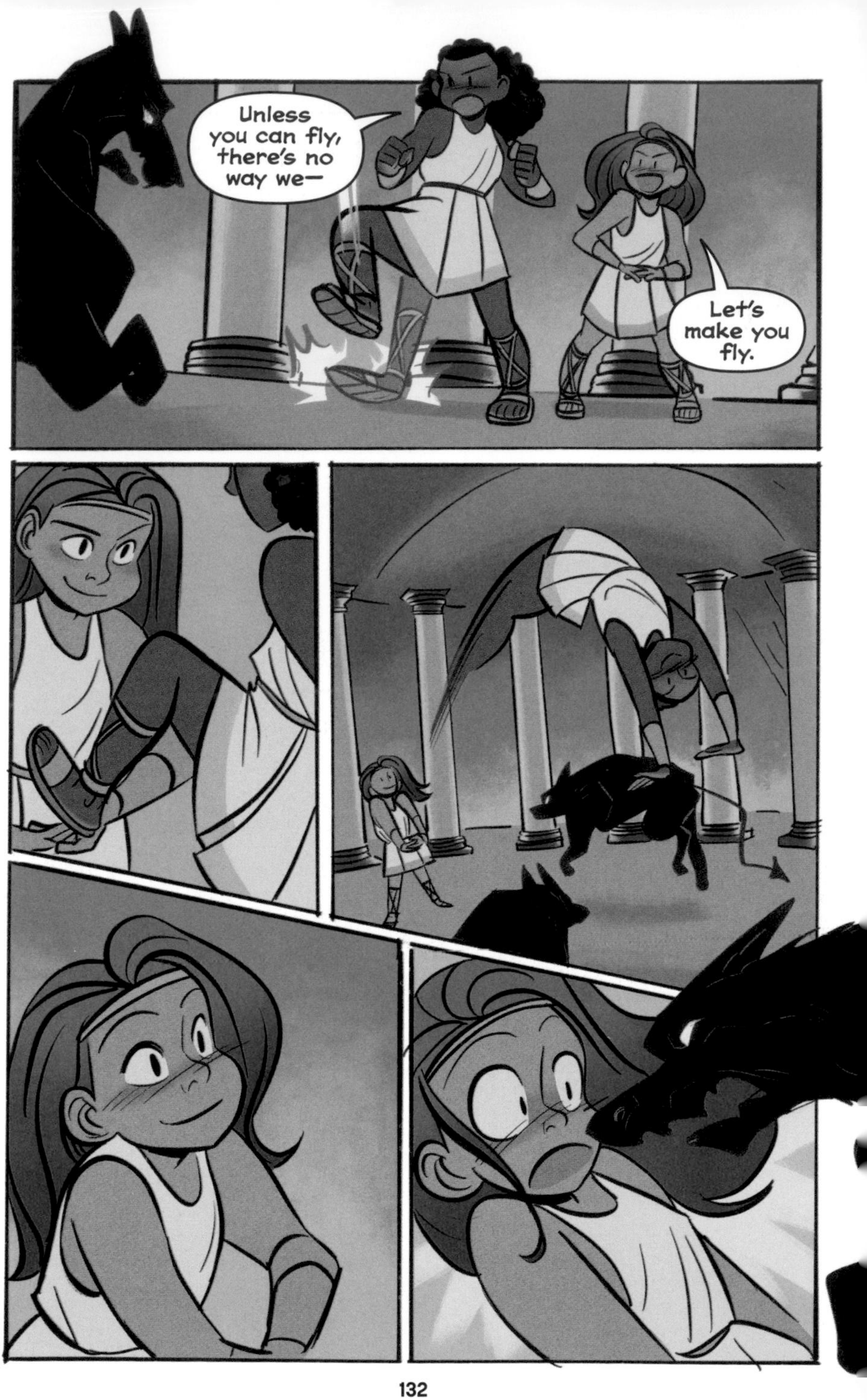
Unless you can fly, there's no way we—
Let's make you fly.

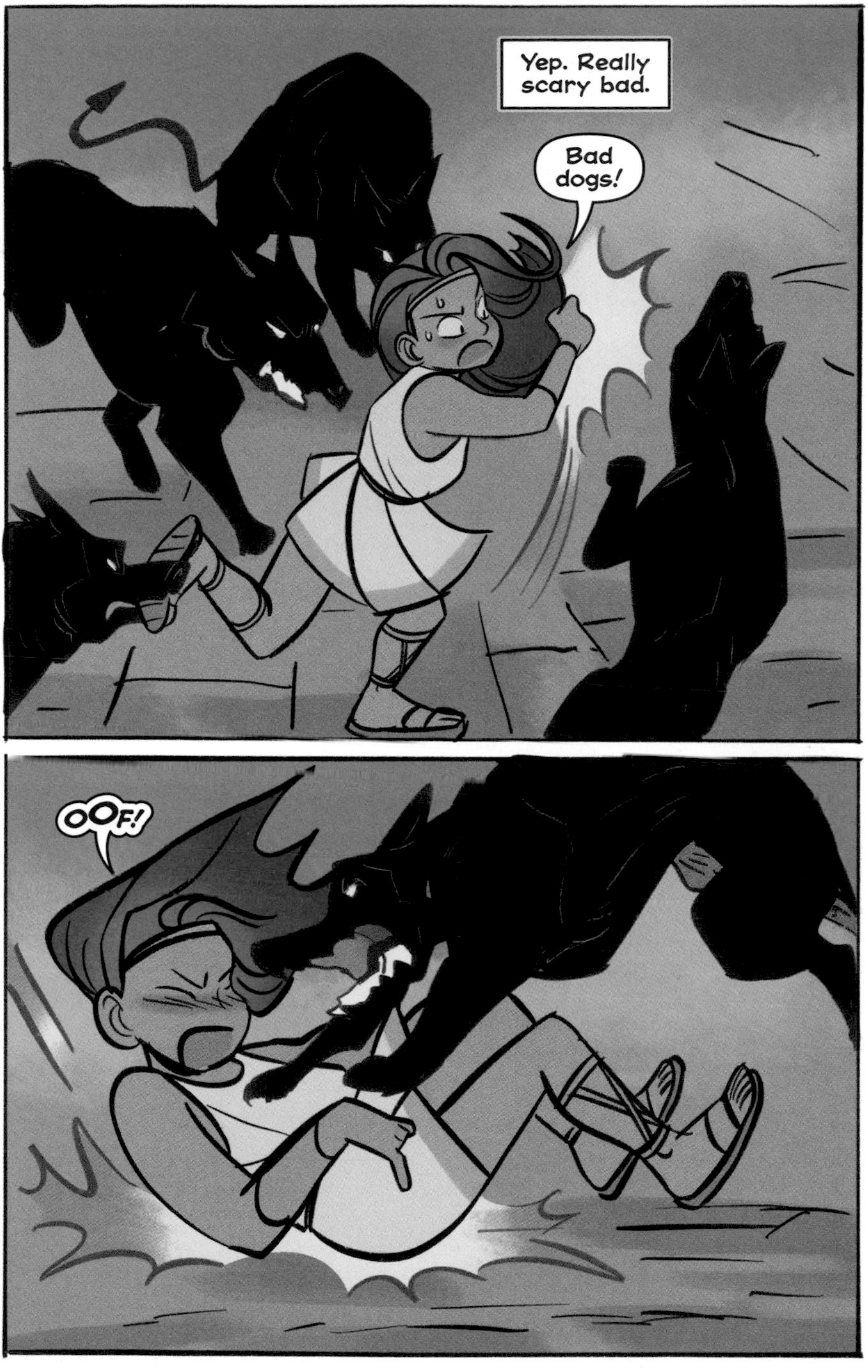
Yep. Really scary bad.
Bad dogs!
OOF!

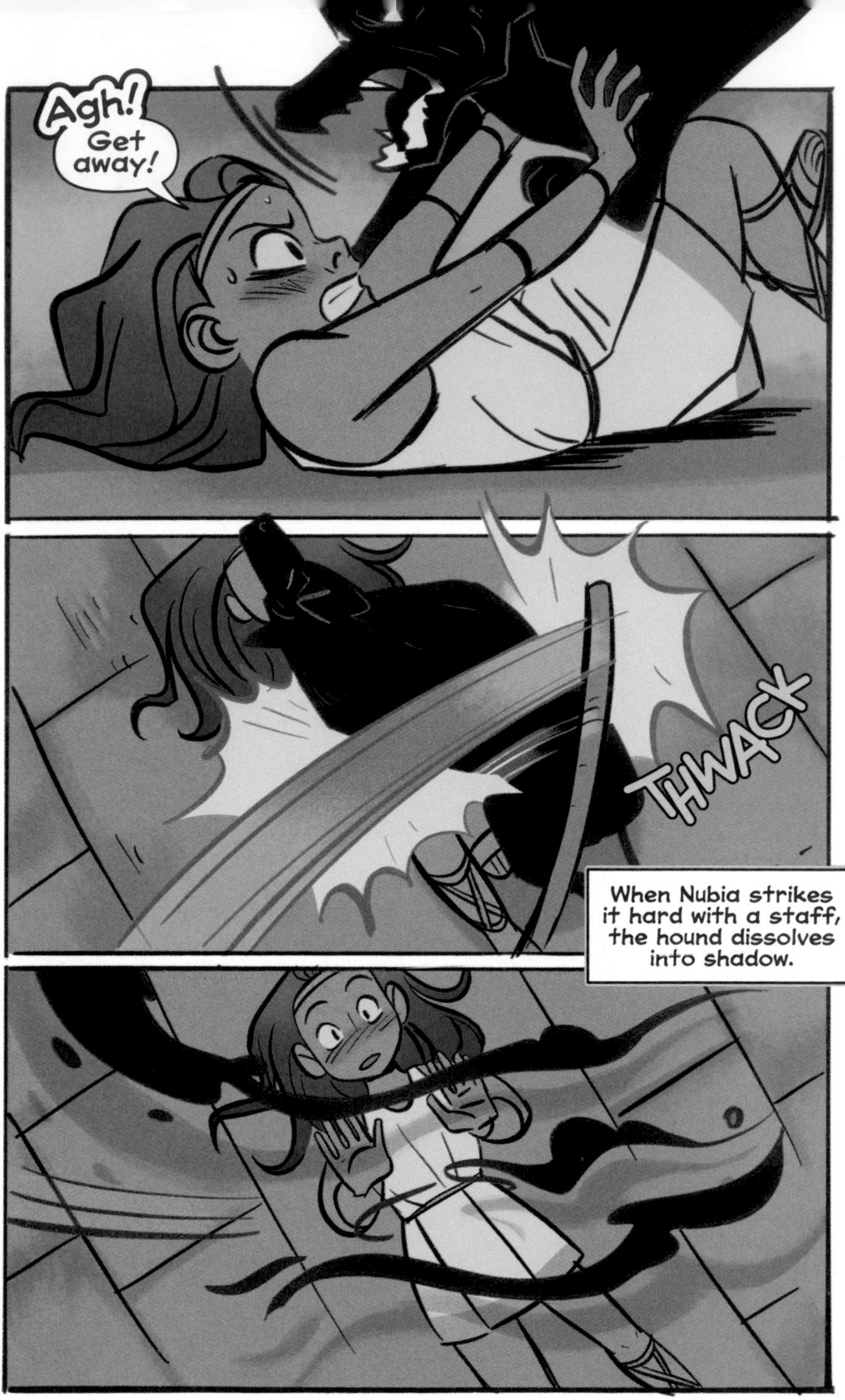
Agh! Get away!
THWACK
When Nubia strikes it hard with a staff, the hound dissolves into shadow.

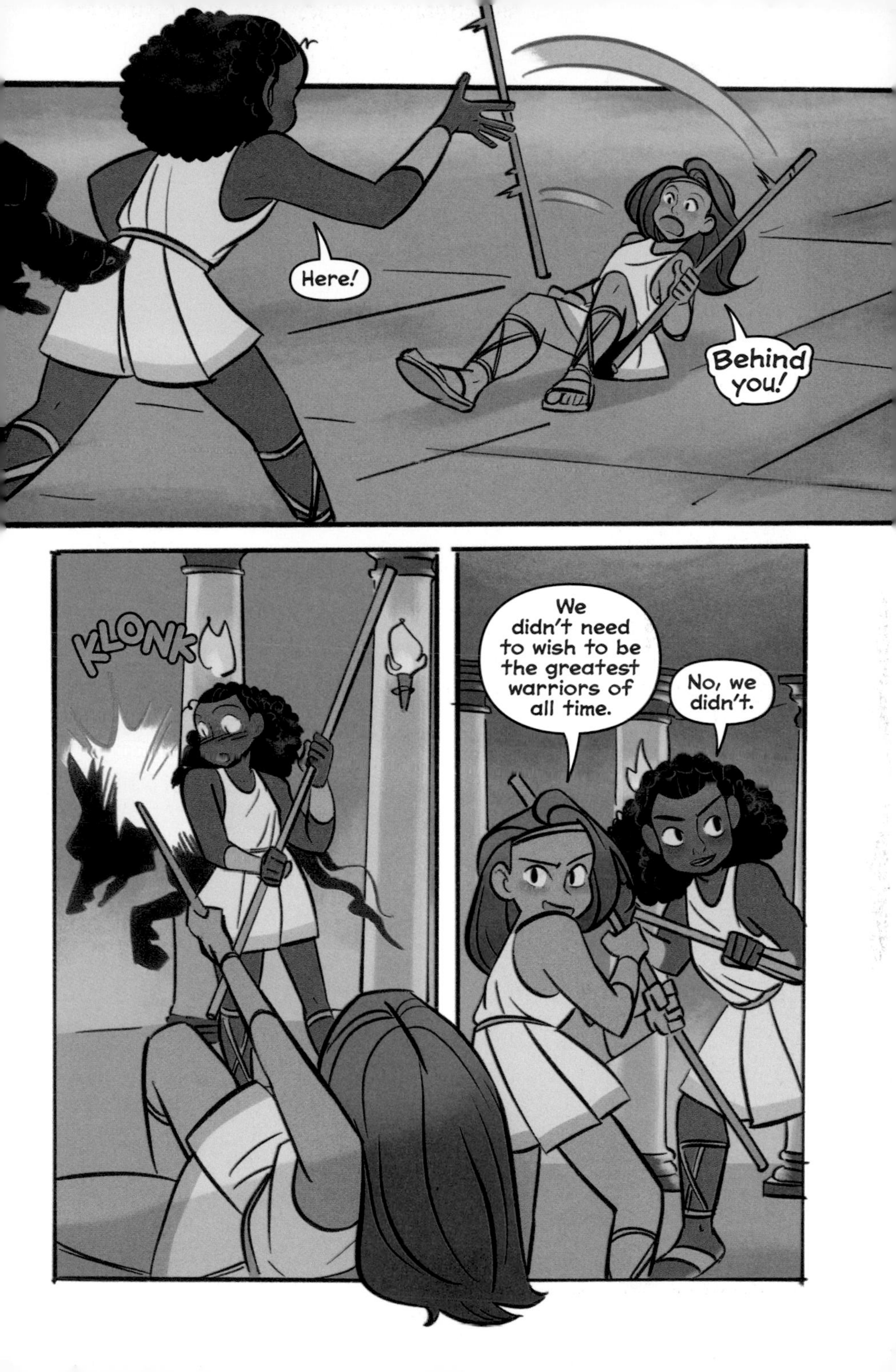
Here!
Behind you!
KLONK
We didn't need to wish to be the greatest warriors of all time.
No, we didn't.

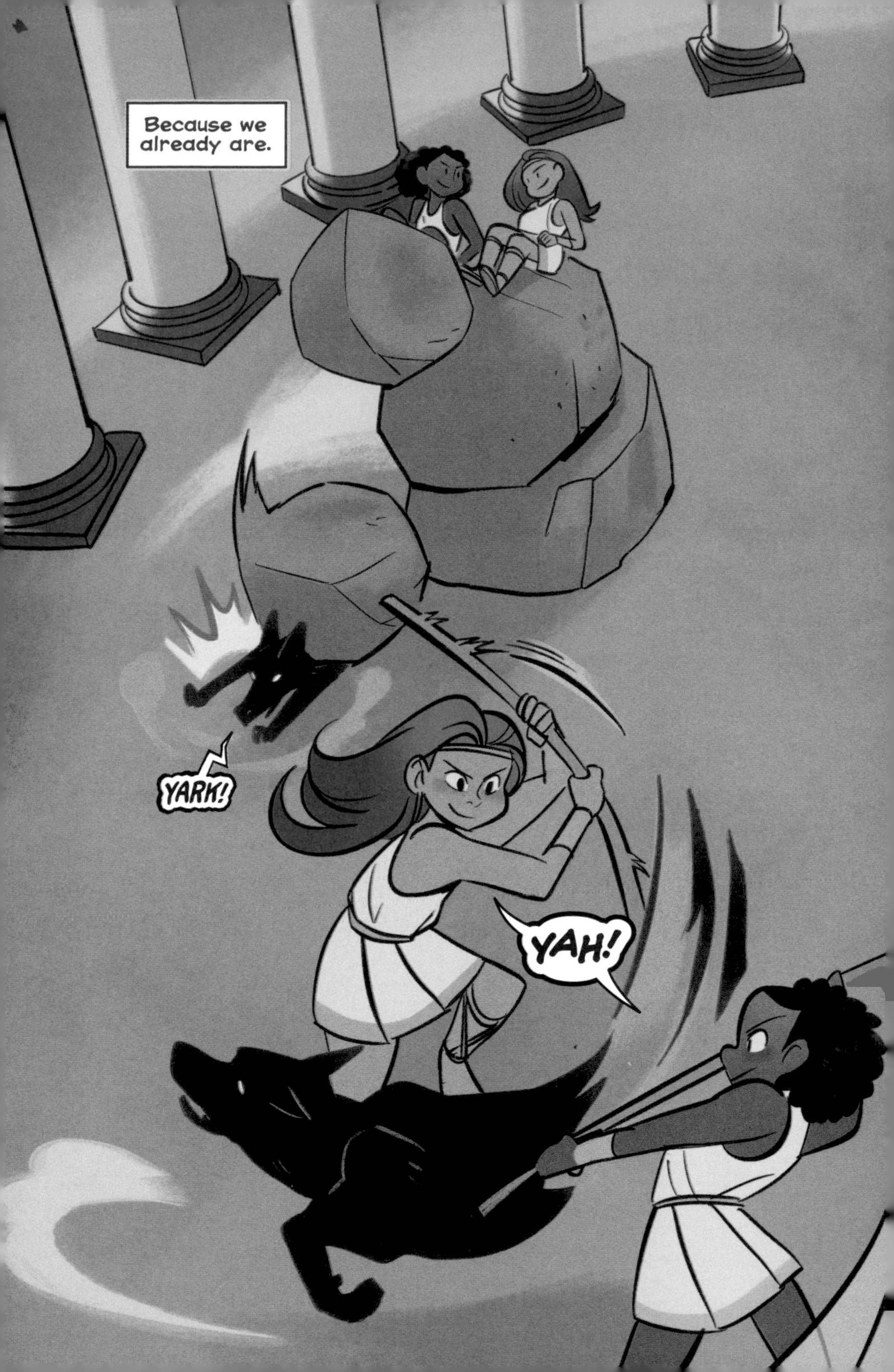
Because we already are.
YARK!
YAH!

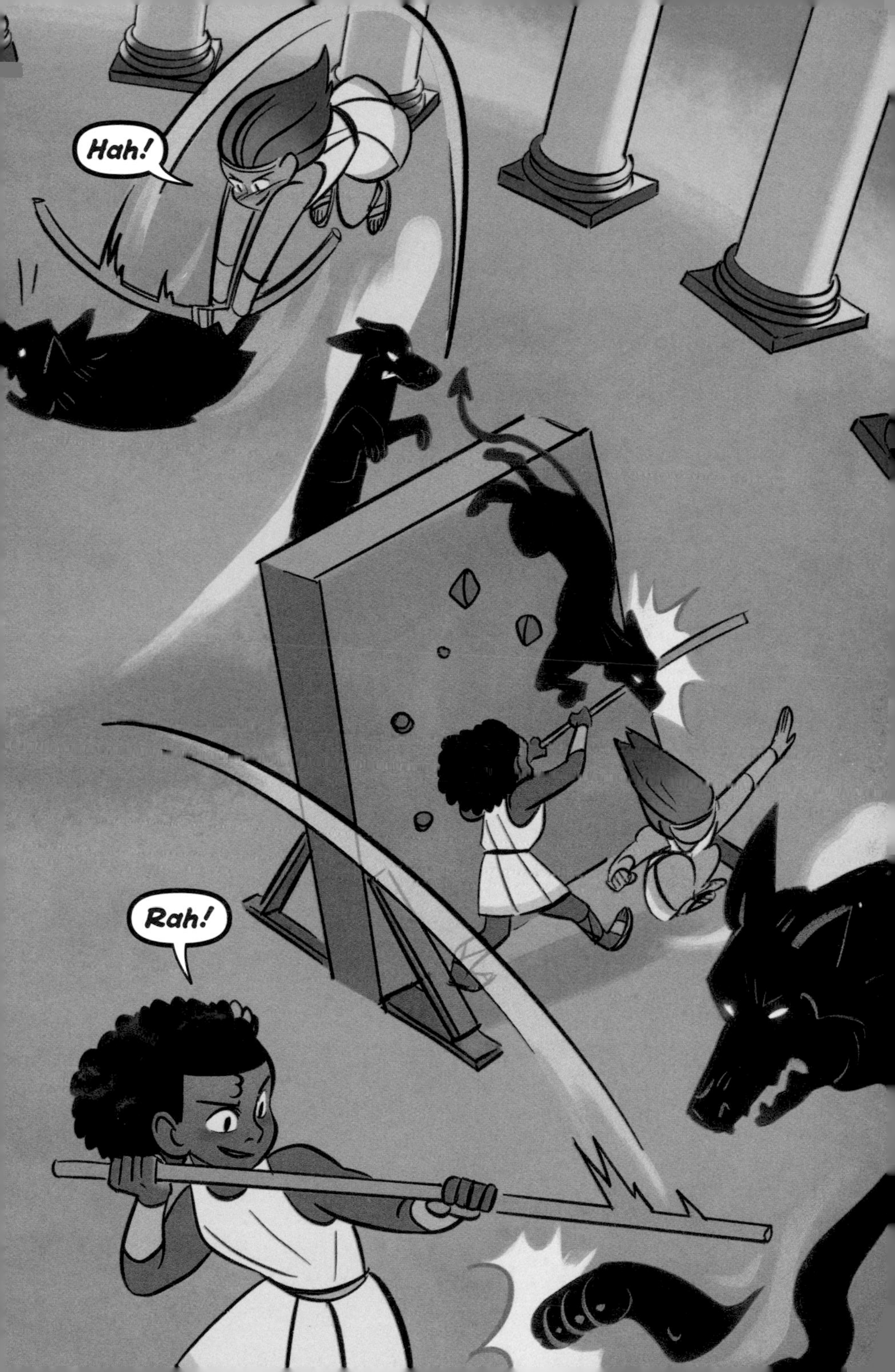
Hah!
Rah!

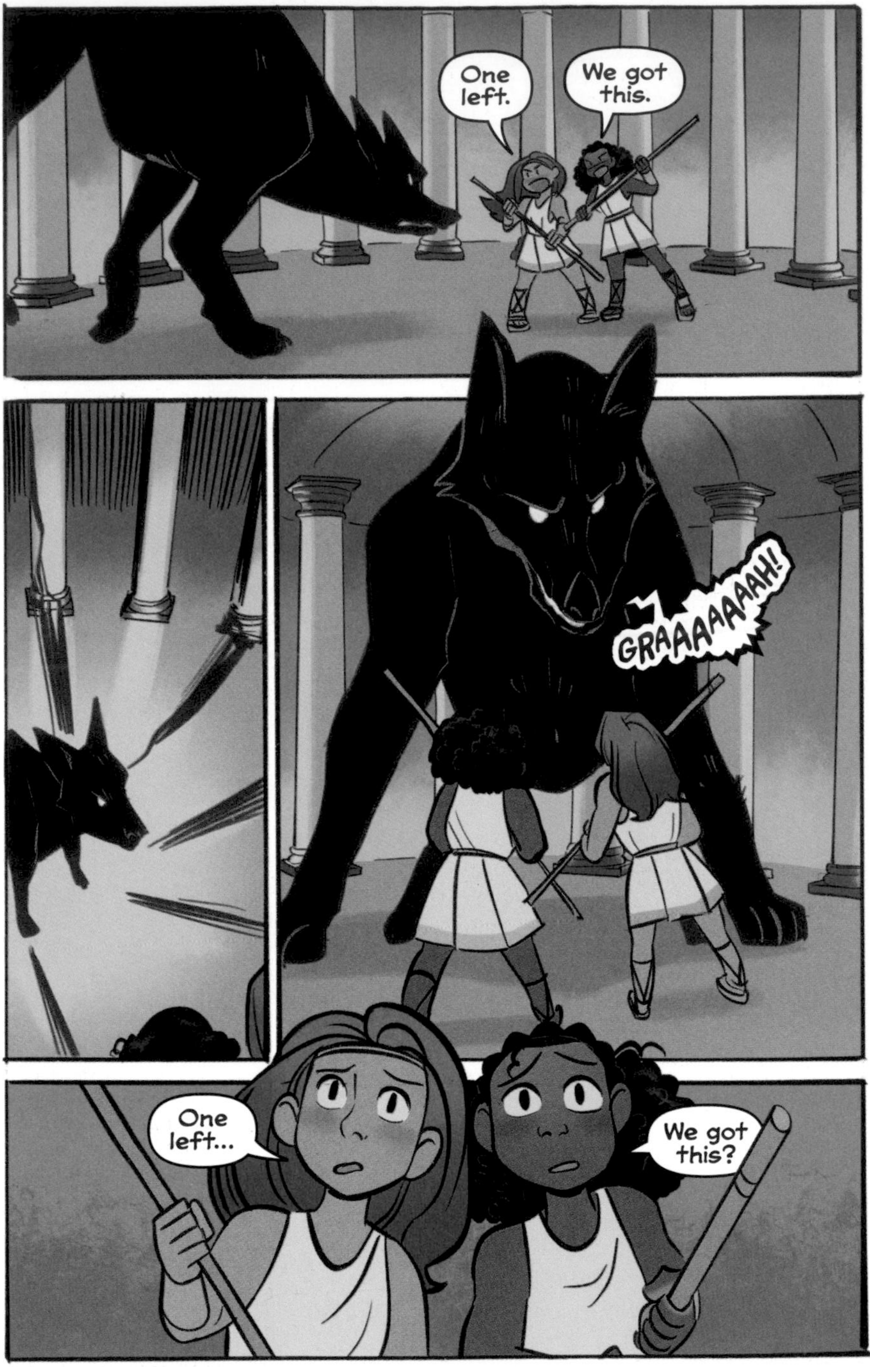
One left.
We got this.
GRAAAAAAAH!
One left...
We got this?

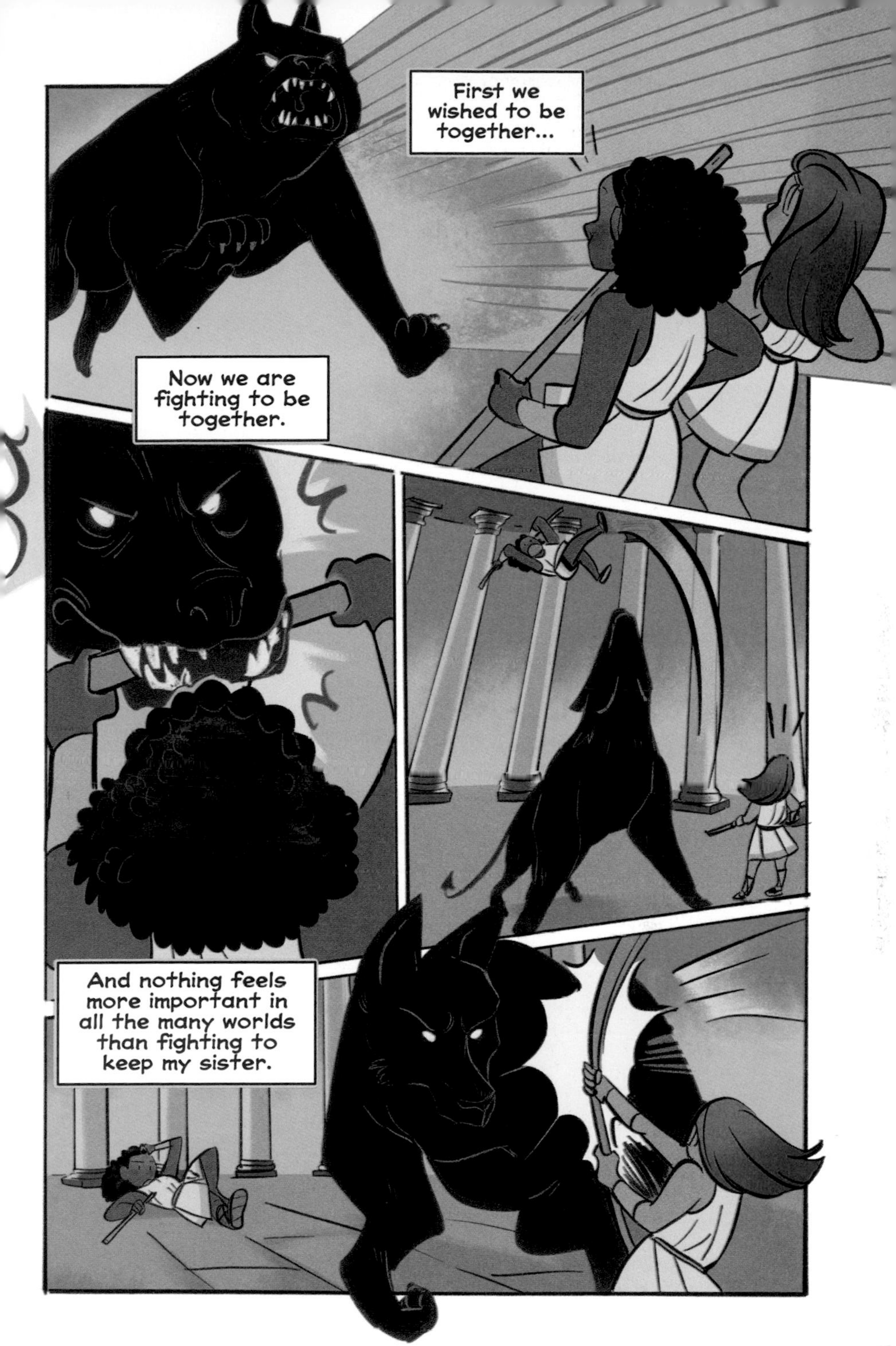
First we wished to be together...
Now we are fighting to be together.
And nothing feels more important in all the many worlds than fighting to keep my sister.

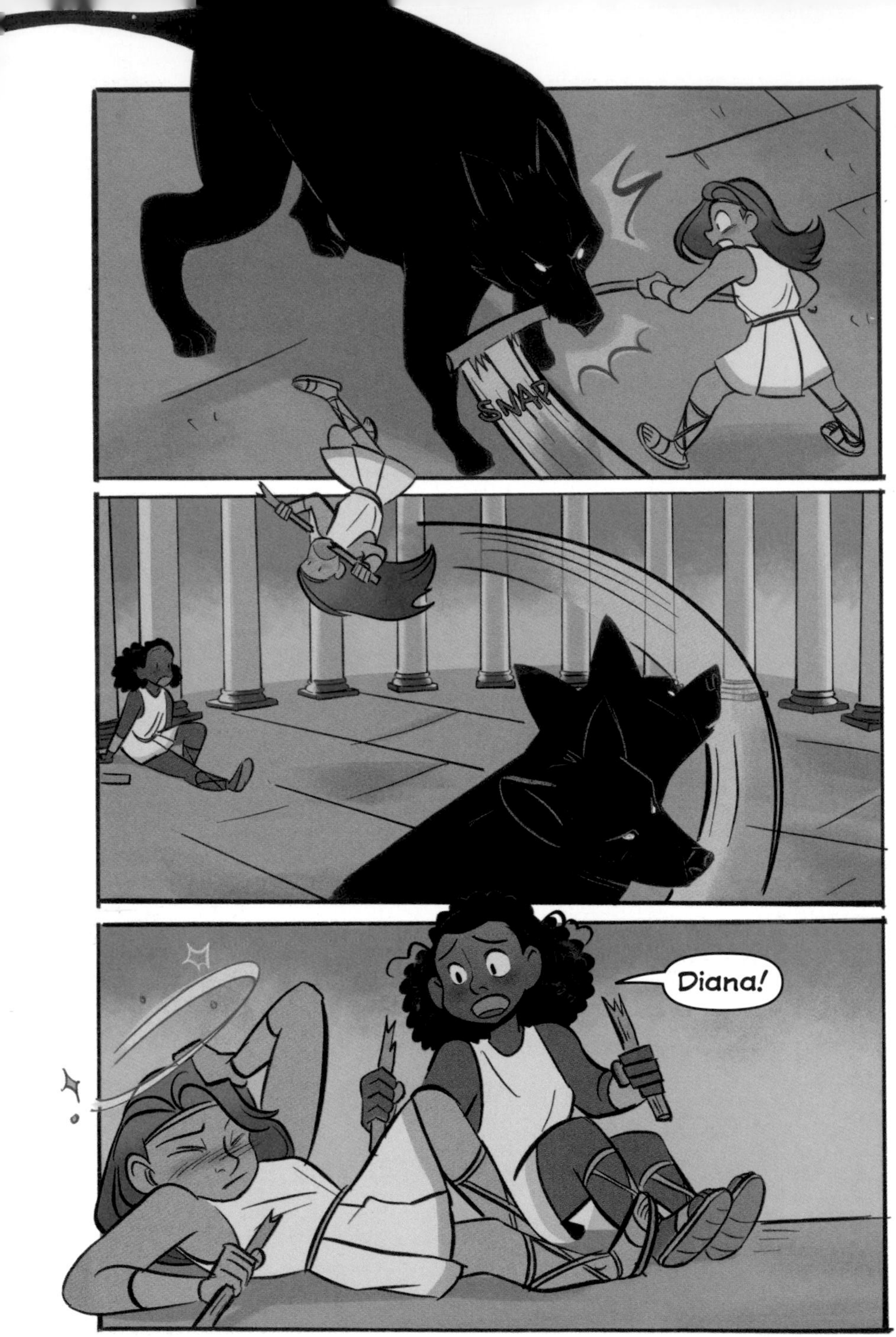
SNAP
Diana!

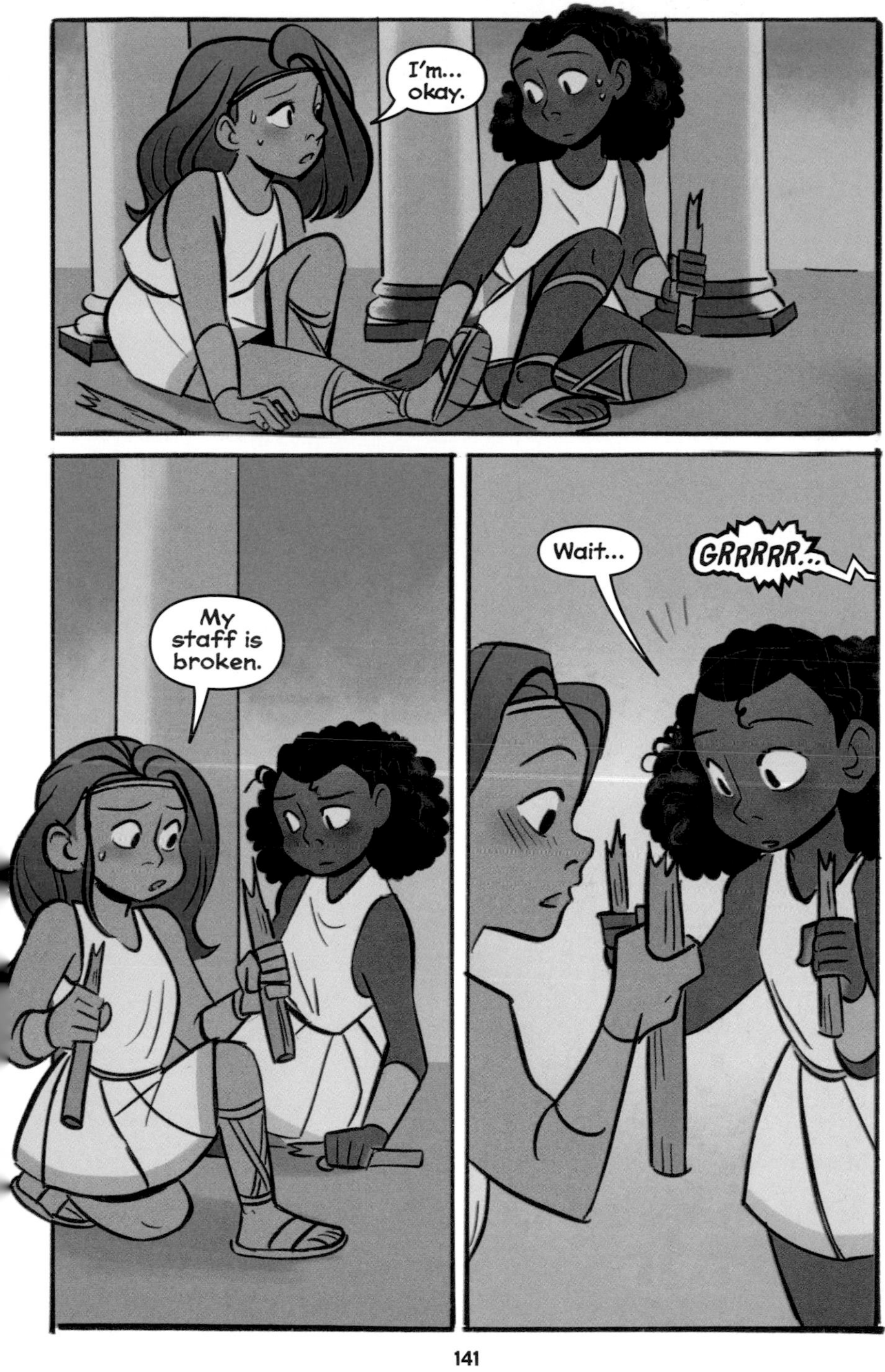
I'm... okay.
My staff is broken.
Wait...
GRRRRR...

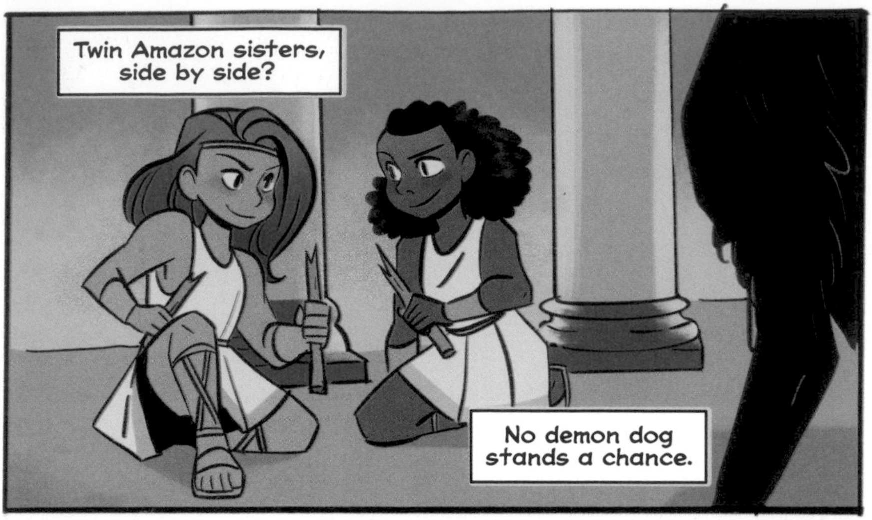
Twin Amazon sisters, side by side?
No demon dog stands a chance.

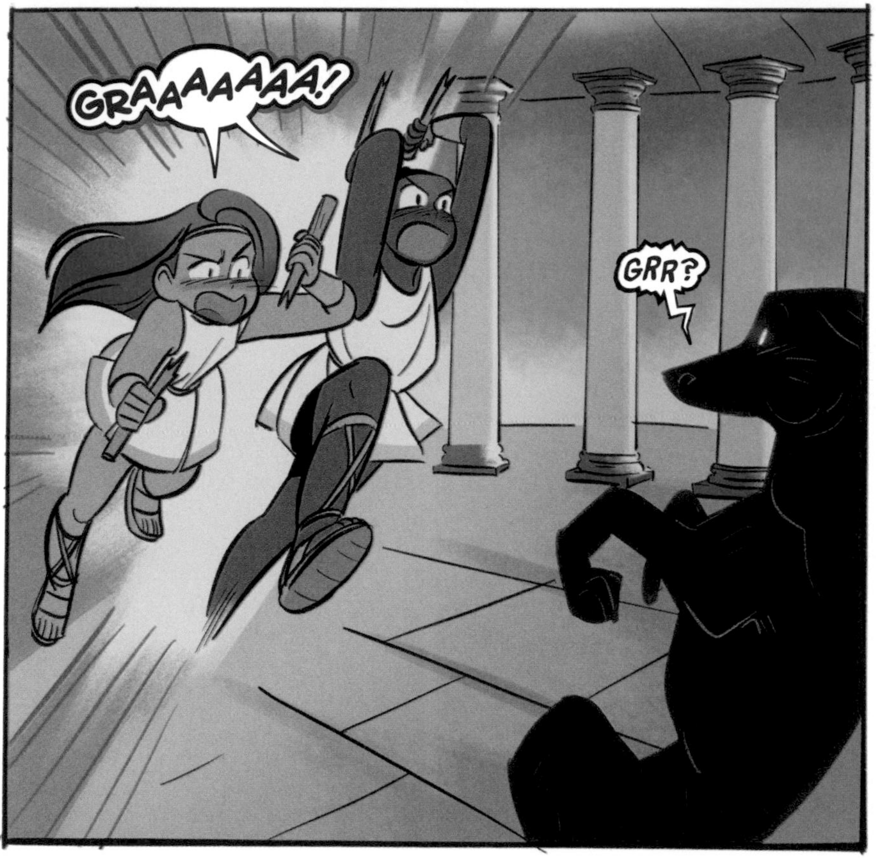
GRAAAAAAA!
GRR?

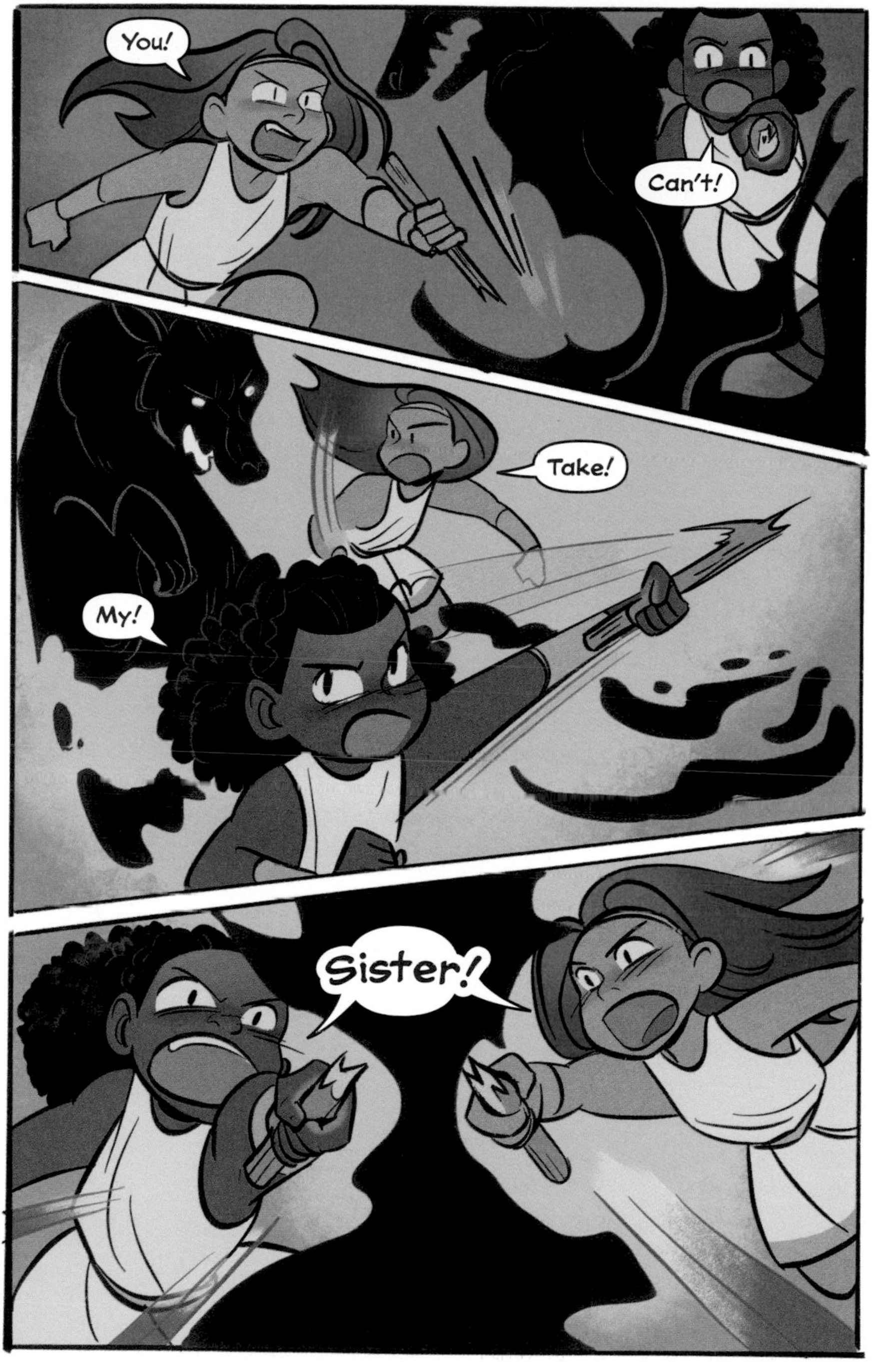
You!
Can't!
Take!
My!
Sister!

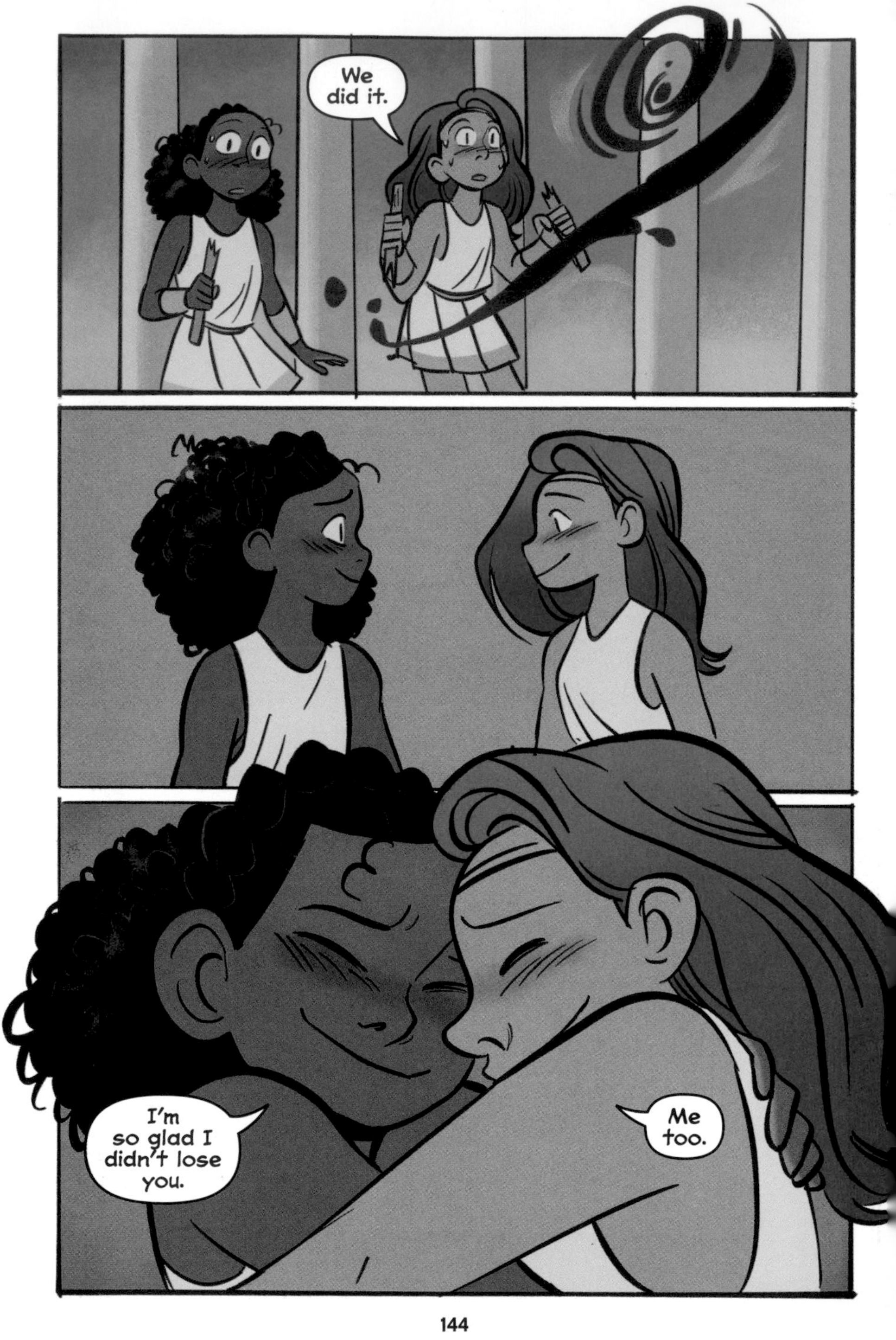
We did it.
I'm so glad I didn't lose you.
Me too.

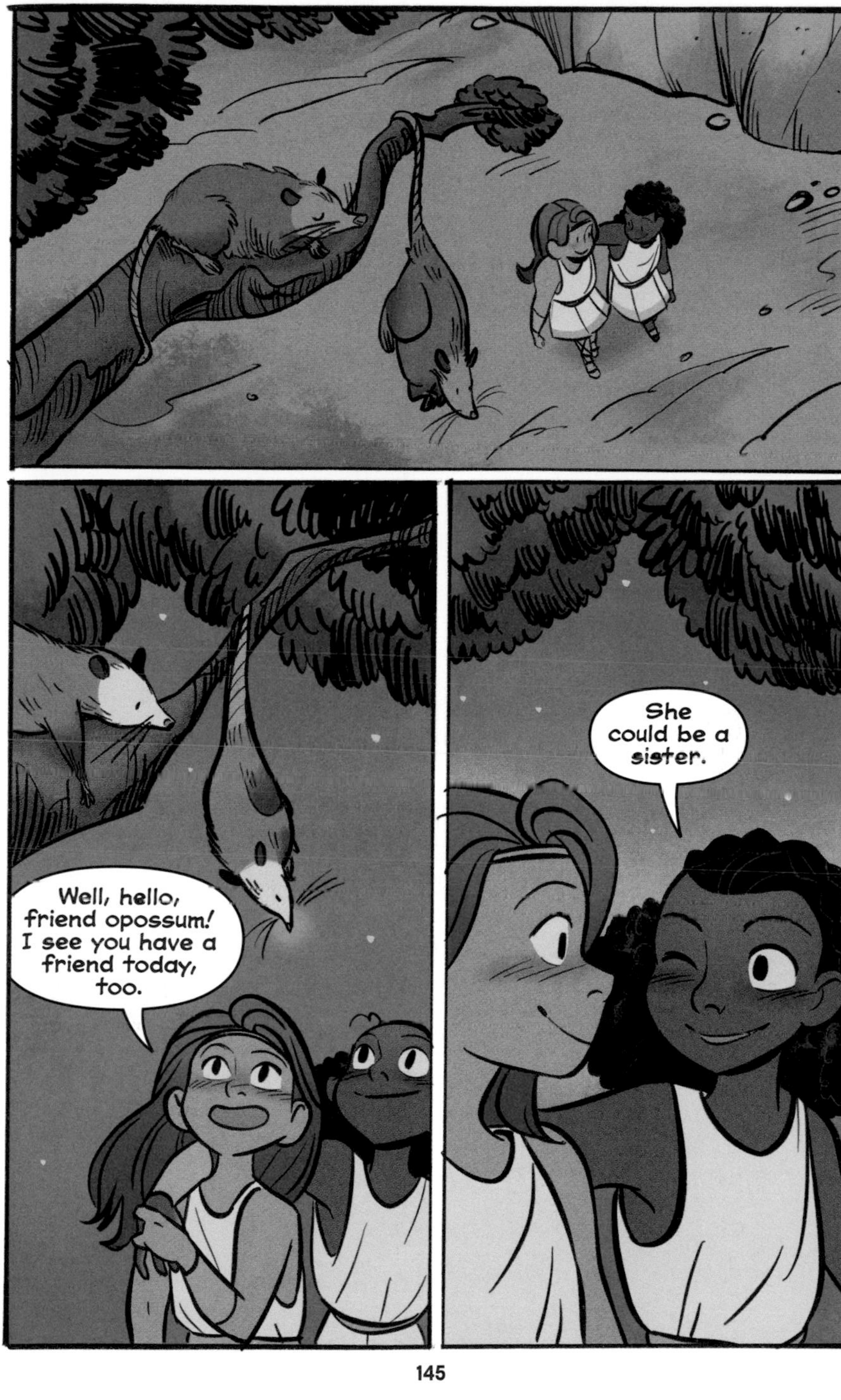
Well, hello, friend opossum! I see you have a friend today, too.
She could be a sister.

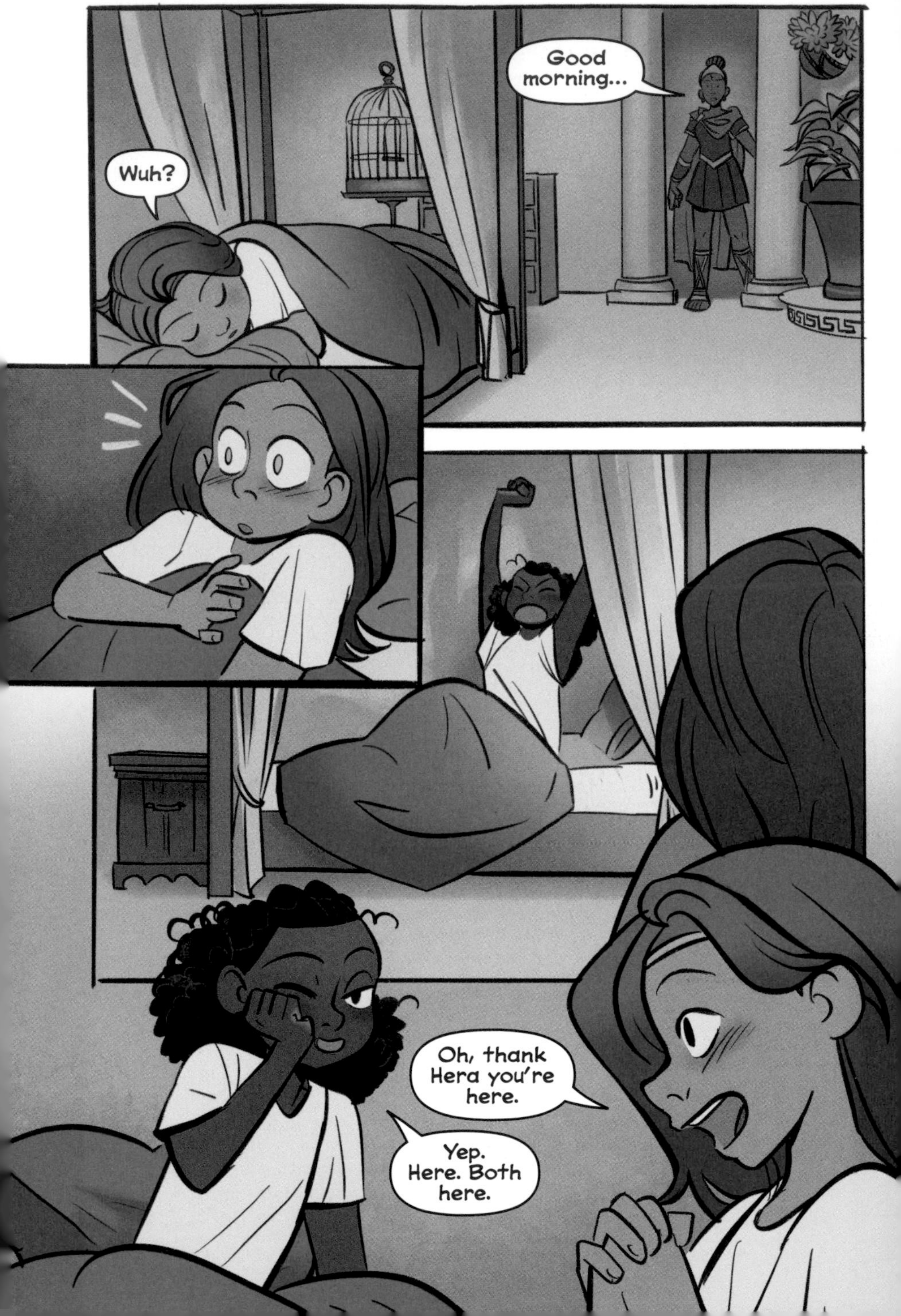
Good morning...
Wuh?
Oh, thank Hera you're here.
Yep. Here. Both here.

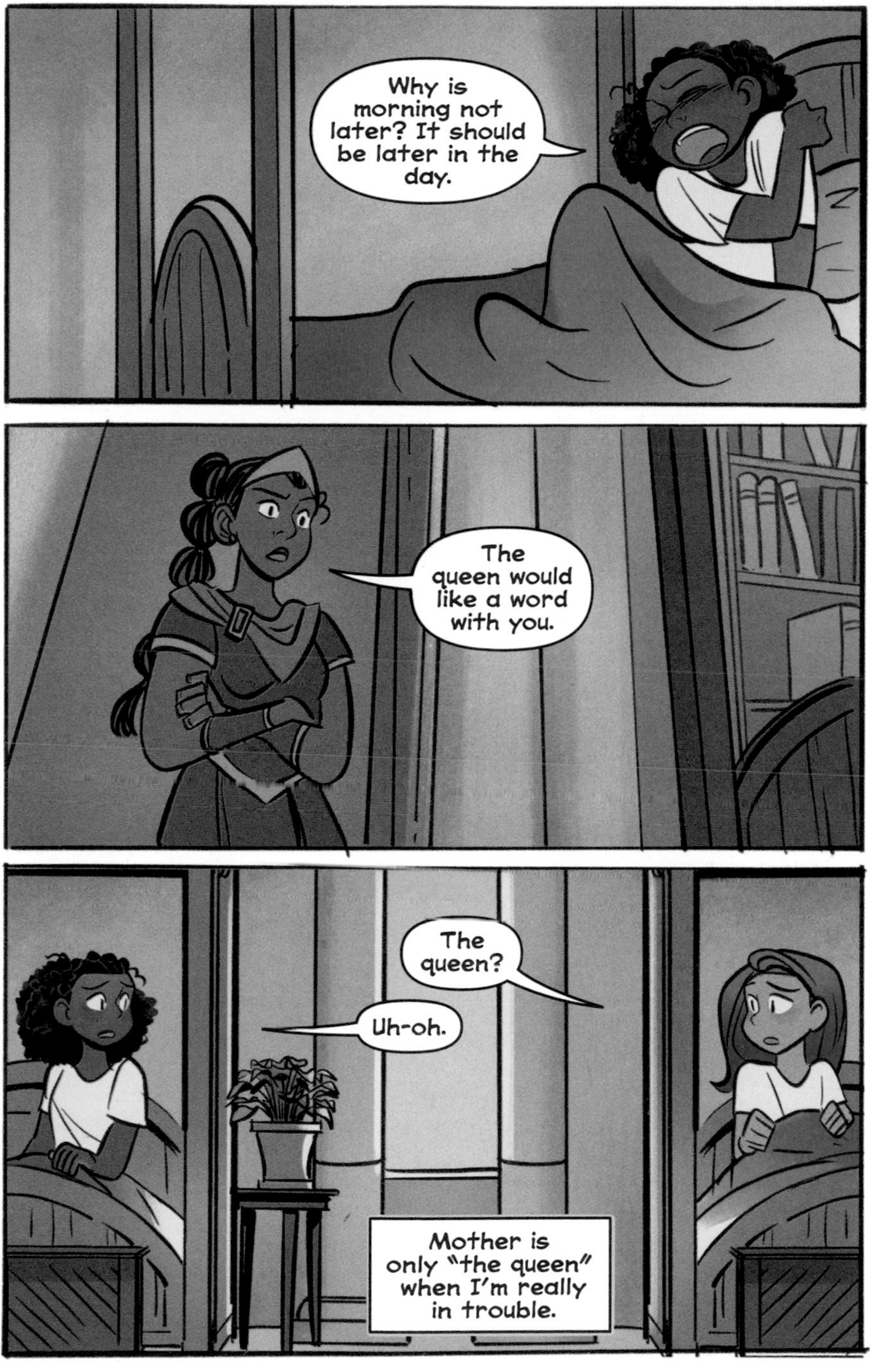
Why is morning not later? It should be later in the day.
The queen would like a word with you.
The queen?
Uh-oh.
Mother is only "the queen" when I'm really in trouble.

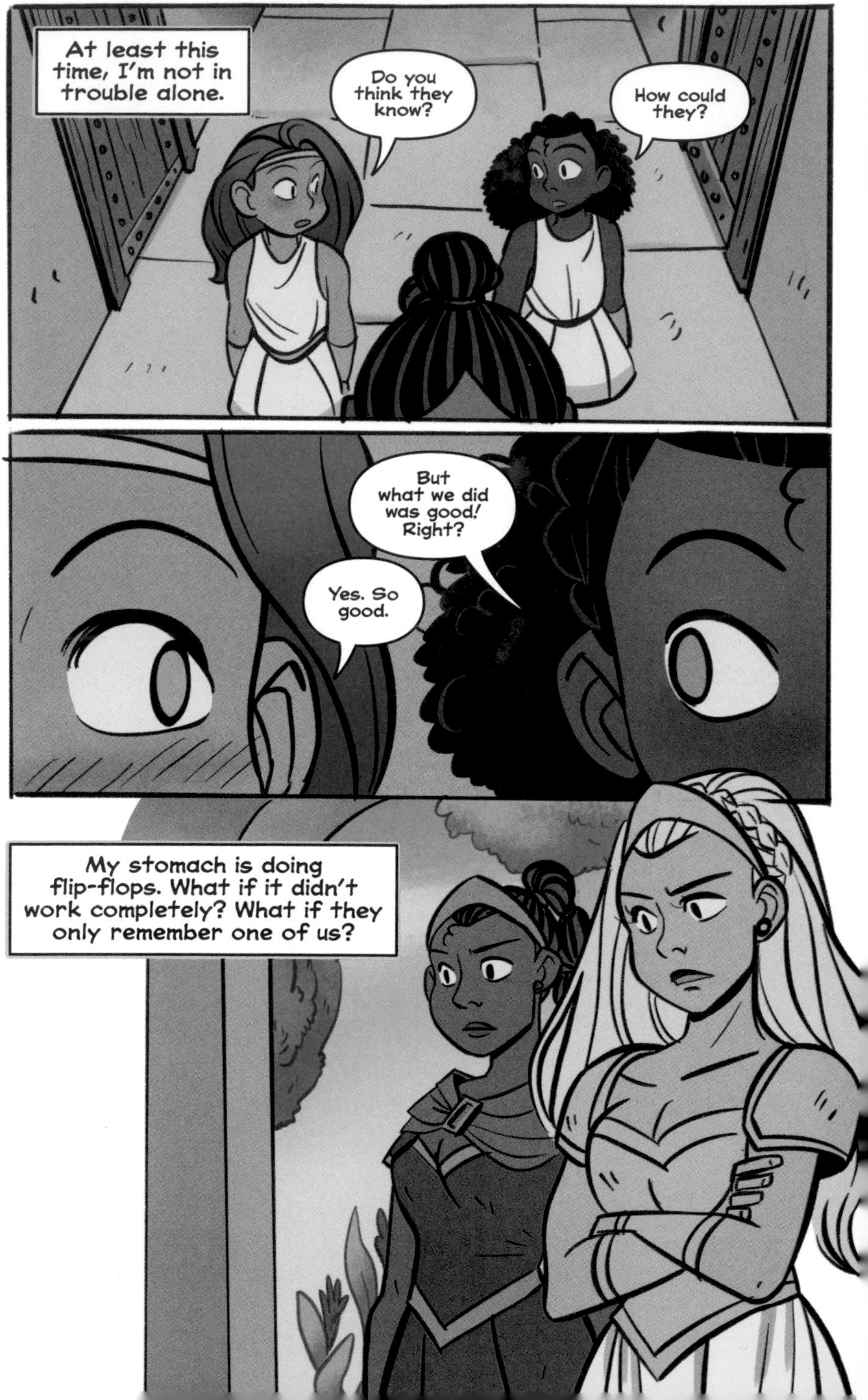

At least this time, I'm not in trouble alone.
Do you think they know?
How could they?
But what we did was good! Right?
Yes. So good.
My stomach is doing flip-flops. What if it didn't work completely? What if they only remember one of us?

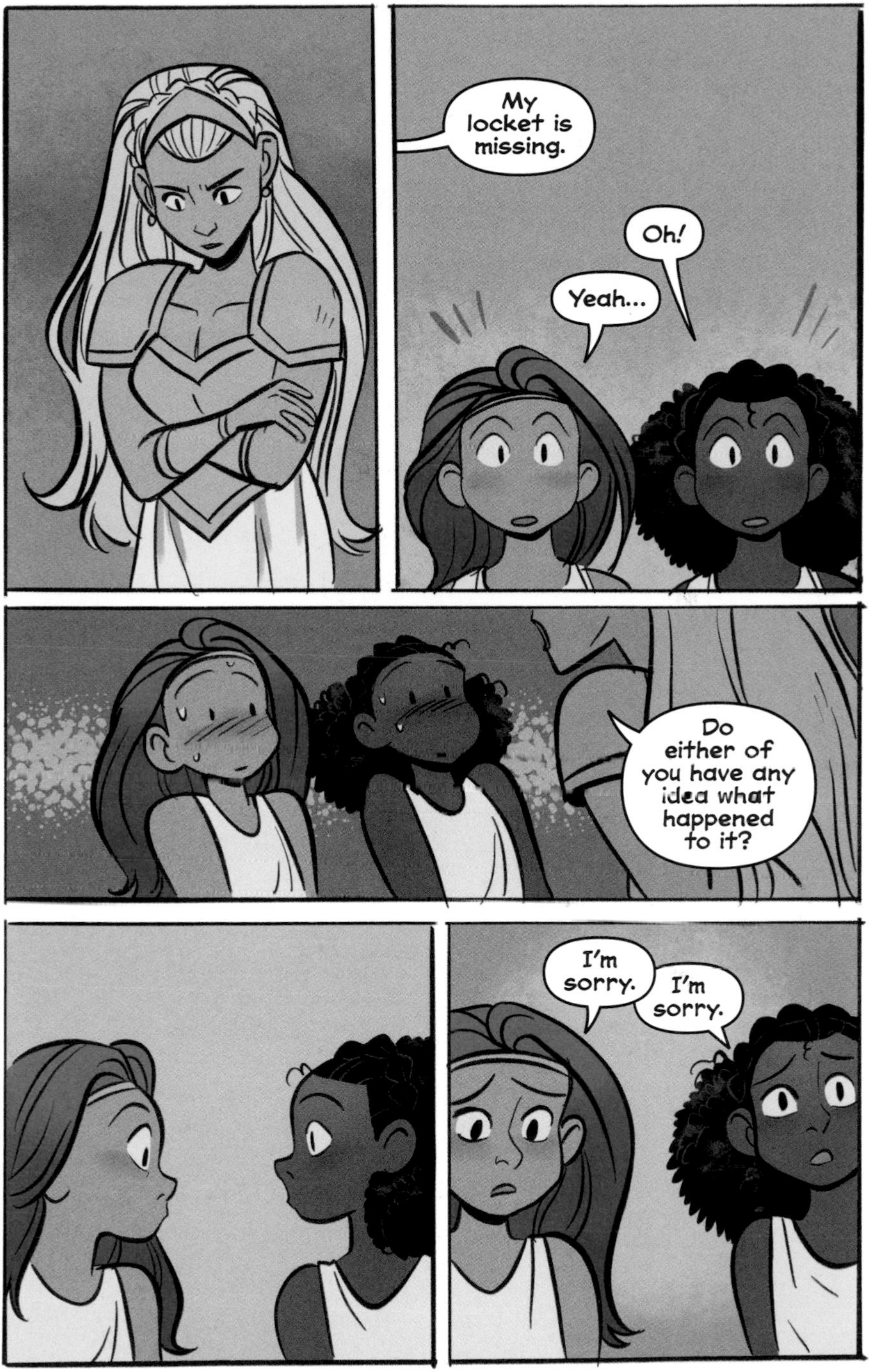
My locket is missing.
Oh!
Yeah...
Do either of you have any idea what happened to it?
I'm sorry.
I'm sorry.

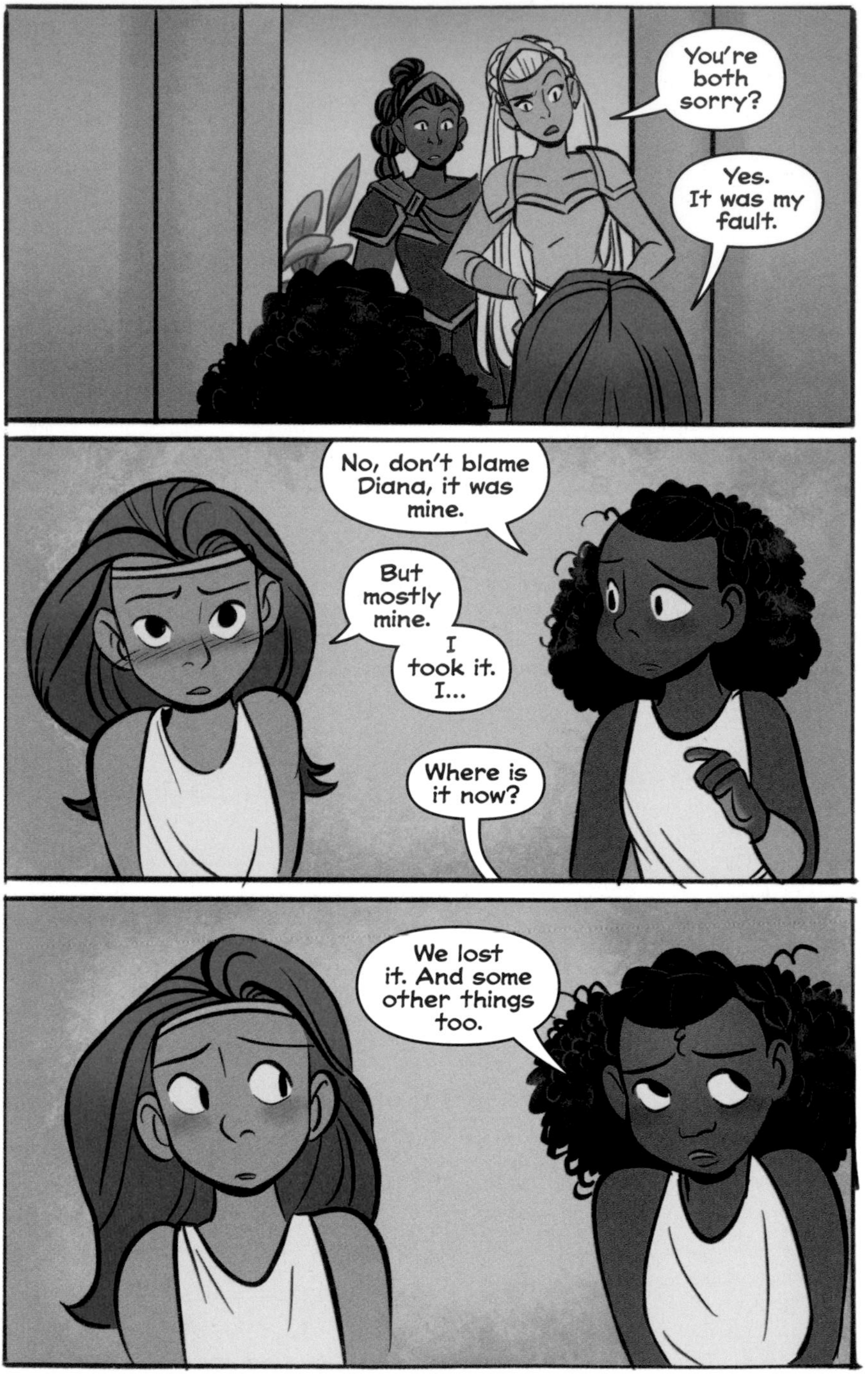
You're both sorry?
Yes. It was my fault.
No, don't blame Diana, it was mine.
But mostly mine.
I took it. I...
Where is it now?
We lost it. And some other things too.

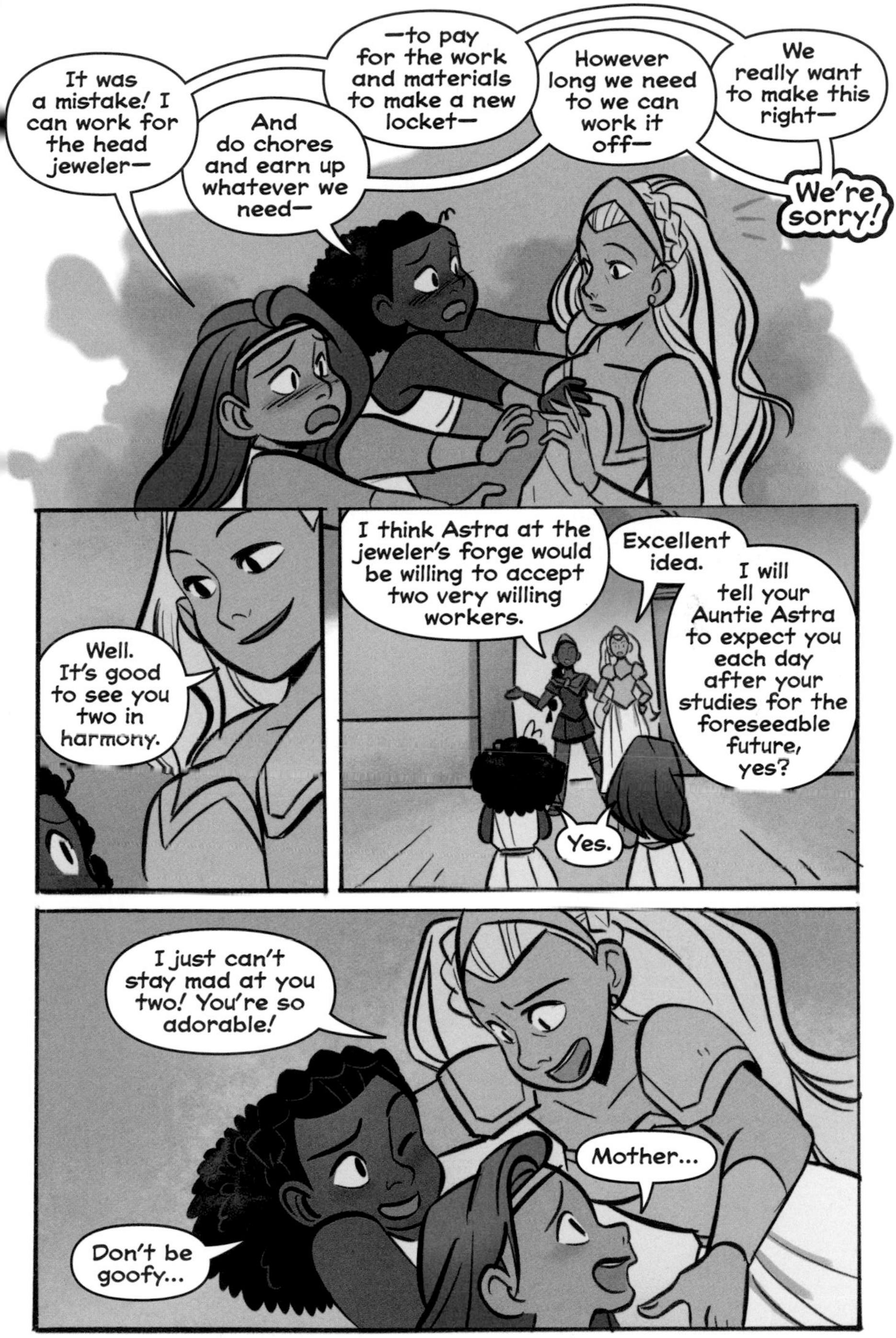
It was a mistake! I can work for the head jeweler—
And do chores and earn up whatever we need—
—to pay for the work and materials to make a new locket—
However long we need to we can work it off—
We really want to make this right—
We're sorry!
Well. It's good to see you two in harmony.
I think Astra at the jeweler's forge would be willing to accept two very willing workers.
Excellent idea.
I will tell your Auntie Astra to expect you each day after your studies for the foreseeable future, yes?
Yes.
I just can't stay mad at you two! You're so adorable!
Mother...
Don't be goofy...

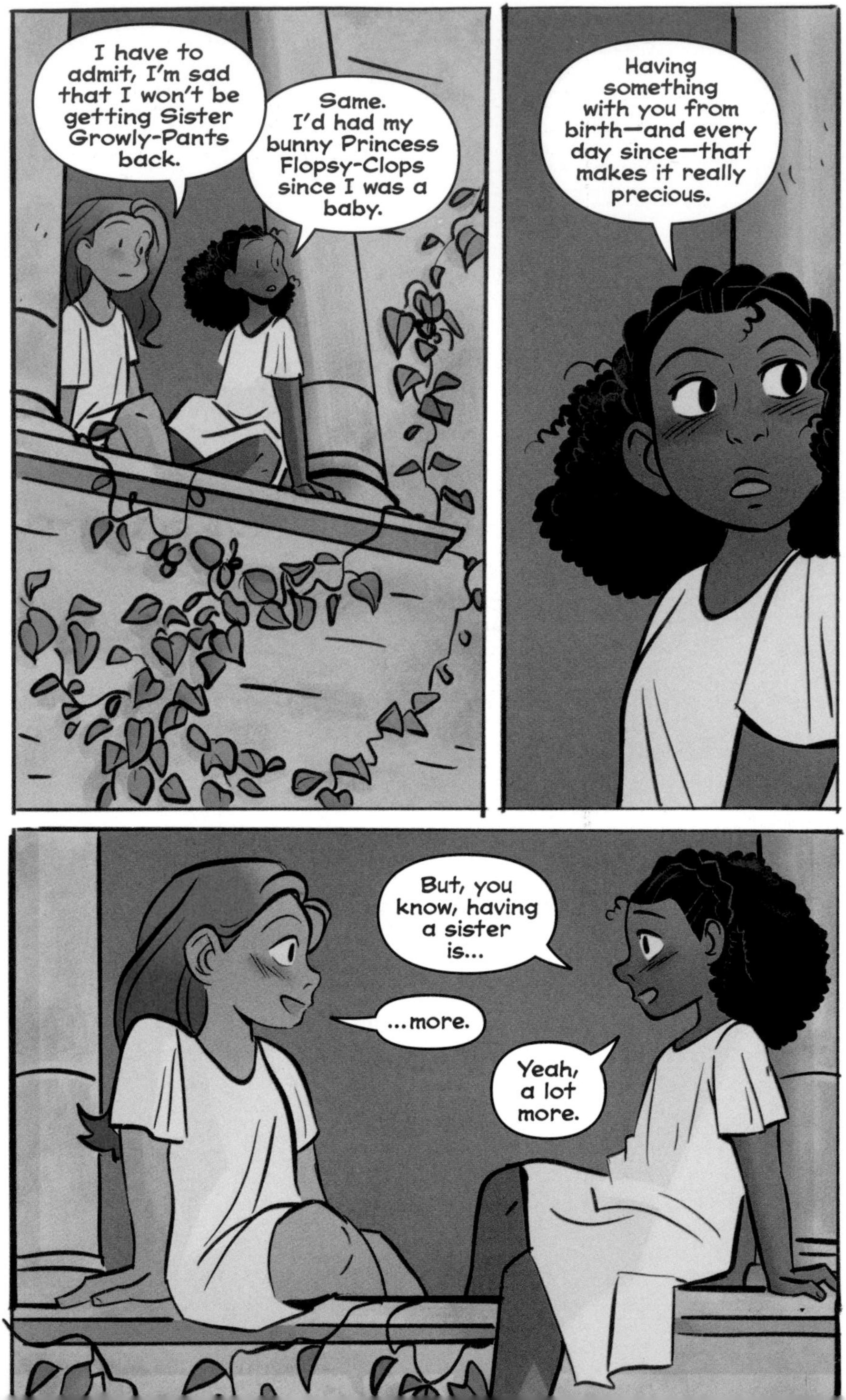
I have to admit, I'm sad that I won't be getting Sister Growly-Pants back.
Same. I'd had my bunny Princess Flopsy-Clops since I was a baby.
Having something with you from birth—and every day since—that makes it really precious.
But, you know, having a sister is...
...more.
Yeah, a lot more.

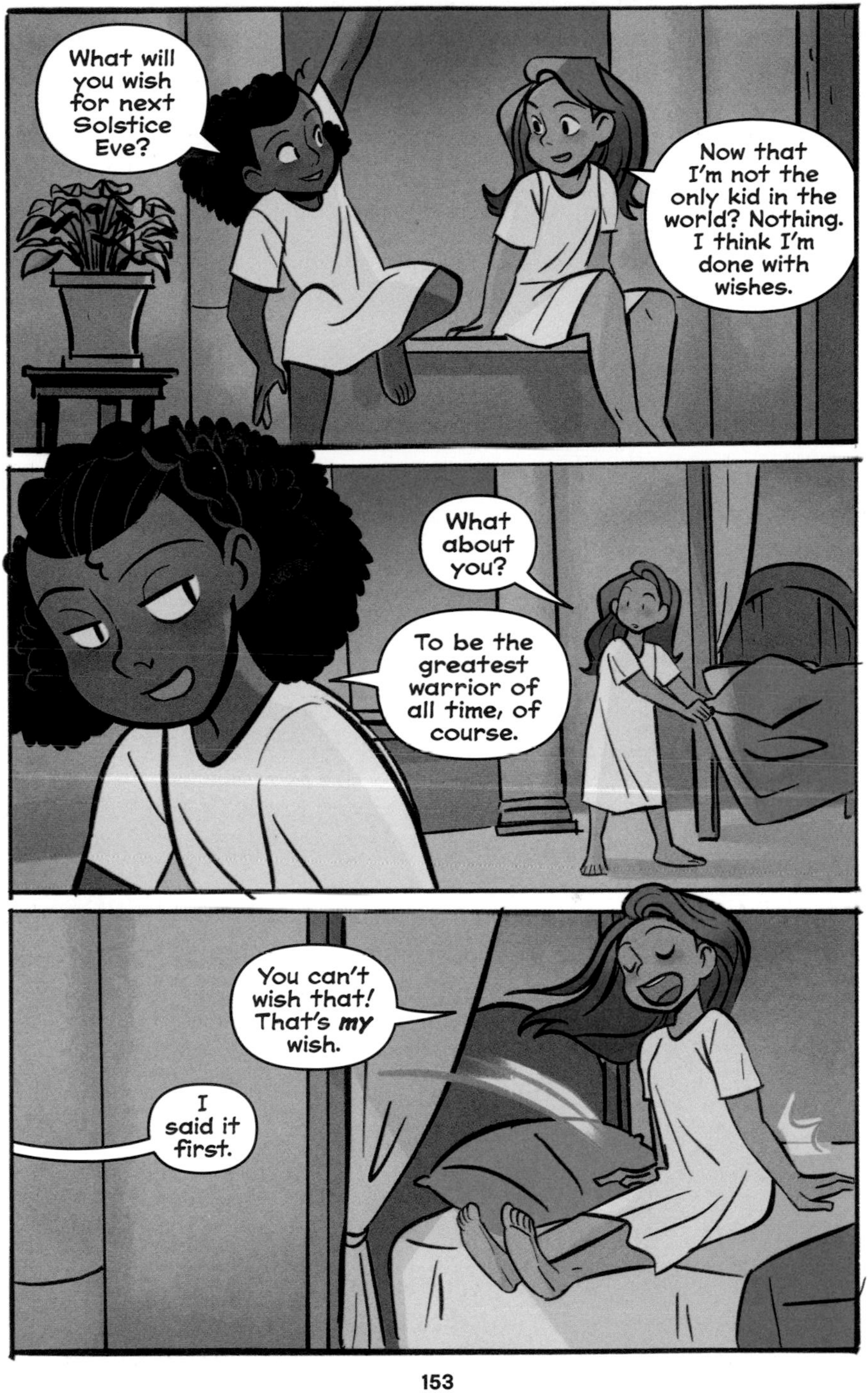
What will you wish for next Solstice Eve?
Now that I'm not the only kid in the world? Nothing. I think I'm done with wishes.
What about you?
To be the greatest warrior of all time, of course.
You can't wish that! That's *my* wish.
I said it first.

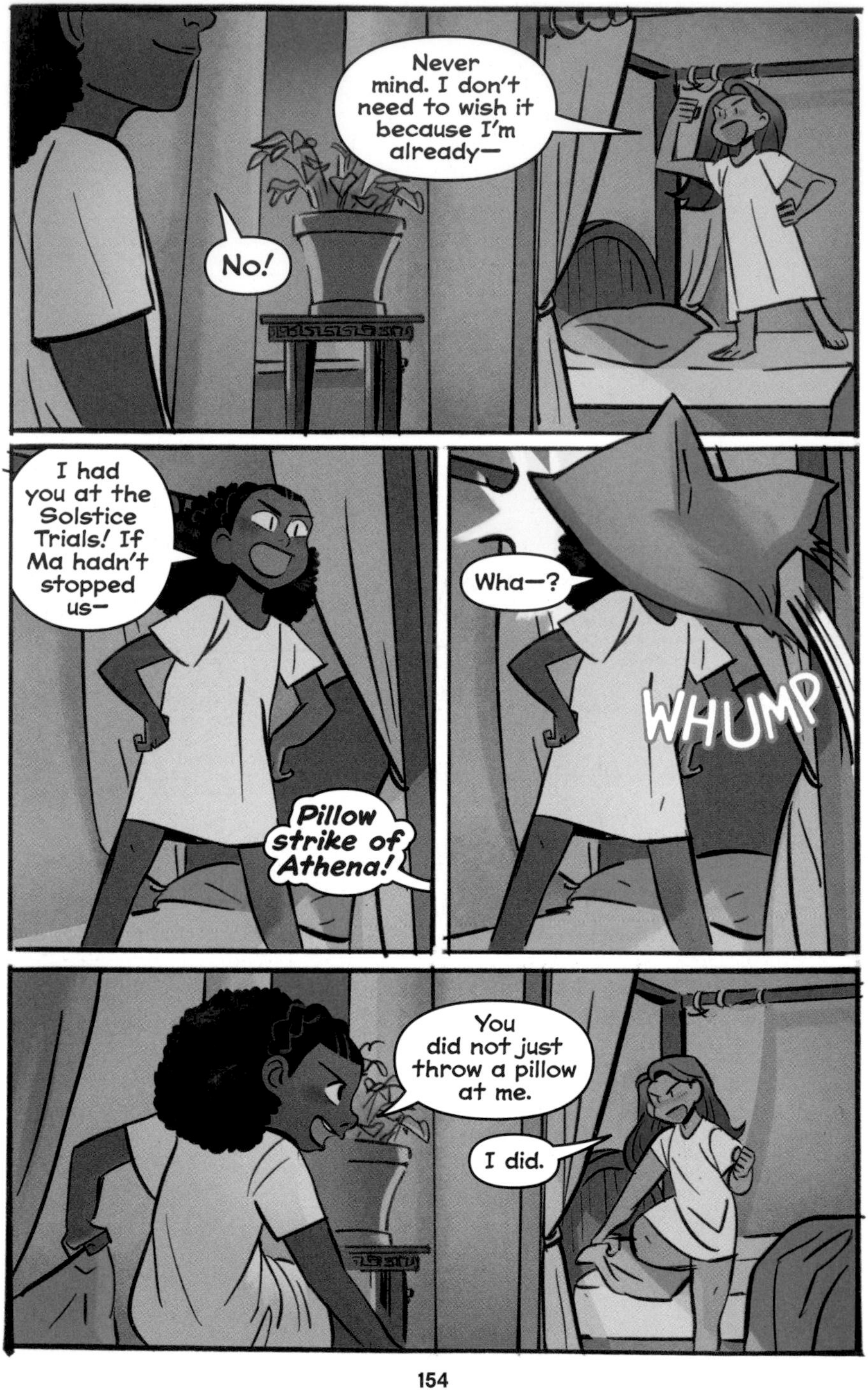
Never mind. I don't need to wish it because I'm already—
No!
I had you at the Solstice Trials! If Ma hadn't stopped us—
Pillow strike of Athena!
Wha—?
WHUMP
You did not just throw a pillow at me.
I did.

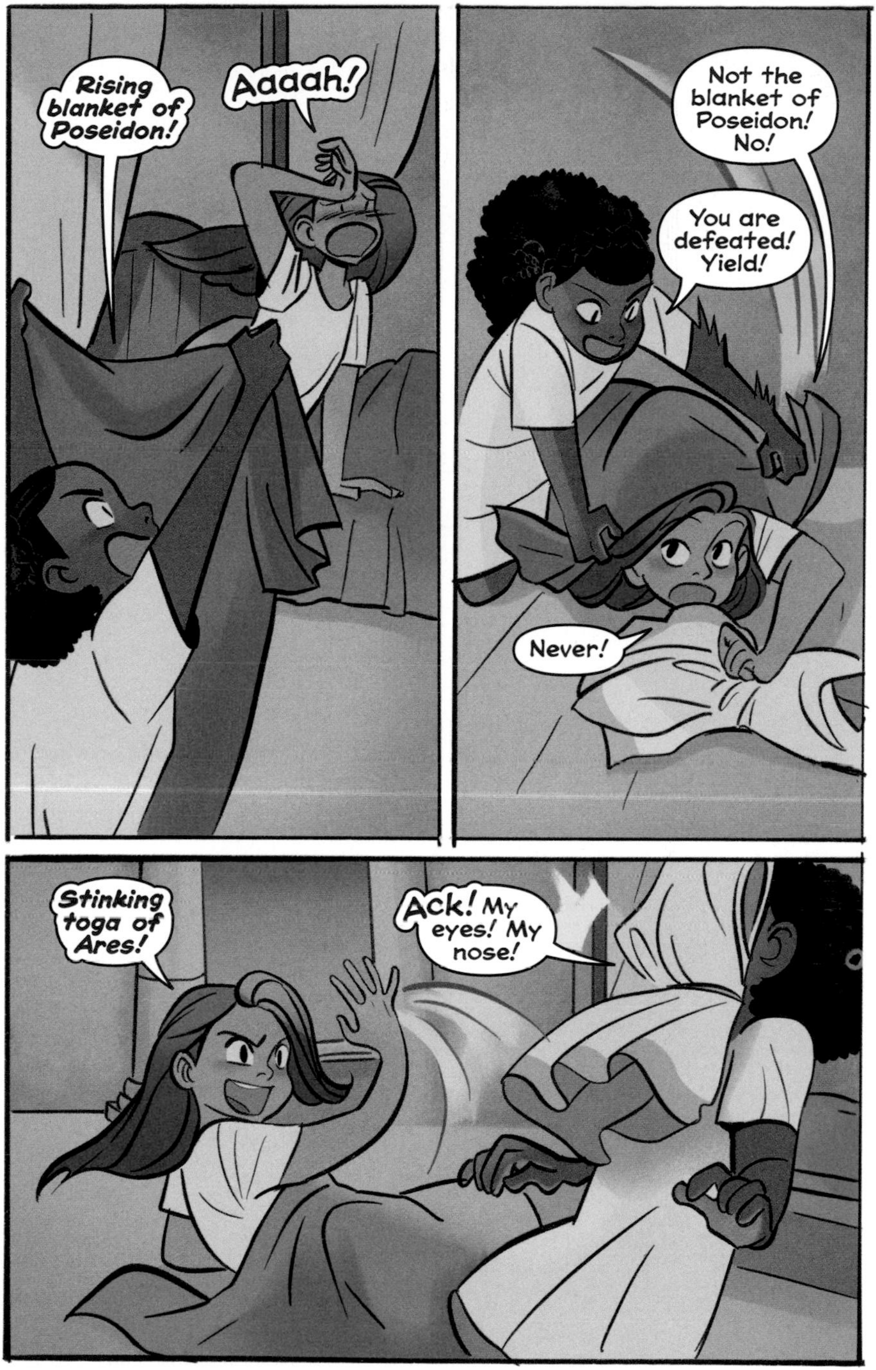
Rising blanket of Poseidon!
Aaaah!
Not the blanket of Poseidon! No!
You are defeated! Yield!
Never!
Stinking toga of Ares!
Ack! My eyes! My nose!

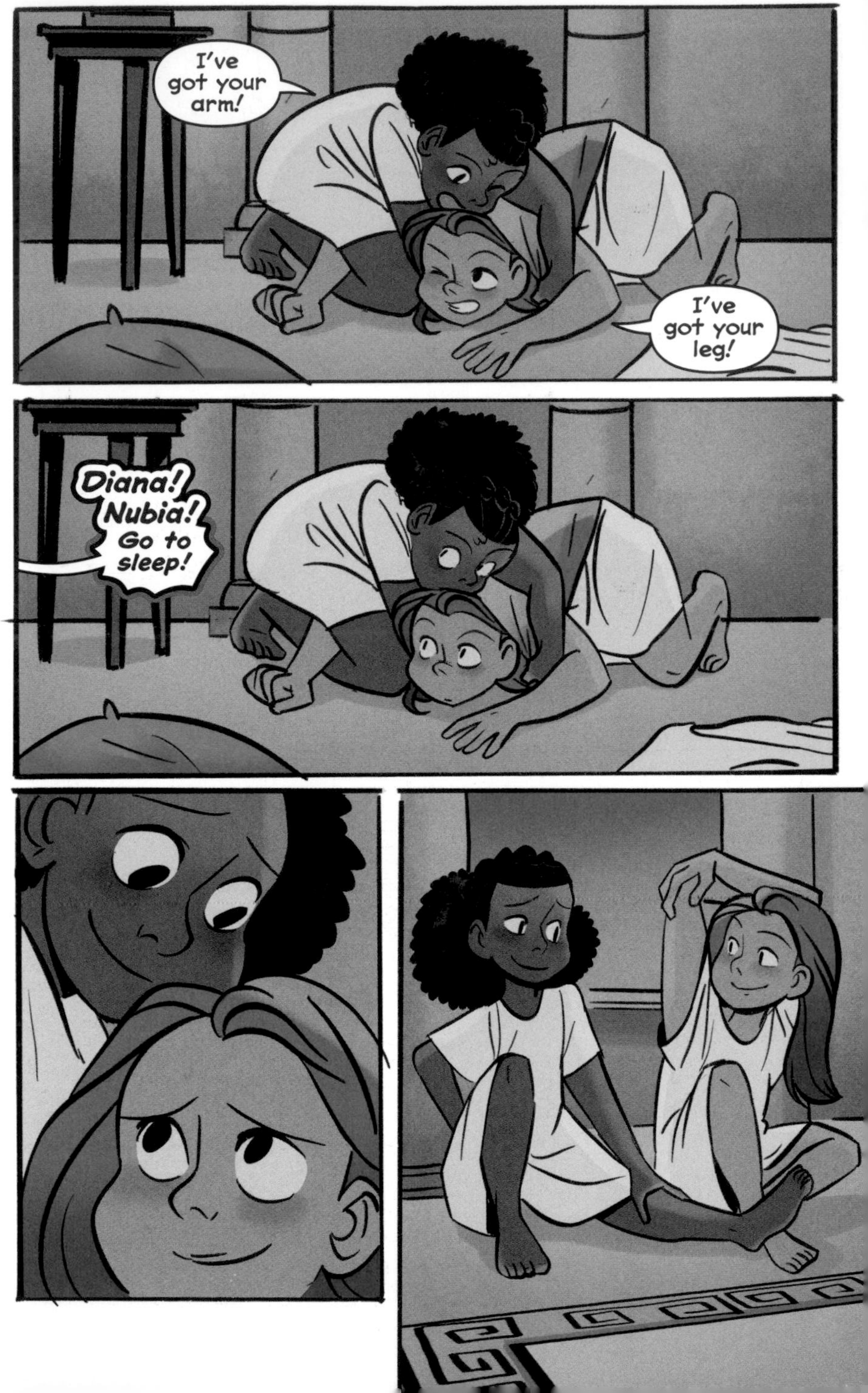
I've got your arm!
I've got your leg!
Diana! Nubia! Go to sleep!

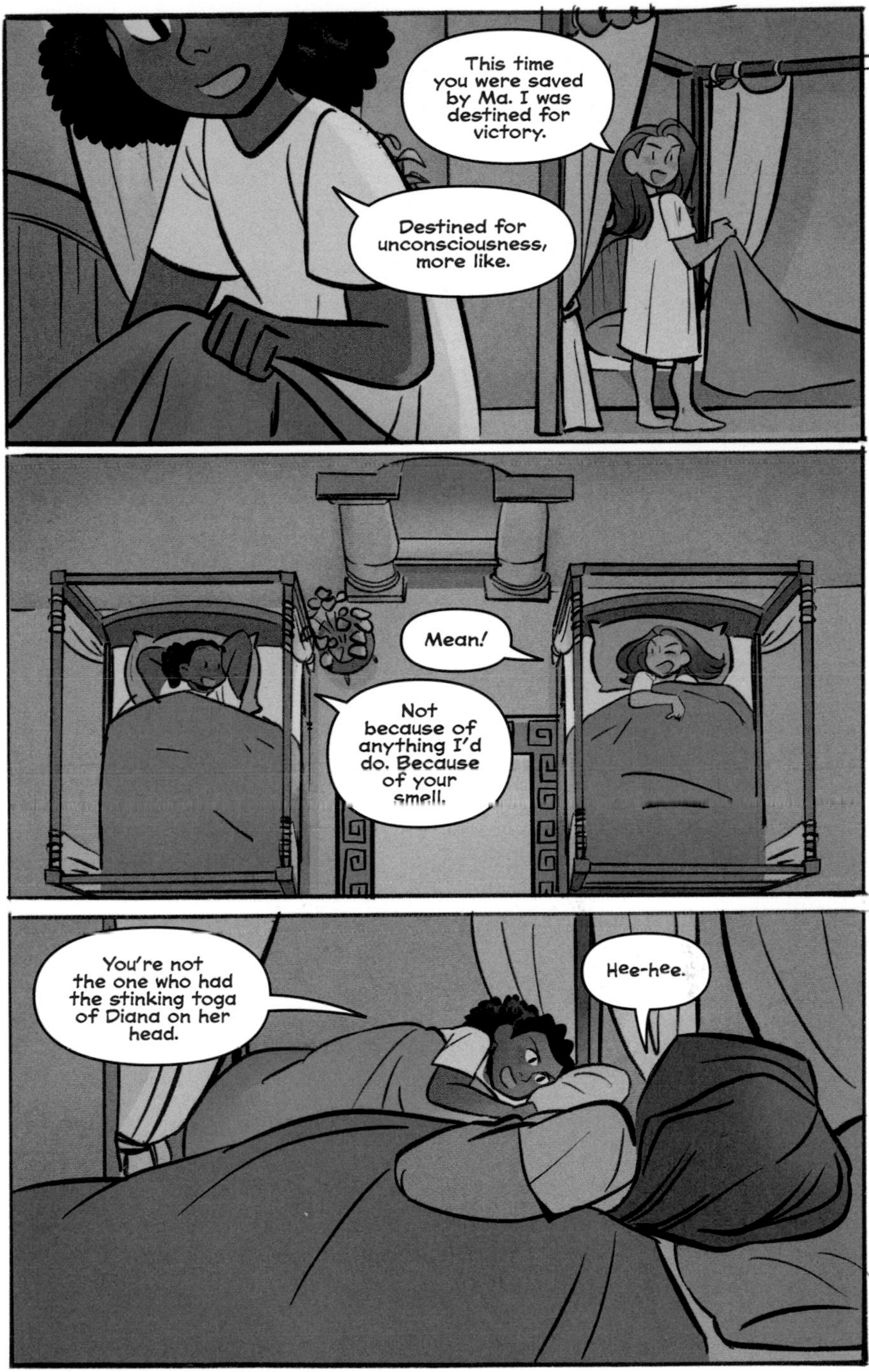
This time you were saved by Ma. I was destined for victory.
Destined for unconsciousness, more like.
Mean!
Not because of anything I'd do. Because of your smell.
You're not the one who had the stinking toga of Diana on her head.
Hee-hee.

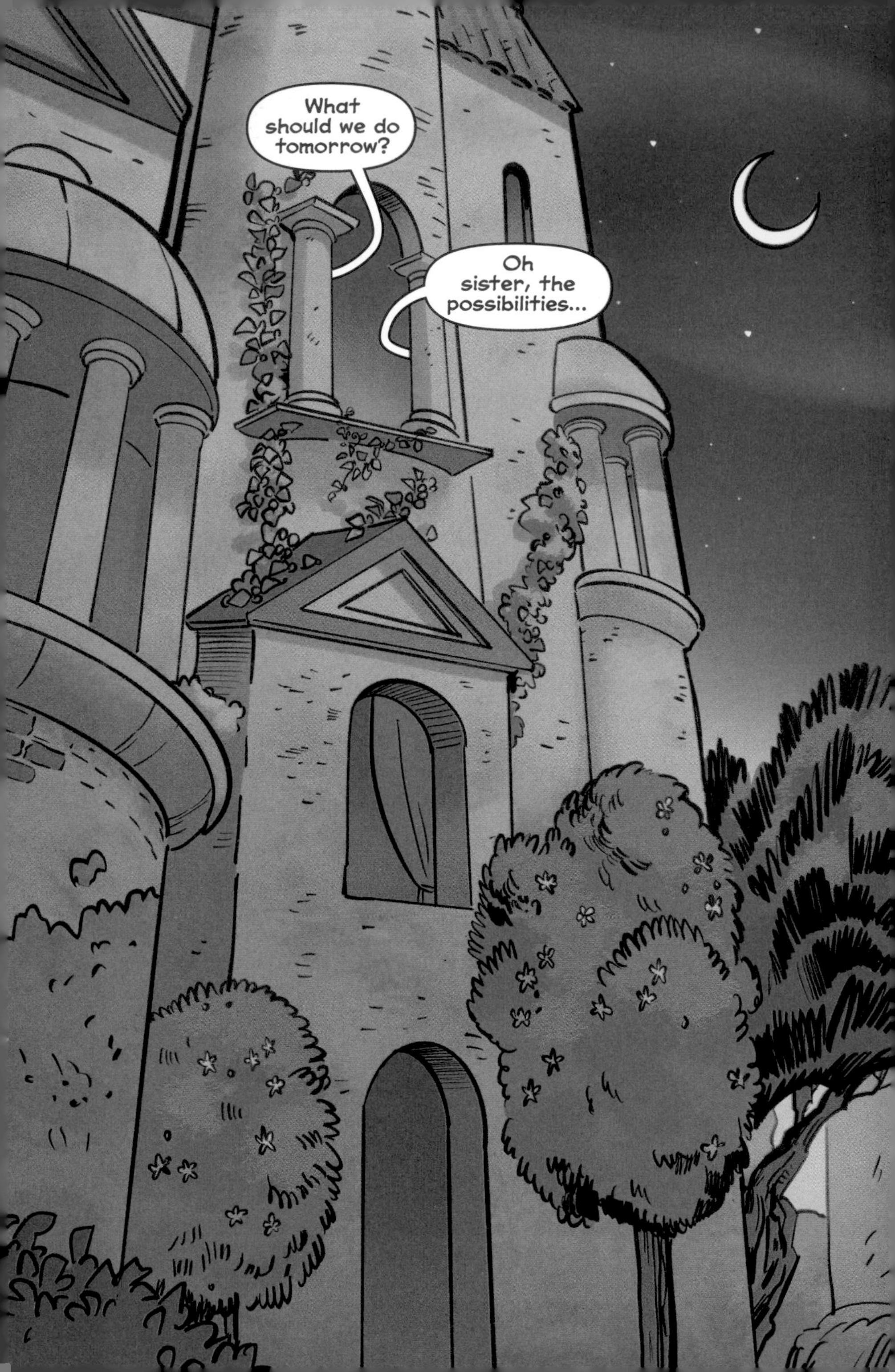
What should we do tomorrow?
Oh sister, the possibilities...

Shannon Hale and Dean Hale are the wife-and-husband writing team behind *Diana: Princess of the Amazons* (with Victoria Ying), *Amethyst: Princess of Gemworld* (with Asiah Fulmore), Eisner Award nominee *Rapunzel's Revenge* (with Nathan Hale), the *New York Times* bestselling series The Princess in Black (with LeUyen Pham), and two novels about Marvel's Squirrel Girl. Shannon Hale is also the author of the Newbery Honor-winning novel *Princess Academy*, the graphic novel memoirs *Real Friends, Best Friends*, and *Friends Forever* (with LeUyen Pham), and many others. Shannon and Dean live in Utah with their four children, including twin girls who have definitely probably coexisted in this universe since birth.

Victoria Ying is an author and artist living in Los Angeles. She started her career in the arts by falling in love with comic books, which eventually turned into a career working in animation. She loves Japanese curry, putting things in her shopping cart online and taking them out again, and hanging out with her gray tabby. Her film credits include *Tangled, Wreck-It Ralph, Frozen, Paperman, Big Hero 6*, and *Moana*. She has written and illustrated the City of Secrets graphic novel series, and a forthcoming YA graphic novel called *Hungry Ghost*.

Lynette Wong began her art career as a concept artist working in a gaming studio, but her one true love has always been comics and sequential art. During her time as a concept artist, she has shipped many titles including *Street Fighter V, Killer Instinct, Marvel vs. Capcom, Bake 'n Switch*, and *Nightstream*. Lynette now lives her comics dreams as a colorist for graphic novels, her debut being *Squire* and *City of Illusion*. She resides in Malaysia and often gets distracted going down rabbit holes on Pinterest boards.

Becca Carey is a graphic designer and letterer who has worked on books like *Redlands, Vampirella/Red Sonja, Buffy the Vampire Slayer*, and more super-secret fun projects to watch out for. She loves terrible horror movies and having conversations with her dog and has proudly read *War and Peace*, but couldn't tell you a thing about it.

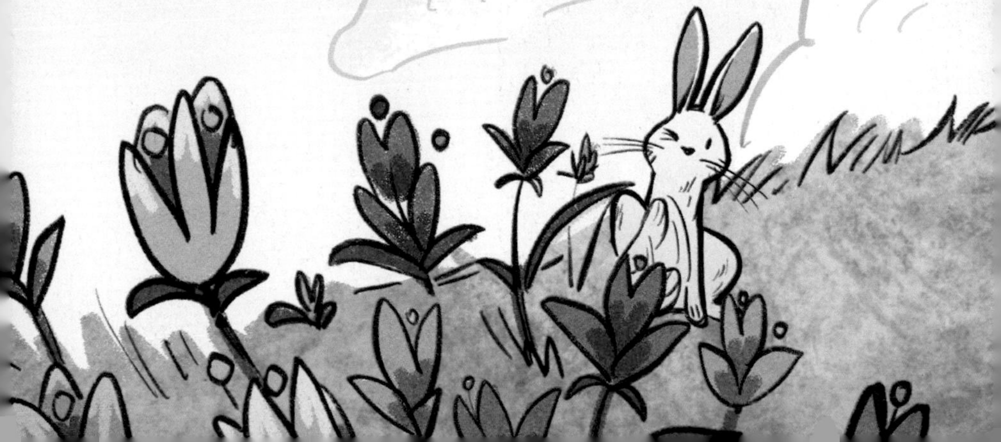

Diana: Princess of the Amazons
Shannon Hale, Dean Hale,
Victoria Ying
ISBN: 978-1-4012-9111-2

Amethyst: Princess of Gemworld
Shannon Hale, Dean Hale,
Asiah Fulmore
ISBN: 978-1-77950-122-6

NEW YORK TIMES BESTSELLING AUTHORS
SHANNON HALE
&DEAN HALE
DIANA: PRINCESS OF THE AMAZONS
ILLUSTRATED BY
VICTORIA YING

New York Times bestselling authors
SHANNON HALE and DEAN HALE
AMETHYST
princess of gemworld
art by
ASIAH FULMORE

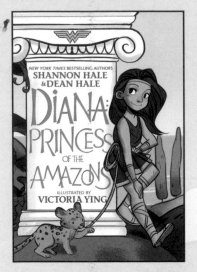

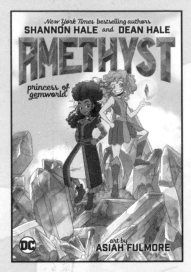

Want more tales of sibling rivalry or budding friendships? Check out these stories from DC Books for Young Readers!

WRITTEN BY
KATE KARYUS QUINN
& DEMITRIA LUNETTA
ANTI HERO
ILLUSTRATED BY
MACA GIL

NEW YORK TIMES BESTSELLING CO-CREATOR OF LUMBERJANES
GRACE ELLIS
LOIS LANE
and the
FRIENDSHIP CHALLENGE
illustrated by
BRITTNEY WILLIAMS
"Grace Ellis and Brittney Williams are a dream team bringing you a zippy, funny story of friendship and mystery!"
—Noelle Stevenson, National Book Award finalist for Nimona

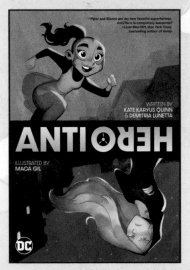

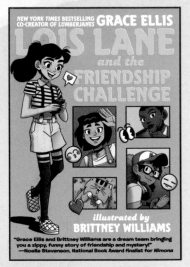

Anti/Hero
Kate Karyus Quinn,
Demitria Lunetta, Maca Gil
ISBN: 978-1-4012-9325-3

Lois Lane and the Friendship Challenge
Grace Ellis, Brittney Williams
ISBN: 978-1-4012-9637-7